MIDNIGHT
SINS

The Urbana Free Library

To renew materials call
217-367-4057

12-08

	DATE DUE	
NOV 2 0 2010		
NOV 0 1 2011		
AUG 2 3 2012		

MIDNIGHT SINS

CYNTHIA EDEN

BRAVA

KENSINGTON PUBLISHING CORP.
www.kensingtonbooks.com

BRAVA BOOKS are published by

Kensington Publishing Corp.
850 Third Avenue
New York, NY 10022

ISBN-13: 978-0-7582-2604-4
ISBN-10: 0-7582-2604-7

First Kensington Trade Paperback Printing: December 2008

10 9 8 7 6 5 4 3 2 1

Printed in the United States of America

For Ashley—
The friend who gives me gossip, laughter, and understanding.
Thanks for being you, lady!

Chapter 1

The guy in the bed had enjoyed killer sex.

Detective Todd Brooks stared down at the naked man. The guy's hands were tied to the bed frame with a thick, white rope. His arms were stretched above him, and his legs sprawled across the mattress. An open condom wrapper littered the floor to his right, but there was no sign of the condom, or of the person who'd bound the man.

Poor dead bastard.

"Someone cleaned up." The rumbling voice came from his partner, Colin Gyth.

Todd grunted and let his gaze drift over the bed. Yeah, Colin was right. Someone had done a Class A job of screwing their crime scene. Maybe the forensics unit would be able to find more evidence, but he wasn't going to hold his breath.

His eyes narrowed as he studied the slight impression that marred the sheets on the left side of the body, an impression that could have been the outline of a woman.

But whoever the mystery lady was, she sure as hell had gotten out of Dodge.

"Heart attack?" Colin murmured, crouching near the foot of the bed.

A possibility. The guy looked fit enough. He was muscled, appeared to be in his late thirties, but, yeah, he could've had a heart attack. The sex could have gotten a little too wild, the bondage game too intense.

It could have happened that way.

Could have.

They'd been called to the dingy hotel less than an hour ago. A maid, a currently hysterical teen girl, had discovered the body. There was no ID in the room, no wallet, no personal belongings—even the poor asshole's clothes were gone.

The desk clerk had him registered as Jon Smith. Not damn original, and not particularly helpful in this situation.

At least the clerk had managed to catch a glimpse of the woman with the guy. A blonde. Long, curly hair. Tall.

Great breasts.

It would have been too much to ask, Todd supposed, for the guy to have actually glimpsed her face.

Where was the woman? Had she been a hooker? Someone the guy had picked up for the night? A street-smart woman who'd taken advantage of a man's death by stealing him blind? Or maybe she'd been his mistress, meeting in secret while her husband was none the wiser. When her lover had expired, she could have freaked.

Yeah, those ideas were definite options.

Or rather, they *would* have been great options, if this hadn't been the third dead, naked male that he and his partner had found tied up like this in just over a month.

Rubbing his eyes, Todd said, "We're going to need a damn thorough autopsy on this one." Because coincidences like this, they just didn't happen. Not ever.

He couldn't overlook the possibility anymore that there might be a new killer preying on the streets of Atlanta. Or that the killer might be one of the rarest breeds—a female serial.

"How the fuck is she doing this?" He asked softly. Had to be drugs. Something the killer slipped into the men's drinks. A little concoction that made their hearts beat too fast. Or maybe just stop. "I want Smith doing the autopsy and supervising the tox screen."

He glanced up and found Colin watching him with those eerie blue eyes of his. Tension had been heavy between him and Colin for a while now, and Todd knew part of the problem was coming from his end of the partnership—but, damn it, he couldn't help the stiffness that swept through him every time he had to confront Colin. Things just hadn't been the same, not since Todd had made the mistake of suspecting Colin's girlfriend in a murder case.

Jesus. Couldn't a guy ever screw up and just be forgiven? Did Colin want him to bleed? "Uh, Colin?"

Of course, there *was* the other problem—the one that had made him wake up those first few nights after the close of the Night Butcher case, his body soaked in a cold sweat of fear—

Todd sucked in a deep breath and caught the heavy stench of death. Okay, now wasn't the time to piss and moan over the damn nightmares or flashbacks or whatever the hell they'd been. He had a case to handle.

Colin blinked and seemed to shake himself out of his own dark thoughts. "I didn't think Smith was back from sick leave yet."

Sick leave. Todd's lips twisted. He was sure that wasn't exactly what she would call the extended enforced absence.

"Yeah, she's back." His gut tightened as he said the words. Smith, the best medical examiner in the state, had been taken hostage on their last big murder case. She'd been held prisoner by a fucking psychopath, and when they'd finally managed to rescue her, the woman had looked like a broken doll.

But the lady had a core of pure steel, and Todd was sure glad she was back at the Crypt—because they damn well could use her help.

Her replacement just wasn't as good with the stiffs.

"Shit." Colin shook his head, a muscle tightening around his jaw. "This is the last thing the city needs now."

Todd exhaled, knowing he was right, but there was no denying the evidence. A killer was out there, preying on men.

Giving them pleasure and hot sex, then stealing their lives away.

Damn. What kind of woman could do that? Sex and death . . . not a combination many could handle.

But apparently, it was perfect for someone.

And it was going to be his job to find her, and to stop her.

By any means necessary.

"Detectives!" A uniformed cop stood in the doorway, his face flushed with excitement. "I've got something for—" His gaze darted to the dead man, and all the bright red color drained from his cheeks in an instant.

Had to be the kid's first body.

At least the scene wasn't too bloody.

Todd sighed and stepped forward, deliberately placing his body in front of the corpse. "Whaddya got?"

The cop swallowed and his Adam's apple trembled. "F-found ID in a Dumpster out back. M-man's wallet. Woman's p-purse."

A hot lick of excitement pumped through Todd and had every muscle in his body tightening. *It couldn't be this damn easy.* There'd been no evidence left behind before—and the cops on duty had sure as hell searched every garbage can and Dumpster in the vicinity.

The kid's quivering, white-gloved hand raised a driver's license. A Georgia license. One glance was all it took to identify the small photo.

Different haircut. Same face.

His eyes narrowed as he studied the ID. Michael House. A quick calculation put the guy's age at thirty-five.

Same age as Todd.

House's address was easily recognizable. One of the wealthier streets, one of those lined with the big antebellum homes.

So why had the guy been slumming on the wrong side of the city?

His attention shifted to the purse. A small leather bag. Delicate and probably expensive as hell. He reached for it, aware of Colin crowding beside him. His gloved fingers brushed across the soft surface, pushed inside.

He touched the hard edge of a wallet. Pulled it out. Black. A high-end label branded on the side.

So the woman had gone slumming as well.

Carefully, he opened the wallet. Just because the uniform had found the purse near the victim's belongings didn't mean the purse belonged to his missing lady. Could have been anyone's purse, especially in this neighborhood, but—

A hard burst of air exploded from between his lips.

But the woman on the ID had long, curly blond hair. Just like the desk clerk had described.

Coincidence? Damn unlikely.

The lady was also a world-class looker. The photo was small, grainy, but the woman—he'd never seen anything like her before.

Perfect.

The word seemed to whisper through his mind.

Her face was a perfect oval, her cheeks high, her nose a small, straight ridge. Her full lips were parted and seemed strangely red in the picture.

Oh, hell, yeah, he could all too easily imagine a woman who looked like her being able to seduce men to their deaths. It was all there—in her wide, bedroom eyes, in the sinful lips.

She was the kind of woman a man would die to taste—and maybe, just maybe, three men had.

"Too easy," Colin said and Todd knew exactly what he meant. Finding her ID—shouldn't have happened.

Nothing had been left at the other crime scenes. Not a hair. Not a piece of fabric from the killer on the victims' clothing. No fingerprints.

Nothing.

So why the hell had the woman left her ID behind this time?

His gaze met the green stare of the young cop. "Tell me, *exactly*, where you found this."

"I-in the Dumpster. Right behind the storage room."

"She might as well have left it in the hotel room." Colin shook his head. "I don't like it."

Well, Todd didn't particularly like *anything* about the case. "It's a lead." A strong one. "And I'm going after her." It was his partner's job to back him up. They were supposed to trust one another implicitly.

But he hadn't exactly trusted Colin for months now, not completely—with pretty fucking good reason—and he knew the feeling was mutual.

Colin stared at him for a moment, eyes shuttered. Finally, he said, "We'll put out an APB. Let the uniforms see if they can find her and bring her in to the station—"

"No." Not an option. "*I'm* going after her." He couldn't explain the sudden, driving compulsion within him, but he was going to find the woman.

He needed to find her.

Sex and death.

The woman in the photo sure as hell hadn't looked like a monster, but an angel's face could hide the soul of a devil. Every cop learned that lesson.

Cara Maloan. The name on the ID was different, exotic. The woman, well, she was probably homicidal, but he was going after her.

His job was to catch killers, and that was exactly what he planned to do. Pretty face or not.

He checked the card again, running over her vitals. Five foot nine, 140 pounds. Age . . . twenty-eight. Blond hair. Blue eyes.

Fucking beautiful.

And deadly?

"Let's get the hell out of here," Colin said, straightening his shoulders. "I'm damn tired of finding naked dead men."

So was he.

Time to play their usual game of good cop, bad cop.

Todd was very, very good at playing the game.

The mysterious Cara was about to find out that she couldn't screw with the Atlanta PD.

She was giving up sex. No, she *had* given up sex.

As of tonight, she'd officially reached the one month, sex-free mark.

Cara Maloan slumped on her couch, her eyes trained on the flickering images of a naked couple as they flashed across her television screen. The man and the woman were gasping, moaning, their hands ripping clothing away in the midst of their frantic sexual heat.

"Hell." So *not* what she should be watching. With a flick of her fingers, she turned off the TV, then tossed the remote across the room.

Unlike that hormone-driven couple, there would be no more fast, hard matings for her.

Giving up sex. That was the path for her..

Of course, the fact that she was a full-blooded succubus and derived her power from the sexual act—much like a vampire from blood drinking—the way Cara figured it, she'd be in for some serious hard times.

Her head fell back against the couch cushions. She was so damn screwed.

Or actually, she wasn't, and didn't have any future plans to be—that was her trouble.

Why—*why* did she have to be different from the rest of her kind? Why did every sexual encounter leave her flushed with power, but aching and empty deep inside?

Why was she such a freak?

The other succubi she knew, they flaunted their sexual power, reveled in it, while she—

Feared it.

Hell. Her long nails dug into the couch cushions, gouging at the soft fabric.

She was an aberration, she knew it. Not a predator like she should be. Too weak. The demon blood in her body should have made her a perfect hunter.

But she'd never really enjoyed the hunt, and *that* was her whole problem.

She sighed. At least she had a backup plan in place. Since she wasn't going to be having the hot, wild sex that her kind craved, she still had to get a power fix. Thanks to her job, she'd be able to get that surge. The sensual rush wouldn't be as strong, but it would be enough for her to keep living.

Damn it, why do I have to be so different?

The peal of her doorbell, followed by the hard, fierce pounding at her door, jerked Cara from her pity party.

She frowned, glancing quickly at the glowing clock on her DVD player—1:16 A.M.

Who the hell would be coming to see her now?

Cara rose, stomped into the foyer and then to the door. Her left eye peered through the peephole as her fingers curled against the wood frame.

Her glowing porch light illuminated two men. Big men. Strangers.

She stepped back, her gaze narrowing.

The door shook as a powerful fist pounded against it once again.

As a rule, Cara wasn't afraid of humans. She was stronger than them, *a hell of a lot stronger*, and had once taken down a six-foot-three, 280-pound asshole with one touch.

She might not enjoy the game of hunting as much as her brethren, but she *did* know how to use her powers to defend herself when necessary.

Keeping the chain in place at the top of her door, she swung the dead bolt and opened the door two inches.

A badge was immediately shoved into the opening. "*Cara?*"

Frowning, she said, "Yes." The badge was right before her eyes, all shiny and official looking.

"Cara Maloan?"

She nodded.

The badge disappeared. "I'm Detective Todd Brooks of the Atlanta Police Department." A pause. "I want you to open the door and let me inside."

She couldn't see much of his face from the angle she had. Just a hard jaw. Sharp cheekbone. Brown hair that was cut brutally short.

Let me inside. His words rang in her head and she blurted the question that immediately sprang to mind, "Why?"

His hand rose, pressed against the door. It was a strong hand, long-fingered, bronzed from the sun. "I don't want to talk about this outside. Your neighbors might overhear."

Doubtful. Her yard was big. Private. That was why she'd bought the house.

Besides, she wasn't exactly clear on what "this" was. Her fingers tightened around the doorknob. "Who's with you?"

"My partner." A touch of impatience coated the man's drawl. "Now I'm trying to ask nicely here, Ms. Maloan. Let me inside."

What would happen if he stopped asking so nicely? A hot spurt of fire stroked through her gut.

Uh, oh. She did *not* need to get turned on by a dark, rumbling voice.

She also didn't need cops on her doorstep.

Cara released the chain and hurriedly jumped back as the door was shoved open. Then the men stormed inside, and her heart pounded too fast as a shiver of fear skated down her spine.

It wasn't the guns in their hands that made her wary, though they were a definite concern. Bullet wounds hurt like a bitch—she knew, she'd been shot once. Not exactly a stellar memory.

No, it wasn't the weapons that made her tremble. It was the men.

The first guy, Detective Brooks, he was tall, a couple of inches over six feet, and leanly muscled. There was power there, in the tight lines of his body, a strength that hung in the air around him, and, damn but the guy was handsome. Sharp, clean lines defined his face. A straight nose, a chiseled jaw and chin. His top lip was a little too thin, but strangely sexy. And his eyes, they were dark brown. They looked . . . warm.

A deception, she was sure, but there was something about him . . . something hot. Dark. A curl of heat unfurled within her, and a rampant thought raced through her mind. *I want to taste him.* All of that wonderful power swirling just beneath his surface. He'd be delicious.

The demon inside her trembled with hunger even as the woman fought to hold on to her control.

With an effort, Cara managed to shift her attention to the

other cop. He stood farther back, his bright blue stare trained on her. The guy looked like some kind of football player—big, muscled, but his face resembled that of a predator. Tight, sharp. High cheekbones, broad forehead, and a jaw that was clenched.

He was a good-looking guy, in a rough, scary way. One of those guys who looked like he could beat the shit out of a man and never even break a sweat.

Despite his obvious power, he didn't spark a hunger within her. Not like the other man did.

Cara swallowed. "I-I don't think the guns are really necessary." What in the hell was going on? Her heart was beating in a double-time rhythm now, nearly shaking her chest. Her breath began to pant out as she eyed the weapons. Okay, for the first three seconds, the guns had just been an annoyance, but the longer the two jerks kept holding the weapons, well, the more nervous she was becoming.

As fear and adrenaline flooded through her, she began to feel the sting of her power racing through her veins.

The second cop, the partner yet to be named, suddenly emitted a hard growl. Her gaze flew to his face. His nostrils flared, as if he were catching a scent in the air.

Oh, damn, damn, damn.

Her pheromones. When she got scared or excited, she lost control of them. Mortal men usually responded instantly to the scent of her kind—sometimes, they could respond *too* strongly.

The scent of a succubus could be a powerful weapon in seduction . . . or in death.

The guy's nostrils widened again. He'd definitely caught the scent. So he should—

He took two quick steps back, shaking his head.

Cara realized she was in serious trouble. Only other supernaturals could hold out against her scent. Actually, in her experience, only shifters could resist the smell. Demons, vamps, and charmers—well, they usually flocked to her like she was some kind of tasty dessert treat.

Shifters. Hell. They were some of the most dangerous and

often homicidal supernaturals. This cop, the one who looked like he routinely ate nails, or perhaps even small children, he was one of those two-faced killers. Not a good thing.

But what about Detective Brooks? She turned her head slowly, wary of finding another killer in her midst.

His dark stare was locked on her. His eyes were wide. His nostrils flared slightly and she knew that he, too, had caught the new scent. Her scent. Sex and woman.

Cautiously, she took a step toward him. If he was like the other guy, he'd move back.

Detective Brooks took a step toward her, licking his lips.

Oh, that was a good sign, that was—

His gun lifted, pointed straight at her. "What the hell are you doing to me?"

For a moment, her heart stilled. *Damn it.*

Human, but, unfortunately for her, a *sensitive* human. One with enough latent psychic talent to be trouble.

The night had just gone to hell.

"Don't get too close to her." The order came from the shifter.

Her chin lifted as she raised her empty hands "I'm not exactly armed."

"Aren't you?" The shifter rumbled and Cara ground her back teeth together.

He was pissing her off. They both were, and she still didn't know why they were in her house. "Look," she gritted, "I want to know what's going on and I want to know *now.*"

The human smiled at her, flashing a set of perfectly white, even teeth, and a dimple in his left cheek. "We have some questions for you."

Bullshit. "Then get rid of the guns." She was practically waving her empty hands in their faces. It should be obvious to the morons that she wasn't hiding any weapons.

What was going on?

He inclined his head slightly and then *finally* lowered his gun. "Ms. Maloan, I'm going to need you to come downtown with us."

Oh, she didn't like the sound of that. "Why." A stark demand. She was tired of this crap. They'd all but forced their way into her home, aimed guns at her, terrified her. She wanted to know *why*.

"Does the name Michael House mean anything to you?" He asked, holstering his weapon.

Ice chilled her blood, but she kept her face expressionless. "Should it?"

His smile dimmed. "Where were you tonight between eight and ten?"

Fuck. She knew where these questions were heading and she also knew the situation wasn't going to end well for her. "Here." Her hands fell to her sides.

"Alone?" The doubting question came from the shifter.

Cara gave a stiff nod.

"Did any neighbors see you? Delivery guy? Anyone?" Brooks asked. Brooks—that was his last name. She couldn't remember his first name, and for some reason, that fact seemed important.

She should know the name of the man who was about to haul her off to jail. After wetting her lips in a quick, nervous move, she admitted, "I don't think anyone can verify my story. I got home a little after five." No one had been out when she'd pulled up into her drive. Just her luck. Usually, one of her neighbors would have been out doing some kind of yard work, but the *one* time she could have used their nosiness to her advantage, well, fate screwed her. Her lips twisted as she admitted, "And I didn't order any dinner or anything. I just, ah, stayed here."

Brooks's stare raked her body, lingering for a moment too long on her breasts. She was wearing an old black tank top and a pair of sweatpants. Hardly sexy. Not succubus material. But—

His pupils flared and she knew he liked what he saw.

Under other circumstances, she might have been inclined to play.

But she'd just sworn off sex, and while the detective had managed to stir her interest, he'd also pissed her off.

"If you can't confirm that alibi, I'm afraid we might have a little problem on our hands," Brooks murmured, and took another step toward her.

She could smell his cologne, a rich, masculine scent. Or maybe it wasn't cologne. Maybe it was just the man. "I still don't understand what's happening here." Though she had a very, very strong suspicion.

Not Michael . . .

"We found your purse. Your wallet. ID." The words came from the shifter cop.

Shifters. She'd always been wary of them. Most supernaturals were. They were born to lie. To deceive. And some of them were just plain crazy.

She'd never met a cop shifter before. The shifters she'd encountered had been more of the run-from-cops kind.

So he'd found her missing purse. Big deal. "Well, good." Not that she really cared. She'd already replaced the ID and gotten a new bag. She didn't have credit cards, so she'd lost a bit of cash. "Where is it and I'll—"

"We found it at a crime scene."

Her mouth snapped closed. *Michael.* "Just . . . ah . . . what kind of crime scene?" Her hands were trembling, a weakness she didn't want the men to discover. She balled her fingers into fists.

Brooks took two gliding steps toward her, closing the distance between them. Cara tilted her head back, gazing up at him.

"We found your bag at a murder scene, lady." The warm smile was completely gone now. Only the hardened cop remained. "Wanna explain that to me?"

She shook her head. She couldn't explain it. "I—I—my purse was stolen two weeks ago—"

"And you reported the theft, right?" The shifter asked, voice doubtful.

Another negative shake of her head. The purse hadn't mattered enough to report, and she certainly hadn't wanted to go out and start attracting attention from cops.

Though it looked like she'd managed to capture their attention anyway.

"Why do you do it?" Brooks asked, leaning toward her. He drew a ragged breath, as if inhaling her scent, then muttered, "You're so damn beautiful, I bet it's like fucking child's play for you to lure those men to you."

It always had been easy. She'd been born as a lure. Since his words were a bitter truth, Cara stayed silent. Reeling the men to her, no that had never been a problem.

None of the men had ever cared enough to *stay* with her.

An eternity of pleasure, but a life lived alone. That was her lot in this world. The lot for all the succubi. She was just the only one not loving the deal.

"Do you get off on it?" Brooks asked, voice silky smooth. "Do you like the power? Like the control in bed?"

She swallowed. Sometimes, she wanted to lose control. To be taken.

His hand lifted, brushed across her cheek in a caress that lanced her flesh with its heat. "And at the end," he said, pressing in even closer, so close that for a moment she thought he was going to kiss her, "when the pleasure is pounding through you, how does it feel to kill your lovers?"

What? "No, listen, I've never—"

He grabbed her hands, yanked them up, and held her tight. Not hurting her. Trapping her. "How do you do it? Drugs? An injection?"

She twisted her hands, trying to break free. "I don't know what you're talking about!" A lie. Killing a lover was so easy.

But not her way.

"*Right*, princess."

Her eyes narrowed at the mocking tone.

"You don't have any idea why we're here. You don't know Michael House, and you have no idea how your ID came to be at our crime scene."

"Wh-what—" She broke off, struggling to clear her throat. "What happened to Michael?" A murder scene, he'd said he found her bag at—

His lips tightened. "I thought you didn't know him."

"*What happened?*" She wrenched her hands away from him.

"Come down to the station, and I'll be glad to tell you."

She hurried back a few steps, and stumbled into the shifter. Damn it, how had he moved so fast? When had the jerk circled behind her? "I'm not going anywhere with you."

One dark brow lifted. "Wanna bet on that?"

Not particularly.

The shifter's hands landed heavily on her shoulders. She jumped at the contact. His touch was cold to her skin, where Brooks had felt burning hot.

Brooks held her gaze. "You can do this the easy way and come with us willingly—"

"Or you can fight," the shifter growled in her ear, "and still wind up finding your ass downtown."

Oh, she didn't like him. Didn't like either of them. Her skin began to prickle as rage and power swept through her.

"Easy." The whisper was so soft she might have imagined it. The shifter's voice. Barely breathing in her ear.

She drew in a ragged gasp of air at the sound, drawing the cold oxygen deep into her lungs. *Control.* She couldn't shatter in front of them. They were *cops.*

Cops who were suspecting her of—what? Assault? Murder?

If she put up a fight, and used her power, she'd never be safe in Atlanta again. She'd have to run, and she wouldn't be able to stop running for a long, long time.

She wasn't the type to run. Never had been.

Her chin lifted as she made her decision. "I'll do it the easy way."

Brooks's lips began to curl.

"For now."

That wiped the smug smile right off his handsome face.

After she shoved on her shoes, they led her outside, into a starless night.

What would happen at the station? The thought flew through her mind, followed instantly by another, darker worry, one that had her mouth drying. *What's happened to Michael?* She hadn't seen her ex-lover in months, and now, Cara feared she might not ever see him—alive—again.

Chapter 2

She didn't look like a killer. Her blue eyes were too clear. Her skin too soft.

She smelled of sex and embodied the best wet dream of his life.

But she didn't look like a killer.

Which meant she probably was.

Brooks watched Cara through the two-way mirror. She sat in the interrogation room, legs crossed, fingers idly tapping on the wooden table. She'd been in there for over thirty minutes now. Alone. Every few moments, a ripple of anger or impatience would appear on her face, then disappear seconds later as her cool mask slipped seamlessly back into place.

Cara Maloan was even better looking than her picture had suggested. In fact, the woman was truly damn near perfect. Hell, yes, he could all too easily imagine her being able to lure those poor assholes to their deaths.

He'd never seen a woman more sexual. Even in the loose jogging pants and tank top she wore, there was no disguising her appeal.

The minute the door of her house had swung open, he'd realized an important fact. He wanted her.

Then he'd caught a whiff of her scent. *Jesus Christ.* He'd never smelled anything so good. Rich, like a woman's sensual cream, but sweet, like flowers or champagne. A combination that had blasted straight to his cock.

He hadn't just wanted her then. He'd *hungered* for her.

And the lady was probably a killer.

Damn if he didn't just have the shit-poorest luck in the world. Or at least, that was what his father would have told him, rest the old bastard's soul.

Todd exhaled and wondered for a minute what his dad would have thought of this case. Of Cara.

His dad. Tough and twisted sonofabitch that he'd been.

Todd had never meant to follow in his footsteps, but fate sometimes had a way of screwing up the best plans that a guy could make.

The door behind him opened with a squeak. He glanced over his shoulder, found his partner watching him with an inscrutable stare.

"You got the photos?" Todd asked.

Colin lifted the manila file.

Todd turned back to the glass, gazed once more at Cara. "It's a real crying shame that a woman like her is a murderer." Because he was still hard for her. Could still smell her.

"We . . . should be very careful with her."

There was a hesitancy in Colin's voice that made the hair on Todd's neck rise. Stepping away from the observation window, he turned to fully face his partner. "What do you know?" Colin had held out on him during their last major case. The knowledge still stuck in Todd's throat, and he wasn't going to sit around and let the same shit happen again.

Colin's stare darted to the woman. "I know she's dangerous."

A hard laugh broke from his lips. "Yeah, well, so do those poor bastards she killed." And he knew it, too, but that fact didn't stop the wanting. What the hell was wrong with him? He'd never been attracted to a suspect before.

Then again, he'd never had a suspect like *her* before.

"Something's off with her," Colin said.

Now he snorted. Yeah, Colin was sure one to talk about something being *off.* "Well, that's 'cause she could be a female serial, and we both know that breed is rare." He remembered a report he'd read back in the academy. Female serials accounted for only 8 percent of all the serial murders. The other 92 percent of the kills were by men.

But women were also said to be a hell of a lot more methodical and precise about their killing. *A hell of a lot more careful with their crimes.*

Maybe there were more female serials out there than the guys in the suits thought. Could be those women were just too damn good at covering their tracks.

Todd rubbed the bridge of his nose. "I think we might need to bring the doc in on this one."

Colin stiffened.

The "doc" in question was actually Colin's current lover, Dr. Emily Drake. She was a well-known psychologist in Atlanta, and the department had recently begun using her as a profiler.

Yeah, it would be a good idea to bring her in and see what she thought of their killer.

Colin's gaze was still on the woman. "Yes," he said softly, "maybe we should."

But first . . . Todd reached for the file. "I wanna see how she reacts to these pictures, and then we need to get started on a photo lineup." They'd taken Cara's photo shortly after she arrived. They'd add it to some more images, show the pics to the desk clerk.

His partner nodded. "Already got a call in to the team." He sighed. "But I'll tell you now, man, I don't think that guy will be able to ID her. Even if the man hadn't been spending all his time staring at her chest, he reeked of booze."

He'd noticed the heavy odor, too. "Right now, there's not much choice for us."

"I know." Colin sounded as disgusted as he felt, and for a moment, it was almost like the old days, before the brutal case that had blasted them apart and sent Todd's world spinning.

Todd's fingers tightened around the folder. "The uniforms will still bring him in. Who knows? Maybe we'll get lucky."

"Maybe."

In the meantime, "Let's find out just what else our lady has to say about Michael House." Because she knew the victim. He'd caught her slip, just as Colin had. Todd was going to make absolutely certain he learned all the secrets Cara was hiding.

A pretty face had never swayed him before. It sure as hell wasn't going to stop him from doing his job now.

She was furious . . . and afraid. And the fear made her even angrier.

They'd left her in the ten-by-eight-foot room for half an hour. The minutes had crawled by as she'd sat and waited.

Something bad had happened to Michael. She knew it. Wasn't going to be dumb enough to deny the obvious. She also knew that the cops thought she was involved.

Not an ideal situation.

Her fingers tapped against the wooden tabletop. She'd been isolated from the moment she entered the police station. If only she'd been allowed to see some of the other cops, she would have been able to use a bit of her power. She wasn't gifted with the power of *complete* mind control—only level-ten demons could totally control the thoughts of humans—but she was still pretty damn good at planting hypnotic suggestions into the minds of susceptible humans, as were most of her kind. The hypnotic power was one of the succubi's most coveted powers. Right then, she sure had a few suggestions dancing around in her head that she'd like to—

The door to the interrogation room was shoved open. It slammed back against the wall with a thud.

Cara sucked in a sharp breath, but instantly schooled her features. They wanted her afraid, so she'd be damned if she let them see her fear.

Deliberately, she leaned back in the chair. "What took you guys so long?" As if she didn't know they'd been watching her through that ridiculous two-way mirror. Humans. They always thought they were so smart.

But she knew they'd been watching her. Well, no, not them exactly.

Just the first cop. The human. *Brooks*. He'd been watching her almost constantly. At first, she'd felt his stare. Heavy on her skin like a touch. Then she'd turned to the mirrored wall. She'd seen past the illusion—she was used to peering past the veil—and she'd seen him. Standing in the opposite room. Fists clenched. Eyes on her.

His attention had fueled her anger. Her fear. And added a spark to the desire she shouldn't have been feeling.

The man is trying to lock you up. Focus! Oh, damn, but she'd always had a hard time not thinking about sex.

And the guy oozed sex. Rough, wild sex. The kind that made a woman scream as she came.

Cara cleared her throat, and realized that neither of the detectives had answered her question. No big surprise.

The shifter—she'd learned his name was Colin Gyth; he'd finally gotten around to introducing himself during the ride over—walked slowly across the room. He stopped at the edge of the mirrored wall. The perfect position to observe, while not blocking the view from the hidden room.

Brooks stalked slowly toward her. He pulled out one of the two remaining chairs at the table. The legs of the chair scraped against the floor, the sound almost like a shriek. He sat down, positioning himself directly across from her, and placed a folder on the table between them.

Her gaze dropped to the folder and her palms began to sweat.

"Sorry we were gone so long," Brooks said, and his brown eyes seemed sincere.

Liar. She knew the guy wasn't the least bit sorry. The waiting—that had been a deliberate police tactic. One she didn't like.

"I wanted to gather some information to show you." He smiled at her then, a warm, friendly smile.

Goose bumps rose on her arms. "Is this what you do?" She asked, the question slipping out without a second's hesitation.

He blinked. "Excuse me?"

Her fingers tapped against the table top. Her nails were bloodred and sharp, and she had to fight the urge to gouge them into the wood. "I asked if this"—she paused, gestured to him, the table, and the silent shifter—"was what you usually do."

"This?"

"Yeah, this whole idiotic routine where you act like you're the good one. Like you give a shit what I think or want." Cara shook her head and her hair brushed across her shoulders. "Got to tell you, I'm really not buying it." He was good at pretending, she'd give him that, and the bit probably worked great on humans. But for someone with her enhanced senses, it was an insulting waste of time.

She could smell the sweat on his skin. See the anger that tightened his eyes and mouth. Past the falsely warm gaze, she could see the core of power and the lurking fury.

Good cop? More like furious, hard-as-nails asshole.

Cara leaned forward, slapping her hands down on the table. "Why don't we cut the games?" She asked. "Just get to the part where you tell me why the hell you drug me out of my house in the middle of the night."

He stared back at her. One moment. Two. Then he pushed the file toward her. "I want you to take a look at the photos for me, okay? See if you recognize anyone."

Gyth shifted slightly, a ripple of muscle and menace.

She didn't want to look inside the file, but her fingers reached for it, anyway. Flipped it open and found—

Michael.

It was a black-and-white shot of him. Shoulders, neck, and head. His eyes were closed. His face devoid of all expression. For a second, one wild second, she thought he might be sleeping.

But the hope died immediately as the truth hit her hard, making her stomach knot and her lips tremble. "He's . . . dead." She bit her bottom lip, trying to stop the tremble. She didn't want Brooks to see her weakness.

She'd been afraid he was dead, from the moment they'd mentioned his name—

Michael. He'd been the first to make her want more than just fleeting pleasure.

"What happened to him?" Cara was proud of the fact that her voice didn't quaver. The words were stilted, a bit cold. But *she* was cold. Ice cold, all the way to her soul.

"Don't you know?" Brooks asked softly.

A shiver worked over her body. "I didn't have anything to do with this!" She'd never hurt Michael.

"Didn't you?" Brooks leaned forward. "Earlier you told me that you didn't even know the guy."

"No, I didn't." She'd never denied knowing Michael. "I just asked you if his name should mean something to me." Not a lie.

His lips thinned. "Why didn't you just tell me you knew who the guy was?"

Good question. Not so easy to answer, but she tried, saying, "I was scared, all right? I didn't know what was happening, didn't know what you wanted from me—"

"So you decided to lie to me." Turning slightly, his gaze met the shifter's, for just a moment. "The innocent always lie, don't they, Gyth?"

A growl was the shifter's only answer as Gyth crossed his arms over his powerful chest.

Her hands slammed into the top of the table. "I didn't kill him!" Then she shoved her chair back, needing more space. She didn't want to look at that picture anymore. Didn't want to think about Michael. If she did, Cara was very afraid that she'd break apart.

It was obvious the detective was out for blood, but she'd be damned if she'd give him any of hers.

"You can have a lawyer, you know." Gyth spoke softly from his watchful position.

Yeah, she knew she could. They'd told her in the car. Said she could get an attorney if she wanted.

But Michael had been the only lawyer she knew. "I don't need a lawyer. I haven't done anything wrong!" This was an absolute nightmare. Cara squeezed her eyes shut, hoping she was just dreaming. Her kind dreamed, too—just like humans. Powerful, dizzying dreams.

But never a dream like this one.

Her dreams were sexy, often wild—but they were *not* nightmares.

"You got him naked," Brooks said, his voice driving into her mind and causing her eyelids to snap open. "You tied him to the bed."

She shook her head. "I was home. By myself."

"Then what did you do? Drug him? Inject him with something?"

Her lips parted in confusion. "What are talking about?"

"How did you do it?" He rose, stalked around the table and loomed over her. "How did you kill him, without leaving a mark on his body?"

No! A sudden, terrifying knowledge swept through her, and for an instant, Cara was actually afraid that she might pass out. Her body began to sway.

In a flash, Brooks grabbed her arms and pulled her up, holding her tightly against him. "Cara?"

She shook her head, unable to speak. No, no, she had to be wrong. *They* had to be wrong.

"Damn it, she's ice cold!" His voice exploded like a shot.

His hands ran up and down her arms, soothing her, warming her, and she wanted to lean into him. To follow that warm scent and put her head on his shoulder, or against the crook of his neck. The temptation was strong. So strong.

But he was just playing a game. She had to remember that. He was trying to confuse her. Pretending to be the good cop one instant, and the bad guy the next. He wanted to trip her up, and she'd already made one mistake with the detective.

She wouldn't be making another.

Gathering her strength, Cara pulled away from him. "Don't touch me."

His gaze held hers. Emotion burned in that dark stare. Anger. Worry. Lust.

Swallowing, she lifted her chin. "I'm done here." And she

was. She'd played the good citizen. Let them haul her to this crappy station. Sat and waited on their slow asses. Then she'd let them accuse her.

No more.

Brooks stepped away from her.

"I think the two of you"—her disgusted gaze flew from one man to the other—"have more than ruined my night. For the record, let me tell you a few things—and I'd suggest that you both listen very, very well." Cause she sure as hell wasn't going to repeat herself.

"I kn-knew—" She stammered just a bit, managed to collect herself, and continued, "Michael House. But I haven't seen him in several months. I didn't have anything to do with his death, and like I've told you *twice* already, I was home, alone, earlier tonight."

"Then how'd your bag wind up at the crime scene?"

Her lips twisted. "Hell if I know." But that fact worried her. "Someone took the bag in the park almost two weeks ago. I've already got new ID. No, I didn't report the theft, there wasn't anything of enough value to worry about in the purse." She pointed her finger at the infuriating human's chest. "You're the cop. Run a check with the DMV—or whoever those people are—you'll see that I got a new driver's license last Monday."

"Oh, baby, you can count on me running the check."

His voice had dropped when he called her "baby." Gotten husky, intimate.

Cara balled her hands into fists. Her heart thundered like crazy, and she knew that her pheromones were about to fill the room. She fought to hold the scent in check—she'd learned how to control the fragrance when she'd been a teen. She'd momentarily lost control back at her home, and if she didn't hurry up and get the hell out of the station, she'd do it again.

"If you're not charging me with something," she snapped, "then I'm leaving."

She waited. Held Brooks's stare, and tried to hold back the growing tide of hunger that rose in her body.

Damn it—why him? Why did she feel this attraction for a man who obviously thought she was a criminal—a murderer? Why did her body tighten and need quicken her blood?

"I hope you're not planning on going too far," he said, the words a threat.

Her gaze narrowed. "I'll go as fucking far as I want." No, she didn't have any plans to leave town, but she wasn't about to tell the too-handsome and too-damn-annoying detective that fact. "I didn't kill Michael, and the way I figure it, if you actually had any kind of real evidence that linked me to the crime, you would have booked me by now." Instead of making her play the waiting game.

His jaw clenched and she knew she'd scored a hit with her last words. Giving a hard nod in the direction of the shifter, Cara headed for the door.

"You didn't look at all the pictures . . ." Brooks said softly.

His words froze her. "I saw all I needed to see."

"Did you?" This came from the shifter. He'd sidled around, came to stand right next to the still-closed door.

She shot him a fuming glare, then glanced back over her shoulder at Brooks. "Look, Detective, I don't exactly know what gets you off." *But you'd like to know, wouldn't you?* A sly voice whispered in her mind. Deliberately, she ignored the voice and the hunger that seemed to flare in tandem with her anger. "But I don't particularly enjoy staring at pictures of dead friends."

His brows rose. "Oh? So the other men were your friends, too?"

"What other men?"

His nostrils flared as he stepped toward her, that damn manila file in his hands. She could see the pulse point on his neck beating furiously. Her pheromones were in the air.

He licked his lips. "The ones we found in the other hotel rooms, tied to the beds, just like Michael House." Then he lifted a glossy photo sheet, showing her the picture of another man—shoulders, neck, and head, eyes closed, lips parted.

"I have no idea who that is." And she didn't. The man had

been good-looking, was still handsome, even in death. Strong bones. Sensuous lips. But she'd never seen him before.

"And him?" Another photo. Another guy with good looks and death's kiss on his lips.

"Never. Seen. Him." She jerked her gaze away as fast as she could.

"All three men were killed in the same way. All three were stripped. Bound. Then, their hearts . . . stopped."

But that didn't make any sense. Her kind had never needed to bind prey. The seduction was bind enough. "When?" She didn't have an alibi for Michael. *Damn, but just thinking about him hurt.* She blinked quickly, trying to fight the tears. "When were these men killed?" Please, please let it be a time she could account for—

"Travis Walters," he lifted the second photo he'd shown her. She refused to glance at it again. "Killed last Friday night. Just like Michael, it was between eight and ten, and—"

Relief swept through her, nearly making Cara dizzy. "I was singing," she whispered.

"What?"

She ran a hand through her hair, frustrated, tired. What time was it anyway? "I'm a singer. Last Friday, I was working at Paradise Found. Go ask the bartenders, the waitresses," she told him, her voice soft but underlined with steel. "I was on stage all night, *so I couldn't have killed that man.*"

"And where were you on the eighth?" This came from Gyth. "It was a Thursday night and—"

"Singing." The reply was automatic. She usually performed at night, Wednesday through Saturday, at the club. She'd started working there only a little over two months ago, but she loved the release of singing. The pleasure of the stage. It was almost as good as sex. *Almost.* "Go to the bar, it's on Tyners Ave—"

"We know the place," Gyth cut in, sounding less than thrilled.

Well, good. Then they could confirm her alibi and this whole terrible mess would be over. "I hope you find the person who did this," she told Brooks, and meant the words with every ounce of her being. "But you need to stop looking at me, because I *didn't kill those men.*" There was really nothing left to say. The closed door waited before her. She reached out and yanked the knob to the left.

A few uniformed cops milled around in the small hallway. They stepped forward when they saw her. She knew the move wasn't because she was a threat to them. No, all the uniforms were males, and her scent drew them to her like a homing device.

"Exit," she snapped, and they all pointed to the right. She brushed by them, wanting to get away and get her scent under control as quickly as possible.

Cara didn't look back as she fled. She didn't want to see Detective Brooks again. The way she figured it, he'd already done enough damage to her for one night.

No, she didn't look back, though a part of her wanted to.

Beneath the rage he'd stirred, the greedy lust still burned. Sometimes it was like that for a succubus. Sometimes, she would stumble onto the perfect prey. A man who could make her want with just a look and who promised a pleasure so powerful it was a temptation to the very soul.

But she could control her needs. She'd vowed hours before to give up sex, and though the lust had caught her off guard, she'd regain her balance. As soon as she was away from the arrogant cop, the heat would lessen.

So she didn't look back. Not once, not even when she heard him softly call her name.

He wanted to stop her. To run after her and catch her and stop her from leaving him.

He wanted to berate the others, who watched her with hungry eyes and lustful faces, even as he knew his eyes matched theirs and his face mirrored the same need.

Damn it, what was the woman doing to him? His guts were tied in knots, his hands actually shaking, and with every breath he took, he tasted her.

Shit. He was in trouble.

He called her name, an instinctual response. She didn't stop. Never glanced back. Just kept moving that shapely ass of hers and walking as fast as she could.

As she fled.

Well, hell, he didn't really blame the woman. If the lady was innocent, and he had to admit that he was starting to think she was, then he'd just come across as a major asshole.

"Shit." This time, his disgust was voiced aloud. He slanted a glance at Colin. "Think the alibi will hold up?"

A grim nod. "She wouldn't have said it unless she could prove it. The facts are too easy to check, and she has to know that."

Yeah, that was what his instincts were telling him, too. So why had her bag been dumped at the site? What was going on?

A setup?

Or was the lady dead guilty and just jerking him around?

Either way, he had to know.

Glancing down, he realized it was edging close to 4 A.M. And Cara didn't have a way home.

Perfect.

He hadn't really planned to let her out of his sight. Not yet, anyway. Not until his questions were answered—*fully*.

He stepped forward, intent on catching her.

And was brought up short by Colin's steely grip on his arm. "It's not a good idea, Brooks."

He fought the fierce need to shove the guy off him. He didn't have time for this crap. Cara was getting away. "Why not? She's a suspect, I'm not just going to let her walk—"

"Don't bullshit me," Colin snapped. "You're hot for the woman. You have been from the moment you saw her."

His temper began to spike. "Get your hand off me, *partner*." His gaze held Colin's glittering stare. One moment, two.

Colin dropped his hold.

Todd's jaw clenched and he gritted, "I can want a woman and still do my damn job." He'd always managed to get the job done, no matter what the hell was happening in his personal life.

"Just don't think with your dick around her." Colin's face was rock hard. "That woman's dangerous. Hell, she could be fucking deadly."

Yeah, he knew that. He also knew that her lips had quivered when she first saw Michael House's photo, that her hands had trembled—and that she'd tried to hide both responses.

When she'd attempted to leave and he'd stopped her with more photos, there had been tears in her bright eyes. Tears that she refused to shed.

The woman didn't act like a killer. There had been genuine shock and sorrow on her face when she'd learned of House's death.

There were some reactions that couldn't be faked, no matter how good the actress.

"I'll go to Paradise Found and check her alibi," Todd said, determination filling him. After he got a few hours of sleep, he'd head out and make absolutely certain her alibis held. But, right now, there wasn't much time to spare. The uniforms had almost been salivating over Cara. If he didn't hurry, she'd probably crook her finger and have one of them volunteering to give her a ride home.

And that outcome just wasn't part of his plans for the few remaining hours before dawn.

"Uh, maybe you should let me check at Paradise," Colin told him, and the hard edge had lessened in his voice. "You and Niol don't exactly have a good track record."

Niol was the annoying bastard who owned Paradise Found. The last time Todd had been near him, the guy had attacked him. Sort of. Todd still wasn't exactly certain how he'd flown ten feet across the bar when he couldn't actually remember Niol ever touching him.

No question, the man was weird as hell.

And he really was a bastard.

But Todd didn't have time to waste talking about Niol then. "I'm going after her," he muttered, and figured that was really all he needed to say to Colin.

His job was now very simple. Either he proved Cara's innocence and got to looking for the real killer . . . or he proved the beautiful lady's guilt.

He hurried from the station, her sweet scent still filling his nostrils and a helpless need tightening his gut.

Colin Gyth watched his partner disappear, shaking his head. This wasn't going to end well. Not. At. All.

He thought about calling in the captain. Giving him a heads-up on the situation.

But then Colin dismissed the idea almost immediately. He didn't know enough about Ms. Maloan to go to the captain, not yet.

And if her alibis checked out, well, then he might never have to tell Captain Danny McNeal that their suspect wasn't human.

"Be careful," he whispered the words too late, because Brooks was already gone. But his partner had no idea what hell a woman like Cara could wreak.

Luckily for Brooks, *he* did—and Colin wasn't about to turn his back and let his partner go down in flames.

Todd caught Cara's arm just as she started to climb down the narrow steps leading to the street.

She turned on him, her face furious, "Damn it, enough, just let—"

"I'm sorry." The words seemed torn from him. Yet he *was* sorry. He'd been doing his job, but sometimes, well, sometimes he didn't like the man he became when he was with suspects.

You have to be willing to fight dirty to take down the devil. His father's words. He'd always hated the truth in those words.

"Ms. Maloan . . ." No, he didn't like that. Too formal, and they weren't going to be formal. No, they were going to be damn intimate. He knew it. "Cara, I was doing my job."

The street in front of the precinct was deserted and slick from the light rain that had fallen during the night. The streetlights glared down on the area, sending pools of light shining onto the gleaming black surface of the road.

"You're still doing your job," she charged, pulling her arm free. Her hair was wild around her face and he wanted to touch it so badly that his fingers shook. "You're just playing the good cop now, trying to gain my trust."

She was right. He was still working the case, but there was more to it than that. More that he didn't understand. "Let me take you home."

Her glare would probably have frozen a lesser man. "I think I'd rather walk."

Todd doubted that. "It's at least twenty miles, Cara, and it's not like you'd be going through the safest neighborhoods."

She huffed out a breath. "Don't expect me to believe you're worried about me. I'm a killer, remember? I seduce men, then murder them. A walk on a seedy street should be nothing for me."

Clamping down on his rising anger, Todd tightened his grip on her. "I was following the evidence," he said, "and if I hadn't brought you in for questioning, I wouldn't be a good cop, now would I?"

Her jaw remained stubbornly set.

"Look, I understand that you're angry—"

One golden brow lifted. "I don't think 'angry' really covers my feelings here, Detective."

"Fine. Furious. Pissed. Whatever. But the fact remains that you need a ride home"—he dug into his pocket with his left hand, pulled out his keys—"and I've got a car ready."

Her gaze dropped to his keys. Her lips thinned. "Fine, but you'd better not ask me another damn question about the case during the ride, got it?"

Oh, yeah, he "got it." Todd smiled. "Come on, my car's around back."

She stepped closer to him

He released his hold on her arm, and his hand rose, brushed lightly across her cheek. *Damn, but the woman's skin was soft.*

Cara stilled.

"And my name's Todd," he said quietly because she hadn't said his first name yet, and he wanted her to say it.

Wanted to hear the name fall from those kiss-me lips.

Her lips firmed. "Good for you, *Todd*." Then she stepped around him and marched toward the parking lot, giving him one stellar view of her firm ass.

Todd swallowed, then sent up a fast and furious prayer that he wasn't about to fall for a killer.

Because he had very definite plans to get close to Cara. He wanted her in his bed. Had from the beginning. But he wasn't going to be stupid enough to let down his guard with her.

He'd get her to trust him, to reveal all her secrets.

And if he had to do so, he'd use those secrets.

He just hoped he wouldn't have to hurt her.

Or that he wouldn't find out that her perfect bedroom eyes belonged to a soulless killer.

The cops were letting her go.

From the shadows, the killer watched Cara climb into the black Vette. Saw the detective stare down at her a minute too long.

The bastard was already falling into her web. Just like all the other idiots.

The plan was working perfectly. The body count was growing and the cops were fucking clueless.

Humans were so blind. Never seeing the reality around them until it was too late.

Soon, it would be too late for Detective Brooks. The poor human was on the list now.

But the cop wouldn't die right away. No point in a kill this soon—and Todd Brooks deserved to get to play this wonderful game a bit longer.

Brooks would play, and so would that bitch Cara.

Then death would come, in its blinding glory.

The killer could almost taste the sweet release.

Soon.

Chapter 3

"You don't need to get out," Cara said when Todd braked at her house. Her voice sounded higher and sharper than she'd intended. "I'll be fine now." She thought about thanking him for the ride, then discarded the idea.

Yes, she knew the guy had been doing his job when he questioned her, but she wasn't going to overlook the fact that he'd been one serious jerk.

Being in the car with him had unnerved her. They'd originally gone to the police station in a patrol car. She'd sat in the back. Like any good criminal.

The confines of Todd's Corvette were far too intimate. The leather seat felt soft and sleek beneath her, and with the windows rolled up, the scent of leather and man filled the car's interior.

Cara reached for the door handle.

"Wait."

Her fingers curled into a fist at the command, her fingernails biting into her palm. She glanced at him and found his stare trained on her.

The car was cloaked with shadows, but she could still see his eyes. The strong lines of his face. Cara licked her lips. "What?"

"You feel it, don't you?" A whisper that seemed like a caress against her skin.

She shook her head. "I don't know what you're talking about." She could lie, too.

His lips quirked, just a bit. With a flick of his fingers, he unhooked his seat belt and leaned toward her. "There's something here."

The promise of hot, wild sex. Of power and magic rushing into her body and making her scream with pleasure.

But she'd given that up because after the burn of fiery release, she hated the ashes of cold reality.

The reality that a man wouldn't love a demon, no matter how enticing her physical appearance.

His hand lifted, reached for her.

Her fingers flew out and locked around his wrist in a fierce grip.

Silence. Then he said, "I just wanted to touch you."

He sounded sincere, *but* . . . "I thought you just wanted to send me to jail."

He didn't deny her words. Didn't fight her hold. Good thing, too, because the way she was feeling, Cara would have shown him just how strong a succubus could be.

Instead, his eyes dropped to her lips. "I wonder," he spoke with words little more than a growl. "Do you taste as good as you smell?"

The damn pheromones. "It's not me that you want." The admission was hard.

"Ah, baby, but I'm going to have to disagree." He was close, so close that she could feel the light brush of his breath against her face.

"You don't understand—"

He kissed her. A soft, fast press of his lips against hers.

Cara's fingers tightened around him as desire began to heat her blood.

"Not enough." His lips were just above hers. "I need another taste . . ."

And she wanted more.

When his lips met hers again, her mouth was open. Ready. The kiss wasn't as soft this time, and she was glad. She could taste the hunger on his lips, his tongue. A hunger that matched her own.

There was no questing search as his tongue slipped past her lips. Just need. Demand.

A moan trembled in the back of her throat even as her mouth widened for him. Her tongue met his, licking, stroking. Her nipples began to ache and swell as the fire blazing inside of her grew.

She *knew* she shouldn't be doing this, but Cara couldn't stop. The cop was the wrong man for her. The situation was wrong.

But the need felt so right.

Power began to fill the air as his lust grew. Such sweet, tempting power. She could feel it, surrounding her. She could have that power. All of it.

She just had to take it.

Take him.

No. She'd sworn to fight that part of her life.

Cara pulled away from him, twisting her head to the side. "I—we have to stop."

His breath was ragged. So was hers. Cara realized she still held his hand. Instead of a punishing grip, her fingers caressed his flesh. She snatched her hand away from him.

"Easy." He didn't retreat and he kept his stare on her. "It was just a kiss."

That was how the sweetest temptation always started. With a soft kiss.

He was aroused. No denying the obvious. It was in his voice, and if she glanced down, she knew she'd see the outline of his swollen cock.

But she was aroused, too. The feel of his lips and tongue against hers had stroked the dark hungers within her, and the feel of his power in the air . . .

Resisting was the hardest thing she'd ever done.

Her chin lifted. She'd started a new life. Or she was trying to, anyway. Lusting after the detective, well, that hadn't been part of her finely crafted plans. "I can't do this," she told him, but couldn't help wishing that she could.

He smiled at her then, and with the streetlight drifting into the car, she could see the wink of his dimple. "Seems to me like you can, baby. You were doing one hell of a fine job just a minute ago."

Her chin rose another notch. "What I *meant* was that I *won't* do this." She reached for the door handle. *Second time is the charm.* She managed to shove open the passenger side door. Her body twisted, her feet touched the pavement and—

"You want me as much as I want you."

He had her there.

"Circumstances are shit now, no denying that."

She looked back at him.

"But I'm not just gonna walk away from you. Hell, even if you weren't hip deep in this mess, I *couldn't* walk away from you." His eyes blazed with intensity.

Cara stood, rising quickly from the car. The chilly air bit into her arms as she left the warmth of the Vette. "You don't have to walk away from me," she said, her voice clear. "I'll walk away from you." Then she took one step, another. Her back was ramrod straight, her head up. She left him like that, not looking back, even though her body ached for him.

"Running, Cara?"

His taunt didn't stop her. Damn it, but she could still taste him. She pushed open her gate—the one she'd never bothered to keep locked—and she took careful steps up the curving path until she finally reached her front door. It was only when she crossed the threshold of her house that Cara drew in a deep, clear breath.

And admitted to herself that, hell, yeah, she'd been running.

Because Todd Brooks scared her. Oh, he didn't scare the demon inside her. The demon could handle just about anything.

No, the demon wasn't particularly worried, but the woman was scared spitless.

Moments later, she heard the growl of his car pulling away. Her shoulders dropped as relief swept through her.

Safe.

For now.

Detective Brooks had finally called it a night, but she knew he'd be back.

Sooner or later.

The faint light of dawn snuck through her blinds just as Cara finally crawled into bed.

Her gritty eyes closed, shutting out the light. The bed was soft beneath her, the sheets faintly cool.

Sleep pushed down on her as exhaustion swept through her body. One deep breath, two, and the dreams claimed her.

The dreams . . .

She didn't know the apartment. Didn't recognize any of the furniture. Cara walked slowly across the floor, her bare feet soundless as they crept over the hardwood.

Where was she? She thought of calling out, but fear stilled her tongue.

Dream or reality? The question bored into her mind as she ventured forward. Succubi always had such strong, vivid dreams. Sometimes it was nearly impossible to tell the dream world from the real one.

A door waited in front of her. Wooden, painted white. Partially open.

Her hand lifted. Pressed lightly against the wood and sent the door swinging inward with a soft creak.

A man's room. The furniture was dark, heavy. Clothes—a shirt, pants, socks—were tossed haphazardly onto the floor. A king-size bed with rumpled covers waited in the middle of the room. An *occupied* bed.

Cara took a step toward the bed, then another, her movements almost helpless. She knew who would be in that bed, of course. There really wasn't any doubt in her mind.

She could smell him.

She'd thought of him before her eyes closed. Still tasted him on her lips.

His dark hair was a sharp contrast to the white pillowcase. His eyes were closed, his features softened in sleep.

Todd Brooks.
Dream or reality?
The floor creaked beneath her feet.
His eyes flew open. Locked on her.
"Cara?"

Too late, she realized what was happening. But it had been such a long time since she'd taken a walk in dreams.

He grabbed her arm, pulled her toward him and had her tumbling into the bed. "You're not real," he muttered. "Damn it, I know you can't be, but I'll take what I can get." Then his mouth was on hers. Hard. Hot. His tongue thrust deep and a growl rumbled in the back of his throat.

His arms wrapped around her, holding her tight. His chest was bare, the muscles strong and warm against her. She wore a thin nightgown, just like the one she'd jerked on before stumbling into bed.

Her nipples pebbled, aching, and the stiff points pushed against the soft silk of her gown.

She straddled him. The bedsheets covered his hips, but she could feel his arousal nudging against her core.

The man was most definitely aroused.

No. No. This shouldn't be happening. She had to stop, she—

His fingers eased under the spaghetti straps of her gown. His callused hands felt so good as they eased over the length of her arms, pushing down the gown and baring her breasts.

He tore his mouth from hers. Eased back so that he could get a better view of her. "God, baby, you're the best dream I've ever had."

The man had no idea.

She could feel the spark of magic in the air as his lust grew. His hunger swirled around her in waves of pulsing need. Her skin began to tingle with the promise of such pleasure.

And such dark power. Hers to take.

The strength it would give her . . .

But she shouldn't. Cara shook her head, fighting for her

own control as arousal had her sex moistening and her back arching in silent demand. No, this was wrong, she—

His lips closed over her breast. Pulled the mound deep into his mouth. Sucked.

Cara shuddered as her fingers dug into his arms. His teeth pressed against her, lightly scoring her flesh, and then he was licking her, long, hungry swipes of his tongue that had her moaning and twisting against him as she fought for more, *more*.

His hands slid down her body. Eased over her stomach, where the gown had pooled in a soft heap. His knuckles brushed across her belly button. Smoothed over her abdomen.

"Todd—" His name broke from her lips. She didn't usually speak while dreamwalking. It was too dangerous. Power was in her voice. A command that had his head snapping up and his eyes flying to hers.

His cock was rock hard now and she realized that she was moving her hips against his. Rocking back and forth. Faster with each stroke of her body.

Red stained his cheeks. His pupils dilated as she watched. And his lips gleamed with a faint sheen of moisture.

Cara fought for sanity once more. "No, I-I can't—"

In a instant, he tumbled her back onto the bed. "It's a dream, baby. We can do anything." He kissed her again. A kiss so sweet and soft that she swore she felt her eyes fill.

If only . . .

But some dreams could turn into nightmares far too easily, and if they didn't stop soon, Todd would learn that lesson. Every moment she stayed with him, she was stealing a little of his life force. Taking a bit of his power as she stole into his mind.

She'd sworn not to take from a lover again.

Damn it, she hated to take!

It reminded her that she was little more than a parasite, living off the power and pleasure of others.

Her hands lifted, caught his face in her palms. She wanted to keep kissing him, to let the passion rage.

Not a choice for her.

His head lifted. His gaze met hers. "You feel so real."

Her lips curved in a smile she knew was sad. "Close your eyes for me."

He obeyed at once, but then, she'd put force into her voice, a compulsion he couldn't resist. Humans were always at their weakest in the dream state.

Her index finger smoothed over his lips. Then she tilted her head, just a few inches, and urged his mouth back to hers. His lips were parted as he readied to kiss her—

She blew a light stream of air into his mouth. A soft, sweet stream that she knew would taste of magic.

His eyes opened, bleary, confused.

"Sleep," she whispered the command.

Then she closed her own eyes, and left the dream.

"Oh, damn." Cara's eyes jerked open and she glared up at the ceiling.

What in the world had just happened?

A walk in dreams. She hadn't snuck into a man's dreams in over five years. She'd vowed never to enter without permission again.

Then she'd gone and plunged straight into Todd's head.

Damn.

Jumping from the bed, she ran toward her mirror. Her reflection stared back at her, eyes wide, hair tangled, skin faintly glowing.

Glowing. Crap. She'd taken from him. Stolen his power as her spirit had seduced his body.

Her head began to shake. A hard back-and-forth motion. She'd taken, and he'd awaken weak now.

"I didn't mean to do it," she whispered, confessing to an image that just stared helplessly back at her. Dreamwalking took focus, intent—hell, often a meditative state. Stealing into the dreams of others was a skill that succubi didn't master until well after sexual maturity. It was one of their greatest weapons, and by far one of the most dangerous.

Cara swallowed and tasted the ash of guilt on her tongue. She'd been dead tired, certainly not possessing the strength needed to slip into a human's secret dreams. She *never* should have been able to cross the miles and find Todd's mind.

It shouldn't have happened, but it had.

She'd just have to make absolutely certain it didn't happen again, because, if it did, she wasn't certain she'd be able to hold on to her control.

The temptation to take the handsome detective was just too strong.

"Shit!" Todd woke up, instantly and completely conscious. Damn it, he was alone.

His hands fisted over the sheets. He could have sworn that Cara was with him. Holding him. Kissing him.

A dull ache pounded in his temples as he rose from the bed. Not enough sleep, he figured, glancing at the clock to find out that he'd been in bed a total of four hours.

Not nearly long enough.

He ran a hand over his face, and, for a second, he could have sworn that he smelled her.

Cara.

The woman was seriously fucking him up. The last time he'd had a dream that hot about a woman—well, hell, he didn't think he'd *ever* had a dream that intense.

He could still feel her satiny skin beneath his fingertips, still feel the curves of her breasts.

His cock was hard and heavy with need. A need that he knew only one woman could slake.

Shit.

Todd headed for the bathroom. He needed a cold shower. It would wake him up and chase the woman from his mind.

He yanked on the water, sending the powerful stream jetting full blast, then he stepped back, caught the flash of his reflection in the mirror—

He frowned. *What the hell?*

His gaze swept past the faint scars on his chest and side. Instead, his stare dropped down to his left arm. His eyes narrowed as he studied the five small half-moon marks on his flesh. Wounds that looked just like they'd been made by a woman's nails.

"No damn way." He lifted his right arm. Studied the biceps. Saw the same small wounds.

In his dream, Cara's fingers had bit into the flesh of his arms as she'd held tight to him. Her nails had pierced his skin and he'd been aware of the faint sting, and of the pleasure of feeling her hips press against his.

But that had just been a dream. A hot fantasy that followed him while he slept.

He ran his fingers over the marks. Felt the raised skin.

"No damn way," he repeated, even as a wave of unease rippled through him.

No other woman had caused the wounds. He'd stopped seeing his last lover, another cop at the precinct, just over a month before.

His stomach knotted. So how the hell had he gotten a woman's scratch marks on his arms?

Cara.

Chapter 4

The lady's alibis checked out.

Part of Todd was thrilled by that news—a very, very large part—because the confirmation meant that the delectable Cara was now fair game for him.

Another part was seriously pissed, and worried. If Cara wasn't the killer, then the murderer had set her up. No other explanation jived for him.

A killer who liked to play games—*damn* bad news.

It was Wednesday night. It had been two days since he'd last seen Cara, since he'd gotten to touch those perfect lips and feel her soft tongue stroke against his.

He'd stayed away, knowing he had to keep his distance until he verified her alibis for the murders. Sex with a suspect wasn't something he particularly wanted complicating his life.

But the lady had been cleared now.

According to Colin, five waitresses and two bartenders had placed Cara at Paradise Found right at the time of the first two kills. And one very nosy, sharp-eyed, elderly neighbor had backed up her story about being home alone during the time of House's murder.

Ms. Murphy, former schoolteacher and extreme art enthusiast—judging by the dozens of canvases in her den—had cheerfully told him that "I saw her come racing home right after five. In that bright red car of hers. Went in, stayed in." A beetled frown had pulled down her white brows. "I thought a man would come and see her, but," a rather disappointed sigh followed, "no one came that night."

"So she was home from a little after five until ten p.m.?" He'd asked.

She'd jerked her thumb to a canvas covered in dark gray paint. "I was on the porch, trying a new technique. I call it night painting . . ."

"Uh, huh."

"I was there till midnight." Her fingers, stained with paint, had floated in the air between them. "Cara never left. I'd swear my life on it." The lady had stuck with that story even after repeated questioning from both him and Colin.

The desk clerk had also been shown a photo lineup. The guy had stared at the line of six blondes, and shaken his head. "I-I don't think I s-see her." His words had been husky, the beer still strong on his breath.

"You don't *think* or you *know* she's not there?" Colin had pressed.

The bleary eyes had cleared for a moment. "She ain't there."

So, now, it appeared that Cara was in the clear.

Absolutely perfect.

A car horn sounded nearby—close enough to have Todd jerking in his seat. He was parked outside Paradise Found. He swore softly as he realized he'd been sitting in the car, staring at absolutely nothing, for the last ten minutes.

But, well, he had a few problems on his hands. He had to convince a woman who thought he was a major asshole that he just might be dateable.

Might.

He also had to catch a killer.

His life was damn busy these days.

With a harsh exhalation of air, Todd finally left his car. His weapon pressed into his back as he walked, and as he drew closer to the dark doors of the club, he couldn't help but remember his last trip to the bar.

He'd had the unfortunate pleasure of meeting Niol for the

first time then. Strange bastard. Since Colin had been the one to verify Cara's alibis at Paradise Found, it had been nearly two months since Todd's last, very memorable, visit to the club.

He wasn't exactly looking forward to seeing Niol again.

How the hell had he done it? Todd wondered. *How had the bastard managed to toss me across the room, without seeming to move so much as a finger?* That day, when he and his partner had come to interrogate Niol, things had gotten out of control, fast.

One minute, Todd had grabbed the guy's shoulder. The next, he'd found himself across the room, lying on top of a shattered table.

He'd known there was something odd about Niol from the first moment he met the guy. Every nerve in his body had gone on alert and the hair on his nape had risen.

That fierce awareness happened to him sometimes. Usually, it happened when the shit was about to hit the fan. When a perp was about to pull a gun or when all hell was seconds away from breaking loose.

He liked to think of it as his body's warning system. A strong instinct. Whatever it was, it had never led him wrong before.

He hadn't felt that response with Cara—at least, not at first. But when he'd walked into her house and gotten closer to her, all his systems had sent out a flashing alert.

He'd originally thought his gut was telling him the woman was a killer. Now, well, now he wondered if his body was just trying to tell him that the lady was pure danger to his soul.

"What the hell do you want, cop?" The snarl came from one of the bouncers, a guy who'd planted his body squarely in front of Todd's path.

Smothering a sigh, Todd glanced up, way up. *Shit.* He knew the tattooed giant in front of him. The asshole had been guarding the door the last time he'd paid a visit to Paradise Found. "I want in," he said simply.

The bouncer laughed at that, a deep rumbling laugh, and he

nudged his sidekick, a short, dark, heavily muscled guy whose nostrils were currently flaring as he leaned in close to Todd.

"Not our kind," the smaller one mumbled.

What the hell? Todd pulled a twenty out of his pocket. Shoved it at the giant jerk. "Open the damn door."

A smirk. The cash disappeared in a instant. "Yer funeral, cop."

The doors opened. The scream of a guitar pierced his ears and the rumble of voices danced into the night.

He paused on the threshold. "Your boss in?"

"Your lucky night, man," from the shorter guy. "Niol's gone hunting."

And just what did that mean?

Then he forgot about the question as he caught sight of a woman with long, golden hair.

Cara.

He stepped into Paradise, and heard the crackle of laughter behind him.

The bar was packed. Literally teeming with bodies. Men, women. Most of 'em looked like they were anywhere from twenty to forty years old. Some were huddling in shadows. Some were all but having sex on the dance floor.

As he walked toward the bar, his nostrils twitched as he caught a familiar scent. It was . . . blood. He'd worked enough crime scenes to know that coppery stench. Where was—

The man to the left of him lifted his head. Blood streamed down his chin. The woman in his arms moaned, turning her head just a fraction. Todd saw the marks on her then. Two deep holes in the side of her neck.

What the fuck?

He reached for his gun. "Get the hell away from her!"

There was a brief murmur at his yell, and one or two people glanced his way, but for the most part, he was ignored—even by the asshole who had attacked the woman.

The woman in question did look at him, though. Her face twisted into a snarl, and her lips lifted to reveal teeth that looked too damn sharp. "Fuck off, human!" she snapped, then grabbed the guy and stormed into the crowd.

"What?" He blinked, not sure what had just happened. No, an assault had occurred, he needed to help her and—

"It's not what you think," Cara's soft, sensuous voice trailed along his nerve endings and cut right through the roar of the bar.

His fingers still gripped the gun. He turned slowly toward her, not sure if he was really ready to face her again, even though he'd come to be bar just to see . . . her.

Shit. She was even more beautiful than he remembered. Her hair was soft and loose around her shoulders. Her face pale and lovely, like something out of a damn magazine ad. Her lips were a flash of crimson, and he wanted them on his.

She wore a short black dress. A tall pair of black boots. Her legs were bare, too tempting and so damn long.

It was all too easy to imagine grabbing her, lifting her up onto the bar that was less than five feet away, and getting her to wrap those sexy legs around his hips.

And if they weren't surrounded by a room full of weirdos who apparently got off on biting one another, well, he might just do that.

"Put the gun away," she ordered quietly. "You're not in any danger now."

His eyes narrowed. "That guy attacked the woman."

"No, they were just having a little foreplay." She pointed with her index finger.

He glanced across the room. Saw the couple snuggled into a corner, and watched as the woman lifted the man's wrist to her lips and bit down, hard.

"*Jesus.*"

She laughed then. A soft, rippling laugh. "No, he's one you definitely won't find here." Then her face slowly sobered and a faint line appeared between her brows. "What are *you* doing here?" The light seemed to dawn as her eyes narrowed. "Checking me out?"

Todd put his gun back into his holster and pulled his jacket over the weapon. "Already did that, baby."

He heard the sharp inhalation of her breath. "And?"

"And your alibis held—for all three murders." A fact that he couldn't help but be grateful for right then. The lady was in the clear. The faint scratches on his arm seemed to burn.

"Of course, they held," she said, brows snapping together. "I told you, *I* didn't kill anyone."

He noticed then that her eyes looked a little red. As if she'd been crying. "You okay?"

"No, I'm not." Her lips pressed together, then she said, "I went to see Michael's family today. They're really torn up."

Yeah, he'd seen them, too. They were grieving their hearts out, and they wanted answers, answers he couldn't give them. Not yet.

They seemed like a good family. The mother, a stylish older woman, had stared blankly at him as tears trickled from her eyes. Michael's father, his own eyes rimmed red, had wrapped his arms tight around the woman's frail shoulders, his gentle hold belying the rage Todd so easily read on his face.

A good family. One that had loved their son.

Todd hadn't belonged in a family like that since—aw, hell, he'd *never* been in a family like that. He was pretty much alone in the world now, and really, that was fine.

He didn't want the kind of pain he'd seen in the Houses's eyes.

Cara shook her head. "But if you already know I'm clear," her husky voice wrapped around him and banished the image of the family's grief, "then what are you doing here?"

Looking for her. He shrugged. "Can't a guy go to a bar to unwind after work?" Seemed a simple enough explanation to him.

"Not to this bar," she said instantly. "Not if the guy is you."

What did she mean by that?

"I don't really think this is . . . ah . . . quite your usual scene," she continued. "Maybe you should leave."

He blinked. "Excuse me?" Was the lady trying to kick him out?

The band stopped playing then as the music faded into silence.

"Hell, I'm on." Worry flickered across her face. "Are you going to leave?"

Not a chance. Especially if Cara was about to perform. "I want to watch you." The words came out as more of a demand than he'd intended.

"I-I'm not very good. Average, really. You won't be missing anything if you leave—"

"I'm staying." Yeah, the club wasn't his usual style, and he could feel most of the patrons glaring daggers at him, but Cara was there, he wanted her, and he wasn't fucking leaving.

"Fine." She shoved her index finger into his chest. "Just don't start anything, okay? Stay at the bar—and . . . stay out of trouble, you understand me?"

Then she was gone, pushing through the crowd as she headed for the small stage. He watched her for a moment, admiring the soft sway of her hips as she moved. The lady really had an incredible ass. One that he would love to get his hands on.

She climbed up onto the stage. A faint light flickered over her head, making her blond hair shine.

Todd eased back, grabbed a bar stool and prepared to watch. There was a tap on his shoulder. He turned around, "What—"

"Whiskey." The bartender—a young guy, probably in his early twenties—pushed his favorite drink across the gleaming bar top.

Todd's fingers curled over the glass. "Thanks."

"Compliments of the house."

The warning bells that had rung before in his head were suddenly back—ringing so loud they were nearly deafening. "Niol's here?" Was the bastard somewhere watching him?

A slow shake of the bartender's dark head. "Got standing orders to have drinks available to you and the other cop."

"Gyth?"

"Yeah." A brief smile curled the guy's lips. It wasn't a

friendly smile. More like a dog showing his fangs to an intruder who'd wandered into his yard. "Though if I had my way, neither of you bastards would be at *my* bar."

Well, he was making friends left and right tonight. Todd lifted the drink in a small salute and wondered vaguely if the guy had poisoned him. "Good to know."

The bartender's eyes narrowed to beady green points. "Watch yourself, cop. You'll find a lot of enemies here."

Yeah, he already had.

Todd drained the whiskey in one long gulp and felt the burn of the alcohol slide straight down his throat.

Then he heard her. The first light whispers of her song spread through the bar.

The voices and the laughter died almost instantly when she began to sing.

He spun around, his gaze zeroing in on her. The band played behind her. No more grating guitar cries. Instead, the band members poured out dark, bluesy music on their instruments.

Her fingers curled around a microphone. Her voice trembled faintly as she sang, and her eyes met his.

He couldn't have looked away then if the bartender had put a gun to his head.

Caught.

Oh, yeah, the lady had most definitely snared him.

Her voice grew stronger then. She didn't belt out the lyrics or croon or any damn thing like that. She just . . . sang, with a deep, husky voice that made his body tighten.

The song was a bit wild, the lyrics lusty and free as she sang about loving a man not meant to be. Her body moved slowly, the sway of her hips gentle and easy. Her left hand lifted, brushing against the air, and he could swear he felt that touch on his skin.

She wasn't the best singer he'd ever heard. It took him two and a half minutes to realize that. Her voice wasn't perfect on the notes. But she had something. A fire. A power that wrapped around the words and made even the freaks back in the corner stop to listen.

When the song ended, a taunting smile curved her lips. The room seemed to tremble as everyone watched her, and for a second, the light above her flickered and Cara actually seemed to glow.

He blinked, trying to clear his eyes, and in that moment, the illusion faded.

Cara stepped into the shadows, went to whisper to one of the band members.

Again. The order whispered through his mind. He wanted to hear her voice again. *Needed* to hear her. When she finally stepped back to the center of the stage, his shoulders slumped in relief. Then she began to sing again, spinning her web and rousing the hunger within him.

He didn't go to her when she finished her set. Todd just waited at the bar, watching her every move.

His stare had been locked on her since she'd taken the stage, and when she'd sang, Cara realized that she'd been singing for him.

Power floated all around her in the room. It filled her, teased her flesh. She sang to take that power. To build the tension in the bar and to feed off the waves of energy given by the supernaturals.

Since she hadn't been indulging in the pleasures of the flesh lately, singing was her only release. Niol knew that. He'd offered her the chance to sing at Paradise Found so that she could keep up her strength. Feeding from the crowd had actually been his idea. An experiment at first. One that had worked surprisingly well—well enough for her to decide to abstain from sex.

"Take a little from them all," he'd told her, his eyes as black as night. "They'll never know."

And even if they did know, what would they do? She didn't take enough power to hurt any of the patrons. She used her voice, injecting just the right amount of sex appeal and desire into her lyrics, and she let the crowd respond.

Then she took their excess sexual energy—it came to her as

if drawn by a magnet because *she* was the one controlling the lust. Her lyrics made her a sexual Pied Piper, and she pulled the raw energy of the bar patrons' lust right to her—and she used it to strengthen her own body. In a place like Paradise Found, where you could often even smell the scent of sex in the air, it was easy for a succubus to feed.

So far, her arrangement with Niol had been working very well for her.

Or rather, it *had* been working well, until the detective had shown up.

Keeping her focus had been nearly impossible when Todd was so close by. She hadn't wanted to sing to the crowd. She'd wanted to be alone with *him*. Wanted to see if the passion between them would burn as brightly as she suspected it would.

Damn it, the man was a temptation that she couldn't afford.

She walked to the bar. Stopped just in front of him. Her heart raced and her body trembled with the rush of power she'd gotten from the crowd. "What did you think?"

His gaze dropped to her lips. "I think every man in this bar wants you." A statement given with absolutely no hint of emotion.

"I was . . . talking about my singing."

"So was I." He leaned back against the bar. "Why here, Cara? You could probably be singing in any club in Atlanta that you wanted. Hell, you don't need to be on Niol's stage—"

"This is where I belong." She wouldn't give him any more of an explanation.

His lips thinned. "But I don't belong here, right?"

A little sadly, she shook her head.

"You know, I'm getting damn tired of feeling like there is some kind of secret shit going on in this town that I don't know about."

Understandable. For a second, she was tempted to tell him the truth.

But she really doubted the guy would believe her. Oh, yes, it would go something like, "I'm Cara, an immortal succubus.

Just so you know, this whole bar is full of demons and vampires and witches. Oh, and your partner, Gyth? He's a shifter. Yeah, he can turn into an animal at will."

He'd *definitely* buy that.

"And just what is it that you think is going on?" She asked him instead, and motioned with a slight flick of her hand for a drink from the bartender, Cameron.

Cameron's eyes faded to black for a moment as she stared at him and his glamour lessened. True demons had completely black eyes. Iris, cornea, even the sclera were all as black as night. But, so as not to scare the tender humans, most demons used a glamour to hide their real eye color.

Just as she hid hers.

Cameron pushed a martini glass toward her. Shot a glare toward Todd's back.

Cameron had never been a particular fan of humans, but he was generally harmless. She'd known the other demon for years. The guy might look like he'd just cruised past twenty-three, but she knew the truth about him.

The two of them had so damn much in common. *Too* much.

She shook her head, a slight move directed at him, and Cameron stepped back.

Todd sighed, a rough exhalation of air. "Hell if I know what's happening around here." He caught her hand, rubbed his fingers over her knuckles. "Maybe I'm just paranoid."

Or maybe not.

With her left hand, Cara reached for her drink. Took a quick sip to ease the dryness in her throat.

"You lied."

She nearly choked on the sweet liquid. "Wh-what?"

His lips curved into a half smile and his dimple peeked at her. "You can sing."

"I-um, th-thank you."

His fingers smoothed over her hand in a featherlight caress. The band began to play again. The music was sexy, slow. Soon, she knew they'd switch into another driving, hard rhythm. Niol's orders. He loved to mix things up at his club.

Besides, Niol subscribed to the theory that music tended to soothe the savage beast, and since so many beasts visited his club, he liked to play music that appealed to them all.

"Do you want to dance?" Todd asked, leaning close to her so that his breath feathered over her cheek.

Power still pulsed within her. A sensual energy that made her want to slide closer and rub her body against his. If they danced, she'd be able to do just that. She could touch him as much she wanted. She could feel the hard strength of his body along the length of hers.

Oh, but that sounded good.

Too good.

She took another sip of her drink. Then asked, "I take it I'm not a suspect anymore?" She wanted a straight answer, just for clarity.

He paused, a barely perceptible hesitation, before he said, "Nothing is pointing to you right now."

Not the answer she'd been hoping for. She really would have liked more of a "You're completely clear, baby, I'll never suspect you again" response. Her gaze held his as she tried to figure him out. "You're not, by any chance, trying to seduce some kind of confession out of me, are you, Detective?"

A slow shake of his head. "No, I'm just trying to seduce you, period."

Her fingers tightened around the glass.

"You want me," he continued. "I want you."

If only things were that simple.

He took the glass from her hand. "Dance with me."

One dance. Surely she could stay in control for just *one dance*. Cara turned away from him and led the way onto the already full dance floor.

Couples swayed together in time with the beat of the music. They looked like simple men and women, but Cara knew they weren't. Spells were being cast around them. Whispers of seduction and temptation filled the air. When Todd took her into his arms and pulled her tight against his chest, she wondered if perhaps she'd underestimated his power.

His pull was strong.

Though she was tall, Todd still towered over her, but when he held her, he bent his head and drew down close to her face. His body was a solid mass of muscle. As they moved, she felt the hard bulge of his cock rising against her.

She didn't pull back. Didn't fake any kind of false modesty. She pressed against him and enjoyed the sensual touch. She wished then that she'd been born different.

Human.

Humans were so lucky. They could love and hate and fear and lust, and not have those emotions destroy them.

Unless they chose to be destroyed.

For her, there was no choice. Never had been.

His hands smoothed down her body, came to rest at the base of her spine.

"Todd . . ." She liked the feel of his name on her tongue, but she had to warn him, before things went too far. "I'm not a safe woman to want."

"I know." His hands were a heavy, warm weight. "But I'm not exactly a safe man." His hold tightened, for just an instant, and a lick of pure passionate fire shot through her.

Her sensually aware skin tingled, her pulse raced, and though Cara knew she was playing a dangerous game, she couldn't seem to stop herself.

He said he wasn't safe. Was he talking about the fact that he was a cop? Or something more?

"I'm not a nice guy," he continued, the words hard, but so soft they carried only to her ears. "I've done things—" He shook his head, "I've done what I *had* to do in order to bring criminals to justice. I've fought. I've lied."

Todd's confession didn't particularly surprise her.

His lips thinned. "I've even killed." His gaze met hers. "If you can't handle that, you need to tell me now."

She could handle it. The problem was that he wouldn't be able to handle *her*. A pang of sadness filled her as she stared up at him. "You like to fight evil, don't you? Like to make sure that the good guys win and that the bad guys get just what they deserve."

"I do my job," he said simply and his fingers pressed into her hips.

"Is everything black-and-white to you? Good or evil? Is that the only choice?" His answer was so important to her.

Because, like him, she'd done desperate things in her life. Fought. Lied. And as for the killing . . .

"Not anymore," he murmured. "Nothing's simple any damn more and—"

A soft vibration shook his hip and reverberated through her. *His cell phone.*

Todd's jaw clenched and his fingers dug into her hips.

Her time to play and dream had ended. Cara shook her head and stepped away from him, breaking his hold. "You'd better check that." The slow, moody music ended. From the corner of her eye, she saw Brock pick up his guitar. She knew what song would come next even before the screech of the instrument cut through the crowd.

Todd grabbed his phone, glanced at the glowing message and swore softly. "I've got to call Colin."

Of course, he did. Evil never slept. At least not in this city.

"Thanks for the dance." Her hand lifted and stroked down his cheek. A soft murmur of pleasure whispered past her lips as she felt the faint sting of stubble along his hard jaw.

He caught her hand. "It doesn't have to end with a dance."

"For me, it does." His hold was tight, but not unbreakable. "I'm not the kind of girl who has flings." Not anymore. Hell, she didn't have much of *anything* anymore.

But once upon a time . . .

"I could change your mind."

So confident. Such a silly, human trait. She kept her eyes on his, feeling the rush of psychic power flow through her. Hypnotism had always been one of her gifts. "I could change yours," she breathed the words as she decided to put an end to the game. No more temptation for her. No more wrong side of the town for him.

"Forget about me, Detective. Go back to your life. Fight your evil, and forget about me."

In the past, she whispered her words and made men into puppets, eager to follow her commands. Long ago, she'd been so good at giving her sweet suggestions.

Until she realized she didn't want puppets.

Todd's eyes widened and he shook his head. Once. Twice.

Sensitive. She'd nearly forgotten about his latent powers, but he wouldn't be able to resist her order, no one ever had, and—

"Your eyes . . ." The words seemed torn from him. "They aren't blue. I thought they were . . . but . . ."

Shit. He shouldn't be realizing what was happening. The guy sure as hell shouldn't have noticed that her eye color flickered with that burst of power.

What was happening?

Cara yanked her hand away from him.

He blinked.

The phone vibrated again with a hard buzz of sound.

"Go." An order from her, one without any hypnotic suggestion because her suggestions weren't working on him.

She could dreamwalk into his mind, plant a suggestion when his defenses were down, but she couldn't control him when he was awake and aware.

Never. Happened. Before.

A man she couldn't control. A human.

If her hypnotic power didn't work on him, if he could still choose on his own, then that meant he hadn't come to her just because of her pheromones and the soft, silent lure that a succubus sent out to prey.

Part of him, at least, and from the awareness in his eyes, she'd say a very *large* part, had chosen to want her.

Very, very scary.

And very arousing.

He wanted her.

"I'll see you again." He sounded absolutely certain.

When she'd told him to forget.

Her hands trembled.

He leaned forward. Kissed her hard, fast, and deep. His tongue claimed hers, seduced.

She was the one who should have seduced.

Then he was gone. Pushing through the crowd and leaving her alone.

As she'd been for so long.

Todd wasn't precisely sure what had just happened. One minute, he'd been staring down at Cara, thinking about how soft her lips looked and how badly he wanted to taste her again.

The next, he'd been looking into her eyes and realizing that the color looked too dark.

Not blue any longer—black.

She'd been talking to him, whispering something that had seemed very important at the time.

He couldn't remember the exact words, but he'd known something was wrong as he gazed down at her.

He'd shaken his head, focused all of his energy on her, and reality had snapped back to him.

Glancing over his shoulder, he found her still standing on the dance floor. A sad, almost lost expression covered her face. He hesitated.

Cara caught sight of him then. Her shoulders stiffened and a mask of indifference swept across her features.

Then she turned and disappeared into the throng of dancers.

Damn it.

He stalked toward the empty booths lining the rear of the bar. Lifted his phone and punched in the number for his partner. Colin answered on the second ring.

"Tell me this is important," Todd barked.

"It is." A pause. "We've got another body."

What? Jesus, already? He rubbed his eyes, felt a throb in his temples that matched the loud beat of the drums in the background. "Where?"

"Dayton Hotel. Off Marcus Street."

"I'm on my way." The killer was moving too fast. He wondered what poor bastard had fallen into the woman's grasp this time. "I'll be there in ten minutes." Marcus Street was close by. Hell, he'd probably be there in less than five.

The back exit was just a few feet away. He hurried forward, shoved open the heavy metal door, and stepped into the back alley.

The human detective burst out of the back door of the club. The killer froze.

Shit.

Their shoulders brushed, a quick touch. The killer hid a smile and grabbed for the door.

The cop hesitated. "What are you doing back here?"

Nosy bastard. If he didn't watch it, his time would run out—and the detective would find himself just as dead as the other fucking idiots. "Gettin' air." It was dark in the alley, and the cop wouldn't be able to see much.

Humans were so wonderfully weak.

And playing with them was so much damn fun.

For a moment, the temptation to attack the detective rose, sharp and hot—

But no, it wasn't time yet for Brooks to die.

Not just yet.

The back door swung open and the killer stepped inside Paradise Found. Waited a beat as the door swung shut. Then smiled.

Perfect. Just in time to catch the best succubus singer this side of the Mississippi.

And to dream of killing her.

Ah, such sweet dreams. Dreams of blood and death and rich, wonderful power.

Would Cara like those dreams? She'd be seeing them, perhaps dreamwalking into them, soon enough.

Then she'd be dying, just like all the others.

Revenge was so wonderfully sweet.

Chapter 5

"We've got a copycat," Colin announced the minute Todd walked to his side in front of the Dayton Hotel.

It was the last thing he'd been expecting. "What? How the hell is that even possible?" The guys in the department had been extra-Captain-McNeal-will-chew-your-ass careful. Nothing had been leaked to the press . . . yet.

So there should be no damn way to have a copycat killer striking in the night.

"Come on." Colin spun on his heel and stalked toward the line of hotel rooms on the east side. "See for yourself."

They strode past the uniforms scoping the scene. Colin pulled on his gloves as they slipped into the room.

Todd's gaze zeroed in on the body. Male. Muscled. Naked. Looked to be in his mid-thirties. And tied to the bed.

Same victim. Same MO.

Well, not exactly. The bedcovers were pulled up high on this guy. Past his pectorals. In the other cases, the bedspreads and sheets had pooled right over the men's groin areas.

Todd slanted a quick glance at Colin. Saw his partner's nostrils widen, just a bit.

"You smell that?" Colin asked.

Todd inhaled heavily, and caught the scent of . . . blood. He stepped forward, his gaze now sweeping over the victim's body like a hawk's.

A tech lifted the covers then, snapped a picture, and Todd got a good look at the guy's chest.

Blood coated his flesh.

"Sonofabitch."

"Yeah." Colin stepped closer. "The uniforms first on the scene didn't touch anything. They just called in the body, said a naked guy had been found tied to a bed with white hemp rope—"

"And no one even checked to see that the guy had been butchered." Fuck. Okay, so the uniforms hadn't wanted to disturb the crime scene—smart.

But, *damn*.

The lady hadn't been playing with weapons before.

So much blood. The poor bastard in the bed had died hard.

"I'd say the guy's been dead less than an hour," the tech told them.

Colin grunted. "The guy at check-in has him signing in at nine."

So the time line fit. Okay, but . . . "Was there anyone with him when he checked in?" Todd asked.

Colin gave a hard nod. "Talked to the clerk right before you got here." A dark brow rose. "He saw a woman with long blond hair. A woman who kept her back turned away from him most of the time."

What was going on? Serials didn't change their MOs. Not this fast.

"It can't be a copy," he muttered, "no one knows about the scene, and—"

"That little redhead, what's her name? Hannah? Holly? You know, the reporter who replaced Darla on *News Flash Five*?"

Todd nodded cautiously. *Holly Storm.*

"I saw her nosing around the scene of the second kill. The captain sent out a gag order." *A damn strong one.* Colin shrugged. "But maybe the lady got some info from one of the uniforms."

"It would've been on the five o'clock news if she had."
He'd seen her at the scene, too, skulking around in typical reporter fashion. But Holly hadn't broadcast any hard-hitting
stories yet—because no one on the force had given her so
much as a five-second sound bite—and the public wasn't even
aware that there was a crime wave *to* copy.

Something else was going on.

The scene didn't *feel* like a copy.

"Someone has to know." Colin pointed to the bed. "Someone knows and they're trying damn hard to make the scene
look the others."

"Uh, guys?" The tech's voice, breaking with excitement.

Their heads jerked toward him. The guy lifted up a knife,
blade still bloody, gingerly holding it by the hilt. "I think
we've got the weapon."

Well, damn. Now that was sure as hell *not* like the other
scenes.

But then, neither was the bloody body.

Either they were dealing with a whole different killer—one
who liked the bondage games just as much as the last woman,
only she liked for her prey to bleed—or their case had just
gotten a very, very big break.

"Let's get it to forensics." They needed to scan that baby
for prints, ASAP. The odds that there would be a match in the
system were slim, even *if* the perp hadn't wiped the hilt clean.

Still it was a solid lead, something that they could run with
on the hunt. The fire of the chase began to heat Todd's blood.

It was dawn before Todd made it back to his place. He
stripped, then all but fell into the bed.

He caught her scent then. A light, lavender fragrance hanging in the air, mixed with the wilder scent of woman.

Cara.

Hell, it was like the woman was right there with him.

As he closed his eyes, he whispered her name, and wondered if he'd dream of her again.

Or if he'd slip back into the past and dream of sharp teeth

and savage claws. A nightmare that he couldn't escape from as he watched a man transform into a beast in a blinding fury of crunching bones and savage pain.

He wanted Cara, not that shifting demon from hell. The demon who had his partner's eyes.

She opened her eyes and found herself in his bedroom once more.

Dream or reality? This time, she knew the answer right away.

Light filled the room. Chased away the shadows and clearly showed the man on the bed. He was naked. She could see the muscled expanse of his chest. The faint marks near his shoulder, the white line too close to his heart, and the jagged imprint on his side. Old wounds—the price of his job.

A light covering of dark hair arrowed down to his groin— right down to the heavily aroused flesh of his cock.

The guy emanated so much sexual tension it was a draw she could all but taste in the room.

But she still shouldn't have been in his dream. Cara frowned even as she stepped forward almost helplessly. She hadn't entered his dream deliberately. Once she'd gotten into bed, she'd closed her eyes and let exhaustion claim her.

She should have slept in blessed darkness.

Not been sent to him.

What was going on? It was like she had no control over herself or her powers when she thought of him.

"Come closer, Cara," he whispered, and her eyes lifted in surprise to find his hungry stare on her.

Shouldn't have happened. Even in the dream state, she should have needed to command his eyes open.

Cara hesitated, confused. *But the time before, he'd been awake and aware—just as he was now.* She just hadn't truly realized the significance of that act—until now.

The man had too much power for a human, and if she had any sense, she'd be transporting out of the dream state as fast as she could.

Instead of licking her lips and inching toward the bed.

His gaze dropped and raked over her. His stare was so hot her flesh seemed to burn.

"You're wearing too many clothes."

Just a thin gown, like before. No underwear. She lifted her hands, caught the silk, and pulled it over her head.

Todd swallowed.

She tossed the gown onto the floor. "Now I'm not." The good part of her, the part that had sprung to life just a few years back, screamed at her that this was a mistake. She shouldn't be in his mind without his permission. Shouldn't be planning to enjoy a sensual game with him. Shouldn't be so eager to taste him, his lips, his body, his very soul.

But the other part of her, the wild, dark demon who lived in her heart, she all but growled with eagerness. *So much strength and power.*

Cara wanted him.

And she would have him.

If only in her dreams.

His dreams.

She eased onto the bed, then crawled up the mattress until she crouched over him. Her index finger lifted and trailed a path down the center of his chest. Her gaze darted over the faint scars and, for a moment, a pang shot through her.

Humans could be hurt so easily.

"God, this feels so real," he muttered. "I can smell you, all around me." He reached for her, fisting his hands in her hair and dragging her up for a hard, deep kiss. A kiss that made her forget about the scars and know only raw need. "And I can damn well taste you," he bit the words off against her lips. Then he kissed her again. Harder. The thrust of his tongue claimed her mouth, and she responded greedily, stroking him and widening her lips.

Her hands caught his shoulders. Broad. Powerful. She pushed up, levering her body so that he lay beneath her while she straddled his hips. "Tell me what you want." An order. Magic seemed to shimmer in the air.

He caught her hips and closed his fingers over her flesh.

The heavy weight of his hands forced her moist sex against the rigid length of his cock. "You know what I want."

"Tell me," she said, her voice husky. "I need the words." She craved them. It made the dream more real.

"I want to taste your breasts. Lick your nipples."

Her breasts ached with need. Too sensitive. She arched toward him. "Do it." A challenge.

His back rose from the bed. His lips closed hungrily around her left nipple. Sucked hard. Licked.

Bit. A light, sweet bite.

Cara shuddered and rubbed her sex over his cock. The slick cream from her core covered his thick length. The wet heat made it so easy for her sex to slide over his erection.

And it would be so easy to take him inside.

His mouth was on her other breast now. Wild. Desperate. Licking and sucking and the rough rasp of his tongue felt so good. She pressed her breast closer to him, wanting more.

Needing everything from him.

"Wh-what else?" The words were gasped. Her sex throbbed with need. Her entire body seemed to vibrate with tension and sensual hunger.

It had been too long since she'd fed from a man's release—and known the fierce pleasure of her own. "What else . . . do you want?"

His head lifted, lips wet with a soft sheen of moisture. The look in his eyes caught her breath. "I want you spread beneath me."

She lifted slightly on her knees. His hands still held her hips. The fingers of his right hand were just below the half-moon birthmark on her left side. She rose a few inches higher, breaking the flesh-on-flesh contact of their sexes. Cara gazed down at her body. At the ivory skin. The light hair that shielded her sex. Then her gaze drifted to his body. Golden skin. Rippling muscles. Thick, full cock. She licked her lips. "What about above you?"

His gaze dropped. His eyes narrowed as he stared at her sex and his lips parted. "I want to taste you."

She could all too readily imagine the warm swipe of his tongue on her flesh. "That's just—"

A sharp, shrieking cry erupted in the room.

Cara jumped in surprise.

Todd swore.

The damn phone.

The dream connection began to fade as the phone rang again, and its piercing call pulled Todd closer and closer to reality.

And farther away from her.

Saved by the bell, again. Cara's lips tightened. *More like screwed by the damn bell.*

She climbed from the bed. Her body ached with unfulfilled need, even as the demon greedily lapped up the sensual currents still permeating the air.

Put him back under. He can't fight you in the dream state. A dark, insidious voice whispered in her mind. *Finish. Take your pleasure. Give the man his.*

His hand snaked out, caught her wrist in a steely grip. "Stay with me."

A reluctant shake of her head. "That's not how it works."

The phone pealed again, the sound even louder as it broke the veil of fantasy.

His eyes seemed so aware as he gazed at her. Hunger and need raged in those dark depths. She wasn't certain just *how* aware he was of what was happening between them. Did he sense that it was so much more than just an erotic dream?

"You need to be careful." It was the woman who spoke, fighting back the demon's snarling demand and her dark wishes. "I'm not who"—*what*—"you think I am."

His fingers tightened around her. "Then tell me who you really are."

Her lips curled as the phone shrieked again. "Lover," *he could have been,* "I'm not even human."

A final demanding cry from the phone swept away the dream and carried her spirit back to her body.

* * *

I'm not even human.

Todd's eyes shot open and he reached for the phone, nearly knocking the nightstand onto the floor. "Damn it, *what*?" A bleary look at his bedside clock showed that he'd managed to sleep for two hours this time. Two whole fucking hours.

And screw it to hell, but he'd been enjoying that dream. Or at least, he had until Cara had whispered her little secret at the end. Just what in the hell had that been about? How fucked up was his subconscious? First the damn wolf nightmares—the fucking claws and teeth—and now this shit.

Couldn't a guy just have a good sex dream anymore?

"Ah, Detective?" The rough, slightly arrogant tone had him slapping a hand to his forehead.

Captain Danny McNeal. *Aw, hell.*

"Is this a bad time for you, Detective?" Annoyed now— and it really didn't pay to annoy the captain.

"Sorry, Captain. I was . . ." *fantasizing, having almost unbelievable sex . . .* "sleeping."

A grunt. "Well, Sleeping Beauty, if you can manage to drag your ass down to the station—"

His back teeth clenched. *Drag his ass.* Fucking nice. He'd worked most of the night to protect the people of Atlanta. He deserved to let his ass get some sleep now.

"—Smith has some info on your case."

Now *that* had him finally snapping to full wakefulness. "Be right there." But he was talking to the dial tone because McNeal had already hung up on him.

Bastard.

Todd met Colin on the steps of the precinct. His only consolation was that his partner looked like shit. Exactly the way he felt.

Smith's timing could have been a hell of a lot better.

Or, depending on the victim's perspective, he guessed it could have been worse.

But he knew the rules. The case came first. Then sleep.

As long as he could function adequately at his job and not jeopardize any civilians, well, he was good to go.

He and Colin rode the elevator silently down to the Crypt. The Crypt was Smith's domain. It housed the medical examiner's office as well as all the cold slabs, so the place always chilled him to the bone.

When the elevator doors slid open, he expected to hear the usual soft strains of Smith's jazz music, but, instead, a heavy, thick silence filled the air.

Colin hesitated. "Maybe you should talk to her alone." His face was tense, lips tight. "I don't . . . know if she's ready to see me yet."

Now that was damn odd. As far as Todd knew, Colin had rescued Smith from that psycho who'd taken her.

At his raised brow, Colin said, "Bad memories, you know? She just got back, I don't want to stir anything up for her." The man looked seriously uncomfortable.

"You haven't talked to her since she's been working in the Crypt again?" Todd had gone down the first day to check in with the good doctor. She'd seemed quiet, her face a bit too tense, but otherwise, she'd appeared just fine.

Colin gave a curt shake of his head. "Not yet."

"Well, hell, man, there's no time like the present." He sauntered down the small hallway, grabbed the handle of the door, and opened it with a quick pull. "After you."

Colin lifted his chin. Marched forward. "Damn it, I don't want her to freak out."

Yeah, well, Smith had never really struck him as the "freak out" type. More the serious, smart, and very-much-together genius type.

Colin entered the Crypt first, then Todd swept inside behind him, calling out, "Smith! We're here—"

She stepped out from behind a row of filing cabinets. Her dark gaze immediately went to his partner, and a tremble seemed to roll over her entire body.

"*Smith!*" He lunged forward, certain that the ME was about to faint.

Colin beat him to her. He grabbed Smith, holding her easily and then pushing her down into a nearby chair. "Easy."

She sucked in a deep gulp of air. Her skin, light, creamy brown, had completely healed from the attack. The bruises had faded. The scratches and cuts had healed. Smith looked like her old self. Gorgeous face. Exotic eyes. Hair dark as night.

But the fear that he saw lurking in those dark eyes, that was new. Before, Smith hadn't been afraid of a damn thing.

He'd admired that about her.

"Get your hands off me," she told Colin, her voice a growl. "I'm *fine*."

He backed off immediately.

Smith's fingers, delicate, ringless, rose to clutch the arms of the chair. Her body wasn't shaking anymore, and when Colin eased back across the room, some of the fear faded from her gaze. Well, well. What was this about? Apparently, he wasn't the only one who got nervous around old Colin these days.

But then, after seeing the guy transform into a four-legged dog with teeth a shark would envy, Todd figured he had a right to be a bit on the edgy side.

After all, it wasn't every day that a guy found out his partner could lick his own ass. Or rip a man's throat out with his teeth.

Smith's body trembled "How's your doc doing?" She asked Colin, and there was an edge to the words that Todd couldn't quite define.

Colin lifted his brows. "Good. If you went to see her, *like you should*, you'd know that."

Her full lips curved into what was definitely not a smile. More a snarl. "I'm afraid I'm not quite the type of patient she's used to."

Now what the hell was this? Todd stepped between them, lifting his hands. "Uh, yeah, it's obvious you two have some shit to talk about, and that's just great." He turned his attention solely to Smith. "But I'm tired as hell, and just want to know about the case right now, okay?"

Smith gave a hard nod. "Fine."

That seemed to be her favorite word, but from what he could tell, the lady was definitely not *fine*. Okay, so he'd been mistaken about her.

A trip to the psychologist sure might be in order for the ME. Well, actually, she'd already been to one. The department had demanded that she go see a counselor before coming back on duty. He just wasn't sure the person she'd seen had helped her.

Maybe Colin's lady could. Dr. Drake sure seemed to know what she was doing.

Smith pushed out of her chair. The wheels squeaked as the chair rolled behind her.

Todd stepped forward instinctively.

She lifted a hand. "Don't even think about it. I just missed breakfast, okay? My blood sugar is too low."

If that was the way she wanted to spin it . . .

Smith moved toward her desk. "Prelim is done on Michael House." She lifted a file, handed it to Todd. "I could've just sent this up, but . . . I needed to talk to you." She cast a quick look in Colin's direction and after a brief pause said, "*Both* of you."

From the corner of his eye, he saw Colin nod.

"So what's the verdict, Smith?" Todd asked. He'd read the file later—every word—but when he worked a murder, he always liked to talk face-to-face with Smith—or Phillips, if that idiot was subbing for her—because he could learn more from the death doctors that way. His gaze darted to the left as he wondered where House's body was. In the vault behind him? Sewn back together all nice and neat?

He really didn't know how Smith did her job. Fighting criminals, finding the bodies, that was hard enough. But working with the dead, every day and night, hell, that was a whole other ball game—a gruesome, give-you-nightmares game.

"Well, I haven't got the tox screen back yet. Even with a rush order to the lab, it's going to take longer . . ."

"What have you got?" The woman was hedging.

She exhaled. "Not a hell of a lot." For an instant, she looked just like her old self. "The guy was in good shape, a nonsmoker. Thirty-five. No diseases or defects—"

"We *know* this," Colin broke in, voice tight, arms crossed over his chest. His usual intimidating stance.

"No, I don't think you get me," she snapped right back at him. "The guy was in *good* shape. There was no sign of coronary artery disease—"

"Wait a minute—you're telling us the guy didn't die of a heart attack?" Todd asked, his own heart beginning to race faster.

Smith hesitated. Cast another quick look at Colin. "I'm saying the guy's heart was in great condition. Hell, the *best* heart I've ever seen in my ten years down here." She rubbed the back of her neck.

"How did he die, Smith?" Todd pressed.

"I can't determine the cause of death yet. I told you . . ." Impatient now, her eyes narrowed, "I won't have the tox screen for several days yet."

Colin slowly uncrossed his arms. "So you brought us here to basically—what? Say the guy was healthy? No offense, Smith, but you could have told us this shit on the phone." He was obviously angry, and Todd was starting to feel the same way.

Too little sleep. Too few leads. Too many bodies. And, shit, if he went back up to the captain, told him their latest vic was a prime specimen of health who'd just happened to drop dead in the middle of some sex games, McNeal would kick his ass all the way back down to the Crypt.

"There was no sign of trauma. No contusions." She shook her head. "The man's body was in perfect condition. Inside, and out." Another hesitation. "At first."

"He was—*what?*" His temples throbbed. "What do you mean, 'at first'?"

Smith reached for her white gloves. "Detectives, there is something you've got to see." She walked across the room, her feet hurriedly tapping on the white tiled floor. She stopped beside a gurney. Her hands reached for the plain white sheet that covered the body. "I took him out of storage a few minutes before you arrived."

Todd hurried to her side. Colin flanked him.

She pulled the sheet down, a faint tremble in her hands. "Check out his chest."

Michael House's flesh was chalky, the dried-out color of the dead. And on his chest, right over his heart and cutting across Smith's careful stitch work, a very clear impression had formed.

The outline of a hand.

"No fucking way." Todd leaned down for a closer look. Caught the cloying scent of the body. Fought to control an instinctual gag.

"Those are what I think are fingers." Her gloved hand moved to the top of the marks, her index finger tracing the pattern. "The side of the hand. The palm."

He could see it. Perfectly.

"When I began the autopsy, this injury wasn't there." Her hand paused over the dead man's chest. "I sewed him back up, started the arrangements to contact the family, then I checked him again and the mark . . . just appeared." Smith's lips pursed for a moment. "It was lighter in the beginning. This is the darkest I've seen it."

It was the weirdest damn thing he'd ever seen.

"Bruising can be caused postmortem," Smith spoke softly, thoughtfully. "I've heard of a case where a guy's body was pulled from a river. Later, bruises appeared on the arm that the cop grabbed to haul the guy out of the water."

"Are you saying that you pushed House's chest too hard?" Colin raised a brow, waited.

"No." Her eyes narrowed. "I'm saying this mark you see right here," she tapped the spot, "appeared in five minutes. This isn't just some bruise—"

"No, it isn't." Todd was adamant on that.

The mark *wasn't* a bruise. He'd learned long ago that bruises could often show up after death and he'd certainly seen his share of those while haunting the Crypt with Smith. But this—this was different. This was the faint tracing of a hand in black, like someone had put a hand against the victim's chest and literally drawn a line around the edges. The interior of the mark was empty, and if the mark had been the result of a blow, Todd figured there would have been a middle pressure mark or deeper finger grooves.

Shit. It was almost like fucking art. The perfect design of a hand. He exhaled. "Were the other bodies like this?"

Smith's hand lifted. Balled into a frustrated fist. "No idea. That idiot Phillips marked 'em as natural causes. Both heart attacks. He had the bodies in and out of the Crypt—too fast."

The bodies were already in the ground now. It would take a court order to exhume them and see if the handprint was on their chests.

His gaze dropped once more to the print. It was like someone had just touched the guy, and killed him. "You're sure—absolutely one hundred percent certain—there was no internal trauma to the chest?"

She bared her teeth in a hard smile. "I'm sure I can do my job, Detective."

Yeah, he knew she could, too. Smith was the best and they were damn lucky to have her and her kiss-off attitude on staff.

He studied the mark, frowning. *Fucking odd.* He lifted his hand, let his fingers hesitate over the outline.

Smaller than his by a few inches.

But then, he'd been a quarterback long ago—back in the day—and he knew he had big hands.

"What the hell are we dealing with here?" He growled quietly. "How is this even possible?"

From the corner of his eye, he saw Smith's stare snap toward Colin.

Todd stiffened and the hand he'd raised over House's chest clenched into a fist. Slowly, he lifted his head and turned his attention to his partner. "There something you need to tell me?" He was damn tired of the games. Maybe they should just put their cards on the table. 'Cause going on everyday like this, acting like he didn't know Colin's secret—acting like everything was, to use Smith's word, *fine*, well, that just wasn't going to keep playing for him much longer.

Not with more weird shit happening—like this handprint on a man that for all intents, *shouldn't* be dead.

Colin shook his head.

"You seen this before, *partner*?" Todd asked, not ready to let the topic drop yet. No way was he going to let the guy hold out on him during *this* investigation.

Colin's jaw tensed. "I've never seen anything like this print before."

Todd wanted to believe him.

Partners *should* trust each other.

Yeah, and there also shouldn't be any secrets between partners. For a cop, there was no one on the streets who was closer than a partner. No one else watched your back like a partner. No one protected your ass like a partner.

And when you found out a partner had been deceiving you, well, nothing hurt as bad.

Todd's shoulders stiffened as he dragged his stare away from Colin and glanced back at Smith. "Any other tests you can do on him?"

"I'm running more blood work." She rolled her shoulders. "This—we need someone with a little more expertise in this area, okay?" Her gaze darted once more to Colin. "I'm out of my element here and—"

"What? Smith, *he's a stiff*!" It didn't get any more in her "element" than that! Todd tried to rein in the anger that wanted to shoot out of him. "The dead are your life."

She frowned at that. "No. They aren't." She shook her head. "Look, maybe we should call in a heart specialist, get a second opinion—make certain I didn't miss anything—"

"You're not the missing type, Smith." Colin's voice was certain.

Damn straight she wasn't. Todd opened his mouth to respond, then caught the faint quiver of Smith's fingers.

Shit. This is her first case back—the lady has to be nervous as hell. "Take your time, Smith," he told her, his voice softening. "Go over the body again, see what you can find."

Her eyes narrowed and for a minute, he thought *she* was going to be the one shooting out anger, but instead, she gave a jerky nod. *Okay, the lady obviously wasn't big on getting sympathy.*

Todd glanced at Colin. "We've got a problem, man—"

"Yeah . . . we're gonna have to see the other bodies."

No choice. Exhuming the dead was a bitch—getting the court orders, dealing with the grieving families—but there was *no choice.*

"Have you told McNeal about the print yet?" Colin asked.

"I was leaving that to you guys." Smith pulled the sheet back over the body. Her chin lifted and a brief smile curved her lips. Not really a smile so much as a feral baring of her teeth. "Thought you'd like to give him the info on that."

Great. Well, they'd have to break the news to the captain pretty fast if they wanted to get going with the bodies.

Colin turned toward the door, paused. "I don't have to tell you how important it is to keep these details quiet." He glanced over his shoulder, his eyes locking on Smith.

"No, you don't." Her shoulders straightened and a bit of her old fire flared in her dark eyes. She jerked her thumb toward Todd. "But you do sure as hell need to tell your partner what you're up against this time."

"Smith . . ." A warning.

Todd tensed. He had that shitty, I'm-in-the-dark feeling again. "Tell me what?"

"Not a damn thing," Colin snapped. "You already know everything about this case that I do."

"But you didn't on the last one, did you, Brooks? Gyth shut you out of the loop and went after the killer on his own."

Colin growled and the hair on Todd's nape rose. "Listen up, Smith," Colin snapped. "The way I see it, you really ought to be damn glad I *did* go after the killer." He turned toward her, facing her fully with clenched fists. "Otherwise, you wouldn't be examining dead bodies anymore." He paused, then said, "You'd be the dead one." Harsh. Cold.

Smith flinched. "You're an asshole, Gyth."

Todd's eyes widened. Okay, yeah, he had his problems with the guy, but fur notwithstanding, Colin was *his* partner. And Todd took his loyalties seriously. Maybe too seriously. "Ah, Smith, the guy did save your life."

She never glanced his way. "You don't understand what's happening, Brooks."

Maybe. Maybe not. "Then why don't you clue me in?"

Her lips tightened.

Fuck. "I thought so. Colin, let's get the hell out of here." He tucked the file under his arm. "You've got issues, Smith. Go see Dr. Drake. We need you back to your old self."

She swallowed. "I'll never be that woman again, Detective. All the therapy in the world won't bring her back."

"How do you know? Letting someone else inside your head could be the best thing you've ever done." He strode to the door. Shoved it open, but didn't exit. *Not the sympathy kind, but too damn bad*. He liked the woman, respected her, and wasn't going to watch her spiral. "I'm worried about you, Smith." And he was. She was too intense. Too high strung. And holding rage that was all but seeping from her pores. "Get some help. Go see Dr. Drake."

Emily Drake was, after all, the best in town.

The late-afternoon sunlight trickled through the blinds as Cara lay on the soft leather couch. She stared up at the ceiling and tried to figure out just what she should say.

Ah, hell, *just get it over with*. "I've met someone."

Dr. Emily Drake, known to her clients as the Monster Doctor, and currently the only psychologist in the South to knowingly treat the *Other*, slowly lifted her head. "Tell me about him."

Cara licked her lips. "He's a cop." Damn. Hadn't she heard somewhere that the Monster Doctor was dating a cop? What if the guys knew each other?

"I see." A delicate pause. "And does he know what you are?" The doctor's pen was poised an inch above her notepad.

Turning her head slightly, Cara let her gaze fall on the doctor. As usual, Dr. Drake's black hair was pulled back into a severe bun. Her thin, wire-framed glasses were perched on the edge of her nose. And her green gaze was trained on Cara. "Does he know?" Cara repeated the question softly, then shook her head. "No, even though I've . . . dreamwalked with him."

The pen skittered across the paper as Dr. Drake jotted down a quick note.

"I didn't mean to," Cara said at once, then winced. Even though the doctor's expression hadn't changed, she still felt the need to explain herself. To justify stealing into a man's thoughts. "I swear, Dr. Drake, I never meant to join him in dreams."

"Then why did you?"

If she couldn't be honest here, in the safety of Dr. Drake's quiet office, she couldn't be honest anywhere. "I want him." The want was a gnawing ache inside of her. An ache that grew worse every moment.

"It's all right to desire a man, Cara. We've been over this before."

No, this was far different from the men before. "I-I gave up sex." Said in a rush.

Dr. Drake's eyes widened and her pen stilled. "Cara, you know you can't do that. It'll kill you."

"No, I don't think"—*okay, she hoped*—"that it will. I've got an arrangement with a friend. He has this place for the *Other*. I've been singing there for a while. When I'm on stage and have the focus of the crowd, I can the pull their sensual energy to me."

"But will that be enough for you?"

"I don't know, it seems to be working so far. I mean, it's not like there are a lot of succubi around here that I can ask if I'll be able to survive—"

"No," Dr. Drake's quiet voice cut straight through her words. "That's not what I meant." She put the notepad face-down. Leaned forward. "Your kind exist for sex. It renews you. Powers you. I don't know if the situation you have will keep working for you, though it's certainly a novel approach for a succubus," she murmured. "But is it *enough* for you? Are you happy stealing wisps of pleasure, or do you want your own release?"

Her own. Her lips pressed together to keep the words back, but she knew when Dr. Drake lifted one brow that the psychologist understood.

"And you want it with him, don't you?"

Hell, yes. She wanted sex with her cop so badly that she was losing control of the demon inside and slipping into Todd's mind. "I can't control him." Or herself. "I can dreamwalk with him, but I can't compel him, not when he's awake. No hypnosis, no—"

"Control is important to you, isn't it?" She eased back in her chair, casually reached for her pad once more.

"Yes."

"Because of what happened before? When you weren't able to stop your sister's murder?"

Ah, damn, but she hadn't even seen that one coming. Leave it to good old Dr. Drake to knock her right between the eyes. "Yes." A jealous lover. A *human* lover had killed her sister. A man who had managed to learn far too much about her kind, and the weaknesses that demons possessed.

Nina. It hurt too much to think of her now, even years later. Her twin. The only other being who'd ever truly loved her. Who'd understood her. Inside and out.

Killed by that bastard.

She'd made certain he got exactly what he deserved. Sometimes, she could still hear his screams.

She squeezed her eyes shut. *No.* She wasn't going back there, not now.

All humans weren't evil. She knew that. Had long ago come to terms with the fact that monsters resided in men, just as good spirits, good souls, could reside in the bodies of monsters.

Such was the way of her world.

"Do you think that because you can't control him that this man might one day betray you?"

"I don't know. Maybe." The guy had suspected her of murder and he'd sure been quick to haul her off to jail.

"You came to me in the beginning because you were tired of puppets. Tired of men who turned away from you the moment you stopped using glamour and magic."

Her nails dug into the cushions of the couch. "Yes."

"But now, you have a man you can't control, one who certainly won't be a puppet. You want him. Tell me, does he want you?"

She could still taste his hunger. "Yes."

"Then you're going to have a choice to make, Cara. You can keep living this new life you've made for yourself . . ."

The life without sex. Stolen pleasures. Empty nights.

"Or you can take a risk with a man beyond your control."

She pictured Todd in her mind. Dark hair. Sculpted jaw. The chest she'd yet to kiss. The cock she wanted to taste.

Beyond her control.

She'd be vulnerable with him. And if he learned her secret, he could destroy her.

But demons didn't exactly have a reputation for playing it safe. She'd been trying, but it had been hell.

Though she liked to pretend that the demon and the woman were really two separate parts of her, the truth was, deep down, she was all demon.

The demon, well, she wasn't afraid of a risk, and she was very, very hungry for her pleasure.

A pleasure only to be had with one man.

A man beyond her control, but easily within her reach.

If she just dared to reach for him.

The demon decided she'd dare. Oh, yes. She would.

"Is the city in the clutches of another killer, one who preys on the sexual fantasies of men? The cops aren't talking, but rumors of the Bondage Killer are rampant on the streets . . ."

The reporter's words stopped the killer cold. He turned around slowly, his gaze jumping to the television screen. He listened to her, stunned . . . and enraged.

Fuck. Fuck. Fuck.

Fury nearly choked him when the redheaded bitch said she was broadcasting live from the Dayton Hotel, "the scene of a brutal murder."

But not *his* kill.

"A body was discovered here last night. A male body. The man was naked, and he'd been bound to the bed."

Oh, hell, no.

Not his.

The reporter's eyes seemed to bore into his as he glared at the screen. She lifted her microphone. "Tune in later tonight for more details on this savage crime. Until then, this is Holly Storm for *News Flash Five*, signing off."

His fingers slammed onto the top of the remote and instantly, the TV screen went black.

Not his.

He threw the remote against the wall.

This wasn't part of the plan. No one should have died at the Dayton Hotel.

Fuck.

His fingers shook. His ears rang. And his control began to shatter.

He knew exactly who was trying to take over his game.

Not gonna happen. No one was gonna to screw with his plans. He'd waited far too long for his vengeance. Planned far too carefully.

A bitch wasn't gonna steal his power.

Time for the game to change. Time for a solo act. Time for more death.

With the next kill, *he* would be the one to steal the victim's life away.

No matter how much she begged . . .

Chapter 6

He was watching her again.

That night, Cara stood on the stage, feeling the swirls of magic and power around her. Desire beat in time with the music of the band. Driving higher and higher in the crowd, and in her own body.

Todd was in Paradise. She hadn't looked at him yet, but she could feel his dark gaze on her body and pleasure filled her.

He'd come for her.

Slowly, she began to shift her attention around the room. Singing softly, the blues carried in the air as she voiced the old lyrics.

There. He was at the bar. Staring up at her. Face hard. One hand wrapped around a shot glass. He was dressed casually, in a pair of jeans and a button-up shirt.

She wanted him naked.

She was tired of pretending to be good.

Tired of fighting the need and hunger.

No more.

Giving up sex just really hadn't worked out so well for her. One temptation, one *very* strong temptation, and she'd been screwed.

The song finished on a long, deep note. She drank in the energy, inhaling deeply as she bowed briefly to the crowd.

Not enough. Tonight she needed so much more.

And she'd have it.

She replaced the microphone. Nodded to the band. Moved easily across the stage, her skirt swirling around the top of her thighs as she walked. When she lifted her hand to the stair railing, she saw the faint glow on her skin. She wondered if Todd would notice it. Hoped that he didn't, because she didn't want to give explanations this night.

She just wanted to give pleasure—and take her own.

She felt other stares on her as she sauntered across the room. One man even reached out and touched her shoulder, but Cara froze him with a look.

There was only one guy in the bar who interested her, and he was the one she was going to claim.

Todd's gaze never left her as she drew closer. He lifted the whiskey. Drained it in one fast gulp right before she reached him. The glass clattered against the bar.

"Hello, Detective." She thought about asking him how the case was going. She'd heard talk in the bar about a body being found at the Dayton Hotel. She wondered if the murder was connected to the others.

"Cara."

It was the way he said her name that got to her. Hunger. Lust. Tenderness.

She decided not to ask about the case. She didn't want to hear about another poor soul who had been killed, not then. She wanted the few hours of the remaining night to belong only to the two of them.

These precious hours just after midnight. Playtime for the *Other*.

"You were good tonight."

She motioned for Cameron to bring her usual drink. The sweet, ice-cold brew that she sipped after each performance. "Thanks." Tonight, she'd been singing just for him. Had he noticed?

Cameron put the drink on the bar. Narrowed his eyes on her. Screw him. She neither wanted nor needed his approval. Hell, she never gave him a hard time when he hooked up with human women.

Cameron's lips tightened when he caught her cold stare, but then he backed away. "Your choice." The words were whisper soft.

"Thanks, Cameron." And, yeah, it was *her* choice.

Or rather, Todd was her choice.

Cara leaned over the good detective, deliberately rubbing her body against his as she reached for her drink. She liked the way he smelled. The fresh scent of soap. A hint of after-shave. Man.

"We need to talk," he told her, and his voice was harder than before. His hands lifted, caught her just above her elbows.

She took one slow sip from her drink. The icy liquid eased down her throat. Cara licked her lips and noticed the slight widening of his nostrils. He was catching her pheromones again. He knew the scent was richer, knew something was happening. She could see it in his eyes.

See the same hard lust she felt.

"We are talking," she told him, wondering what his next move would be. She was putting on a bold front with him now, but the truth was, she was nervous as hell inside. If she had sex with him, if she gave in to her instincts, it wouldn't just be about fun and games and a rush of sweet, sensual power.

You have a man you can't control. Dr. Drake's words echoed in her mind.

"You're different tonight." His hold tightened.

Yes. "Why did you come back, Detective?"

"Todd." A pause. "I like it when you say my name."

A costly admission. It gave her more power. He should know that. "Todd." She obliged him softly. "Why are you here?"

"Maybe I like the band." His lips hitched into the briefest of smiles and that sexy dimple winked at her. "Or maybe it's the singer."

Oh, but the guy was smooth. Humans were often so gifted with their words. Especially the men.

She'd known human men who could lie their way into almost anyone's bed. But—

But Cara didn't get the feeling that Todd was lying to her. She took another sip of her drink, conscious of the warm weight of his hands on her arms. She wanted those hands on other parts of her body. She wanted them out of the bar and back at her place.

She wanted Todd any way she could get him.

Cara lifted a brow. "So what is it that you want to talk to me about?" She could hear him easily in the bar, even though voices and music surrounded them.

He brought his face close to hers. Stared into her eyes and said, "My dreams, Cara. I want to tell you all about my dreams."

The glass nearly slipped from her fingers. "Dreams?" He remembered them?

Men weren't supposed to remember dreams of a succubus. Pleasure, passion—those were the only impressions meant to stay in a man's mind. The succubus herself, well, she should be forgotten.

"You've been in my head," he said. "Awake, asleep, I just can't escape you."

And she couldn't escape him. "Do you want to escape?"

He brought his lips down onto hers. Kissed her once. A slow, leisurely taste of her lips, then a deep thrust of his tongue into her mouth. The human sure knew how to work his tongue.

When his mouth lifted, she wanted to moan at the loss.

"No."

At first, she didn't understand. Was he rejecting her? Then he said, "I don't want to get away from you." His eyes narrowed. *"I just want you."*

"Do you usually get what you want?" She bet that he did.

"Sometimes I do." For a moment, his lips tightened. "Sometimes I don't. Guess that's the way it is for us all, right?"

The way for humans.

"We can play the game, Cara," he told her, rubbing his hands up and down her arms in a rough caress. "I can be the gentleman. Take you out on a dates. Movies. Theater. Whatever you want."

He was what she wanted. The lust between them burned too bright for a slow courtship. She needed release. Pleasure.

Him.

Was it because he was a sensitive? Was he somehow magnifying the feelings of desire? It could be possible. Human psychics were rare. She'd only encountered a handful of others. Dr. Drake was by far the strongest she'd ever met.

Todd was strong, too, but his power was different.

Maybe because he didn't even realize he had it. If he channeled his magic—

Well, she wasn't exactly certain what would happen.

Her gaze dropped to the hands that still held her. She lifted a brow.

With a muttered curse, he released her.

Able to move more easily now, she pushed her glass back across the bar. Gave an almost imperceptible nod to Cameron. Despite his pissy mood, she'd managed to grill him about the detective earlier in the evening. Grudgingly, Cameron had admitted that the cop was known for being on the level. Not one to take a bribe or to "misplace" evidence. And, apparently, if the gossip around town was anything to go by, Todd had quite a reputation with the ladies. Not that she'd been particularly surprised by that news.

Cameron had also said the guy was a straight-up asshole, but Cam usually said that about human males.

Judging by Cam's continued glare, she figured he was clinging tightly to his asshole theory.

"I've never really had much use for gentlemen," Cara murmured, and the words were true. Of course, she hadn't really met that many gentlemen.

"So what do you want?"

She leaned toward him. Put her hand on his chest so that she could feel the fast thump of his heart. "I want to get out of here. Go someplace dark and quiet. And I want you with me." Under her. In her.

Now that she'd lowered the walls around herself just a bit, the lust was bursting though her body like water that had been contained behind a weak dam.

His jaw clenched. "You sure?"

"Very." She smiled at him, stepped back. "But the choice is yours, Detective." He was the one taking the bigger risk. He just didn't know it yet.

She wouldn't hurt him. She never hurt her lovers. Well, unless she meant to do so.

And she'd only meant to kill once.

A life for a life. Primitive justice, but it had been what her sister deserved.

She shook her head slightly, trying to push away the past. Now that she'd started thinking of Nina, that terrible night kept slipping into her mind.

This really wasn't the time to think about death and darkness. With Todd, she only wanted to think of pleasure and life.

She held up her hand. Offering, waiting.

"There's something different about you," he said. "I know it."

He was right, but he had no idea just how very different she could be. Perhaps she'd show him.

He reached for her hand.

The choice was made.

The whore had the cop under her spell. From the shadows, he watched as Cara and her detective left the bar . . . the human had his fucking hands all over her.

The fool didn't know who—*what*—he was touching. And he sure as hell didn't know what price he'd pay for his pleasure.

The others hadn't known, either. They'd fallen so easily for Cara and her lying eyes. Fallen . . . then died.

A smile curved his lips even as his hands clenched into fists.

Cara should have learned by now—the humans weren't for her.

Just how many would he have to kill before she learned her lesson?

Dr. Emily Drake stepped out of the elevator and into the dimly lit parking garage. It was late, well past midnight, but her vampire client hadn't been able to make it into the office any sooner. And Marvin had insisted on seeing her. Seemed he'd almost taken blood from a human the previous night. The near miss had so rattled him that Marvin had been physically sick ever since.

Poor Marvin.

A classic bloodphobic vamp.

But the guy was making some incredible headway. At least he wasn't afraid of the actual blood anymore.

No, now he could drink the blood just fine, provided he didn't have to get it straight from a source.

As she walked, Emily clutched her keys tightly in her right hand. The garage was all but deserted, the fluorescent lights flickering above her. Her car waited up ahead, maybe fifteen feet away, and—

Someone else was in the garage.

The certainty came to her on an icy wave of knowledge as Emily's psychic gift flared to life.

Hell. Who was—

She spotted the Jeep then. Parked behind one of the large columns. Nearly hidden from prying eyes. The perfect place to wait for unsuspecting prey.

Her shoulders slumped in relief when the driver's side door opened. *Of course.* She should have known *he* would be there. When she worked late, he usually showed up, even if he was working on a case.

"Colin." He stepped toward her, and for a moment, the glow of the shifter caught her stare. All shifters carried that glow, and as far as she knew, she was the only person on earth able to actually see it. The glow was a soft shine, kind of like a second skin. It was the beast glowing.

He opened his arms to her, man and beast, and she went to him without a second's hesitation. He pulled her tight against the hard length of his body. Held her close against his heart. Just the way she liked for him to hold her.

"I thought you were going to start walking down with one of the security guards," he growled, lowering his face to the curve of her neck and biting lightly.

Same old argument. "I can take care of myself, you know." She was far from helpless. The guy should've realized that by now.

His head lifted. His blue gaze met hers. "Just do it for me, okay? For my sanity, will you promise to only come in the garage this late if you've got a guard?"

Emily gave a grudging nod. She didn't like having to wait on security, but she would—*for Colin.* Hell, she would've waited that night, but she'd been in such a hurry to get home and see . . . him. "If I get the guards to escort me, does that mean you'll stop stalking the garage?"

He didn't answer. Just kissed her. A hard, deep kiss that had her moaning and wishing they were far away from the cold garage and instead in a warm, comfortable bed.

Her fingers curled over his shoulders, and when he broke the kiss, she was the one who almost howled in frustration.

"I need you to come with me to the station," he said, voice soft.

Her eyes widened. "Wh-what?" Not the sensual night plans she'd been hoping for.

His stare was solemn. "I think we may need you on another case, baby."

At his words, and at the darkness she saw lurking in his gaze, her sexy excitement began to fade.

"The place is deserted now. McNeal asked me to bring you in, see if you could look at the files."

Her fingers clenched around the strong muscles of his arms. "Just what do you think we're dealing with here?"

His hands smoothed down her back. There was tension in his touch and in his face. In the faint lines around his eyes and the tightness around his mouth. "A being that can kill a man with a touch." A hard exhalation of air. "Know anyone like that, doc?"

Yes, unfortunately, she did. The cold from the garage crept through her bones, settled in her heart.

Cara.

Todd followed Cara back to her place. She waited for him on the steps of her house, anticipation building in her and making her heart drum far too fast.

When he joined her, lust had hardened his face.

She kissed him. Because she needed to. Her tongue snaked into his mouth, teased his. Pleasured.

Oh, but the night ahead was going to be so *good.* Because she was finally going to be bad.

She broke the kiss, gazed up at him. "No regrets, Detective?" There was still time to call it off, if that was what he wanted.

"Not a damn one." He grabbed the keys from her hand, managed to unlock the door, then all but dragged her inside.

She'd always loved a strong man.

His mouth was back on hers before the door slammed shut behind them. Tasting. Devouring.

Cara had known it would be like this between them from that very first moment. She'd sensed it from the first look, and she was tired of fighting a hunger that just grew every minute.

The Monster Doctor had been right when she told her, weeks ago, that some instincts shouldn't, *couldn't,* be suppressed.

It was time for more pleasure.

Her fingers found the front of his shirt. Jerked. Buttons popped off and flew and she growled into his kiss.

His head rose, a hard smile curving his lips. "So that's the way you want to play?"

Then his hands were on her. Not her shirt. On the fabric of her skirt. He shoved the soft cotton up, and then his hand was on her thigh. Fingers stroking.

Her chin lifted and her breath panted out a bit faster. *Higher.* Just a few more inches, and he'd touch her just where she wanted him to—

His fingers trailed over the crotch of her black lace panties. He licked his lips. "You're wet."

Because she was so turned on that her body was about to explode. The sexual tension between them was so thick she could see it in the air and the powerful rush from that need was driving her wild.

So much wonderful energy.

His fingers curled around her underwear. Gripped. Yanked.

The fabric gave way with a soft rustle. Then his hand was on her sex. Parting her folds. Fingers sliding into the creamy warmth.

Her skirt was bunched at her waist. Her high heels pressed hard into the floor. Her breasts, aching, swollen, pushed against the cups of her bra.

And she was about thirty seconds away from her first release with the good detective.

The very *good* detective.

His thumb caressed the hard button of her need and he drove a finger, broad and long, into her core.

Her lips parted on a moan, but he caught the sound with his mouth, drinking it in and then thrusting his tongue deeply past her lips . . . just as he thrust his finger into her body.

One finger.

Another.

The man had *big* hands—long fingers, strong.

So good.

A slow thrust. Withdrawal. The swipe of his thumb against her clit. A thrust, harder, knuckles deep—

The release hit her. A fast, hard pop of pleasure that didn't satisfy. Oh, no, not even close. It just made her hungrier.

Her sex clenched around his fingers.

Oh, but this was going to be fun.

Cara brought her hands between them. Pushed against his chest.

His lips tore from hers. He gazed down at her, cheeks stained with color, lust on his face. Then he blinked, shook his head. "Cara, you look . . . different. So fucking beautiful, but—"

Shit.

The sensual energy was literally absorbing into her skin. The faint shine of the magic would be noticeable to him this close.

But not as noticeable if the lights were off.

She broke free of him, hating the loss of those clever fingers. Moving fast, she hit the lights and plunged the room into darkness.

He swore.

Stepping forward, she grabbed his hand. "Come with me."

A rusty laugh slipped past his lips. "Right now, I think I'd follow you to hell."

She stumbled at that. Had to choke back her instinctive protest. Finally managed to whisper, "The bedroom will be far enough for me."

He was giving her too much, too soon, and she was so greedy that if he didn't hold back more, she just might try to take everything.

They were at the foot of the stairs. Her porch light shone through the picture window, casting just enough illumination over the steps for them to see and move easily.

The rooms at the top of the landing were in darkness. Perfect. They hurried up the stairs.

His hand was warm against hers. The door to her bedroom stood partially open. With her left hand, she shoved against the wood, and it opened fully with a soft creak.

She stepped forward, heading for the brass bed she loved.

He didn't move.

"Todd?"

Her vision was sharper than a human's. Even in the dark, she could make out his form. See the tension he held in check.

"Why do I want you so much?" He asked. "I swear, I can't even breathe right now without tasting you." He moved a few inches forward, and the moonlight spilling through her bedroom window fell over his face.

Her pheromones filled the air. No way to control them now.

But she could smell his scent, too. The warm, rich scent of man. With every breath that she drew, she inhaled him.

And she could taste him on her tongue.

"You feel it, too, don't you?" He asked, and there was a demand in his voice.

It. The need. The lust that was almost overwhelming. Hell, yes, she felt it, too.

"I'm safe, Cara. I need you to know that. I use protection, *always* use it."

Good to know. She was immune to human diseases, but he wouldn't understand that if she told him. And it was honorable that he wanted to tell her of his health.

A gentleman.

It made her want him even more.

She tugged against his hold.

"Cara?" He released her.

Her fingers immediately went to the waist of his jeans. Found the buckle of his belt. She unhooked it, then she began to work on the snap of the jeans.

"Don't." An order.

She tilted her head back. "It's gonna be pretty hard for this to work with your pants still on there, stud."

A surprised bark of laughter rumbled from his throat and Cara's own lips curved.

Damn. How long has it been since I even felt like smiling with a man?

"Ah, baby, don't worry. The jeans will *definitely* be coming off." His fingertips trailed over her arms. "But I'd rather get you naked first."

She liked her plan better, *but* . . . Cara's fingers rose, began to lift up the hem of her shirt. She tossed it onto the floor. Unfastened the front clasp of her black bra.

Humans and their inventions. Sometimes they could be damn clever and sexy.

Her breasts sprang free. The nipples were tight with arousal. She wanted his hands on them. His mouth. But first—

With a swift move of her fingers, she shoved her skirt down her legs. It pooled around her ankles and she stepped out of the trapping fabric. She kicked her shoes across the room. "Better?"

He growled.

She took that as a yes.

"Your turn." Then her hands were on him. Unsnapping those jeans. Sliding down the zipper. Discovering a pair of boxers beneath the rough fabric of the jeans.

Then finding his cock. Aroused. Long. Wider than her wrist. Warm to the touch and pulsating with desire. She stroked him, a long caress from root to tip, and heard with pleasure the sound of his ragged breath.

"Don't tease, Cara." An order given with glittering eyes.

"I'm not." She stepped back. Moved to the edge of her bed and felt the mattress against the back of her thighs. Her hands were literally itching to touch him. To give pleasure. To take pleasure.

And power.

Just a touch. So simple. So gentle.

A touch could bring paradise or pain. Such was the way of her kind.

Lucky for Todd, she wasn't too much into the pain. Never had been.

"Tell me, Detective," she used the title deliberately, "just what do you like? A woman in control? Or do you like to keep the power?"

He swore softly. Shed his remaining clothes with an economy of motion. "I don't care much for games," he muttered, and she saw him reach into the back pocket of his jeans. He pulled out his wallet, reached inside for something. Probably protection. After a moment, he stalked toward her and tossed a small packet onto the bed. "I just care about getting you under me in, oh, the next five seconds."

Her lips parted to reply—

But he had her pinned to the bed, legs spread, arms anchored to the soft mattress above her head in, oh, three seconds.

The man might not like games, but he sure liked being in command.

The ridge of his arousal prodded against her sex. Todd was more than ready. So was she. He could thrust deep and hard into her right then and she wouldn't—

"I've dreamed about you."

Dreams he shouldn't have remembered.

"I want to know if your breasts feel as good against my tongue, in reality, as they do when I'm dreaming." Keeping his hold on her wrists, he lowered his head, the faint stubble of his five o'clock shadow scraping across her flesh in an electric caress that made her gasp.

His lips closed over her left nipple. His mouth was warm, wet, and his tongue, as it curved around her areola, so damn skilled.

Todd Brooks certainly wasn't an amateur when it came to pleasures of the flesh.

Good. Neither was she.

A moan filled the air. *Her* moan. She lifted her hips, rubbing against him and loving the friction of his body against hers.

His mouth opened wider and he began to suckle her. Strong. Hard.

"Todd!"

His head lifted. "You taste the same . . . just like my dreams." He turned his attention to her other breast.

Oh, *damn*. Sensual energy filled her body. She pulled her arms down, easily breaking his hold. "I can show you . . . ah, *that's good* . . . a reality that's a hell of a lot better than any dream."

His mouth moved to her stomach. Began to kiss a heated path over her flesh. "You seem like a dream. A beautiful, fucking dream that I have no business having."

Underlying his words, there was a hint of anger that puzzled her. But then she felt the stir of his breath on the curls that shielded her sex and she forgot about the anger. His hands caught her thighs as he shifted his body. He pushed her legs farther apart, spreading her even more.

"I never got this far in my dreams."

A damn shame to her way of thinking. She would have enjoyed the hell out of this particular act. Damn phone call.

"Before I take you tonight, I've just got to taste you, right here." He parted her folds. Pressed his lips against the throbbing center of her need.

Then she felt the warm, wet lap of his tongue. Swirling around her entrance. *Oh, damn, but that was great. Great.*

His tongue drove deep inside her.

Her hands clamped in his hair, held him close, just where she wanted him.

His fingers were working her sex now. Plucking. Teasing. Rolling her clit between his thumb and index finger. And Todd kept using that wonderful tongue to lick her—then to drive deep into her sex.

Not just great. Damn fabulous. She was going to come again. A hard, blast of release that would send power rocking through her. She was going to—

He pulled away from her. The moonlight spilled onto his face. Cara saw the need. The fierce desire. "When you come this time," he gritted, "I'll be buried as deep in you as I can get."

Sounded like a fine plan to her.

His right hand reached for the foil packet. He ripped it open with his teeth. Rolled the latex up the length of his cock.

He pushed his aroused flesh between her legs. The head of his erection prodded her straining entrance, just slipping inside her sex.

Her lips curved into a full smile as she gazed up at him. This was what she'd thought of giving up? She must have been absolutely crazy. *Or really, really desperate.*

Todd worked his cock inside of her—*slowly.* One inch at a time. There was sweat on his brow, glistening on his body. He was trying to stay in control. Not wanting to hurt her.

Sweet, silly human.

As if he could ever hurt her.

Besides, she'd always liked it a bit rough. Not pain, of course, she didn't really like that, but rather hard pleasure.

Cara twisted her body, rolling suddenly and taking them near the edge of the bed. When their bodies halted, she was on top of him, knees on either side of his hips, and his cock was buried fully inside her.

"That's better," she whispered, and she began to move. She lifted her body up, then drove down. His hands clamped on her hips, fighting her for control of the tempo and depth.

Her sex was tight and swollen from her previous climax, but she was more than ready for him, and he filled her so wonderfully well that every move had her body tightening with delight around him.

The thrusts became increasingly harder. She moved faster and faster. His fingers bit into her waist. The power in the room beat at her, *at them*, the waves so strong that a faint hum filled the room.

The release was close. A spark of electricity shot through her body. Blue sparks flickered in the air around them.

Todd's eyes had squeezed shut, so he missed the burst of light. He never stopped thrusting. And she never stopped taking him.

So much energy. Hers for the taking.

Just as he was.

His eyes opened as he pushed up, caught her breast in his mouth and lashed the nipple with his tongue.

"Todd!" Her delicate inner muscles clamped tight around him and the climax that had been just out of her reach flew toward her.

Her right hand slammed down on his chest, driving him back against the bed. The power would come now, come crashing over them both.

She probably should have warned the guy before. She should have—

"*Ah!*" The scream was hers. Exultant.

He bucked beneath her, roared his release and the driving power of his lust pounded powerfully in the heart that drummed just below her hand.

The sensual power broke free. As they climaxed, as the pleasure lashed their bodies, the feelings magnified. They shuddered, gasped.

Cara threw back her head, wild with the rush, but her hand never left his chest. Her body stayed joined to his, and as the magical waves shook her, her head dropped over his.

Her lips found his. Carefully, she breathed her magic into him. Shared the power.

She'd never given any of her sensual power to another before.

But she didn't want to just take from him.

He wasn't like the others.

His heartbeat, already too fast, began a mad, driving beat.

Her tongue stroked past the entrance of his mouth. Found his. She kissed him until the powerful rush of magic and climax began to ease.

Then she lifted her head and forced herself to meet the gaze that she knew would hold a thousand questions.

Because Todd had to have just realized that sex with her was far, far from normal.

His chest ached, and a goddess rose above him.

Her small hand slowly lifted, and his heart finally began to slow down.

Jesus. He'd just had the best fucking climax of his life,

hands down. For a second there, he'd actually been afraid that he might pass out. A damn embarrassing admission for him.

But in between the pleasure that had made his back bow off the bed and his toes tingle, something else had happened.

When she'd placed her hand over his heart, for a moment, it had felt like she was branding him. And he'd felt . . . her.

Her hunger. Her need. The feelings had been heady. His body had trembled with an unknown power.

A power he couldn't wait to feel again.

Damn, but he felt fucking good. Like he'd slept for twenty hours good.

Like he'd had the best orgasm ever good. One that had been far, far from normal . . . because he'd felt her release, too.

And that shouldn't have been possible. How the *hell* had it been possible?

"I-I don't want to talk now."

Her voice dripped honey and sex. Still within her depths, his cock began to stir again.

His arms skated down her spine. He needed to touch her. Everywhere.

Was her skin glowing? The pale flesh seemed strangely luminous in the dark, and her skin sure felt warm to the touch. But a human's skin didn't glow like it was lit by a fire from within.

I'm not even human, lover. The words from his dream whispered through his mind.

No, no, that—

"We can talk in the morning. I'll explain everything to you—tomorrow. If you . . . want to know about me."

Oh, yeah, he did. He wanted to know everything.

But not at that moment. He shoved the doubts and questions aside. For that night, they were just going to be a man and a woman. Two people who wanted each other very, very badly.

Dawn could bring out the truth.

For now . . .

Reluctantly, he lifted her body off his hips—and it was so easy. Like the woman was as light as a feather.

He was so ready to go another round.

"Don't leave."

What? Did he look like a moron? "I've gotta clean up." *Find another condom.* "Then I'm coming back to bed." He reached out a hand. Traced the line of her nipple. "Because I'm not even close to being done with you." Would the next climax be as strong? Would he actually feel the power of her release again?

It was almost like he'd touched her soul.

He'd never been so close to another person. He knew that he should be scared, or at least a little alarmed, but—

He wasn't. At least, not yet.

Though for a minute there, when her hand had pressed against his chest, he'd had an uncomfortable flash of poor Michael House.

He'd been too far gone to stop then, but apprehension had risen in the back of his mind, for just a moment.

Fucking ridiculous.

Cara wasn't a killer. Her alibis had checked out. She was the best sex he'd ever had—the perfect lover—and he was a damn lucky man.

"Hurry back," Cara whispered, and the husky sound of her voice made his cock twitch. He saw the white flash of her teeth as she smiled.

"Because I want you inside me again," she said.

That was sure as hell where he wanted to be.

Yeah, dawn could bring reality. For now, he'd take his goddess and the dreams she offered to him.

The killer returned to the scene of the Dayton murder.

Going there was stupid—no denying it, but there really hadn't been a choice for him. The compulsion to go to the scene had been too strong to resist.

A line of yellow police tape marked off the room. The door

was closed. Sealed shut. The same garish plastic tape criss-crossed the windows.

He gave a moment's thought to breaking into the hotel room, but decided the risk just wasn't worth it. The body was long gone, so there really wasn't a point to forcing—

A police cruiser circled the parking lot. *Shit.* He made a quick slide back into the shadows.

Damn it. It shouldn't have happened this way. The plan had been different.

That poor bastard hadn't even been on the list.

A door opened to the left. A young girl peeked out, then pushed a cleaning cart forward.

Perfect.

"Excuse me, miss . . ."

The girl let out a quick squeak of surprise.

He stepped into the light. The cops were gone. It was safe now. For the moment, anyway.

"I want to ask you a few questions." Power pulsed beneath the words.

The girl's eyes went blank. She wouldn't remember the questions later—so she'd get to live.

"Y-yes, sir . . ."

And he would get his questions answered.

Because before he dealt out his punishment, he had to be certain of the crime.

Good partners were so very hard to find.

Only a few women enjoyed the bittersweet mix of sex and death.

"Tell me about the body you found. Every. Single. Detail."

The girl began to talk and his hands balled into fists with every slow word that she uttered.

He'd known, of course, the instant he'd learned the man's name.

But when the sweet young thing before him started talking about the blood and the knife that the cops had found . . .

Fuck. The last betrayal he'd expected.

By the one woman he'd trusted.

Oh, yes, he was gonna make the bitch pay.

She'd been his perfect bait.

Pity.

Now he'd have to add her name to his list.

"Thanks, sweetheart," he told the girl softly, and bent to give her a light kiss—and to steal a wisp of power.

The girl swayed before him.

He stepped back, left her. He couldn't very well kill her—finding a woman's body wouldn't fit the MO he'd created.

Not that the last murder fit, either—*because of that whore.*

But he'd show her. He'd find her, and make the bitch beg. Let her know that, before the cold hell of death, there could be such sweet, hot pleasure.

Chapter 7

"I need to know," Colin told Emily as he paced the small confines of the precinct office. "Just how many supernaturals out there can kill with a touch."

Emily kept her gaze on the crime scene photos. "You're certain a more . . . human method wasn't used to kill these men?"

He sighed. "Hell, doc, I don't know." He came behind her, settled his warm, strong hands on her shoulders and began to gently knead her flesh. "The tox report isn't back yet on the last victim."

Oh, God, but his hands were skilled. She closed the folder. Tried to stop picturing the dead. "What about the first two victims?"

"Smith was out. Phillips ruled 'em natural causes. Heart attacks."

"But you don't think that's what happened?"

"Michael House has a handprint on his chest. Not a bruise, an actual outline of a hand. His heart—his whole body, according to Smith—was in perfect condition. No reason for a guy like him to up and die."

"Unless he was given drugs or—"

"Or one of our local supernatural assholes has decided to start fucking with the humans again."

She had to wince at that because, technically, he was a supernatural who happened to be, ah, *fucking* with a human.

"Tell me what supernaturals out there can kill with a touch," Gyth repeated, his voice hardening, "and I'll start tracking those bastards down."

Yes, he was very good at tracking. *Hunting.* It was the nature of the beast he carried. Her lover was a wolf shifter, a fierce breed, and once he started hunting his prey, he wouldn't stop until he'd run the killer to ground. "I'll need some time to think, to check my books and—"

"You already have suspicions, doc." He wheeled her chair around, crouching at the same time so that when the chair's wheels stopped moving, she found herself staring straight into his bright eyes. "So spill it."

Her lips tightened. "There are . . . several beings who could potentially murder this way." *Potentially* was the key word. Just because the *Other* could kill that way, well, it didn't mean that any of them had.

One black brow lifted. "And they are?"

She had to be careful here. She couldn't break her client confidentiality, but she had to give him as much knowledge as she possibly could. Fighting monsters was never easy. Her shifter knew that. "An incubus. A succubus. Both could—"

"Wow! Wait!" His eyes widened. "The sex demons?"

A slow nod. Most *Other* had heard of the incubi and succubi. Even if they hadn't had, er, personal contact.

Because once a being *had* personal contact with one of that particular breed, well, it was said that the experience was unforgettable.

And, unfortunately for some, very addictive.

"I thought those two were supposed to get high off pleasure."

Emily frowned at that. "They don't 'get high,' as you put it." She sniffed. "They literally live on it. Like vamps and blood."

"Shit." He rubbed his chin. "So how do they go from pleasuring someone to killing 'em?"

Not an easy move. "Most of them don't," she said, placing deliberate emphasis on *most.* "But, sometimes, certain succubi—or incubi—" *though from what she'd learned the fe-*

males were reputed to be far more dangerous than the males, "well, they can get . . . carried away in the heat of the moment."

His gaze dropped to her lips. "Yeah, that can happen."

Her heart rate sped up. "No, ah, not like that. The power they get through sex isn't enough for them. It's really . . . more like stealing life. The pleasure they get, it's life. It's power. Energy. If the succubus or incubus doesn't shut off the flow of power, if they keep linking with the prey," not the best word choice, probably, but it was all she had, "they can literally drain every last drop of life from the body—"

"And leave a dead man in the bed." A muscle flexed along his jaw. "Hell."

"Succubi and incubi are generally mid-level demons. Fives or sixes. They can only kill like this when sex is heavily involved." Normally, humans didn't have too much to fear from the lower-level demons. It was the all-powerful level-tens that made real nightmares into reality for humans.

"Trust me," Colin said. "Sex has been heavily involved in these cases."

Yeah, she'd kind of figured that from the naked bodies and bondage. But . . . "A level-nine or -ten demon could also do something like this—with the right set of circumstances, anyway. You know they can control minds—"

"Assholes like Niol? Yeah, I know they get off on playing with humans."

"—but they can place a suggestion a human's mind, literally, for death."

He huffed out a hard breath. "You're telling me a level-ten can tell a person he's going to die, and then the poor bastard would just keel over?"

"Theoretically, it *should* be possible. The body would temporarily mimic whatever suggestion the demon gave— whether it was a heart attack or a stroke. The victim would think he or she was truly having the attack. And if you think it, well, sometimes that can just be enough to kill you."

Colin stared at her in disbelief. Poor guy. For a supernatural, he still didn't quite understand the way the world worked. She tried to reassure him. "But I-I've never known of an actual case like that." Though just the thought of that much power scared the hell out of her.

"But you *do* know of a case where a sex demon has killed someone." He pounced on what she had said, and what she had not.

Emily stared straight at him. Now this was the hard part. Colin was her lover, the shifter she loved, but he was also a cop, and she wasn't about to break her professional standards. "I really couldn't say."

"Then, baby, you've just said enough."

Her back teeth ground together. "There is another who could kill this way. The *cazador del alma*—"

"What? What the hell is that? Spanish?"

"Yes, it roughly means soul hunter. The *cazador* has the touch of death. He finds those whose time has run out. He touches them—"

"And he fucking kills them. Just great." Colin shook his head. "So I've got some hunter out there who can kill humans at will—"

"*Cazadores* don't usually kill humans," Emily felt obliged to tell him. "They usually are the ones who go after *Other* when they go bad." Though the *cazadores* were extremely rare these days.

"These vics were human." Absolutely certain.

"Then they wouldn't be a *cazador*'s usual prey."

"Not unless the guy is just another crazy bastard—which is a definite possibility. *Shit.*" Colin glanced back at the table and the closed file. "I need to know which of these assholes is in *my* town."

"They aren't going to advertise their presence." The deadliest beings often kept the lowest profiles, striking out only when necessary. "Look, there could be others, let me research—"

"Oh, you do your research, baby, and let me know everything you find out. In the meantime, I'm gonna start hunting and—" His eyes widened. "*Sonofabitch.*"

"Colin?"

He growled. The sound more wolf that man. "We fucking had her in the station."

"Who?"

He jumped to his feet. "A succubus. I'd bet my life on it. I could smell her—damn, the scent alone was enough to—" He broke off, rather wisely, Emily thought.

But she still had to ask, "Enough to what?"

"Enough to make me back the hell away from her, fast. Because she wasn't you."

Oh, very good answer. She rose quickly, grabbed his T-shirt, bunched it in her fist, and dragged him close for a hard, deep kiss.

One good thing about wolf shifters. Their loyalty was sacred to them, just as sacred as a mate.

The bad thing, well, that would be that some of them were psychotic. Luckily for her, Colin was as sane as they came, just with a decidedly aggressive streak that made him perfect as a cop.

"I've got to call Brooks, let him know—"

Now here was the problem. "Just what, exactly? That you think you have a suspect and she's a demon?" Emily hesitated. "He still doesn't even know the truth about you yet, does he?"

A fast shake of his head.

"So how do you think he'll take the news of a demon stalking the streets?"

Not very well. They both knew that answer.

Colin exhaled. "I'll talk to the captain. See if he wants me to work this case on my own."

She didn't like that idea one bit. "Partners are supposed to watch each other's backs. You're *not* supposed to be out there chasing down killers on your own." A cold knot lodged in her stomach. Emily knew that Colin was physically one of the strongest supernaturals around, but he wasn't invincible. As far as she knew, no one was.

So she'd feel much better if someone was out there patrolling with him while he hunted.

"You can't keep him in the dark forever." They'd had the same argument before. "I know your last partner screwed you—"

"No, baby, he tried to *kill* me when he found out what I was."

"Brooks isn't Mike, okay? You don't know what he'll do."

"It's not just my call, Em. Once Brooks finds out the truth, the shit will hit the fan about *everyone*."

Yes, it would.

"I'll talk to the captain," he repeated, "and see what he wants me to do. But I'm also going to have another chat with the succubus."

"She might not be involved." Her voice was carefully expressionless now. "You should wait for the tox screen—"

"Oh, I'll wait for the results, but I got the feeling she knew exactly what I was—"

"When you backed away, she knew." She could tell him that much.

"Hell." Disgusted.

Emily cleared her throat. "Shifters have such an overdeveloped sense of smell that her pheromones came off smelling too sweet to you. When you retreated, she knew what you were." Humans and demons always went closer, eager for more of the heady scent.

But not her shifter . . . he'd acted just as the others of his kind had done before him.

"You sure seem to know a lot about the sex demons." His head cocked to the right. "How certain are you that the info you have is accurate?"

Since her knowledge had come straight from the mouth of a succubus, pretty damn certain. "Something else you should know," she told him, knowing she had to tread carefully. "Sex demons—they are very, very territorial. I'd be surprised if there are more than a few in the city."

"In that case, I'll damn well be having my little talk with Cara as soon as possible."

Cara.

The name rang in her ears.

Oh, damn.

The rising sun shot streaks of pink and purple across the sky as the lights filtered though the clouds and illuminated the horizon.

Cara paused in the swimming pool, her body easily staying afloat. This was really her favorite time of the day, when the shadows had to give way to the light.

She turned slightly, and dove deep, heading straight to the bottom of the pool. The water was warm—she always kept it heated—and it closed around her like the arms of a lover.

Todd.

She'd left him sleeping upstairs. A smile had been on his lips. Cara had kissed him, a soft, light kiss before she left.

A part of her was afraid that would be the last kiss she ever gave to him. It was easy to pretend you didn't care about reality in the heat of passion. When pleasure was only moments away, it was fine to focus on the moment. Hell, she did that all the time.

But Todd was a cop, and he wasn't just going to ignore the . . . peculiarities of the night before.

Of course, she had been holding back on the guy. Things could have gotten so intense that she could have had the man begging.

Or screaming with his pleasure.

Though they'd both come pretty close to that.

When she touched the bottom of the pool, Cara pivoted and shot toward the surface. Her eyes were wide open as she swam, and she saw the outline of a man standing near the edge of the pool.

Todd. Her heart rate kicked up a notch. Her head broke the surface and she sucked in a deep breath of air. Tendrils of steam rose from the water.

He'd dressed in the rumpled clothes he'd worn last night. His hair was tousled, and there was a hard set to his mouth.

"Do you always leave your lovers at dawn?" He asked her quietly.

She swam to the edge of the pool. Slow, unhurried movements. She reached for the wall. Curled her fingers over the edge and stared up at him. "Do you always whisper my name when you sleep?" He had, right after she'd kissed him, and that soft sound had pierced straight to her heart.

Fool. He's not going to care when he knows the truth. They never care.

In fact, humans were usually horrified when they found out what she really was.

Narrow-minded jerks. Okay, now she was starting to think like Cameron, but it wasn't as if she could help the way she'd been born. She didn't blame humans for having skin that could injure too easily or—

"Lately, yeah, I probably do." He crouched down, his powerful thighs bunching. "I missed you when I woke up this morning."

The guy sure knew how to say just the right thing.

She swallowed. "I, uh, usually swim at dawn." Oh, jeez, could she have sounded more like a stuttering fool and less like a calm, cool demon?

"I'll remember that. Maybe I'll join you one day."

"You could . . . join me now if you wanted."

His gaze heated at her words.

Cara lifted her hand, pointing to the high privacy fence that surrounded her yard. "Don't worry about a suit. No one can see us." Though she wouldn't have really cared if they could. Modesty had never been a particular concern of hers.

"Damn, but you tempt me, woman."

Yeah, that was the point.

His hand reached out, caught her by the back of the neck and his lips took hers, pressing tight in a fierce kiss. His tongue moved swiftly to claim hers, stirring the hunger she'd thought was temporarily sated.

Her wet hands wrapped around his arms. When his lips lifted from hers, she whispered, "Come into the water with me."

His gaze was so dark. So intense. Todd pulled away from her. Rose. Stared down at her with a face drawn tight.

She wanted him so badly that her body trembled.

And the light of dawn was beginning to glow brighter.

His hands went to his shirt. Only a few buttons remained, thanks to her frantic efforts last night. Slowly, he unhooked them and dropped the shirt onto the cement.

He kicked off his shoes, tossed away his socks. Then, gazing down into her eyes, he stripped off his jeans and boxers.

Oh, yes. The man was absolutely perfect to her. She licked her lips. Her stare raked down his chest. Over the sculpted abs and down to the narrow flare of his hips—and to the broad shaft of arousal that jutted toward her.

This might just turn out to be the best swim she'd ever had.

"How deep?" He asked, and for a wild, hungry moment, she thought he was talking about sex.

Then she was actually able to think past her lust. "Uh, twelve feet here and—"

He dove into the pool, arching his body and cutting straight into the water with an economy of splash.

She spun around, wanting to catch him when he came up and feel all that bare male flesh against her body. She was in a bikini, but it would be easy enough for him to pull away the spaghetti straps and—

He caught her around the waist. Tugged her beneath the water. Her hands flew out, slid over his shoulders, and she found him staring at her, body perfectly poised, eyes blazing with need.

Oh, but she liked the way he played.

His hands went to her top. Untied the straps with a quick flick of his fingers. Her bared breasts were desperate for his touch, the nipples tight and hard in the water. He caught the tips with his fingers. Caressed. Teased.

Made her want so much more.

Todd and Cara shot to the surface at the same time. The moment air filled her lungs, Cara was ready for him. She kissed him, sealing her lips tight to his—

Right before they sank beneath the water.

His fingers went to the bottom of her suit. Found the same easy ties to untangle. When the fabric floated away, he touched her sex. Pushed those strong fingers between her legs and made her hips strain toward him as he strummed the center of her need.

They kicked to the surface together. His hands were still on her. Her lips still on his. Her mouth lifted slowly.

Then he pushed her back against the wall of the pool. Spread her legs ever wider and thrust two fingers deep into her core.

Cara hissed as the pleasure lashed her. But she wanted more than just those fingers inside of her. "Todd . . . I need you."

"Ah, damn, but you are the sexiest thing I've ever seen." His mouth pressed against her throat. Bit. Sucked the flesh.

"Don't . . . ah . . . play." But playing felt so good. "Make love to me."

His head lifted. "I don't have any more protection with me." He sounded horrified.

Hell. Pregnancy wasn't a major concern for her, but now really wasn't the time to get into an explanation of her genetics.

The lust was riding them both too hard. Now was the time for relief. "Guess we have to improvise," she whispered. It wouldn't be as good as having that thick erection of his driving into her, but she was discovering that just about any sensual play with Todd was better than everything she'd experienced with others.

The man sure as hell knew how to please a succubus. A rare talent.

But she also knew how to please a man. Her fingers found the small nubs of his nipples. Tugged lightly. A growl rewarded her efforts, and she trailed the tips of her nails down his chest. The pressure of her nails wasn't enough to hurt him or mark him, but just enough to sensitize his flesh and let him know what was coming.

Well, *he* would be coming. And so would she. But first—

Her fingers eased over the skin of his abdomen.

"Cara . . ." His voice had become guttural now, and the fingers inside her were still working her sex in a fierce, possessive drive.

Her climax was close.

Time for his.

The air crackled around them. The already warm water in the pool heated perceptibly as their passion flared.

She found the length of his cock. Long. Hard. She wrapped both hands around him, squeezed. Tested the length, moving from root to head. Again. Again.

The fingers driving inside her began to move faster.

So did her hands.

He kissed her. Drove his tongue into her mouth in perfect time with the thrust of his hand.

Her sex contracted around his fingers. Her skin began to prickle as the sting of energy in the air surrounded her, so rich and sweet she could taste it . . . just as she tasted him.

Her hands pumped his flesh. Squeezed tighter. Stroked harder. His body stiffened against her, the muscles bunching as he spiraled ever closer to his release.

Her fingers closed over the top of his shaft, caressed the sensitive head beneath the warm water.

Oh, but she was close—

He tore his mouth from hers, stared down at her, breath ragged and hard.

His thumb pushed against her clit and his fingers thrust deep again.

The fire within her erupted into a blaze as Cara choked out his name and greedily took the pleasure he offered . . . even as she pumped him to his own climax.

His cock tightened, jerked. The face above hers flushed and she felt the hard jet of his orgasm.

Cara kissed him again, riding the wave of her orgasm, his, and funneling that energy right back to Todd so that his body shuddered as the fiery pleasure seemed to last and last.

When the climax ended, dawn had arrived in full force. Light blazed across the pool, sparkling on the waves.

Damn. It was a miracle they both hadn't drowned.

Todd blinked and gazed down at Cara's glistening face. He was so screwed.

Her full lips trembled. Curved into a smile that looked gorgeous, and a little lost.

So screwed.

But he felt good. Fucking fantastic, in fact.

He kissed those lips of hers. God, but he loved her mouth. The sweet bow of her top lip. The plumpness of her lower lip. The way her mouth fit against his. The way she tasted.

Her fingers stroked his cock. A final caress before she eased her hands away.

Todd exhaled. "Cara . . ." Now that the fog of lust was starting to clear, he knew they needed to talk.

But, if he didn't get away from the naked temptation of her body, he'd forget about talking, *again*, and pounce on the lady one more time.

"I like you." Cara's words stopped him. "You're . . . different, Todd Brooks."

And she was far beyond any experience he'd ever had.

"That's why this is going to be so hard," she whispered.

He frowned. "What are you talking about?"

Now the smile on her lips was just sad. "We should get dressed."

She disappeared under the water, sliding beneath the clear surface and swimming around him, before reappearing in the shallow end of the pool—close to the steps that led up to the cement and the waiting patio. He swam slowly behind her, the tension in his gut thickening.

Todd knew he wasn't about to have the best conversation of his life.

He sure as hell hoped the lady wasn't kicking him out. Not yet.

His gaze zeroed in on the graceful line of her back as she rose from the pool. Dipped low to the curve of her ass. He hadn't showed her ass the attention it deserved yet, but he would. He'd show—

She turned a bit, reaching down to grab a towel off the chaise, and he caught a glimpse of her birthmark. A perfect half-moon birthmark above her hip. Left side.

Shit.

Goose bumps grew on his flesh, his warning system going off too late.

In less than five seconds, he was out of the pool. Splashing water and storming toward her. "What the hell is going on?"

She whirled at his snarl, holding her towel in front of her. "Ah, Todd—"

He grabbed the edge of the towel, wrenched it away. Last night, it had been so dark in her bedroom that he hadn't noticed the mark on her hip. But now, in the bright light of the new day, there was no mistaking it.

Just like in his dream. A perfect fucking match.

Impossible.

No, it *should* have been impossible.

A woman couldn't just . . . walk into his dreams.

And a man couldn't transform into a wolf—but Colin had. He'd seen the transformation with his own eyes.

Just like he now saw the damn birthmark.

"I dreamed of that mark." He stared at the smooth white skin. Skin that contrasted so richly with the dark half-moon. He lifted his gaze to her face. Found her watching him with worried eyes. "How'd I do that, Cara?"

The hair on his nape had risen. Oh, yeah, his alarms were ringing now. Shrieking, actually.

Her hand lifted. "Give me the towel."

Todd realized they were both dripping wet and still naked. And that he was aroused. Confused as hell, but increasingly aroused.

He tossed the towel back to her.

She wrapped the terry-cloth around her body. "On the other side of the pool, there's a small storage room. You'll find some towels in there."

"Cara . . ."

"We'll talk, okay? Just . . . you need to get dressed first."

Fine. He spun around, military-style. His gaze flickered over the still water of the pool, saw her bikini floating on the surface. His stomach clenched.

Damn it. Todd headed for the storage room. Found an oversize towel. Swiped away the water and secured the towel at his hips. *Not dressed, but good enough—for the moment.*

He went back to face his temptress, and ignored the growing chill in the air.

She stood at the edge of the pool. Hair slicked back. Eyes bright.

He stopped about three feet away from her. Waited. Questions tumbled through his mind. One after the other. How had he known about her birthmark? And when he'd woken that first night, with scratch marks on his arms, just what the hell had been happening?

Had their encounters been dreams . . . or had they been all too real?

And why the fuck did he still feel so good? Energy and heat pumped through him, making him feel stronger than he had in months.

"I haven't been completely honest with you, Todd."

No shit. Her voice was soft. Tense. Her gaze darted to the left a moment, then returned, almost reluctantly, to his. "I'm not the woman you think I am."

"Then who the hell are you?" Why was she talking in riddles? He wanted to know about her birthmark, not—

Her left hand lifted, toyed with the top of the towel. "Tell me, Detective—"

Oh, now he was back to *detective*? Like she hadn't been moaning his name less than five minutes ago.

"—do you believe in monsters?"

Her question drove the breath from his lungs. *"What?"* Oh, Christ, he sure hoped she wasn't gonna tell him that—

"Do you believe in monsters?" She repeated the question and licked her succulent red lips. "You really should, you know."

"And why is that?" His heart pounded like a drum, the dull beat echoing in his ears.

"Because according to some people, I'm one of the worst monsters you'll ever meet."

Chapter 8

He jerked on his clothes, so furious that his hands shook. "Look, baby, if you want to blow me off, that's fine, but don't give me some bullshit about being a monster—"

"It's not bullshit," she said, blond brows rising in what could have been a flare of annoyance.

"—because I know all about real monsters, okay? I deal with them every fucking day. Rapists. Child killers. Fire freaks who burn down homes with nice old ladies inside—"

She flinched.

"Unless you're about to tell me that you *did* kill Michael House," *and Jesus but he hoped she wasn't*, "then don't screw around with me by throwing out labels that I understand one hell of a lot better than you do." She'd hit his weak spot, and he was furious. Todd knew all about the evil in the world. Had known about it since his fourteenth birthday, when he'd watched that bastard Costa smile and shoot his mother straight in the heart. Monsters. Yeah. He knew all about the bastards, and the evil that lived in what they pretended were souls.

"I didn't kill Michael." She licked her lips again. Stood there with that towel wrapped around her and looked so damn good that he ached. "But I *am* a monster, Todd. I-I'm a demon."

He'd just finished dressing when she made her announcement. He shook his head, slowly. "Run that one by me again, baby." No way the lady had just said—

"I'm a demon, Detective. A real, honest-to-God," her mouth curved slightly at that in a wan smile, "demon."

Todd stared at her, not quite sure what to say. The automatic words, *You're crazy*, trembled on his lips.

And he would have said those words to her—*two months ago*.

Yeah, back then, he would have laughed at her claim. Asked what her punch line was.

But that was two months ago.

Back before the dangerous night when he'd trailed his partner to the warehouse district on the darker side of Atlanta and watched his partner of two years stop being a man—and become a snarling, deadly beast.

A wolf.

Todd hadn't said a word to anyone about what he'd seen. He'd followed Colin because the guy was his partner, and partners backed each other up.

He'd been shaken as hell. Stunned.

He'd planned to follow the wolf into the warehouse, help him, but the captain had paged him, said that he had to get back to the station ASAP—and that he knew where Todd was.

The order had been blunt. *Get your ass out of there before you get Colin killed.*

So he'd left. He'd taken a heavy knowledge with him—a knowledge he hadn't shared with anyone—because, well, who would believe him?

At first, he'd had so many dreams about that night. Memories of that brutal shift. The snap of bones and the growl of the beast had haunted his nights.

He'd kept at his job, though, damn it. Bit back the instinctive fear that roused its head. And he'd stuck by his partner's side, even when he'd been pissed and confused as all hell.

He'd thought that Colin was an anomaly, but now—

"Did you hear me?" Cara raised her voice. "I-I just told you that I'm a demon."

Todd blinked. First werewolves, now demons. But Cara didn't look like a demon. No horns. No tail. No forked tongue. Or was all that stuff he'd heard as a kid just bullshit?

"This is the point where most guys get really afraid and leave, as fast as they can." She hesitated. "Uh, Todd? Can you say something? Are—are you all right?"

"No, I'm not all right," he gritted. "My lover just told me she's a damn demon." Not the best news he could have gotten, but at least she hadn't confessed to being a *murdering* demon. "You . . . don't look like a demon."

Now her smile really did break his heart. "Sure I do," she said, and closed her eyes. When they opened a second later, they were black. Completely black.

"Shit!"

Another blink, and her blue gaze was back. "It's just a little glamour," she told him, lifting a brow.

Those eyes. He'd seen them before. The darkness. Black cornea. Retina. He'd seen it with—

Niol. That asshole at Paradise Found. He'd wondered why someone would wear contacts like that, but if Cara was telling him the truth, that meant Niol was a demon, too.

And that fact made a hell of a lot of sense when Todd remembered his strange attack in the bar.

"You're handling this, um, rather well." Cara gazed at him solemnly.

When Todd lifted his hand to shove back his wet hair, he noticed a tremble still in his fingers. *Not that well, baby.* He tried for rational. "Demons aren't real." He knew the statement was a lie the minute the words slipped out. His partner was a werewolf. If werewolves could exist, then why not demons, too?

Shit, but the world was even more messed up than he'd originally thought, and about a hundred times more dangerous.

"Of course, we're real. We've been living with humans from the very beginning." She held up her hand. "And before you start asking, let me just tell you, demons are *not* the spawn of the devil, okay? Total myth, that part. We're just a . . . different race."

Different race. Seemed simple enough—but his thundering heart wasn't quite buying the simple explanation. *Christ.* "What kind of demon are you?" His gaze raked down her body. "And just how much, uh—" What had she called it? "Glamour have you been using on me?" A cold wind seemed to blow over him. The woman was too pretty. Too perfect looking by far. Hell, the only flaw on her body was that birthmark on her hip, and it really wasn't a flaw so much as—well, a mark he wanted to bite.

Too perfect. He'd thought it from the beginning. Just what, exactly, was she hiding beneath the glamour?

Did he really want to know?

"Don't be an idiot!" Cara snapped, and turned on her heel. She stomped toward the chaise and picked up a thin, blue robe. She shouldered into it, letting the towel drop to the ground.

Todd swallowed and absolutely refused to try and catch a glimpse of her naked sex.

"I'm not using glamour to do anything but camouflage my eyes, okay? In case you didn't notice, they're a bit of a giveaway, don't you think? And it's not like I want to go around advertising my true self to the world!"

"Well, your 'true self' is what I'm interested in." Last night, he would have done almost anything to claim her. The lust had been that wild. Now, he couldn't help but wonder . . . how much of it had been real?

A demon. He didn't know anything about demons or their power. It was so unbelievable. So insane, so—

True.

He knew in his gut Cara wasn't lying, and too many facts and situations from over the years were rolling through his head.

So much made sense now. The angry stares in Paradise Found. The strange energy he'd felt there.

"I'm not using glamour to shield my body or my face," she said, hands tightening into fists.

"So that crap about demons having horns and pointed tails is—what? Straight lies?"

"No. It's true for certain very, very old and very, *very* powerful demons."

Hell.

"I'm not a very strong demon," Cara admitted and did her cheeks flush? Was the woman, ah, demon, embarrassed by her weakness?

"And just what kind of demon are you?" He asked her again, and wondered why she hadn't answered him before.

Her mouth opened as if she were going to reply, then she stopped and pressed her lips together.

Uh, oh. Not a good sign. But, just how many demons were there, anyway?

"You're not acting particularly shocked," she said slowly, and, once more—not answering his question. There was suspicion on her face as she asked, "Have you met my kind before?"

Yeah, he just hadn't realized it until now. No wonder he'd felt like half the world had been keeping secrets from him. They had. But not any longer. The rose-colored glasses lay shattered at his feet. "Cara . . ."

"Guys really do generally run at this point." A faint line appeared between her brows. "Like I told you, fast."

"You've told a lot of guys this spiel, huh?" Was that jealousy flaring in his gut? Sure felt like it.

"A few. Those who don't run usually want me to prove that I'm a demon."

"So you do your eye trick."

Her lips tightened. "I can do more than that."

Now he was curious. Kinda like those people who stopped and turned around when they saw car accidents. "Like what?"

"On any human male but you, I'd be able to hypnotize with just a word. Get you to do my complete bidding."

Now Todd had to swallow to ease the dryness in his throat. *And she didn't think that made her fall into the "strong" category?* "So why am I the lucky human?"

"Because you're a latent psychic with more power than you realize." A shrug. "You've got shields up in your mind that you don't even know about."

Now that was a load of shit. He wasn't psychic. Never had been. "Nice try, baby, but if I were psychic, I would have won the lottery years ago and retired to Mexico." How was he even having this conversation?

They'd been climaxing together minutes before. He'd wanted nothing more than to shove deep and hard into her tight sex and now—

Well, now he'd entered the twilight zone, and he'd very much like to leave, please.

"You're not that kind of psychic." He thought he heard her mutter, *idiot*, beneath her breath. His eyes narrowed. She continued, "You probably get feelings, don't you? Little vibes of tension or fear just before you walk into a situation that's dangerous as all hell. But you know *before* you walk in, don't you?"

How did she know that?

"Some folks would call that instinct. A psychic edge. Whatever you want to name it, the fact is that your mind is stronger than others. You've got a gift, one most humans never get, and those that do have it, well, precious few understand just what in the world is going on when the edge kicks into play."

"But you understand, right?"

"All of my kind have the edge. We were brought into this world with it, and we'll leave with it."

He didn't want to talk about what fictional powers he may or not possess. Right then, he just wanted to focus on her. "So you usually do a hypnotic show, huh? No other tricks to prove that you're a demon?" Though proof was really moot at this point, he still felt the driving need to keep pushing at her.

Because she's just knocked my world right off its axis.

No, his jaw tightened. He couldn't lie to himself right then. Colin had rocked his reality months ago. Cara had just broken the shaky peace he'd been living in since that night.

"I have a few other skills," Cara admitted, somewhat grudgingly, he thought. She lifted her hand. A small plume of smoke appeared about two inches above her open palm. As he watched, the smoke thickened, and with a snap, a ball of flames burst in the air. Cara pulled back her hand, smiled at him, and tossed the fire straight toward him.

"Shit!"

He ducked. Felt the rush of fire. Looked up, saw the ball, spinning in the air, fire blazing gold and red.

Then it vanished.

"Don't worry, I wasn't going to hurt you."

He wasn't 100 percent certain he believed that. Especially since the top of his head felt singed.

"You pissed me off," she said, lips twisting. "I shouldn't have tossed that toward you."

"Uh, yeah, you shouldn't have tossed the *ball of fire* at my head." Unbelievable.

His lover was a demon.

Damn. Damn. Damn.

A very sexy demon.

One who apparently had a very bad temper.

And gorgeous legs.

Ah, hell. "So what am I supposed to do now?" He really didn't know.

No, actually, he did know one thing—with absolute certainly. He still wanted her.

"What do you want to do?" Was that hope flickering in her eyes?

He had to ask. "You feel, don't you, Cara?"

She frowned.

"I mean, like me, like humans, you feel. Lust. Anger." Oh, yes, he knew she felt anger. He had the burnt hair to prove it. "Love."

A slow nod. "I can feel. Being a demon doesn't mean I'm not a woman, Todd. I need. I hurt. I bleed. Just like anyone else."

But with a few dangerous extras thrown in for spice. He rubbed his eyes. "Look, I've gotta have some time to think about this." To figure out just what the hell was going to happen next.

Her face paled. "I see."

That cold, stilted voice pissed him off. He dropped his hand and stalked toward her. Todd caught her arms and hauled her up against him. "No, I don't think you see a damn thing." She thought he was running, like those other fools she'd mentioned.

But he was no fool.

He kissed her, driving his tongue into her sweet mouth and growling his hunger.

Her fingers pressed against his shoulders.

He drank in her essence. Fought the growing hunger that roared inside him. "I have to get to the station," he bit the words off against her lips. The tox screen was due in first thing this morning. He had a job to do and—

And he needed to think.

But he was *not* running.

He stepped away from her. "I'll be back, Cara, tonight. We'll finish this—" Whatever *this* was.

She just stared up at him, silent.

What was he supposed to say? The woman had just confessed that she was a demon, for Christ's sake.

No wonder the sex had been so damn powerful with her. She wasn't human.

Just like she'd told him in his dreams.

Oh, yeah, his dreams . . . they'd have to talk about those babies—and she would have to tell him just what the hell had really been happening when he touched her in his sleep.

Cara nodded. "I understand." She shrugged, tried to look as if she didn't care. Failed. "Do what you have to do."

Damn if the stiffness in her shoulders didn't make him feel guilty, when he was the wronged party. He hadn't misled her about being human. "It's the case, Cara. I have to check in by seven thirty. I'm supposed to be getting the tox screen in for House." Okay, he probably shouldn't have told her that. His big mouth was going to get him into trouble one of these days.

"Then you'd better hurry."

No screaming. No yelling. No when-will-I-see-you again questions.

He shoved his hands into the front pocket of his jeans. Marched toward the gate on the side of the house. Hesitated. Shit—he *had* to go. He had to swing by his place, find a shirt with buttons. Then hurry his ass down to the station.

Todd pulled in a slow breath. "This isn't finished." He said the words without looking at her, because gazing at the woman was dangerous to his control.

"No." The word drifted to him on the breath of the wind that feathered over his face. "It's not."

He'd be seeing his demon again, there was no question of that in his mind.

His right hand reached for the gate.

"It was real, you know." Her voice stopped him cold. "Everything that happened between us was real. I wanted you, you wanted me. Just like humans. Only much better . . ."

Much better than anything he'd ever experienced before, that was certain.

"Remember that, when you're away from me. Remember what we had when we were together, and stop thinking that you screwed a monster."

His fury erupted. Todd spun around, hands fisted. "Damn it, I never—"

She was gone. Just the faintest trace of her soft lavender scent remained in the air.

"I never thought you were a monster," he snarled, knowing that she couldn't hear him. "That was *your* word, not mine." He'd thought of her only as . . .

His.

Todd's eyes squeezed shut. Hell, he'd known the woman

was going to be trouble from that first glance, and he'd been so right about her.

Now what was he supposed to do?

Colin was bent over his desk, busily thumbing through files, when Todd walked into the bull pen. As usual, chaos reigned in the detectives' world. Phones rang with shrill cries. Voices floated around the room as questions were tossed back and forth between the men and women who were guzzling black coffee and pushing the sleep from their eyes.

His home away from home.

Todd headed for this small desk, directly opposite his partner's. He'd barely taken two steps when Colin's head suddenly snapped up and his gaze zeroed in on him.

No damn way he heard me. Not with all this racket going on. Todd stared back at his partner, saw the slight flare of Colin's nostrils, then the abrupt tightening of his jaw.

He knew what that telltale clenching signified. Colin was furious, and from the look on his face, that anger was directed straight at Todd.

A sigh broke from his lips. Okay. He was tired of the guy's attitude. He'd put up with enough shit from Colin. It was time to clear the air once and for all—

"Have a good night, partner?" Colin murmured when Todd reached the desks.

His eyes narrowed. "Good enough."

Colin glared at him. "You know you could be fucking up the case."

He knew. Todd didn't know how the cagey bastard knew, but Colin realized that Todd had spent the night with Cara. "She's not a suspect anymore."

Another flare of the guy's nostrils. "You sure about that?"

Very deliberately, Todd placed his hands on top of the old, wooden desk and leaned in over Colin. "It wasn't too long ago when you were screwing a suspect, too, buddy."

"Emily was never a suspect! She was working with us and—"

"—and for a while she looked guilty as hell." His hands shoved harder against the desktop.

"But she wasn't!"

"Neither is Cara!" Not guilty of the murders, anyway, but—

"Gyth! Brooks!" The whiplash of Captain Danny McNeal's voice cut through the fire of Todd's anger. He glanced up, realizing too late that he and Colin hadn't exactly been having a quiet conversation. Most of the eyes in the station were on them, particularly the glaring gray stare of the captain.

Shit.

"In my office," McNeal growled, his completely bald scalp gleaming as he inclined his head toward the open door. "*Now.*"

Todd straightened. This wasn't going to be pretty.

The wheels of Colin's chair rattled as he shot to his feet.

They didn't speak as they crossed the room to the captain's office. Not really much to say at that point.

McNeal slammed the door shut behind them. Marched to his desk. He didn't sit down. Just glared at them, tension evident in the thick muscles of his body.

Todd knew that Captain Danny McNeal had been with the Atlanta PD for over twenty years. The guy was in his early forties and in better shape than most of the men in the precinct. He ran every day, and could be routinely found in the PD's gym, tossing cops over his shoulder and onto the cushioned blue mats.

The guy was a real hardass. Smart as a whip. And known for his fiery temper.

According to the rumors, he'd also been heavily involved with Smith at one time.

But, of course, those were just rumors, and Todd had never really been able to imagine the gorgeous doctor pairing up with the asshole cop.

Just didn't fit for him.

"Are you going to fucking stare at me all day, Brooks, or are you going to tell me why the hell my best two detectives were yelling at each other like two twelve-year-old girls in the middle of my bull pen?"

Oh, damn. Todd winced. The first time he'd ever been compared to a twelve-year-old girl. "I lost my temper, Captain. Sorry." He wasn't going to point any fingers at Colin. Not his style.

McNeal grunted. "Well, learn to keep your damn temper in check! Understand, Brooks?"

"Yes, sir." Though McNeal really needed to learn the same coping skill.

"I got the shit-for-brains mayor and the dumbass DA breathing down my neck right now, yelling about another serial killer being on our streets—I don't need this crap from you two!"

"Understood."

Another growl from deep in McNeal's chest. "Is this partnership working?" He asked bluntly. "Do I need to reassign—"

"No," Todd answered immediately, and saw Colin stiffen slightly from the corner of his eye.

"Hmm." McNeal's gaze shot to Colin. "What do you say?"

"There's no problem with us, sir."

"Just stupidity," McNeal snapped, then finally dropped into his chair. "All right, screw it. You've been warned. Stop acting like fucking idiots and tell me the status on these damn cases."

Todd had to fight the curve of his lips. McNeal was a tough bastard, but he respected the guy, and in other circumstances, he would have even called him a friend.

Instead, he called him boss.

And asshole—behind his back, anyway.

Colin cleared his throat. "Smith put a rush order on House's toxicology screen—"

"And?"

"I just got the results." A pause. "Negative. The guy's system was clean."

"Shit." McNeal's bushy brows snapped together. "So what's the cause of death, then? How's Smith calling him?"

Now Colin looked *real* uncomfortable. "Uh, Smith actually said she'd be down for a briefing on this and—"

"*How's she calling it?*"

A light tap sounded on the captain's door. "I'm busy!" McNeal yelled instantly. "What the hell? Does a closed door look like I want company?"

The closed door opened. Smith poked her head in, frowning. "I know you did *not* just yell at me."

McNeal jumped to his feet. "Smith, I-I didn't know it was you." His voice seemed to drop, just an octave, so that it was no longer a bear growl. Something softer. More intimate.

Well, I'll be damned. Todd studied the captain with barely contained curiosity. Maybe there was a bit of truth to those rumors about the guy and the ME.

Smith's dark stare flashed to Colin. Held for just a few seconds as she said, "I told you I needed to be here for this meeting. I'm not going to be cut out of another case."

"Neither am I," Todd added at once, memories of the last serial killer swirling through his mind. The captain had put Colin in charge and basically sidelined Todd while his partner worked day and night with Dr. Drake.

No. Definitely not happening again. This time, the killer was his.

McNeal's chin lifted. "It's not a matter of cutting you out—either of you. It's a matter of doing what's best for the department."

Bullshit.

Smith closed the door behind her. The two chairs in front of McNeal's desk were empty. Todd stood just to the left of the chairs, while Colin was positioned near the back of the captain's office, right beside an oversized green plant. A plant Todd wasn't entirely convinced was real.

Smith crossed the room. Sat in the chair next to Todd. "What did I miss?"

McNeal stared down at her. "You all right?" He asked suddenly.

Todd saw her shoulders tighten. "Fine."

He almost snorted. He had no idea the lady was such a lousy liar.

He could tell by the doubt on McNeal's face that the captain knew she was lying, too.

But he didn't push her, just sat back down in his chair, and said, "You didn't miss much. Just discussing the tox screen."

The tension in her shoulders eased a bit as she said, "Michael House wasn't given any drugs. At least, not as far as I can tell." She held up one hand, the fingers steady. "Now, I didn't screen for everything—would have been damn impossible to screen for every drug. But I hit the main boys, every mix that I thought could do something like this." A shake of her head. "He was clean."

"So what's the cause of death going to be?"

Her hand dropped. "At this point, the COD is going down as undetermined."

Todd swore. "Smith, if it goes down like that—"

"Then you're off the case," McNeal finished. "Because as far as the mayor and DA are concerned, there will be *no* case."

"I didn't say the victim died of natural causes," Smith pointed out quickly, her voice rising a bit.

"You might as well have." Damn it, the guy had been murdered. Todd knew it in his gut. "What about the hand, Smith? That print on his chest?"

McNeal's fist slammed down on the desk, hard. "What print?"

"It's not a print." Smith turned her head and glowered at him. "It's not like I can scan the thing and get fingerprints." She looked back at McNeal. "It's just . . . an outline. Of a hand."

"Right in the middle of Michael House's chest," Colin said quietly.

"It's a bruise," McNeal dismissed, fingers tapping now on the desktop. "Has to be. The assailant applied pressure to his chest and—"

"It's certainly not what I'd call a normal bruise. Colin . . ." Smith pointed to McNeal. "Show him the pictures."

Colin marched forward. Handed the case file to the captain.

"A normal bruise can appear after a vic's death, but . . ." Smith rubbed her forehead. Todd snaked around the desk to get a better look at the pictures. "Bruises are generally of varying discolorations. This one is the exact same throughout. A perfect black outline. There aren't pressure marks, no damage beneath the surface of the skin."

She stood up, walked over, and shoved her hand at Todd's chest, hard. He grunted under the impact.

"When I hit him, I used the ball of my hand. It gives the most force. Or," another shove, "I can push him back with the tips of my fingers. Just . . . not with as much power" A faint smile tilted the corners of her full lips. "Sorry, Brooks."

"Don't be, Smith. He deserved it." The rumble came from Colin.

Smith had once joked easily with Colin. They'd been good friends. Now, she seemed to shut down at the sound of his voice, her smile fading instantly.

"Neither of those hits would leave a mark like the one found on House." Her hand fell away from Todd. "Even if the perp were over the vic, shoving him down into the bed, it would have been a ball-of-hand contact. There is *no* scenario I can think of that would leave that perfect outline of a person's hand."

"Ah, shit." McNeal's fingers rubbed over his eyes. "Smith, I wish you'd give me this information first. I've told you time and again there is chain of command here and—"

"I put the file in your box long before I gave a copy to Gyth." She raised a brow. "Have you checked your box, Captain?"

"I've been here since four a.m., stuck in a damn three-and-a-half-hour emergency meeting with the mayor and DA," he snapped. "So, no, Smith, I haven't!"

"Well, next time, you should. Especially before you go growling at me about how to do my job! I *know* how to do my job!"

She was all but going across the desk at him as she nearly shouted her words, and the lady *finally* was acting like her old self.

McNeal leaned forward, eyes narrowed.

"McNeal. Smith." It was Colin's steely voice that broke the tension in the room.

Their furious faces immediately turned toward him. Colin cleared his throat, then said, "Captain, as you pointed out to me and Brooks, we really don't have time for this shit."

Touché.

Smith drew in a deep breath. Took a few steps back, then slowly lowered her body into the chair. "Are you going to be able to exhume the other two bodies?"

A hard shake of McNeal's head. "DA will never go for even trying on the order. Especially if House isn't going down as a homicide."

"I checked House's body, thoroughly." She shook her head. "The man shouldn't have died."

The captain's gaze darted to Colin.

Todd tensed when his partner gave an almost imperceptible nod. *What the hell?*

McNeal peered down at the files again. "Well, at least we damn well know the last vic—what was his name?"

"Thomas Monroe," Todd supplied.

"Yeah, well, at least we know Monroe was murdered. Turn your focus onto him."

They *had* been focusing on him, and the other dead men who kept turning up. "There were no prints on the knife, but we did retrieve a hair from the mattress." A long strand of blond hair, and that fit because, "The desk clerk said a blond was there with Monroe." Just like a blond had been in the other hotels with the other dead men.

But why the change in MO? It made no sense. If the perp was the same, why change methods now? Why change them at all?

"The press has gotten wind of the link in the murders." Colin's voice was quiet, tense. "That new reporter for *News Flash Five*, Holly Storm—"

So now he remembered her name.

"—she was at the House scene, too. Must've gotten there

after we left. She talked to the desk clerk. Found out about the bondage, and now she knows about Monroe."

"I saw the damn story at five last night," McNeal muttered. "Shit. *'The cops aren't talking, but rumors of the Bondage Killer are rampant on the streets . . .'* Hell. Like I needed that crap from her now."

Todd winced. He'd also caught the redhead's story, just like nearly every other person in the city.

Holly Storm had finally made her big splash on *News Flash Five.*

"Damn straight the cops aren't talking." McNeal rapped his fingers on the surface of the desk. "My team doesn't talk."

Well, there wasn't exactly much to be talking about.

"All right. Here's how this is going to be handled." He stabbed a blunt finger in the air toward Todd. "You start digging into Monroe's life. See what you can find out about any girlfriends, people with an ax to grind, whatever."

He'd already been doing that. It wasn't like he was a fresh-faced uniform who didn't know how to handle a case.

The finger stabbed in Smith's direction. "I want the completed autopsy report on Monroe ASAP."

"Is there any sign of a print on his chest yet?" Todd asked quickly.

She shook her head. "The killer did a real number on his chest. Seventeen knife wounds."

Now that was a lot of rage.

Usually that much rage was personal.

"Finish the autopsy. Get me the report." McNeal's gaze shot to Colin. "You talked to Dr. Drake about this case?"

"Last night."

"Good." He waved his hand toward the door. "That's all—Smith, Brooks, you two can brief me later on your findings. Gyth, stay so we can talk."

Smith opened her mouth as if to protest. Then she shook her head and mumbled, "I don't think I want to hear this, anyway." Then she marched for the door, head held high.

McNeal's gaze followed her, and his lips pulled down into a small frown.

The door closed behind her with a soft click. No slam. No sign of fury.

But Todd knew she was angry.

Smith didn't like being cut out of a case.

Neither did he.

But, unlike Smith, he wasn't just planning to quietly walk out with his dignity.

Fuck dignity.

This was *his* case. He wasn't going to be pushed to the wayside again. He was a good cop, damn it. He'd busted his ass for years on the force. Taken two bullets. Back when he'd been on beat, he'd even gotten one of the highest arrest rates on record for the city.

"That's all for now, Brooks," McNeal said gruffly. "I'll update you on Dr. Drake's findings later."

Todd didn't move. "I think I'll just listen now. Save you from having to rehash it all later."

McNeal blinked. "I said that's *all*, Brooks."

A clear dismissal.

He was tired of being dismissed, and after the morning he'd already had, he wasn't about to back down.

My lover is a demon. I don't really think these guys can surprise me with anything else after learning that fun fact.

Todd cast a glance at Colin. Found his partner watching him with a tense, worried expression. "After I talk to the captain, I'll come and brief you," Colin told him, voice quiet, but his eyes seemed to blaze a warning.

Colin was trying to save his ass, Todd realized. Going toe-to-toe with the captain probably wasn't a good idea. Colin obviously thought it wasn't, and now his partner was trying to smooth things over.

Pity he wasn't in the mood for a nice, polite smoothing. He turned his attention back to the captain. "What don't you want me to know about this case?"

McNeal smiled. A shark's smile. "Oh, come on, now, Brooks, don't be ridiculous! You're completely in the loop on this case—"

And hell wasn't hot.

"—I just thought your time would be better spent following other leads—"

"Like with the Night Butcher?" He tossed out.

The smile dimmed. "I don't like your tone, Detective."

"And I don't like being kept in the dark." He began to pace, unable to contain the swirling energy in his body. "I'm tired of feeling like I'm only catching half of the things happening in this precinct." *In the world.* "I'm good at my job. Got enough commendations to plaster the damn wall at my apartment." He stopped, right next to Colin. "I deserve to know what's happening."

"You don't really want to know." Colin's voice.

He turn his head fractionally, just enough to meet his hard stare. "What don't I want to know, *partner*? That this world of ours is fucking full of monsters? And that you're one of them?"

Chapter 9

Silence.

Then, "How long have you known?" The question came from McNeal.

Colin just stared at him. His face was completely blank.

"Since the night Smith was taken. I followed Colin, long enough to see him change."

Colin flinched.

Todd spared the captain a glance. "Then you called and demanded I come back."

"Shit." McNeal rubbed the top of his gleaming head. "I knew you were going after him, but I didn't realize just how damn close you'd gotten." McNeal glared at Colin. "How come you didn't smell him? Hear him? You shifters are supposed to have such keen senses!"

"We do." A growl.

"I watched from a good distance. Used night-vision binoculars."

"His scent was already on me," Colin said nearly a second later. "And that night, I was more focused on *Other* things."

McNeal watched him with a hooded gaze. "So how much do you know?"

Not much. "I know werewolves are real—"

"*Wolves?*" McNeal mumbled. "Fucking figures."

Colin cleared his throat. "Ah, we're generally called shifters—not werewolves."

"—and that demons are, too. I know that place, Paradise Found, is some kind of meeting place for them all." And that all this shit was still making his head spin. Because now he wondered . . . how many of the perps he'd busted over the years, how many of the people he'd met—had actually been human? And how many had been something more?

"So you know about your little girlfriend, huh?" Colin drawled.

Todd braced his legs apart as he confronted his partner. "Don't push me, man. I don't care how much fur you can grow or how sharp your claws are, I will take you down." He wasn't particularly afraid of the big, bad wolf, not anymore. The first, oh, two weeks, yeah, he'd been piss scared. But the fear had soon morphed into anger—anger because his partner should have told him the truth long ago

"You're gonna take me down?" Colin shook his head. "Another partner tried that. He's dead, and I'm still here."

What?

"So how do you feel . . . knowing all this, Brooks?" McNeal rose and stalked toward them. "Do you think the shifters are evil? The demons are abominations that need to be put down?"

Cara was no abomination. She was beautiful and sensuous and she made him feel better than he'd felt in years.

Ever.

And his partner could be a bastard, but he wasn't evil . . . just too furry sometimes. "I feel like a veil has been over my eyes for years, and now I'm finally seeing clearly." He might not love everything he was seeing, but he *wanted* to see it all. Good. Bad. Human. Shifter. Demon.

"There's a lot more out there than you can imagine. A whole world of supernaturals—*the Other.*" McNeal was close now. Barely two feet away. "Vampires. Do you know about them? They're real. They can drain a human dry, kill with a bite. And the demons . . . you think you know about them? Do you know about the level-ten demons? The ones who can destroy buildings with a blink of their black eyes? Do you know that level-tens are practically immortal? The older they get, the harder it is to kill 'em. Hell, some can't even be killed by mortal weapons."

"So that makes taking them down a real bitch," Colin added darkly.

McNeal's words were probably meant to scare him. They didn't. They just made him more curious. He'd been trying to block Cara from his thoughts as best he could while he talked with Smith, McNeal, and Colin about the case, but the gloves were off now. No more pretending.

They were talking about the creatures that were roaming the city right under the noses of the humans. Cara was one of those creatures. He wanted to know everything he could about this new world and about her. "What else is out there?"

Cara wasn't a level-ten. She'd said she only had mid-range power. She could make fire. The lady had also said that she could hypnotize humans. Not him, but others.

"Oh, just about any damn thing you can imagine." McNeal never took his gaze off him. "The nightmares that wake you up late at night, the ones that make you break out into a cold sweat—the things out there, waiting in the shadows just beyond human sight—they're worse than your bad dreams. A thousand times worse."

"Djinn." Gyth spoke softly. "Witches. Wizards—"

Instinct guided him as he faced McNeal. There was something about the guy's voice, about the way McNeal eyeballed him. "And just what are you, Captain?"

McNeal's expression never wavered. "I'm an overworked cop who hadn't thought he'd have to be dealing with this crap again so soon."

Not the answer he wanted. That lick of heat powered his blood, the burst of excitement he got when he came close to breaking a case. Or now, breaking his captain. "You aren't human." He wouldn't have really questioned the captain's humanity before. But that had been *before* . . . before he'd watched Colin change. Before he'd kissed a demon and touched a paradise he hadn't known existed.

"Oh, I'm human. Just with a little something . . . extra." A quick glance toward the locked door. "Screw it. If you want to play in the *Other* world, I'll put my cards out for you."

"Captain?" The surprise in Colin's voice was real.

"He knows, Gyth. No sense denying anything now. Besides, the way this town is overrun with *Other* gone bad, you're goin' to need his backup on these damn monster cases—even *wolves* can't go it alone."

"But will he back me up?" The question was directed at McNeal, but Colin's gaze was on Todd.

So he answered. "I always have, haven't I?"

"That was before." His eyes were guarded.

"Yeah, well, the fact that your ass gets furry doesn't really change things for me." A pause. "I'll still watch your back, just like I expect you to watch mine."

A hard nod.

"And no more secrets. I'm sick of 'em."

"Brooks . . ." Now the captain looked worried. "There aren't many humans who understand about the paranormals. You can't just go around talking to anyone—"

What the hell? Did he have "idiot" stamped on his forehead? "I'm learning the rules of this game. It's gonna take me some time," *and a whole lot of adjusting,* "but I'm learning. And I've already figured out most folks are like I used to be. They don't have God's first clue what's happening—and I think most of 'em would like to keep living in the dark."

"Glad you understand that."

"Um." He cocked a brow. "So what are you, captain? A demon? Do your eyes do that cool black trick?"

"Vamps can do that, too," Colin told him. "Not the whole eye, though, not like a demon's. A vamp's eyes change when he goes into hunting mode."

Good point to know.

"I'm a charmer," McNeal said.

"What?"

"A charmer." His lips thinned. "It means I can talk to certain . . . animals."

"Uh, just what kind of animals?"

The captain smiled his shark smile once again. "Come with me for a walk sometime, Detective, and I'll be happy to show you."

Yeah, he'd put that on his to-do list. Right after he caught a killer. "Rain check, Captain." He pointed to the file that had been tossed onto the desk. "So what about our killer? What are we dealing with here?"

Colin rubbed his fingers over the bridge of his nose. "Emily had a few ideas on that one."

Emily? So she was in on this, too?

McNeal must have guessed his thoughts, because he said, "Dr. Drake isn't exactly who you thought she was, Brooks. She's human, but gifted."

"Psychic," Colin supplied.

Todd tensed.

"Her gift only works with paranormals, so Dr. Drake's patients are generally . . ."

Supernaturals. *Other*. The captain didn't have to finish his sentence. "I get the picture."

"Good." McNeal frowned at Colin. "So just who—what are we facing?"

A hesitation that lasted nearly a minute, then . . . "According to Em, the most likely suspect is a demon. Based on the body's appearance and the crime scene, she thinks we might be dealing with a succubus."

Succubus. The name was familiar to Todd. He'd heard about a succubus before, and the male version, the incubus. He'd read about them back in college in one of his medieval studies classes that he'd taken, hoping for an easy A, but managing to drag out a low B.

A succubus was a kind of . . . sex demon.

Cara's image flashed in front of his eyes and an icy spear of awareness pressed right into his heart.

Oh, shit. No way, she couldn't be a—

"Succubus." McNeal whistled soundlessly. "Met one of 'em once. About ten years ago. Sexiest thing I've ever seen." He coughed. "Well, *almost* ever seen."

Cara was damn well the sexiest thing he'd ever seen, but that still didn't mean—

"I've been doing research on succubi," Colin said, eyes hard and intent on Todd. "Talked with Em some more, hit the local occult shops right before I came in." A brief smile. "Those places are always open—works for the clientele, you know."

Todd made a mental note to hit the same shops. A bit of research reading was definitely in order.

"From what I've learned, the succubi tend to be extremely territorial. It's rare to find more than a couple in the same city."

"And do we know of a succubus in Atlanta?" McNeal asked.

Colin looked at Todd. Too much knowledge was in his stare. *No.*

"I said, do we know of a succubus in Atlanta?" The captain repeated, voice rising.

The spear drove deeper into his heart and the pain stole his breath for a moment when Colin said, "Yeah, we do. Her name's Cara Maloan, and she was our original suspect in the killings."

Todd's face burned fiery hot, then shot to icy cold as pinpricks flew over his skin. A sex demon.

"Then get her ass in here, *now.*" McNeal's thin lips tightened. "But be careful. I've heard stories. A succubus can steal a man's mind. Drive him crazy with lust . . . and kill him as he begs for her touch."

The captain's warning came too late for Todd.

A steady rage began to burn inside him. "Cara's not the killer," he snarled.

"Fuck." Grim understanding was in the one word. "Brooks—what the hell have you done to my case?"

He met that gray stare without so much as a blink. "Cara isn't a killer. Her alibis checked out—"

"And if those alibis were given by humans, she could've planted the damn suggestions! Shit, Brooks, she's a demon, you can't trust her—"

He wanted to. "I *saw* her reaction to the news of House's death. The woman *hurt*. She's not a killer." His gut told him that.

"That's your dick talking," McNeal snapped.

Todd stepped forward, body tense.

McNeal glared right back at him. "Gyth . . ." He never took his eyes off Todd. "Bring her in."

He felt, rather than saw, his partner's hesitation. "Her story checked out, Captain—and the alibis—they were given by demons and a witch, not humans."

"Like demons and witches don't lie." McNeal shook his head. "I want Ms. Firon here *to-damn-day.*"

Todd realized that his hands were clenched into fists. "You're wasting time."

"Gyth—get out of here." McNeal barked the order, then glared at Todd a full minute before saying, "Brooks, you'd better start talking—fast—and let me know why I should keep you on this case. *If* Cara's guilty—"

"*She's not.*" Gut, psychic edge, whatever the hell it was— every instinct he possessed screamed her innocence.

The woman *had* lied to him, though. *A sex demon.* Shit. She should have told him—

"You'd damn well better prove she's not involved in these killings—convince me, or your lover is going to find her ass in jail."

She was back in the station again. Back in the same dingy interrogation room. Sitting at the same scarred table and sitting in the same chair that tilted slightly to the right.

And Cara was pissed.

"Why isn't Detective Todd Brooks in here?" She demanded, glaring at the stony visage of his partner.

Gyth shrugged. "Because I've got questions for you."

Screw his questions—and screw him. "Does he know what you've done? That you dragged me out of my house—"

"Politely escorted—"

"Handcuffed me—"

"For your own protection—"

"Cut *my* hair—"

"You agreed to that sample—"

"And put me back in this shitty room—"

He cleared his throat. "Interrogation rooms aren't supposed to be pretty."

Her nails tapped against the table top. "Correct me if I'm wrong, but I was under the impression we'd already done this dance before. My alibis checked out, remember? I even got a nice apology from your partner."

"You left out a few facts when you were here before." He pulled out the chair on the opposite side of the table. Flipped it around. Straddled it as he sat down.

Her eyes narrowed. "What do you mean?"

"Well, like the fact that you're a demon. You didn't mention that little tidbit the first time around."

He'd told her secret. "Todd . . . discussed that with you?" It hurt. In the heart that others had said she didn't have. To think that Todd had run straight from her bed to the station so that he could tell his buddies what a freak of nature she was—

Cara straightened her shoulders. "I want to see him."

"Don't think that's the best idea," he murmured.

Like she gave half a rat's ass what he thought. Her nails scraped over the old wood. "Look, shifter—"

His jaw tensed. "How do you—"

"I want to see Todd. If I don't see him, I'm done talking. Done being the good citizen and putting up with all this bullshit." She'd call Niol, and he'd make the cops sorry they'd even thought to question her. "You don't want to mess with me. I've got friends—you can't even imagine how strong they are. Not even in your darkest dreams."

He leaned forward. "You threatening me?"

Cara shrugged. She was done talking. Unless she got to see Todd.

"He's been watching you." Gyth pointed his index finger toward the mirror. "Listening to you."

Not a newsflash. She could *feel* his stare. He'd been in and out of the other room since she'd been dumped in interrogation. But she didn't want to admit her knowledge to the cop, so she'd asked her questions—

And gotten more damn enraged by the moment.

Todd should have his ass in there. What game was he playing now? What—

"If he wanted to talk to you, he'd be here—"

The door shoved open before Gyth could finish his sentence. Banged back against the wall with a thud. Todd stood in the doorway, face flushed, eyes glinting.

He looked furious. Body tight. Hands clenched.

Just the way she felt. "Been telling stories, have you, Todd?" She asked softly, tilting her chin back just the slightest bit. Seeing him again stirred an ache inside her. The hunger hadn't abated. The need was still there, even though he'd turned on her.

She could be such an idiot sometimes.

"I didn't have to tell him. Gyth already knew." He slammed the door shut with his heel, then stalked toward her.

Ah. Her gaze darted back to the other cop. Shifter nose.

"And how'd you know about me?" Gyth asked.

A shrug. Not like it was confidential information or anything. "When you smelled my pheromones, you stepped back. Demons, humans, vamps—they all come closer."

A growl sounded. It didn't come from the shifter, but from Todd. "So you've got a lot of . . . experience luring men, do you?"

She didn't like his tone. Not. One. Bit.

"But you're a sex demon, right? So screwing men, draining them, even killing them for sensual power—that's just right up your alley, isn't it?"

What the hell was happening? Was this some really nightmarish game of bad cop, bad cop? What had happened to her tender lover?

He'd left when he found out what I truly am.

The air in the room thickened around her. "I don't like the

term 'sex demon.' " Her head cocked to the right. "I find it offensive." As offensive as she found the rest of his words. She'd made love with him the night before. She hadn't just been screwing around.

Her fingers flattened against the table. Deep groves indented the surface, courtesy of her nails. Her gaze held Todd's. "And I am not, *not*, going to apologize for being what I am." She'd been born a demon. Unchangeable fact. She was a demon, one that, after she hit adulthood, needed a certain powerful energy to continue living. Not her fault. Just the hand of fate.

"You're not going to apologize for killing?" Gyth asked. "Damn ballsy of you."

Now she had to be careful. "And just who is it that you think I killed? I've already told you that I had nothing to do with Michael's death, or the others you mentioned and—"

"But you didn't tell us that Simon Battle liked to come to Paradise Found and listen to you sing." Todd was at the edge of the table. Hands fisted. Brows low over his eyes, and jaw clenched tight.

"What? Who?"

"Simon Battle." Gyth slid the eight-by-ten photo across the table. "Victim number one, in case you've forgotten."

Her gaze flickered to the photo. She inhaled sharply. "I don't know him."

"But he knew you," Todd told her. "In fact, according to the guy's friends, he made it a habit to go and catch your show once a week."

"I've only been singing at Paradise Found for a little over two months—"

"And he caught one of your shows every week."

Cara studied the photo, tried to block the pain that shook her. The man's eyes were closed. There was nothing particularly familiar about the guy. He was attractive, with strong features and a faint dimple in his chin. His hair was brushed back from his high forehead.

Yeah, a good-looking, *dead* guy. One she didn't know. Her

eyes lifted back to Todd's. "You've been at Paradise when I sing."

Gyth swore.

She ignored him, continuing, "You know how packed that place can get. With the lights on the stage, it's not like I can see every man in the crowd."

"But they can all see you."

"So?"

He opened his mouth, began to snap, "That's just what you—"

"How'd a human get inside Paradise so often?" Gyth demanded, cutting across Todd's angry words.

Cara blew out the breath she'd been holding. "Humans get in all the time. Those who know about us sometimes like to play."

"And Niol lets them?"

"As long as no one gets seriously hurt in his place, Niol tolerates just about anything."

"You know him pretty well." Todd's voice was controlled now, *too* controlled.

Cara nodded.

"He's like you, right?"

"Not exactly." Niol wasn't an incubus. Just a full-blooded, deadly dangerous warrior . . . who happened to be a level-ten demon.

He'd also been her sister's lover. Years ago.

"What about him?" Gyth pushed another photo in front of her.

She really didn't enjoy looking at photos of dead men. Cara spared a brief glance for the still features of the handsome man, felt pity stir in her heart. "Am I supposed to know him, too?"

"Travis Walters. Until recently, he lived on your block. We found out he moved about five months ago."

"And I moved in less than four." She wanted to jump up, to scream and rage at Todd. How could he be doing this? Did he really think she'd murdered these men? How the hell could he go from making love to her to—to treating her like a prime suspect?

She wanted to punch him. She wanted to scream.

Damn it, she even felt stupid tears welling in her eyes.

This shit sucked!

"Tell me, Cara . . ." Todd's tone was so sharp it could have cut glass. "Can a succubus really kill her lover?"

"You're still alive, aren't you?" She flared, driven to the edge. She was about to snap. One more smartass comment from her lover and—

"Can a succubus kill?"

Cara shot to her feet. "Anyone can kill under the right circumstances." He should know that. After all, he'd admitted his own crimes to her.

"But what about killing without damaging the body? Without breaking the skin at all?" Gyth asked.

Her stare never left Todd. "What am I? Your prime suspect or some kind of expert on demons?"

Todd's lips tightened and gaze dropped to her lips. She saw hunger flicker in those eyes, need. Anger. "You're both."

"And you're a damn jerk." Why did she always have to fall for the wrong man? And, shit—these questions, they weren't just about *her* being a suspect, Cara realized with a sinking heart. Todd and Gyth thought the killer was a succubus.

And they knew she was a succubus.

Oh, hell.

"Is it true that succubi are territorial? That only one or two hunt in a city at a time?" Gyth just kept pressing with his questions. Firing one after the other.

And then she realized what they were doing. Todd was the distraction. Gyth was the real threat. He was hitting her, trying to uncover any secrets she might have.

Fine. If they wanted some secrets, she'd tell them. Nothing too dangerous, of course. But . . . "Yeah, we're a bunch of possessive bitches." A faint shrug. "Usually one, maybe two in a city—"

"How many are in the city now?" Gyth fired.

She paused. Okay, this was gonna look bad, but she'd give them the truth. "As far as I know . . . I'm the only one."

The two men shared a dark look.

Hell. *Jeez, Cara, why not just ask your lover to lock you up and toss that key away next time?*

"As far as you know . . ." Todd repeated carefully. "Does that mean another succubus *could* be in the city?"

"Possibly," she admitted. "*Maybe.*"

"You sense each other, don't you?" Gyth's question was hard.

"Just like you'd know another shifter." She pushed back the hair that wanted to tumble over her eyes. "Look, it's *possible* another succubus is in Atlanta—if she's stayed far enough away from me, I wouldn't have sensed her, so I can't say with complete certainty—"

"What about the men?" Todd asked quietly.

Cara frowned. "There aren't any other—"

"*Incubi.*"

Oh. A shrug. "Yeah, some of 'em are in Atlanta." The incubi outnumbered the succubi nine to one, so they'd had to learn long ago how to share the prime cities. It had been a real bloodbath at first. Too many men. Too much aggressive hunting instinct bred into the blood.

She smiled at Todd, a deliberate, seductive smile, and let her scent out, full-force.

The shifter swore. "Man, be careful."

Too late. Her fragrance was in the air, seducing, and she saw the telling twitch of Todd's nostrils.

Cara put her hand on his chest. Just as she'd done last night, when no clothes separated her from his flesh. His heart thundered beneath her touch. Not just from anger. The desire was there—on his face and in his eyes. "Poor detective. Wanting something that you hate."

His hand flew up. His fingers locked around her wrist in a hard, steely grip. "I don't hate you, Cara."

"But you fear me." And suspected her of murder, apparently, *again*. Damn it. Could things not just work out well for her one time?

"No, baby, I don't fear you." He leaned in closer to her. "I'm pissed as hell—*you should have told me the truth—all of the truth, damn it*—about yourself."

Ah, he meant the little succubus part of her demonhood. "I would have told you—you didn't give me enough time before you ran out—"

"I didn't run! Shit! I had a job waiting on me, fucking cases. I was coming back to you tonight—but then I found out a *succubus* is killing in the city and oh, guess what, my girlfriend just happens to be a succubus—"

His girlfriend? Okay, she pushed that part aside, for now. "Todd—what makes you think the killer's a succubus? We don't kill." *Anymore.* "We get along with humans, we don't hurt—"

"Somebody sure as hell is," Gyth murmured.

"Tell me it isn't you," Todd said, the words fierce, cutting her like a too-sharp knife.

Did he truly think she'd gone on some kind of sex spree and killed those three men?

His skin was warm against hers. The scent of his body reminded her—too much—of the pleasures they'd shared. But his eyes held secrets . . . and suspicions?

Fuck him.

"So was it a game?" The words burst from her as the anger raged past the pain. "Coming to Paradise, dancing with me, going home with me—was it all some trick? You still think I'm a killer and—"

"I think you're a sex demon—"

"*Succubus.*"

"And you just confirmed that your kind aren't exactly tripping over each other in the city."

"I. Didn't. Kill. Them!" But if they *knew* a succubus was involved . . . "And you know what, *Detective,* it sounds to me like someone has been feeding you information about my kind. What's the deal? You got your own demon expert somewhere around here?" Her gaze jumped to the mirrored wall. "Maybe right there?"

"Maybe." The drawl came from Gyth.

Her gaze jerked back to Todd. He stared down at her, too handsome, too fierce.

Too human. Humans and their suspicions. Always so quick to judge.

Her temper snapped. "Arrest me or let me go."

"I'm not letting you go." Todd shook his head.

"Well, then you'd damn well better—"

His jaw worked a moment, as if he struggled to find words then, "I-I believe you, Cara."

"What?" Gyth demanded. "Brooks, are you crazy—"

"She's not a killer." He cut across Gyth's snarl with one of his own. "I fucking told you *and* McNeal that already—"

Her lips parted. *What?*

"She's in here now because procedure demanded it, but Cara's alibis checked out, she's cooperated, and she's not a *damn killer*!"

Okay, the man was making her head swim. "If you knew I was innocent, why did you put me through this shit?"

He jerked his thumb toward the mirror. "So the asshole in there would know you were innocent, too."

She blinked. "Ah . . ."

He faced the mirror. "Reactions, right, Captain? That's what you wanted to see. Well, judge her. *I* say she's innocent. If you think she's a murderer, then come in *now.*"

Don't come in. The words flew through Cara's head.

Silence.

Then a curse from Gyth. "Fucking ballsy."

Todd grunted then glanced back at her. "I have to do my job. *Always.* Remember that."

She was trying to play catch-up, fast. So, Todd had been forced to question her by his captain? He still believed she was innocent?

But . . . from the look on his face, he *was* pissed at her.

Because I didn't tell him I was a succubus.

Damn.

"You had to be questioned, Cara." Todd spoke, voice

softer now, more controlled. "And you had to come in because, hell, Cara, I really do want your help." He glanced at
Gyth. "*We* need your help."

Her knees were shaking. "Just what do you want me to
do?" Her anger had cooled a bit, replaced by confusion, fear,
and other emotions that she didn't want to analyze too much.

Todd sighed and the look on his face told her she wasn't
going to be loving what came next. "Well, first, baby, we're
gonna need you to look at a body."

No, not loving it at all.

He hated battering her with questions. Hated watching the
play of stark emotions run across her face.

For a few moments, she'd looked almost broken. Then the
anger—no, rage—had kicked in.

And the lady had looked like she wanted to kick his ass.

Not the normal pattern for a killer—he sure as hell hoped
McNeal realized that fact, and got off his back.

The captain had wanted to yank him from the case the
minute he'd learned about Todd's night with Cara. He'd ar-
gued for an hour with McNeal, listing every reason, five
times, why Cara couldn't be the killer.

Damn, but he hoped he wasn't wrong.

His gut said he should trust her.

His cock said he should take her.

And his heart said he was in serious trouble.

He was out on a limb now with the captain. A very thin
limb that could break at any point, but the fact was, if Cara
wasn't the killer, then seeing as how it looked like another
succubus was on the loose, she'd be the best person to guide
them in their hunt.

Provided, of course, that she was feeling like helping out
the long arm of the law.

"I need you to see something on the body," Todd told her
softly, trying to pull back the anger that flared within him.

Anger because she'd lied to him—Christ, a *fucking sex
demon.*

Every man in the world probably wanted her.

He *wasn't* the sharing type.

And just how many other humans had she bewitched with her seduction? Was he just another in a long line for her? While she was—well, *much* more to him.

"*What?*" Cara's cry was hoarse. "I don't know about your idea of a good time, Todd, but—"

"You know *exactly* what my idea of a good time is." He wanted her then so badly he ached.

And she still looked angry as all hell.

Oh, yeah, he'd royally fucked things up.

No choice.

Proving her absolute innocence was paramount now.

Keeping away the other assholes on this earth who wanted her—well, that would be his goal number two.

Her plump lips parted as she drew in a deep breath, and if Gyth hadn't been glaring at him, Todd would have leaned forward and kissed her right then.

"Don't even think about it," she said.

He leaned forward another inch anyway. Just a breath of space away from her delectable mouth. He'd never seen a mouth that sexy before, and he knew it tasted as good as it looked. Pushed too far, he taunted, "But isn't that why you sent your sweet smell out to me? Because you wanted me . . . to want you." And he did. Didn't matter to him that the lady was dangerous. A huge unknown element. He. Wanted. Her. Period.

And when this case was finished, he planned to take a few days off and spend them in sheer wild sexual bliss with her.

Provided that he hadn't pissed her off too much in the meantime.

"I—*shit.*"

Her mouth even looked good when she said that.

Sexy demon.

Sex demon.

"I really do need your help, Cara," he said, trying to take his mind off just what being a sex demon entailed. He didn't want to think of her with another man. Other men.

He wasn't a virgin. He'd had more than his share of willing partners, so he sure as hell didn't expect Cara to be pure as the driven snow.

But he did *not* want to think about her with other men. Not even for one fucking moment.

"Rein in the scent." He reinforced the order by tightening his fingers around her delicate wrist. "I don't want the cops in the bull pen going crazy."

"You have no idea what I could make them do," she told him, voice rumbling.

Oh, he was starting to figure it out.

"The last victim, Thomas Monroe, was stabbed." Gyth's harsh words snapped Todd back to the case.

Cara blinked. "But that doesn't make any sense. Not if you truly think the killer's a succubus, anyway."

They were pretty damn certain that was who they were after.

"A death like that," Cara continued, "it wouldn't yield a succubus any power."

His breath caught. "Explain that to me, nice and slow." 'Cause he sure as hell didn't know what she meant, but he knew he didn't like it.

"Look, killing isn't really our way." Her lips twisted. "Anymore, okay? Once upon a time—"

"And that would have been when?" Gyth asked.

"Middle Ages."

Shit.

She read his expression easily. "While I personally wasn't around then, demons always have been. Get used to that fact, Todd. Your life will be so much easier once you start realizing there is much more to the world than you thought."

Maybe. Or maybe things would just be five times harder.

He'd bet his paycheck on option two.

"A lot of demons killed back them. Succubi got a reputation."

He'd read a bit about that earlier. Right after the captain had chewed his ass out and he'd made a frantic trip to the occult bookstore two streets over.

"A lot of innocents were killed back then, blamed for what the demons were doing. The attacks also brought attention to the *Other.* Not really something that my kind wants."

"So the demons decided to take a break from killing?" Not likely.

"There were some ancient demons. Those who've been on earth from nearly the beginning. They don't rule over anyone, but back then, they—they kept an order, so to speak." She nibbled on her lower lip. "I haven't heard anything about those guys in years, don't even know if they're still around."

Great. So if the big bosses weren't controlling folks anymore, then he'd probably keep finding demons with appetites for murder.

"But long ago, those guys sent out the *cazadores del alma.*"

Gyth stepped forward. "I've heard of 'em."

"Yeah, *I* haven't." Todd realized he was still holding Cara's wrist. Stroking her pulse point with his thumb.

He dropped her hand. Put some space between them.

"They're soul-hunters. Born of witch and demon, those guys are incredibly powerful. Have few vulnerabilities. And they're basically the boogeymen who come after *Other* when things get out of control."

"Do these boogeymen ever go after humans?" Gyth asked, eyes hard.

"Not that I know of." Her brows lowered. "Anything's possible, though."

Todd was trying to assimilate the information as quickly as he could. "So let me get this straight. Succubi stopped their sex death party in the Middle Ages because the *cazadores del alma* were sicced on them?"

"Basically."

"And you're saying none of your kind has killed since then?" Not buying it.

Cara hesitated. "I'm saying succubi don't normally kill. Not anymore. There's no need. The sexual culture today is so much more open. Hell, we can get a little rush of energy just by going into a bar—"

Understanding dawned. "Or by singing to a hungry crowd."

"As long as humans are there, *yes*," she said—and did a faint flush color her cheeks? "If there aren't humans in the crowd, it won't work. Demon power doesn't infuse us." A slanted look at Gyth. "Shifter strength can work, just not as well."

His head was aching. Temples pounding. And he'd thought working the cases before was tough. "Fuck it. We're going to see the bodies."

She shook her head, sending the blond locks flying. "I told you, I didn't want—"

"Cara, *I need your help*. House needs you—just look at 'em, okay? I wouldn't ask if it weren't damn important." And just the idea of letting her into the Crypt was unorthodox as hell, but he was desperate. With every word she'd spoken, he'd become more convinced that a succubus was out in Atlanta, killing. And to catch a murderer, or a sex demon, well, he just might have to use . . . a sex demon.

The knowledge Cara could provide to him was priceless, and he wasn't about to let her slip away. Not when he needed her so much.

For the case.

And for . . . well, hell, he just needed her.

She swallowed. "Todd . . ."

"Cara, I need you."

Her gaze held his. One breath of time. Two. Then, "All right."

Relief had his shoulders dropping.

Smith had wanted someone with more "expertise" to look at the print on House's body.

Looked like she'd just gotten the perfect expert.

"What do you think?" Danny McNeal asked quietly as he and Dr. Emily Drake watched the threesome file out of the interrogation room.

Emily stared through the thin mirror. "I think I'm not going to be able to help you very much on this case." Her palms were sweating, but her voice was perfectly controlled.

"Could that woman, Cara Maloan, be a killer?"

Yes. "I can't answer that question." Her shoulders were stiff as she turned to face him. "I'm sorry."

A line appeared between his brows. "What? Why can't—"

"Doctor-client confidentiality." The words were soft.

McNeal's eyes widened, then, "Shit."

Nice sum up, but McNeal had always seemed to possess a special talent with words.

"You didn't go inside," she said softly. When Todd had called him out, she'd felt the electric arc in the air as McNeal tensed.

A growl. "Can't prove she's involved yet." A pause. "And Brooks has never been wrong on a case before."

But he'd never had one like *this* before, either.

Emily glanced back over her shoulder just as the door shut behind Colin. Damn, but this case had taken a bad turn. Cara was a sweet woman. Smart. Unquestionably beautiful.

But sad. So very sad on the inside.

And, even though she couldn't tell McNeal, Cara was also a woman with the complete capacity for killing. Emily had learned about Cara's darker side months ago—when the succubus had finally confessed about her sister's murder . . . and the ensuing death of her sister's lover.

Emily's fingers curled into fists. She sure hoped Todd knew what he was doing. Colin wouldn't slip up—he'd never let his guard down around the other woman.

But Emily was trained to observe other people. To read their emotions, and when she'd watched Todd, she'd seen the hunger in his eyes. The need for Cara.

A need that could prove to be very, very dangerous.

A need that had proved fatal for another.

Chapter 10

"Ah, not so fast, Gyth." Todd brought his hand up, and barred the entrance to the elevator.

Cara frowned at him.

"What the hell are you doing now, Brooks?" The shifter glowered at him.

"Getting time with my lady. We need to talk, *alone*." The words held an unmistakable edge.

Gyth's face hardened. "If the captain finds out . . ."

"Then he can call my ass out again—but I'm talking to Cara now. Take the stairs."

Todd stepped back and the doors slid closed, blocking the sight of the shifter's stony visage. Then he turned around and locked his stare right on her.

All alone now. She looked at him and said, "Asshole."

Todd blinked. "Cara, I told you, I had to—"

"You could have warned me!" She wanted to hit him, hard. "You didn't have to let that jerk shifter haul me off to the interrogation room—"

"I had to fight like hell to stay on the case, Cara."

"I thought you said I was clear—"

"You were! Baby, I wouldn't have slipped into your bed otherwise." Blazing eyes. "But then we found out that we weren't just looking for your run-of-the-mill killer—we're looking for a succubus—and you're the only one in the area who fits that bill."

Damn it.

He stepped closer to her. His left hand shot out. Punched a red button on the elevator control panel.

The big box shuddered to a halt.

"Wh-what did you do?" But she knew.

"We're clearing the air here, Cara." He exhaled heavily. "The captain knows about our relationship. Hell, Gyth knew I'd been with you the minute I walked into the station."

The quiet words rocked through her.

"I don't make a habit of talking about my sex life." His mouth tightened. "I came in today because I was on duty. Apparently, Gyth has one hell of a nose. He"—Todd's jaw clenched—"smelled you on me."

Yeah, those two-faced shifters could do that.

"Kissing and telling—that's not my style."

"But then I'm not your usual 'style,' now am I? You think I'm some kind of freak because I happened to be born a demon and—"

"You're not a damn freak!" She winced at his yell. "Or a monster or—"

"What am I, then?"

His mouth snapped closed.

"What am I? What am I to *you*? A suspect? An itch that you want to scratch? A—"

"*You're mine!*" Nearly a roar.

She shook her head and wondered if her ears would stop ringing soon.

He grabbed her, crushing her against him. "I hate this case. I hate bringing you in. I hate seeing you scared and angry. I hate wanting to rip my partner apart because he questions you—and I hate *myself* because I have to stand there and watch—because if I go too easy on you, the captain will sure as hell suspect you're involved—and that you're using your *sex demon* powers to slip into my mind and make me weak!"

Wow. She knew her eyes had to be wide—and that her mouth was hanging open in surprise. "Todd, I don't—"

"There's the case, baby, then there's you and me."

Well, that was the way it should have been—but... "I keep finding myself in the middle of your case, Detective."

"I know. And it fucking sucks."

He had no idea. *He* wasn't the one who kept popping up as a suspect.

"*Cara*..." Almost desperate. His hands were too tight on her. "Christ, woman, I—" His mouth crashed onto hers. Rough, Demanding.

So right.

A hot flush of excitement spread through her. She was still angry with him, she didn't like the way he'd confronted her during the interrogation, but—ah, damn it, *yes* she still wanted the guy.

The sensual power flowing from Todd in waves wrapped around her.

The man sure had some kind of potent sexual energy.

And *she* was the one who was supposed to be dangerous.

He ripped his mouth from hers, breath rasping out. He freed her hands, only to raise his arms and slap his palms on the wall behind her head, effectively caging her.

She tasted him on her tongue—and wanted more. "A-aren't you nervous?" She asked, wetting her lips and watching his gaze drop with a helpless surge of pleasure. "I mean, you're all alone here with a demon. There's really no telling what I could do to you." He'd sure gone running fast enough this morning.

"And you're all alone with a man who wants you so badly he can hardly think." His mouth hovered over her lips. "Are you nervous?" The question was whispered right back to her.

Yes.

His scent surrounded her, just as she knew the tempting lure of her pheromones surrounded him.

"Is any of it real?" He asked, and there was a spark of unmistakable anger in his eyes. "The lust, the need... is it all a trick?"

"I told you before." She hadn't lied then, wouldn't lie now. Screw her pride. "I want you. Have from the moment I opened my door to you." Her head shook, a little sadly. "That's no trick."

"But what about how *I* feel?" His right hand dropped to capture her jaw. His thumb brushed over her lip. Pushed just past the edge of her teeth. "Are you making me want you?"

Her sex clenched with hunger just from his touch. He stood so close to her that she could feel the hard ridge of his aroused cock pressing against her.

His hand moved, drifting down her neck until his fingers rested lightly over the pounding pulse in her throat. She tried to answer him as honestly as she could, saying, "My pheromones, my scent, they're designed to lure . . ."

"You mean the way you smell like sex and paradise? Yeah, baby, that's a damn big lure."

"I don't release the full scent with you. I mean, I have, when we were making love, there was no way to stop it then, but now, and before, I've tried to control it." Okay, she'd let it slip in the interrogation room—but he'd pushed her *too far.* And he'd certainly caught the scent plenty of other times—but not the full onslaught.

"Just the scent of you arouses men." His voice was thick with tension.

"It can."

"You said you weren't using your magic on me."

"Not to hypnotize you." She hadn't.

Damn, but she wanted the man to kiss her. That mouth of his was so close—

"What about the dreams, Cara? Those sweet, wild-as-hell dreams I had?" His fingers eased over her collarbone. Slid down the vee at the top of her shirt and paused in the valley between her breasts.

"I-I didn't mean to—"

He brushed open the edges of her shirt. Slid his fingertips under the lace of her black bra. Her flesh was so sensitive that when he found her nipple, she gasped with the pleasure that arched through her.

Even as she realized that the seductress was being seduced.

"Didn't mean to what?" he whispered, then his mouth finally took hers. Lips touched. Pressed. His tongue thrust deep. Tangled with hers.

Only to withdraw too soon.

He gazed down at her, and there was no mistaking his need. Or her own.

"What didn't you mean to do?" His voice was gravel rough.

She could still taste him on her tongue. "Come to you, that way. I-I . . . in the past, I've had to focus my power. Project." *Hunt.* "When I closed my eyes, I just went to you." And it had been wonderful.

"It was all real then?" His fingers strummed her tight nipple.

"Yes, in a-a sense." She licked her lips. "The pleasure was real, but it *was* just a dream." She hadn't actually been in his room. Hadn't felt the warm, naked contours of his body.

Well, until last night, anyway.

His fingers stilled on her breast. "How many other men have dreamed of you?" He growled the question at her.

Anger was in his tone. But so was . . . hurt? Cara lifted her hands. Curled her fingers over the hard muscles in his arms. "They don't matter. The only one that matters now is you." She meant that.

Dreams, fantasies, they were like wisps of smoke. Being with Todd, it was real, *he* was real, and the way he made her feel—

Like a real woman.

Not just a demon.

It was her turn to stroke his jaw. The faint sting of stubble rasped along her palm. "I want to be with you. Not the cop and the demon." She was tired of the allegations. Suspicions. "Just the man and the woman." Maybe it wasn't possible, but, damn it, *something* was between them.

And she wanted to find out just what it was.

Could be hard, hot lust. A lust that would burn out with the pounding mating of their bodies.

But maybe it would be more than lust. That elusive something more she'd searched for so long.

Cara rose just a bit on her tiptoes. Wrapped her hand
around the back of his neck and urged his face closer to her.
Their lips met, mouths open. Need burning. She kissed him
with all the raging passion in her, and he met her, kissing
back, full force.

When the elevator lurched, she didn't pay it any attention.
She ignored the soft ding of a bell and enjoyed the slow thrust
of his tongue and the skilled play of his fingers on her nipple.

There was a soft *swish*, and Todd hurriedly stepped back
from her, pulling his hand and mouth away with a muffled
curse.

Cara realized then that they'd made it to the basement. The
elevator had started moving on its own. Damn it.

Todd glanced out of the elevator. His back was ramrod
straight. "No one's here."

She didn't particularly care.

But when he stepped from the elevator, her eyes narrowed
and she followed him. "Todd—"

His eyes burned down at her. "I'm *always* a cop."

The intensity in his voice made her stomach knot.

"The cop and the man, they aren't separate for me. I do my
job, twenty-four-seven. I *live* this job—and I want to trust
you, but—"

But. She felt the word hit her like a slap. "I thought we
were past this. You said you didn't think I was a killer."

"I *want* to trust you." The words seemed to be ripped from
him. "But you didn't tell me the truth about yourself until just
hours ago—and even then, you didn't tell me everything. I had
to get the details from Gyth."

Because she'd been afraid he'd turn away from her. "You
don't understand." She had to swallow to ease the dryness in
her throat. "You don't know what it's like—"

"You're damned right I don't—and you haven't told me."
A door opened near the end of the hallway, and from the corner of her eye, Cara saw Gyth exit what she figured was a

stairwell. The words snapped out fast as Todd demanded, "Tell me this, baby, are the demon and the woman really separate for you?"

No.

Her expression must have answered for her because he nodded. "I didn't think so." Todd wasn't touching her now. Not at all. "We are who we are, Cara. No changing it."

"I didn't say I wanted to change." She'd never longed to be human.

Not really.

"Take me as I am, and that's the way I'll take you."

The grated words had her blinking in surprise. Was he saying—

He kissed her, hard. "And stay the hell out of anyone else's dreams, baby."

Before she could respond, Gyth was there. Glaring at her and Todd, with his nostrils flaring. A moment later, another door opened, one that brought her the scent of death and decay, mixed with bleach and the harsh stench of chemicals.

A tall, thin woman with coffee cream skin—a woman so beautiful Cara doubted she was human—stepped into the hallway. She frowned when she saw them.

"Smith, just the woman we wanted to see," Todd called out.

The woman wore light green scrubs. Behind her, Cara heard the sound of jazz music drifting from the open door.

"I'm takin' a break, Brooks."

He sighed. "We need to look at the bodies."

A stare that was as dark as night locked on Cara. "Who is she?"

Todd raised a brow. "She's the expert you need."

"What?"

"Remember, Smith? You said you were out of your 'element'—well, trust me, for Cara—this is definitely her area of expertise."

Smith's gaze darted to Gyth. "One of yours, huh?"

"She sure as hell isn't!" Todd snapped, just as Cara asked blankly, "One of his what?"

Gyth marched to the doctor's side. Whispered to her. Cara caught the familiar "succubus" and the equally familiar "dangerous."

"No need for whispers," Todd said, grabbing her hand and pulling Cara toward the door. "Okay. I know what's going on, I've been a blind idiot, but I get it now. *I get it.*"

Smith's stare was solemn. "You're not an idiot. You're just human, and I'm beginning to think that we're pretty damn rare."

Oh, but the doctor was very much mistaken. "Actually," Cara murmured, "at the last count," unofficial though it had been, "humans outnumber supernaturals two hundred and fifty-four thousand to one." Give or take a bit.

Smith didn't look particularly pleased or impressed by this bit of news. But after a moment, she turned around and marched back into the slightly chilled room.

Back to where the bodies waited.

Cara pulled in a deep gulp of air, tasted death, and knew this wasn't about to be pretty.

Cara's skin still seemed too pale when she crossed the threshold of the Crypt.

The impulse to comfort her, to wrap his hands around her delicate shoulders and pull her close, was strong. As strong as the impulse to kiss her had been in the elevator.

His shoulder brushed against hers, a subtle gesture to let her know that he was there.

She wasn't facing this alone.

Smith kept glancing at Cara. Then at Colin. Then Cara. The woman looked nervous and . . . angry.

Colin had told him the full truth about Smith's abduction earlier. He knew that one of the *Other* had kidnapped her and tortured her. Before that horrible experience, Smith had no idea that any creatures like shifters or demons really existed.

It had been a brutal introduction for her. One that she had apparently not recovered from yet.

Of course, he couldn't really blame the woman. If he'd been held captive by a sadistic psychopath who also happened to be a damn powerful supernatural being, well, he would have freaked, too.

Not that Smith had freaked, per se. The lady was far too controlled for that. But she'd changed. No denying it. Shut down. Blocked herself off.

She wouldn't be able to live that way.

No one could. Not and stay sane. He knew. He'd tried once—after his mother's shooting. He hadn't wanted to feel again after that. The pain had been too much for him.

Over the years, Todd had learned a hard truth, though. If you weren't feeling, you weren't living, and life was too damn short to sit on the sidelines.

Smith used to know that.

The screech of a wheel caught his attention. His head turned, and Todd watched as Smith pushed a sheet-covered body toward them.

"Just finished some more work on him. Was about to transfer him out . . ."

Then they'd arrived just in time.

Smith's gloved fingers pulled back the sheet. Todd heard Cara's sharply indrawn breath. When he glanced at her face, he saw a faint quiver shake her lower lip.

Maybe demons weren't so different from humans, after all.

She'd deceived him, yeah, no fucking denying that, but his Cara wasn't a killer.

And he didn't need his "psychic edge" to tell him that.

"Lower the sheet more." Her voice was soft but steady.

Smith pulled down the sheet, exposing the surgical marks on Michael House's chest and the dark handprint.

Cara's fingers lifted over him. Hovered above that perfect impression. Her hand was smaller than the print, by at least a few inches.

Cara's fine-boned fingers were nowhere near close to being a match. He hadn't thought they would be, though. He hadn't brought her down there to match hands—he'd brought her there to show her the print—*and to find out what the hell it was.*

"Cover him." A tight order as her hand fisted. Smith jerked the sheet back up. Cara's breath came faster now. Her gaze lifted, shot to his. "You were right, Todd. *Damn it, you were right.*"

He noticed that Smith and Colin craned just a bit closer. "You've seen that mark before."

"I've seen a mark *like* that before."

"How was the impression made?" Smith immediately wanted to know. "The bruising isn't like—"

"It's not bruising." She cleared her throat. "And it was made with a simple touch."

"I don't understand." Smith frowned at her.

Me, either, Todd thought.

Gyth said nothing, but his attention was completely focused on Cara.

"We like to feel the beat of the heart when we take power from someone."

He remembered the soft press of her hand against his chest.

"In ancient Egypt," her voice was strangely calm, almost dispassionate as her gaze stayed on the sheet-covered body, "they believed that the true essence of a man was kept in his heart. His spirit. His soul. All in the heart. Not the brain."

"That's why they used a stick to yank out the brains," Smith sniffed. "Didn't really care about preserving that part."

Todd wondered where the history lesson was going.

"When the brain stops functioning, a person's body is still alive." Cara's gaze dropped to House's covered chest. "As long as that wonderful heart keeps beating, the person *is* alive."

She wet her lips, continued, "To my kind, the heart is life. We want to feel that precious beat. To share the pleasure, the thrill. Sometimes that release of pleasure is so intense," her voice dropped, "so powerful that the urge to keep taking is too strong." Cara swallowed. "If you drain a human while you're feeling the wild beat of a heart, when the human dies, the stain of the touch will remain."

"Then you've seen this before?" He repeated. She seemed absolutely certain, but Todd had to know.

"Something *like* this. Yeah, once." Shadows cloaked her eyes. "But I've heard stories. Before the killings stopped—"

Yeah, well, if she was telling him the truth, the succubus killings hadn't exactly *stopped*.

"—brands like this were found all over France. England. Humans didn't understand what they were seeing back then." A quick glance at a silent Smith. "Now the doctors know it's not just a bruise."

It was a brand. A fucking calling card left by a killer who'd wanted to mark his victims.

"The hand, it's average size," Smith said, "could be a woman with long fingers or maybe a man with sm—"

"No." Cara's denial was absolute. Said at once. She shot a frowning stare at the body. "You all need to understand something—Michael—he was straight. There's no way an incubus could have been with Michael."

She'd know.

"An incubus can only seduce those who would find him attractive. Same thing for a succubus. It's a basic, primitive response." A firm shake of her head. "Michael would never have gone with an incubus. The killer, *hell, the killer's a succubus*."

She swiped a tear from her eye and whispered, "You deserved better than this." She spoke to Michael, her voice the intimate one of a friend.

Or lover.

"I'm sorry, Michael." She sounded completely sincere. Her hands balled into fists.

Damn, but Todd wanted to comfort her.

To protect and to fuck. Two drives that should have been at odds, but with her, they seemed perfectly in tune.

Todd huffed out a hard breath and wondered just what he was going to do about his sex demon.

Smith cleared her throat, looked a bit less hostile as she asked, "Uh, does she need to see the other body?"

Todd gave a grim nod. "Show her." No sense putting it off now. Besides, he'd been the one to come up with the idea of bringing Cara to the Crypt.

He just hadn't realized that seeing her pain would hurt him so much. "Hurry, Smith." He wanted Cara away from that place.

Smith turned toward the vault. Pulled back the gleaming handle and grasped the covered slab. The slab rolled toward them with a rush of icy air.

Cara inched forward. Gasped when Smith revealed the body and she caught sight of the deep wounds on his chest.

"Why would a demon do that?" Gyth asked her, coming to stand on Cara's right side. "If you guys can kill with a touch, why mutilate the man?"

"To make him suffer," Smith said, watching Cara carefully. Like a rat watching a snake that had slithered too close.

Or a very nervous human watching a dangerous demon.

"No need for that." Cara turned her stare directly onto the ME. "We can cause as much pain as we want, without butchering a human."

Nice to know.

She rubbed her arms, as if chilled. "It . . . this doesn't make sense. A succubus *wouldn't* do this. I told you, it's a waste— of energy and power." Her gaze met his. "This isn't—our way. This is rage. Hate. There's no reason to kill this way— not when a succubus could use a simple touch."

Yeah, pretty much his thoughts.

Two different murders. A nice clean death, versus a slaughter.

Because there were *two* killers?

One a sex demon who could kill with the soft stroke of a hand touch and one—one who enjoyed the red splash of blood and the screams of a victim's pain?

Ah, shit.

Two killers—a possibility he couldn't ignore.

Chapter 11

Smith's hands were shaking when the detectives finally left with their little guest.

Guest.

A demon.

Oh, God, but they were everywhere—and, from the sound of things, another one was out there, a crazy psycho like the one who had attacked her. Only this time, instead of ripping out throats, the killer was seducing and murdering.

She braced her elbows on her desk and lowered her head into her palms. The faint strains of jazz swirled around her. The music had once relaxed her.

But the music had been playing when that asshole took her. He'd come into the Crypt, smiled at her, and then lunged.

She'd seen teeth. Too sharp. Claws.

Then she'd seen darkness.

Only to awake to a nightmare.

Her shoulders hunched. Every person she met. Every. Single. Person. She wondered about them. Human? Demon? Shifter? Vampire? Something far worse?

The bodies that came in, she studied then with sharper eyes—and remembered the times bodies had been "transferred" out of her care due to a so-called overload in her department.

Had those transferred bodies been supernaturals? Were they moved so that she wouldn't notice differences in genetics?

She suspected they had been.

The door to the Crypt squeaked open.

Smith gasped, spun around, and found Danny McNeal standing in the doorway.

She shot to her feet and demanded, "What do you want, Captain?" Their personal relationship had ended. *His* choice. He'd ended the best damn thing she'd ever had over six months ago. No explanations. Just a cold, hard cut.

They probably shouldn't have ever gotten involved in the first place. They worked together. He was the captain with the bright future that everyone was always talking about.

She was the ME who carved up the dead.

But she'd wanted him.

He'd wanted her.

And late one night, when she'd gone to his office to give him a report, they'd finally given in to that need.

The passion between them had burned hard for three months.

Then he'd shut her out.

The bastard.

The worse part—he'd ripped out her heart.

Not that she'd ever let *him* know that.

Her chin lifted when he stepped inside the Crypt. "Do you need a case file?"

His gaze swept the room. Returned to her. Turbulent gray. "I need to talk to you."

"Unless it's about one of those bodies," she pointed in the direction of the vaults, "we don't have anything to say." Maybe not the most adult response, but she didn't really give a shit.

She'd been through hell the last few months, and she wasn't in the mood to hear him ramble about crap. Besides, she had a feeling she knew what he was going to say. After the attack, he'd started looking at her kind of . . . funny.

With eyes too intent. Always watching.

After the way he'd kicked her aside, the jerk was probably feeling guilty. Good. He should. He—

"You need to know something about me." McNeal stalked toward her, and yeah, stalked was the best description.

Smith tried to study him dispassionately. Really, her friends had asked her what she'd seen in the guy. He was white, for one thing, and her girls had never been into the white men. And he was older. Nine years.

And bald.

But on him, being bald, being older, even being white—it *worked*.

There was a hardness to him, a strength, in his face, along that stiff jaw, in those eyes. And then there was the aura of power that had always drawn her to him . . .

Jerk bastard.

"What do I need to know?" She snapped. "That you're an asshole? I know that already. That you're sorry I got taken by that freak? Yeah, I know that, too."

"It's not that . . ." McNeal looked damn uncomfortable. "You need to know—"

Now her heart was racing too fast. "What? You're seeing someone else? Great." No, it wasn't, and the pain clawing through her chest told her that. "Look, I don't have time for this. I've got to finish working on the Monroe case and with all these damn monsters around I—"

"I'm one of them, Nathalia."

Her blood iced. "One of wh-what?" But she knew. God, but she *knew*.

"I'm not completely human."

Her knees threatened to buckle. "I *really* don't need this now, Dan."

He took a step toward her.

The back of her legs rammed into the desk when she instinctively moved back.

"*Jesus,* babe, relax, you know I'd never hurt you."

But you did. "What are you?" Not a demon, or a shifter, please not—

A muscle flexed along his jaw. "I'm known as a charmer."

"What? What the hell is that?" A nightmare. That was it. She was having one really wild-ass nightmare—

"My kind—"

His kind?

"—we're highly psychic and have the ability to communicate with certain animals."

Her eyes widened. "Your apartment. That fucking big snake—"

McNeal coughed. "That was . . . ah . . . actually my mother's."

This just kept getting worse. "Your mom talks to snakes?"

A quick nod.

It was unbelievable. No, it *should* have been unbelievable. But she knew it was the truth. "So what do you do?"

"Cats."

"Like what? Meow-meow kitties that—"

"Tigers."

Of course. No soft and friendly little cats for him.

"I found my connection with Shaman, a white tiger who used to be housed at the zoo, when I was a kid."

The man talked to tigers. Her head pounded so hard that Smith was a bit afraid of passing out, and she refused to humiliate herself that way in front of him. "Get out, McNeal."

Another step toward her. This time, the move put him close enough to touch. "We're not all bad, babe."

She stiffened at the endearment and the touch that had her wanting to lean closer to him. "I can't deal with this" *you* "right now."

There was a flash of torment on his face. "I am so fucking sorry about what happened to you. I never, ever wanted anything or anyone to hurt you—"

"But you just didn't want *me*, right?" The words she'd held back for so long burst forth and she was glad. She was tired of pretending everything was fine and that she wasn't human enough to feel pain.

Because she *was* human, even if he wasn't.

The saddest smile she'd ever seen curled his lips. "No, baby, that wasn't it at all."

Liar. She knew her eyes said what her mouth didn't.

"I was afraid if you found out the truth, you wouldn't want me." He glanced down at her, eyes narrowed.

She realized that she was all but flinching away from him. Her body recoiling, knees shaking.

"I guess I was right." He dropped his hand. Stepped back. Then turned and walked away.

Before she found her voice, the door had swung shut behind him and she was left with the sting of memories and the bitter taste of fear on her tongue.

"Brooks."

Colin's gruff voice stopped him just as Todd reached for his Vette. He tensed at Colin's approach, really not in the mood for a pissing match.

But when Colin stood beside him, the guy hesitated. Colin drove his hands into the deep pockets of his jacket. Glanced around the all-but-empty parking lot.

"What is it, Gyth?" Maybe something had come up about the case or about Cara or—

Colin's bright stare turned slowly back to him. "I couldn't tell you." Stark.

Todd didn't speak, just waited.

"When I was in Illinois, my partner—he found out what I was." A pause. "He tried to kill me."

Well, *shit*.

"I couldn't take the risk that you'd—I just couldn't risk another partner turning on me."

Yeah, Todd could see where an attempted murder would make a guy hesitate. "I'm not your old partner. I'm not gonna reach for my gun just because you're . . . different." Too tame of a word for a werewolf.

"Good to know." Colin's eyes held his. "Why didn't you say something, after you saw—"

Because at first, he'd been too damn stunned. Then he'd tried to convince himself it hadn't happened, then he'd gotten so furious and then—"I wanted you to tell me." But now, knowing what Colin's last partner had done, Todd understood more about the guy—and he knew that Colin probably would never have told him.

He tried to kill me.

Shit. No wonder it had been hard for Colin to trust him.

Colin exhaled. "So what happens now? Are we gonna keep working together, or—"

"Hell, yeah, we're gonna keep working together." Like he'd really go to the trouble of breaking in anybody else. Besides, Colin was one damn fine cop.

With a few peculiarities. What had shocked him weeks ago, now just, okay, *still* shocked him. But he was dealing with the situation—or at least learning to deal with it.

Todd narrowed his eyes. "But no more secrets, man. You trust me, and I'll trust you." Simple.

A grim nod. "Agreed." Colin held out his hand. The shake was brief, strong.

"Now get the hell out of here," Todd said, jerking his thumb toward Colin's old Jeep. "You don't want to leave that sexy doc of yours waiting too long."

A smile broke Colin's lips. "No, man, I sure don't—my doc's not exactly the waitin' type." He turned away, then hesitated. When he glanced back at Todd, his smile was gone. "Be careful with *your* lady, Todd. A woman like her, she's got a lot of secrets, too."

Yeah, he knew she did. And he also knew those secrets weren't going to stand in his way. He wanted Cara—and he intended to have her.

Todd heard the soft knock at his door just as he was about to head into the shower. He paused, sent a quick glance at the clock.

Midnight.

His steps were swift as he hurried from the bedroom. He knew the identity of his caller even before he opened the wooden door.

He'd smelled her.

Cara stood just past the threshold, dressed all in black with her hair pulled into some sort of sexy twist. Her eyes were lined with dark shadow, her lips tinted red.

"You missed my first show tonight," she said. Then stepped forward.

He fell back, knowing she'd come fully into his apartment and wanting her there.

Needing her there. "It's still early. Shouldn't you be at Paradise?" The woman usually played at least three sets.

"I told Niol I had business tonight."

"Business," he repeated the word softly. "Is that what I am?"

A slow shake of her head. "I looked for you in the crowd, but you weren't there."

There was something in her voice. "Missed me, did you?"

A faint frown appeared between her brows. "Yes, actually, I think I did."

Well, damn. He hadn't been expecting quite that level of honesty from her.

"We need to talk, Todd and—" Her gaze darted behind him, landed on the pile of books he'd tossed haphazardly onto the sofa. A golden brow arched. "Doing some light reading?"

Shit. "Just some books I picked up. Nothing important."

But she brushed around him, heading straight for the sofa, those delicate hands reaching down and—

"*Demonology: A Hunter's Guide.*" She grabbed another heavy volume. "*Unmasking the Demon.*" As Cara reached for the third book, the one he'd made the mistake of leaving open, a gasp tore from her lips. "And what the *hell* is this?"

He didn't need to see the picture to know what had pissed her off. He could remember the image perfectly. One side of the page featured a sketch of a beautiful, naked woman, hair streaming down her shoulders, lips curled in a smile of anticipation.

Then, on the other side of the page, the illustrator had drawn the picture of a "real" succubus. It was a demon with a long, pointed tail, a body covered in scales, a face like a dog, and a snarling mouth full of jagged teeth.

"Ah, Cara . . ."

She threw the book at him. It missed his head by about three inches. "Is that what you think I am?"

He hoped to heaven not. "You said demons used glamour—"

"I use it to hide my eye color, not to disguise the fact that I'm some kind of freakish hag! Ugh!" A flush stained her cheeks. "That writer is a complete moron, and so are you, if you're buying into that crap. A succubus looks, well, damn it, look at me! Just like a woman."

A beautiful woman. Seductive. Physically perfect.

He lifted his hand to her. "I think you're exactly what you appear to be."

Now she eyed him suspiciously. "And what's that?"

"The woman I want." His head still swam with the new knowledge that he had, but one thing was absolutely clear to him. He wanted Cara.

Her face softened.

"Why did you come here tonight?" He asked, trying to force his gaze to stay on the lines of her face when the hunger demanded that he stare at her body. Those breasts. Such a wonderful size for his hands—and they tasted so sweet in his mouth.

And her legs . . . He wanted them wrapped around his waist. Holding him tight as he thrust deep inside her.

"I didn't just take from you, Todd. You aren't prey to me." She crossed back to his side. "I want you to understand that." Her hand rose to his chest, pressed just above his heart.

At her touch, his cock swelled even more with a flood of arousal. "I thought that was what you had to do. Take energy."

"We can take, but we can also give to our lovers." The heat of her hand seemed to sear him through the thin fabric of his T-shirt. "Tell me, how have you been feeling since we made love?"

Better than he had in weeks. Months. A cautious "Good" was his only answer.

Her lips curved. "We did that. The energy from our bond

spilled into us, renewed us—and made us both more powerful."

That sounded like a pretty good deal to him. "So it's not always like that? What usually happens?" *Not* that he wanted to think of her with others.

The smile faded away. "Usually we take what we want. Humans are left with pleasure, but their bodies are much weaker than before. The weakness can last for a few hours or even days."

"Why didn't you just take from me?"

"I don't know." Stark.

Again, more honesty than he'd expected. Her lips were just a few inches away from his. Her eyes were so blue. A deception, that. He didn't want any more deceptions. "Show me your eyes. Your real eyes."

Her lids lowered in a slow blink. When her lashes lifted, her eyes were blacker than the night. He raised his hand. Traced a fingertip under her left eye. "Beautiful," he murmured, and meant it. With Niol, the dark eyes looked scary as hell, but the darkness didn't detract from Cara's appeal. It added to it. Made her look mysterious, wild.

"I want you." There was no coyness in her. "Naked. Inside me."

That was exactly where he wanted to be.

"I don't want anything between us. I can't catch any diseases that humans have, and I control my own fertility."

Handy.

"I want you, flesh to flesh, with me."

The lady had caught him at "naked."

He bent his head. Kissed her. A slow, tasting kiss. When she moaned, the sound rumbling in the back of her throat, every nerve in his body tightened.

She pulled away from him, licked her red lips. "But first, I want a taste."

Her powerful scent surrounded him. Sex. Woman. Magic. When she dropped to her knees before him, Todd actually felt light-headed for a moment. "You don't have to—"

But her hands were working on the buckle of his jeans, easing down the zipper and then shoving the rough denim and his boxers out of the way.

His cock bobbed toward her. The head was stiff and a drop of moisture already coated the tip of his arousal. Her hands wrapped around his swollen length. Tightened. Stroked.

Pleasure lashed through him.

"Relax," she murmured softly and Todd realized he was growling in anticipation. "I'm only going to give."

Then her mouth was on him. Lips parted and soft. Tongue caressing as she closed her mouth over him.

His fingers wrapped around her head, dug into the silken tendrils of her hair.

A powerful energy snaked through him. Her mouth was heaven. Every sexy move of her lips paradise. But there was more. More than he'd ever felt.

The feelings were magnified, spiraling along his nerves and cells, the pleasure pulsating within him.

Her mouth caressed his cock, her lips featherlight. Her fingers circled the base of his shaft and she moved her hand in time to the seductive motions of her lips and tongue.

Driving. Him. Insane.

His cock swelled even more under her ministrations. His hands fisted in her hair, and each move of her mouth had him nearly begging.

But then she pulled away. Easily broke his hold and leaned back, bracing her palms against the floor as she gazed up at him.

No, damn it, not yet, he wasn't—

"I like the way you taste, Todd. I like it a lot."

He swore he could actual hear the *rip* of his control shredding. He fell to his knees beside her, hands trembling. A roar filled his ears and a growl churned in his throat. A red haze of need covered his eyes and he reached for her with hands that were too rough, far too strong for her delicate skin.

She met him eagerly. Fought with him to jerk off her shirt. To bare those breasts that he loved. Then he shoved her bra out of the way. Caught one tight nipple between his teeth while his right hand fondled her other breast. The heady scent that was pure Cara thickened in the air.

He suckled her, drawing her breast into his mouth, then slipping back to lave her nipple. God, but the woman had great breasts. Pink nipples. Sweet, firm flesh. Not too big. Just right for his mouth.

He dragged his fingers down her body. Managed to push down her pants as she shifted, and Cara kicked off her pumps and the pants in a hard, fast move.

With a last lick, he lifted his head. She wore only black panties now. A small scrap really. Barely covered her mound. His fingers wrapped around her hips, and his eyes zeroed in on that tempting flesh.

She'd gotten to command his body. Turnabout was only fair.

"Spread your legs." A guttural demand.

Cara smiled, pure enticement, and spread those long, slender legs.

He eased down between her thighs, lowering his head right over the dark silk. His nostrils flared as he caught the scent of her cream. The rich promise of hot sex.

The promise of her.

His lips pressed against the silk. A stark kiss. She arched beneath him, sliding more fully against his mouth.

Just where he wanted her.

He could feel the soft nub of her clitoris pressing through the underwear. He rubbed his tongue over the sensitive spot, loving the way she sighed his name with each soft touch.

But it wasn't enough.

The fingers of his right hand caught the silk. Tugged and the fabric tore free. Then her sex was bare. Open. Ready for his kiss.

He put his lips against her first. Explored her creamy flesh. Moved as slowly as he wanted so that he could learn every inch of her. Learn what she liked. What made her moan and twist and shake.

Then he used his tongue, sliding it into the folds of her tight core, taking the rich cream and giving pleasure. He lapped at her. Tasted. Drove his tongue deep. Again and again and—

Todd felt her climax against him with a shudder.

He drank up her release, driving his tongue deeper into her body, hearing her cries and loving the feel of her nails as they dug into his shoulders.

When the shivers faded, his head lifted, just a few inches. Todd licked his lips as his fingers slipped over her mound and stroked the center of her need. Oh, damn, but she was wet and more than ready for him now. The flesh swollen, warm and waiting to be fucked.

Todd drove two fingers deep into her straining sex.

He felt the sudden tightness of her body beneath his with a rush of satisfaction. His succubus wanted to come again for him. Her sex clenched around his fingers, a telling sign that he wouldn't ignore.

Todd pulled away from her, only to reposition his body, lodging the head of his cock against her moist opening. The feel of her sex against his, the creamy warmth, the silken skin, had him gritting his teeth as he thrust forward.

Her hand rose. Covered his heart. For an instant, he stilled.

Then her gaze met his. Black eyes. Dark and deep.

Her lips curved.

He caught her hand with his. Pressed it harder against his chest. Felt the air around him seem to shimmer, to pulse.

He drove into her, burying balls-deep in one hard move.

Then he was moving. Thrusting. Withdrawing. Thrusting. Cara wrapped her legs around him. Arched into his driving hips.

Her face took on a faint glow. A light from within. A faint stir of gentle wind blew against his face, then all over him, and her hand stayed steady and warm against his chest.

His thrusts became harder. Deeper. "I want to feel you come," he gritted. He wanted to feel her release, to see it on her face.

"Then you will," she whispered, and gasped, tipping back her head and squeezing her legs even tighter around him.

The feelings hit him then. The ripples of pleasure that weren't his own. The shattering euphoria that danced along his skin.

Hers.

He didn't understand how, but he was feeling her release. Riding the wave of her pleasure, just as he plunged into her body.

"Ah . . . Todd! Kiss me!"

His lips caught hers. His tongue drove into her mouth.

And his hips pistoned against her.

His climax hit him, rolling over him in a furious burst of power.

When she stiffened and moaned into his mouth, he knew she felt the surge of release, too.

An exchange. Not just taking. Giving.

From both.

He held her tighter. Kept thrusting, trying to wring every drop of sensual satisfaction from their bodies. His skin was slick with sweat, his muscles trembling. But he didn't want to stop.

Not ever.

So when the climax ended, he just kept thrusting. His cock swelled within her. Her legs gripped him tight, and she stared straight up at him with her midnight eyes.

Magic was around him. Pressing in the air. Dancing on his skin. The glow of power lit her body.

And his.

It gave him strength, a stamina he'd never had. Not so quickly. Never as fast—

So the thrusts continued. The strange link that he had with her intensified. He knew what she wanted. Knew exactly where to touch and kiss, without her having to say a word. Their breaths panted out, their hearts thundered in a mad, matching rhythm, and the furious race to climax had them locked tight.

So tight that he could almost touch her soul.

When they came again, they came together. Mouths, bodies.

Spirits.

A demon and a man.

No, a woman and a man.

A perfect match.

He held her, arms too tight, and knew that he'd go to hell for her in a heartbeat.

A sobering thought for a man who'd already fought the devil once in his life—and had the scar to prove it.

"I know you didn't kill House." He spoke in the darkness, when the heat of the passion had cooled, but the magic still fired their blood. "Or any of the others."

They were in his bed. Naked. His body curled over hers, his right hand on her breast. His left arm rested beneath her head.

She turned to look at him. "Do you mean that?"

"Yeah." He'd touched her in ways most men wouldn't understand. Not physical. Her heart. Soul. He'd felt her, down to the core of her spirit. Cara wasn't evil. "You're not a killer." He'd said the same words at the station, but he needed to say them again, now, with her in his arms and her scent on his skin.

She swallowed. "I told you from the beginning that I didn't kill Michael." There was an ache in her voice when she said the other man's name.

Cara had cared House, maybe even loved him. Todd ached for the pain she felt, even as an insidious curl of jealousy rose within him.

But House was gone now, poor bastard. A death he hadn't deserved.

He'd find the guy's killer—because it was his job and because he liked to give victims their peace.

His fingers eased over Cara's flesh. "I can be a hard man, Cara. My job's important to me. Doing what's right. Protect-

ing those who can't protect themselves. I take it all seriously."
For years, the badge had been all he had. He wanted her to
understand him. The darkness inside, a darkness he knew
she'd felt.

Her cheek rested on his arm as she gazed at him. "Why did
you become a cop?"

The memory of his mother's scream burned in his mind.
"My dad was a cop. He worked for the Atlanta PD for eighteen years." Most folks took the statement at face value and
left it at that. A boy, wanting to grow up and be like his father.

Some truth. Some lie.

"But why did *you* join the force?" The dark eyes that
stared back at him saw too much.

Too deeply.

Todd found himself telling her a story he'd never told another. Not even the grandfather who'd wound up raising him.
"My dad worked undercover. Deep undercover. Months
would go by and we wouldn't see him, then when he would finally come home, he'd be a stranger." A hard, brooding
stranger who smelled of alcohol and smoke. One whose eyes
had been flint sharp and whose mouth had never smiled.

"He was a good cop, though. Everyone said so." And there
had been so many plaques and medals in his dad's room. His
mom had polished them every single week, smiling that same,
sad smile as she cleaned them. "I don't know how many guys
my dad put away over the years. Drug dealers. Robbers.
Killers. He made a lot of enemies in his time, the kind of enemies who don't forget or forgive when they've been betrayed."

Cara didn't speak. Just watched him.

"A guy got out one day. Tony Costa. My dad had been undercover in the guy's crew. Busted him for selling coke and for the
murders of two prostitutes."

"And he got out?" Cara asked, surprise in her voice.

The woman didn't understand the human justice system.
"He rolled on some higher-ups. Pleaded to manslaughter for
the prostitutes and wound up serving a seven-year sentence."

He sucked in a deep breath. This was the part that he hated to remember. "I was fourteen when Tony was paroled. I remember because it was my birthday. Mom had ordered me a cake and we were just leaving the house to go get it." He'd been going to have a swimming party. The plan had been to get the cake and go back home to set up before his friends came over.

"Costa was waiting for us in the driveway. He had a gun."

"Todd . . ."

"He made us go back inside. Told mom to call dad. Said to 'get the bastard over there so he could watch.' But dad was undercover, and mom couldn't get him. She told Costa she could call his captain, but—" A lump was in his throat now, choking back the words. "But Costa knew a call to the captain would have cops swarming over him. So he smiled at my mom, and he killed her. The bastard shot her point-blank in the head."

She wrapped her arms around him, turning to burrow her head against his neck. "I'm so sorry."

He felt cold. Even with the warmth of her body pressing down against him, he felt so damn cold. "Then he turned the gun on me."

She froze against him. A burst of wind blew into the room, sweeping over his body, ruffling the sheets and covers.

Her head lifted. "He shot you."

Todd caught her hand. Brought it to rest against the old, jagged scar on his left side. "I tried to run, but the bullet caught me." He'd thought he was dying when he felt the burning lash of the pain in his side. The fiery agony had stolen his breath, then he'd seen the blood. So much blood. His. His mother's. Everywhere. "He left me there. Bleeding out on the floor, with my mother's body only a few feet away." He still had nightmares about that day. Still woke up in a cold sweat, wishing he'd done something to save his mother. Wishing he couldn't still smell her blood on his skin.

"But you survived." Her fingers curled over the white scar. "You got out of there. You *lived*."

"A neighbor heard the gunshots. Called nine-one-one. I

woke up in a hospital, my side stitched up, and found my grandfather sitting beside me."

"And where was your father?" He caught the snap of anger in her voice—and the soft echo of pain, for him.

"Tracking Costa. He came to see me, once, in the hospital. He hugged me and told me that he regretted a lot of the things he'd done in his life." His dad had been the same hard, stranger, but he'd also seemed . . . desperate. He'd put back on his wedding band, a ring Todd had never seen the man wear. "He told me then that 'if you go too deep into the devil's world, only darkness will fill you.' It was the last thing he ever said to me."

"Did he catch the man who'd shot you?" Quiet words in a beautiful face that was suddenly deadly.

The windows were still closed to the night. The magic wind had disappeared now. The air was strangely tense around him.

"Yeah, he caught him. Didn't even try to bring him in. My dad shot Costa in the head and in the heart. Then he turned the gun on himself."

Eighteen years on the force, and his dad had eaten his gun. And left him alone.

"I hated him for leaving me. For years, I didn't understand why he'd done it—"

"He thought it was his fault," she said, her voice soft. "Humans . . . do crazy things when guilt presses on them."

This was the part he didn't like to think about. "I blamed him, Cara. For my mother's death. For me getting shot. If he'd just been at home, taking care of his family like he should have been doing, none of this would have ever happened." The words came from the boy he'd been, though he liked to think the man knew better.

Yeah, he liked to think that. "When I first woke up and realized that my mom was gone, I wished it had been him instead of her." And he'd kept wishing that, even when his father had finally come to see him in the hospital. He'd wished it until . . . "His captain came to see me a few days after I was released. I was staying at my grandfather's." His mom's father had been an affluent, somewhat reserved man who lived in one of the older, richer parts of Atlanta. He'd never approved of his only child marrying a cop, and he'd been fighting hard to get a custody hearing for Todd when the captain had come calling with his dark news.

"How did you feel, when you learned what had happened?" Her naked body pressed against his, and the flesh-on-flesh contact was strangely comforting. Her hand stroked his scar, softly, tenderly, and the mysterious eyes that stared into his held no censure. Just patience. Warmth.

Warmth in darkness.

His skin didn't seem quite so cold anymore, but inside, he still felt like his heart was encased in ice. "I was so fucking glad that Tony Costa was dead. So fucking glad."

She pressed a kiss against his chest. Right over his heart. "But what about your father?"

He'd been furious with him. "He didn't have to die, Cara. There were so many other options for him, *he didn't have to die.*"

"Maybe he thought he did."

"Well, he was damn well *wrong.*" He'd taken the coward's way out. The easy way.

"He might have thought that he'd failed you, your mother. A man who'd spent his life protecting others would have a hard time facing the fact that he'd failed to protect the ones who'd mattered the most."

Yeah, the shrinks had all said something like that. They'd told him that his father had been disturbed, pushed past his reason by the murder of his wife.

But the simple truth was that his dad had *chosen* to put that gun into his mouth.

And chosen to leave the world and his son behind.

He hadn't forgiven him for that, not yet.

Not deep inside.

"You hate him, don't you?" Again, no censure. No judgment of any kind. Just a quiet question and those eyes, watching him.

"For a long time, I did. I'm still mad as hell at him for what he did, but—" The truth? "It takes too much energy to hate. I wish he'd been different. I wish *I'd* been different, but hating a dead man isn't going to make my life any better."

"Will blaming him?"

The direct question made him flinch. Suddenly, part of him wanted to jump from the bed, to put distance between them. And another part wanted to hold her as tight as he could. "It helps me to sleep at night, baby."

"No, I don't think it does." Now she kissed him on the mouth. Not a passionate kiss. Her lips were closed, the touch brief, but soothing. "Nothing makes death easier to bear. *Nothing.*" There was a knowledge in her voice. A pain that hinted at her own loss.

He brushed back her hair, and wondered what had caused the sadness he felt in *her*. A sadness that more than matched his own.

He wanted to ask her. Had begun telling her about his father because he'd wanted her to learn to trust him—as he was learning to trust her.

But now wasn't the time to push her, he knew that. And perhaps he'd already revealed too much about himself, too soon.

"If you blamed him, then why did you become a cop?"

He would tell her this. "Because I needed to prove him wrong." He'd also wanted to save others, as he hadn't been able to save his mother. But he didn't tell her that.

"How?"

"You don't have to give up your humanity to be a good cop. You can fight killers, mon—" He broke off, uncomfortable with that particular word choice. "Evil without becoming evil yourself."

"And trying to make up for your mother's death? That has nothing to do with it, hmmm?"

Insightful demon.

Smart woman. "Yeah, it does." He tightened his arms

around her. The past weighed too heavily on him. He'd opened the door, but too much had spilled through. "Enough of this talk, Cara. It's late, you're here, I'm here, and the dead, they're buried now."

"Sometimes they don't stay buried." Whispered words.

"What?"

She shook her head and brushed her lips against his once more. "Nothing." Her arms wrapped around him, held him tight.

For the first time in years, Todd almost felt at peace.

Closing his eyes, he inhaled her sweet scent.

Susan Dobbs paced in front of the phone booth. She was nervous as hell, but the call had to be made.

She'd driven hard and fast to get out of the city. *He* had too many friends, *spies,* in Atlanta, and she'd been afraid one of them would see her making the call. Hell, she'd even thought about buying one of those cheap, disposable cell phones, but she'd stopped at two stores and hadn't been able to find any in stock.

Just her fucking bad luck.

But it didn't matter—this way was better, anyway. Dozens of people used this phone every day, so the call would never be traced back to her. Besides, once she made the call, she'd keep driving straight down that long, dark road, and no one in Atlanta would ever see her ass again.

Her palms were sweating and her heart pounded so hard that her chest hurt.

He didn't know what she'd done. The last attack hadn't been part of their original plan. When he found out, Susan knew the guy was going to be fucking furious.

But damn it, when was she supposed to ever have any fun?

Taking a breath, Susan reached for the phone. A lock of blond hair fell over her eye, and she shoved it out of the way with her left hand.

Then she dialed the cop's number, a number she'd memorized days before.

Chapter 12

The shrill cry of the phone ripped Todd from his sleep. He muttered, cursed, and tried to reach for the nightstand. Cara was on top of him, her body completely limp, so the phone rang four times before he finally managed to snag it.

"What?" Jesus, the light on the bedside clock said 4:15 A.M. If McNeal was calling him again—

"They lied to you." A woman's voice. High. Thready with what could have been fear.

A burst of adrenaline brought him to instant wakefulness. "Who is this?"

Cara, who was now partially on her side, tensed.

"They lied to you," the woman repeated. "*He* made them lie."

"Look, lady, I don't know what the hell you're talking about and it's too damn late for prank calls—"

"Your demon wasn't at Paradise Found like she told you. The waitresses, they lied. So did the bartender. She slipped away, and they know she did." The words came out in a tumbling rush.

Anger began to fuel his heart. "How the hell do you know that?"

"Because *he* made them lie. Just like he tried to make me."

"Who are you talking about?" But he already knew.

"*Niol.*" A fearful whisper of sound.

"You got proof of that?" Cara was completely silent next

to him, and he knew that she could hear the whole damn conversation.

"He's a demon, just like she is. Demons lie. They deceive."

"Who are you?" He asked again, but he knew the caller wasn't about to reveal her identity.

"I'm a woman who is tired of living with evil. The killings have to stop." A pause. *"She* has to be stopped. Don't let her trick you. She's rotten inside. Just like they all are."

The force of his rage caused his fingers to shake. His hand tightened around the phone. "I want to know just *who*—"

The call ended with a soft click. Then the buzz of a dial tone had him swearing.

Sonofabitch.

As quickly as he could, he used his call return. One ring. Two. The beeping filled his ears, and he counted up to fifteen rings.

The lady wasn't gonna answer his call.

Shit. Not a big surprise. He glanced over at the Caller ID light on his phone. Made a mental note of the number. He'd be pulling a few strings come daylight, and he'd track down the mystery lady.

Light trickled through the window, spilling onto the bed and Cara. She sat up, pulling the covers over her breasts. "Todd?"

He ran a hand over his face. This damn case was really pissing him off.

"She was lying, Todd. I never left Paradise Found those nights, and I sure as hell didn't get anyone to lie for me."

But had Niol? The bastard was as deceitful as a snake.

"Tell me that you believe me." She touched his cheek. "I don't know who that woman was on the phone, but she's the one lying, *not me.*" Her voice was vibrating with intensity.

He caught her hand. Kissed her palm. "It's all right." He'd get to the bottom of this shit. If the woman had been lying in an effort to set up Cara, he'd find out why, and he'd find her. "Go back to sleep." Though he doubted he'd be able to follow suit. Possibilities and worries filled his head.

If Cara was innocent—and he'd bet his badge that his lady was—then someone was working damn hard to make her look guilty. Something like that—it was personal. Always.

So who would hate his succubus enough to want her life destroyed? Enough to kill to see her punished?

He'd find out.

And he knew just where he was going to start his hunt.

With Niol.

Cara lay back against the pillows and closed her eyes. The words Todd had spoken rang in her ears.

And the words he had not drove into her heart.

She'd bared her soul to him when they made love, let him touch the deepest part of her spirit, and the man still didn't trust her.

Perhaps it was time for her to back off. To let the cop have his space.

Or perhaps it was time for her to start showing the world just how powerful a succubus could be.

Because there was only one conclusion she could draw from that phone call.

Some bitch was setting her up for murder.

And she wasn't about to take that shit from anyone.

Cara could play the nice girl. She'd done it for years. But nice went skin deep, and true power, demon power, it cut to the bone.

She was going to find the person out there who was screwing with her life, and she'd make the woman pay.

For poor Michael's death.

For the other men.

For making Todd doubt her.

And for ruining one of the best nights she'd had in years.

The bitch was about to find out just what happened to people who angered a succubus.

The woman had better run, fast. Because once a succubus started seeking prey, she didn't stop until the hunt was over.

*   *   *

"You're really a stupid whore, you know that?" The deep voice came out of the darkness and had Susan spinning around. Her back slammed into the phone.

Oh, shit. He was there. "Wh-what are you—"

He smiled at her, and the sight chilled her. She wasn't afraid of much in this world, but this demon terrified her.

Because she knew he was evil. All the way to the core.

But so was she.

Carefully, slowly, she began to kneel down. Before she'd shot out of town, she'd stopped at the pawnshop and picked up a new knife—one that was strapped on her ankle and sharpened to kill. Susan liked knives—liked having them close. She had since she was seventeen, when she'd used the sweet, sharp blade of her mother's steak knife to stab her stepfather right in his heart.

Right after the bastard had made the mistake of touching her again.

Just a few more inches, and she'd have the knife. She knew the demon's weak spots, and even if she couldn't take him down, she could hurt him enough to get away and—

He lunged for her. Grabbed her right hand. Broke her wrist with a twist of his fingers.

She didn't cry out. She'd stopped doing that years ago. Susan stared up into his black eyes and choked down the pain.

He yanked her up against him. "You've been playing without me, sweetheart." He leaned in close, pressed a kiss to her cheek, and inhaled her scent. "I can still smell the blood on your skin."

She'd washed for hours. Scrubbed until her flesh was sore. But those damn demons, they could smell a speck of blood from a mile away.

Or so the stories said.

Susan thought the stories were half bull, but one thing was undeniable—the demon knew what she'd been up to while

he'd been watching other prey. "Tommy deserved to die."
He'd turned his back on her. *Her*. Tried to walk away and
leave her behind.

No one did that. Not anymore.

And Tommy had sure changed his tune once she'd started
using her knife on him. He'd been begging for her forgiveness
then.

But she hadn't been in a forgiving mood.

"Thomas Monroe wasn't on my list, Susan." His touch was
ice cold.

She'd liked that in the beginning. Liked the chill and the
rush that he gave her.

When they'd started killing, she'd liked him even better. It
was only lately that she'd begun to worry about him, and to
wonder—

What did the good-looking demon who carried the scent of
sex and death have planned for her?

"He wasn't supposed to die."

"Yeah, well, he was on *my* list." She should probably be
playing this differently. Acting cowed. Scared.

Not her style, even though fear squeezed her heart.

The demon smiled down at her, and his scent thickened in
the air around them. Helplessly, she felt her body begin to respond. Her nipples tightened. Her sex creamed.

"You were such a surprise to me, sweetheart." He leaned
his head toward her. Kissed her lips. Pushed her back even
harder against the plastic phone. "So beautiful."

His words were a lie. She knew it. Yeah, she was pretty.
She'd used that physical appeal more times than she could
count in the past, but he hadn't wanted her because she was
pretty.

He'd wanted her because she looked like the other woman,
Cara.

She'd fixed that demon whore. Cara would be ending up in
jail soon.

"You left evidence behind. Very, very sloppy of you, sweetheart."

So she wasn't as smart as he was. Not as good at cleaning up. "The cops don't have anything on me." She forced a smile. "They think it's that singer, Cara. I just called the detective, you know, the one who's been watching her at the club . . ."

His hand dropped to her throat. Caressed the skin. "And?"

"I-I told him that her alibi was crap. That the people at the club were lying." Her heartbeat began to steady as hope raised its head. Maybe she could smooth the situation over with him. He wanted Cara to take the fall for the killings. She'd just given him the other woman on a silver platter.

Surely that made up for a little extra murder?

His fingers began to squeeze her throat. "You're so fucking stupid."

The pain of his steely grasp brought tears to her eyes. She blinked, trying to block the moisture from falling. She could get out of this mess. There was still time.

But her heart had started to race again.

"He's screwing her now," he spat the words at her. "When you called Detective Brooks, she was in his bed." A laugh. Cold. Deadly. "She would have heard everything you said. She'll know what's happening now, Susan. She'll start hunting you."

"W-won't . . . f-find . . . m-me . . ." Talking was hard with his fingers digging into her windpipe. She barely managed to gasp out the words.

Then his hand was gone and she dragged air into her lungs, sucking in the oxygen desperately.

"Of course, she will. Demons are very, very good at hunting. Almost as good as those fucking animal shifters."

But that Cara, she was just a piece of fluff. Susan wasn't scared of her. She'd cut the demon up, just like she'd cut Tommy—

He laughed at her. "You still don't understand what you're up against, do you?"

Now she was getting pissed. "I . . . understand th-that you . . . need me." He couldn't kill without her. She was the bait. The perfect setup. Though the demon might be furious, he wasn't going to do anything stupid. "Look, I th-think . . . the rules between us . . . need to change." The sex was great. Hell, sex was always great after a kill. And he'd been giving her money. Gotten her a nicer place.

But now the shift of power was about to turn, in her favor. Susan let a smile curve her lips.

His eyes narrowed. "Actually, Susan, I don't need you any-more at all."

Just like that, her fate was sealed.

She shoved against him, hard, seeing her death in the dark-ness of his gaze. The bastard laughed again and stepped back, and she managed to twist and yank her knife from its sheath. "You stay the hell back!" She had to hold the blade with her weaker left hand—no way could she use her right now.

"Aw, Susan, why do you want to fight me?" That charm-ing, deceitful smile was on his face. She'd always thought hu-mans lied well, but they couldn't even come close to matching demons.

"Get out of my way!" He was blocking the entrance to the phone booth. But if she could make him move, she could run, maybe make it to her car—

It hit her then. His scent. Teasing her nostrils. Sex. Power. *No, damn it, no!*

Helplessly, she felt her body respond even more to him.

"You don't want to use that knife on me." His voice be-came even deeper.

Damn demon power.

She *hated* demons.

The hand gripping the knife began to lower.

"Good girl."

No. She'd stopped being a *good girl* the night her bastard of a stepfather had climbed into her bed.

"You want me, don't you, Susan?" Still using that hypnotic power of his.

Her nipples were so hard they ached. Her legs trembled. She managed a nod.

"And you don't want to hurt me, do you?"

Oh, but she did.

He lifted his hand toward her as he closed the space between them. His fingers trailed over her breast. Plucked the nipple. "Kiss me, Susan."

Her mouth, open, met his. The kiss was far too hard, far too rough, and she felt the copper of blood on her tongue.

The she felt the press of his hand against her chest.

Right over her heart.

No! The scream echoed in her mind even as she continued to helplessly kiss him back.

His lips lifted. "I'm gonna drain you," he whispered, and sounded like a lover with a caress in his voice. "Every drop of power from you—I'm gonna take it. Then I'm gonna leave your corpse to rot." Another bruising kiss.

Then she felt it. The slow stir of magic in the air. No, God, no, she wouldn't go out like this.

With every ounce of strength she had, Susan focused on her left hand. She just needed to break the demon's power. If he lost his concentration, the pheromones would weaken, and she'd be able to fight more—

And not just twist and moan eagerly like a bitch in heat against him.

"Ah, Susan, you're gonna beg me to fuck you, then to kill you."

The fingers of her left hand trembled as they tightened around the knife.

Distract him. "I-I can still . . . help you," she managed. "I-I can get . . . more men. Don't—"

He laughed at her. *Laughed.* "I told you, Susan." His hands cupped her cheeks. "I don't need you anymore."

She'd screwed up. Played with the devil when she wasn't ready for hell. "B-but I-I can give . . . you the n-next man on . . . y-your list! I-I can give y-you . . . T-Todd Brooks—"

"You already have." He smirked at her. "Thanks for the gift."

Oh, he'd be thanking her. Her breath caught, sweat beaded

her brow, and she managed to lift the knife and plunge it into his side.

Startled, the demon cried out, then stumbled back.

His scent eased, just for a moment, and her head cleared.

Snarling, she plunged the knife straight into his chest. His cry of pain was music to her ears. Susan yanked the blade out and drove it deep again.

Blood sprayed across the phone booth. Dripped down the glass.

She drove the knife into his chest once more. Furious. Desperate. He should be going down. Weakening.

Susan lifted the knife, prepared for another hard thrust.

His fingers flew out and locked around her throat. "Bitch." His breath was ragged. "I'm not one of your fucking humans, Susan." He shook her, slamming her head back against the glass. Stars exploded before her eyes. Bloodred stars. "It takes a hell of a lot more than a few knife wounds to kill me."

She'd see what it took, Susan thought, her world a blur of pain and blood. She'd keep stabbing him until the bastard went down. Straining, she struggled to bring the knife between them.

He should have been weak. His blood was all around her. On her skin. Soaking her clothes. Covering the glass of the booth.

His hold tightened around her throat. The knife was slippery in her hand, wet from too much blood. If she could just—

"I'm glad you came out here, sweetheart," he gritted the words and glared down at her with black eyes. "Nice deserted spot. No one around for miles. The perfect place to die."

Her thundering heart shook her entire body. "Don't! Just—"

Too late. He jerked his hand, twisting her head hard to the right and breaking her neck in one fast move.

The knife slipped from her hand and landed on the floor of the phone booth with a clatter.

He held her a moment, enjoying the feel of her twisted neck beneath his fingers. Then he smiled and let her body fall.

*   *   *

Todd was called to the crime scene on Thomas Boulevard the next morning at a little after 8 A.M. When he'd awoken, Cara had been gone, and he wondered for the fifth time since leaving his place why the woman had disappeared on him without a word.

He pulled his car to a stop, jumped out, automatically reached for the latex gloves he'd brought in his jacket, only to be stopped short by Colin.

There was worry in his eyes. "Where's Cara?"

Todd frowned at that. "Hell if I know." But he'd be finding out, soon.

Colin's lips tightened. "When did you see her last?"

What the hell? "Is this another hit by our killer? Damn it, I wondered why we got the call on this one." So what was happening? There wasn't a hotel around, but had the Bondage Killer struck again? And was Colin trying to pin this one on Cara? *Not gonna happen.* "Look, man, Cara has an alibi, she was with me last night."

"With you?"

"Yeah, at my place, in my bed, until seven this morning." When he'd heard the soft click of the door closing behind her.

"I wasn't saying she committed this crime—"

"Then what were you—"

Colin grunted. "You sure she was with you until seven?"

What the fuck? "Yeah."

His shoulders seemed to relax. "Thought it was her at first, but the smell was off, the freckles weren't right and—"

"What the hell are you talking about?"

Blue eyes held his. "Go see for yourself."

Well, he'd been trying to do just that when Colin had stopped him. Shouldering past his partner, Todd headed for the phone booth just beyond the crossing lines of yellow tape. Even from the distance, he could see the blood lining the glass. "Shit. Someone really did a number on the vic—"

"Not the victim's blood," Colin said from behind him. "The victim died from a broken neck."

He was at the phone booth now. Todd glanced down, and felt as if he'd just taken a knife to the chest. "She . . . looks like Cara." Not a perfect match. But the hair was the same. The nose. The brow. This woman's chin was bit more curved and she had a line of freckles on her nose, but—damn, it was a close resemblance.

"The uniforms on scene recognized her from the station . . . or they *thought* they did. They called the captain—he told me to get down here ASAP."

It could have been Cara.

The woman looked so much like her that she could have been her sister.

A woman who was a copy of Cara, murdered near a phone booth just hours after his mystery call.

No damn way that was a coincidence. Clearing his throat, he asked, "Have you run the phone records?"

"Just sent out the order." A pause. "When I got the call from McNeal, he told me not to notify you yet. I-I didn't know what was happening, and I thought you should be in the loop—" Colin broke off, shaking his head. "Man, if I'd known that he thought it was your lady, I *never* would have called you in—"

Your lady. The remorse in Colin's voice was undeniable. "It's not Cara." But, what if it had been? What if he'd arrived and found her bloodstained body, lying broken in the phone booth.

No. His hands fisted. He wasn't even gonna *think* about shit like that. His lady, as Colin had so aptly put it, was a strong demon. No one would hurt her.

No one. Todd forced his gaze away from the woman's face. Sweat beaded his brow.

Do the job.

He had to focus. Do what needed to be done.

Then he could get the hell out of there.

Not Cara.

He moved forward, being careful not to disturb the victim. His gaze locked on the small identification square just below the phone. The plastic screen that covered the phone number for the booth was spattered with blood, but he could still make out the numbers.

He exhaled heavily. *A damn match.* He turned his attention to a still shaken-looking Colin. "I think you're going to find my number was the last one dialed."

"*What?*"

"I got a call last night, this morning, hell, around four a.m." The call could've come moments before the victim's time of death. "A woman told me that Cara's alibis were crap. That the staff at Paradise Found were lying."

"And why would they be doing that?"

"Because Niol told them to."

"Shit."

"The call came from this number." He pointed to the small sign. This case just kept throwing him one damn surprise after another. He whistled as he glanced around the booth and saw nothing but blood. "The lady must have done a hell of a number on her attacker."

Thank God it hadn't been Cara.

"There was a knife beside her body," Colin said. "It's already been tagged and bagged."

The stench of blood had him swallowing and stepping back. Well, a knife would explain the blood, if . . . "Shouldn't there be another dead body here?" He asked quietly. Someone had sure bled out like a stuck pig, and no human could survive that kind of blood loss.

No human. He met Colin's stare, understanding hitting him with the force of a blow right to the face.

"It takes a lot to kill certain people," was all Colin said.

Not people. *Other.*

Sonofabitch. "Just how fast," he asked quietly, too quietly for the other cops to hear, "do demons heal?"

"From wounds like this?" Colin exhaled, then said, "A couple of days. Unless it's one of the level-tens—and even for one like that, healing would take some time—at least twenty-four hours."

Then he'd better move, fast. "You got this scene secured?"

"Yeah, yeah, I got the scene. Smith's on her way. So is the captain." He whistled. "Bastard's gonna bawl my ass out when he finds out you were here." A wince. "What I deserve, though, man, I'm sorry, if it had been her—"

"It *wasn't.*" He turned away from the body. The scene would be safe. He could trust Colin to handle this end for him.

Todd yanked off his gloves and began heading for his car, his long strides almost a run.

"Brooks! Damn it! Wait!"

He paused, but only for a moment. "If the killer can heal as fast as you say, then time's running out, partner." Every minute that passed was more time for the killer to heal. "You lead things here."

"And where are you going?"

He turned his head and met Colin's stare. His partner wasn't going to like this. "I'm heading to Paradise."

Colin started cursing. "No, wait, not without backup—"

"Take care of the body," he said. "And this time, I'll take care of Niol."

The bastard really hadn't been on his list of suspects, until that call came last night. After mentioning the demon's name, the lady had met one hell of a violent end.

Coincidence? He didn't buy those anymore.

Oh, yeah, it was past time for him to see the devil.

And to find out if he bled.

"I want to see your boss." The two assholes at the door just smirked at Todd when he gave his order.

I'm not in the damn mood for this. He brushed back the edge of his jacket, let his holster show. "I said *I want to see your fucking boss.*"

They stopped smirking. The big, bald one—*Jesus, did that guy ever sleep?*—stepped toward him, arms crossed over his barrel-like chest. "Niol's busy now."

Busy doing what? Trying to staunch the flow of blood from

knife wounds? "Let me in." No, he didn't have a warrant, probably couldn't even get one, but he wasn't leaving until he talked to Niol.

He no longer even thought for a moment that Cara was a suspect in the Bondage case.

But she could very well be a victim.

God but that dead woman had looked so much like her . . .

"I've got another dead body, one that points to Niol, and unless you want every *human* cop in Atlanta stationed at this door, twenty-four-seven, you'll let me inside."

The bald bastard stared him down. Todd glared right back at him. Finally, the guy cursed and lifted his radio. Then he muttered, "Tell Niol company's coming."

He stepped back, clearing the way.

Todd grunted as he brushed by him and the other bouncer, a tall, lanky fellow with beady eyes who glared daggers at him.

Inside, Paradise Found was quiet. Dead quiet. The last time he'd come during the day for a confrontation with Niol, the place had been exactly the same.

Apparently the local ghouls weren't much for daytime partying.

Now if he could just find that ass—

A door marked 'PRIVATE' opened to the left. Niol stepped forward, carefully shutting the door behind him. He quirked a brow as his gaze met Todd's. "Ah, Detective, I was wondering when I'd be seeing you again. From what my bartender Cameron tells me, you've become quite the addict here. But then, your kind tends to get addicted so easily."

The bastard didn't look injured. His dark hair was brushed back from his high forehead. His black eyes glinted as he stared at him. "Cameron says that, huh?" Cameron talked too damn much. Todd's gaze slanted toward the bar. No sign of the punk.

But he wasn't there for Cameron, anyway. Another fight for another day.

Time to cut through the bullshit. "I've got a dead body—"

"Another one?" Niol drawled, breaking across his words. "You boys at the Atlanta PD sure do keep busy."

"The victim looks a hell of a lot like one of your singers, Cara Maloan."

Not so much as a flicker of his expression. "Really."

"Yeah, *really*." He clenched his hands. "I've got reason," *damn good reason*, "to believe the victim managed to injure her attacker before he killed her."

"He? You're sure the killer is a man?"

No, he just had the damn strong suspicion that Niol was the killer in question. "This victim called me last night." Hadn't been completely proven yet since the woman who *could* prove the call was stone dead, but lying to Niol wasn't a crime. It was perfect bait. "Told me that you'd been getting your workers to lie about Cara's alibis."

Now Niol frowned and took a few steps away from the closed door. "I haven't told anyone to lie."

"Then maybe you used some of that demon bullshit power of yours and made 'em think they were telling the truth."

Niol tapped his chin. "Finally figured things out, have you, Detective? It certainly took you long enough."

He hated this asshole.

"But your education is still very much lacking." Niol sauntered toward the bar. "Demon magic doesn't generally work on other demons. And my staff here, well, aside from the occasional witch—who, by the way, would be immune to my power, too—well, they're all pureblood demons."

As if on cue, Cameron suddenly appeared behind the bar, looking a bit pale as he pushed a dark red liquid toward Niol and a whiskey toward Todd.

"I'm not here to drink," Todd snapped. Not even 10 A.M. What was with these demons?

Niol took a slow sip from his glass. "No, of course not. Thanks, Cameron." He glanced at Todd. "You're here to find out if I've got some kind of wounds, right? From the attack?"

"Yes."

Cameron headed toward the back of the bar, disappeared.

"I don't think I have to show you anything. I mean, a demon's body is his own, now, isn't it?" A taunting smile curved his lips once again. "I think you're playing out of your league, human. Way out. Perhaps you'd better leave and send the shifter back. At least he's strong enough to handle all the players in the game."

Todd's control snapped. He could still smell that woman's blood. See Cara's face. And he wasn't in the mood to be jerked around by a demon. He lunged at Niol, grabbed him and slammed the guy back against the bar. "Don't fuck with me!"

"Why? Aren't you fucking with one of my singers?"

He'd break him apart. He pulled back his fist, ready to wreck Niol's face and—

"Stop, Todd!"

Cara's voice.

His head snapped to the left. There she was. Standing just outside the door Niol had exited moments before.

His arm shook with the effort of holding back his punch. "What are you doing here?" He didn't release Niol and didn't drop his hand, though part of him was surprised the demon wasn't using his mojo to send him flying across the room.

Cara glanced down at Niol, then back to him. "I work here, remember?"

"Not today, you don't." Wednesdays through Saturdays. He'd confirmed her schedule long ago.

"Um, good memory, cop," Niol murmured.

Cara's chin lifted. "I still have to come in and get my check and—talk with Niol about the band."

And spout lame-ass lies to him.

"Take off your shirt," he snapped.

Cara blinked. "Uh, Todd—"

"Not you!" She'd damn well better not think of stripping in front of Niol. His fist dropped and his hands clenched the front of Niol's black shirt. "Him!"

Niol's eyes—eyes that were just as dark as Cara's when she dropped the glamour, but lacking the warmth he saw in her stare—narrowed. "Despite what you may have heard, Detective, I really do prefer to be wined first. And I prefer my partners to be female."

Fucking asshole. "Cut the crap and take off your shirt."

The scent of sex and lavender floated around him as Cara scrambled to his side. "Niol didn't kill that woman. He didn't even know about her until I told him—"

"*What?*"

"Demon hearing—"

"Another part of your lacking education," Niol said at the same time.

"It's much stronger than a human's. Not shifter strong, of course, but . . ." She shrugged. "I heard everything you said to Niol."

Hell.

"And I heard everything that woman told you on the phone."

"I know." And that part, he *did* know. Cara had been right beside him when he got the call—even a human would have heard the conversation. "What I don't understand is why you would have come running to him." That she had done so made Todd angry.

Furious. Okay, fucking *pissed*.

She shouldn't have turned to Niol, she should have turned to *him*.

"Cara and I go way back." Niol's voice held the intimate tone of a lover and it made every muscle in Todd's body stiffen. "She trusts me."

The guy didn't have to say the rest. It was implied. *And she doesn't trust you.*

"Take off your damned shirt." He wasn't there to find out which of them knew Cara better. He wasn't there to play the jealous lover, though he sure as hell could have nailed that part.

"Take your hands off me," Niol snapped, and the mask that he'd been wearing began to crack as shards of anger pierced his words.

Todd stared down at him. Waited one beat, two.

Then he released him. "Your turn. Get the shirt off."

Niol glared at him. "I don't have to do a damned thing for you—"

"For me." Cara touched his arm and the move had Todd biting back a snarl. "Just show him, for me."

Niol caught her hand. Brought it to his lips and pressed a kiss to her knuckles. "Only for you." Then he rose, yanked the black T-shirt over his head, and exposed a chest that was completely unmarred. He lifted a brow at Todd. "That good enough for you, or do I need to drop my pants, too?"

The phone booth had been small. The blood splatter marks had been high on the glass—so the perp must have been injured in the upper portion of his body.

Not below the waist.

"Not necessary," he growled.

Niol winked at Cara. "And what about for you, my love?"

"*Not* necessary," Todd answered for her.

Cara shook her head, mouth tightening. "Look, stop acting like a jerk. Niol did what you wanted, he's shown you every courtesy—"

And just how many courtesies had he shown her? "I found a woman's body less than an hour ago. A woman who looked almost exactly like you."

She flinched.

"Her body was in a phone booth outside of town. She'd been left there, like some kind of broken doll."

"The woman who called you—she's really dead?"

"Yeah, I think it was her." Odds were damn high that it was.

Her eyes squeezed shut for a moment, then she opened them and said, "You don't understand what's happening here, Todd." She licked her lips. "You'll think it's crazy, but I-I believe someone's trying to set me up for murder."

Not crazy. "And you came to Niol?"

"*He* hasn't told anyone to lie for me! My alibis were good. That woman," she swallowed, "if-if that's the one whose body you found, *she* was lying. And there's only one reason she'd call like that and lie to a cop."

"Because she wanted to take Cara down," Niol said, making no move to put his shirt back on. Instead, he reached for his drink, and took another slow sip. "The vics were all linked to Cara, weren't they, cop?"

All but the last one. Thomas Monroe—and his murder hadn't fit the MO.

"So you've got these bodies, these men who are all somehow tied to Cara, even if *she* didn't know them, and they wind up dead. Men in the peak of health. *Dead*." He tapped his fingers on the bar. "And they bear the mark of a sex demon."

"Succubus," Todd snapped.

Niol quirked a brow. "Interesting, isn't it, that all the clerks at the hotels just happened to see a blond woman fitting Cara's description—"

"How the hell do you know about that?" Todd demanded.

Niol blinked. "You do realize that demons make up a good third of your force, don't you, Detective?" Another sip of his drink, then, "Where was I? Oh, yes, the clerks all described a woman like Cara, the victims are all killed by the touch of a sex demon, and at one scene, well, damn, you even find Cara's ID, all nice and neat and just waiting for you."

Cara's eyes were on his.

"The killer was shoving her down your throat." Another sip. "So to speak."

"It's true, Todd," Cara said, her tone fierce. "Someone is setting me up. I can't prove it yet, but I will, and—"

He grabbed her arm, jerked her toward him. So close. He wanted to kiss her. He wanted to claim her. He wanted to tell Niol to get the hell away from her. Instead, his fingers curled tight around her.

"Todd? I'm being set up, I—"

"Don't you think I fucking know that by now, baby?" Then, because he couldn't stand the stark look in her eyes, he kissed her. Deep and hard, and tried not to feel the swirling cold in his gut.

A cold that was instinct, rearing its head.

His succubus was in danger.

And he wasn't sure if he'd be strong enough to keep her safe.

But he was damn well going to try.

Chapter 13

"I'm really getting sick of this damn police station," Cara growled as Todd pulled her across the bull pen and toward his desk, a desk that was overflowing with paperwork.

"Tough." He raised a hand and waved one of the uniforms over to them. "Mark, I need you to watch her."

Watch her? What the hell was she now? Some kind of dog? Cara set her back teeth.

Mark gave a firm nod.

Todd pushed her toward his chair. "Stay here."

The man was going to piss her off in about five seconds.

"Detective?" Mark frowned up at him. Probably because he didn't know if she was a suspect or some poor victim who needed protection.

She was neither, damn it.

"I've got to find the captain." Todd pointed to Cara. "Keep an eye on her. Do *not* let her leave."

She gritted, "Todd, this is absolutely unnecessary—" The guy had been in some kind of freak mode ever since they'd left Paradise Found.

"It's damn well necessary. Consider yourself in protective custody, baby." He kissed her. Hard. Fast. "Until I can determine what the hell is going on, I'm going to make certain you're safe."

And that was why she was currently surrounded by cops.

She grabbed his hand. "I can take care of myself." He sure didn't seem to be understanding the whole demon part of the equation.

She was a powerful supernatural creature. Not a level-ten, but still strong enough to kick most folks' asses. The guy had to stop judging her by the surface skin.

"You don't know what we're dealing with here." His voice was pitched low, too low for the young cop to catch. "*I* don't know what we're dealing with, and until we know just who we're up against, you're going to be under police protection."

Hell.

"Now, I'm going to find Colin and the captain, and see if they know more about our Jane Doe." A hard stare. "Stay here and stay out of trouble."

His gaze shot to the uniformed cop. "Don't let her out of your sight, Mark."

"Sir."

"And . . . try not to smell her." Said with a frown.

Mark blinked. "Uh, sir?"

Another hard kiss. Then he pulled away from her and marched across the room.

And left her with the junior policeman for protection.

Cara sighed and closed her eyes.

Then she started trying to figure out who hated her enough to kill.

One name came instantly to mind. *Lance Danvers.*

But that bastard was dead. Had been for the last seven years. She'd seen the body. Touched the cold flesh.

Yeah, he was dead.

After all, she'd been the one to arrange his meeting with the devil.

"We got an ID on the victim," Colin said, pushing a file toward Todd. "Susan Dobbs. Her prints were in the system."

"That was fast. I mean, it's been what? Five, six hours since the body was found?"

"This case has the highest priority," McNeal said. "I expect everything to go *fast*."

Duly noted. Todd flipped over the manila folder. Glanced at the black-and-white photo of the woman in her mug shot. "What'd she do?"

"Ms. Dobbs liked to cut men up with knives," McNeal said, leaning back in his chair with a groan of leather. "Started when she was a kid. Made a habit of the killings for the next fifteen years."

Killing with a knife. Sure as hell fit for the Monroe murder. But for the others . . . "She's human, isn't she?"

"Emily thinks so," Colin told him.

Todd's brows snapped together. "Run that by me again."

McNeal cleared his throat. "The doctor, she's good at sensing these things."

Right.

"If Em says the vic's not *Other*, she isn't." Colin sounded absolutely definite.

Okay, well, that meant . . . "Susan wouldn't have been able to kill the other men."

"Not by herself," his partner said.

It was the conclusion they all had no choice but to reach. Todd turned his stare onto the captain. "It's a setup, sir. I don't know who is doing it, and I don't know why, but my gut tells me Cara is deliberately being tied to these crimes."

The captain grunted. "You think the killer was using the blonde to throw suspicion on Cara?"

"She's a dead ringer for her."

"That could just be coincidence," Colin pointed out.

Todd snorted. *Bullshit.*

"The woman could've been a lure, though," Colin continued, tapping his chin. "Em said that vamps use them all the time."

"What?"

Colin stopped his tapping. "A lure. Something nice and flashy to catch the attention of the humans so that they never see the monsters coming until it's too late."

"A succubus shouldn't need a lure." The wheels in Todd's head were turning, fast. A succubus *was* a lure. So why use Susan? Why bring her in unless . . . Todd shook his head. "What do we know about Susan Dobb's personal relationships?"

Colin reached into his pocket and flipped out his notebook. "Her mom's in jail, her father was never on the scene, and—"

"No, her *sexual* relationships. Has anyone checked—"

He closed the notebook. "Bryant did."

Bryant was the newest detective in the department. A quiet guy who'd transferred up from Miami just a few months back.

"Susan liked men—a *lot* of them." His brows lifted. "What? Do you want him to get you specifics?"

Todd slanted him a hard look. "Cara said Michael House was straight. That he would have only gone to the hotel with a woman." A woman who looked a lot like his ex? "*Fuck. A succubus shouldn't need a lure,*" he repeated as excitement pumped through him. He might just be figuring this shit out. "A woman wouldn't need to use Susan, but a man—he sure as hell would."

Colin whistled. "Susan could've brought in the men, tied 'em up with the promise of some wild sex."

McNeal's fingers flattened on his desk. "And instead just made them helpless and got them ready for the kill."

"Yes." One damn good supposition. "Maybe she tied the guys up because if they'd seen who was really waiting for them, they never would have been into the game."

"He could have waited in the closet . . ." Colin's eyes were thoughtful. "Or in one of those small-ass bathrooms." He spoke the last softly, as if to himself.

Hell, yeah, that was exactly what Todd was thinking. "It could have happened," he said. Maybe it *had* happened just that way.

"An incubus?" McNeal asked.

"It would explain the print." Because that was the mark of

a sex demon—succubus or incubus. "If the guy wanted to drain the humans, he would have needed to get their sexual energy pumped up—he would have used Susan for that." The woman had been a looker, just like his Cara.

"So Susie gets the men tied up, gets them horny," Colin murmured, "then our incubus comes in. He gives them a touch and kills the poor bastards."

"As he takes their power and lives—*yes!*" It made sense. Every bit of it made sense. "This guy, whoever he is, I think he chose Susan Dobbs because she looked like Cara. He dumped Cara's purse at the third crime scene so we'd pick her up, and he's been choosing men that are all linked to her."

"Except for Monroe." Colin straightened. "We can't find any link to him and Cara—"

The pieces fell into place. "Because that guy was Susan's kill, hers alone. Think about it." He paused a moment, then lifted his fingers as he counted off the reasons, saying, "She stabbed him. She's got a long history with knives, we all know that. She left the room a wreck, left evidence behind—"

"The scene was nothing like the others," McNeal agreed grimly.

"*Because the killer was different.*" Todd knew it with every cell in his body. "*She* killed him. I bet if we dig, we'll find a connection between her and Monroe, something personal." The woman had snapped—killed in an undeniable fit of rage. There had been so many knife wounds in the guy's chest . . .

"Shit. So what, we had some damn team killing together—" McNeal began.

"Until Susan broke the rules." He thought about the cold, quick death Susan had received. "Then she had to be punished." But just who had punished her? The lady had tried to lead him to Niol, but the demon appeared to be clean.

Though appearances could sure as hell be deceiving. He was learning more about the truth of that old saying every day.

"If Monroe wasn't a planned kill—"

"Then our guy probably got real pissed at Susan." Because she'd broken his control. Destroyed the layout of his nice, neat little game. "So pissed that the lady wound up with a broken neck."

"But if we're dealing with an incubus, why didn't he just drain her?" Colin shook his head. "He could have gotten her energy and—"

"She fought him." Todd could still see the blood staining the walls of the phone booth. "Maybe he intended to use the touch on her, but Susan had her knife, and once she started stabbing, he snapped her neck."

McNeal sighed. "Damn it, I'm tired of this shit in my city. What ever happened to keeping a low profile? Why does this asshole want to stir things up?"

"Why is he going after Cara?" Todd fired back.

Colin rolled his shoulders, a ripple of movement. "Gotta be personal."

Yeah, that was what he figured, and what scared him.

"Niol was clean?"

He nodded curtly at the captain's question. "Doubt I'd ever say that, but there weren't any wounds."

Colin lifted a brow. "And the guy's not a sex demon."

"Incubus," he corrected, almost automatically. "Just what the hell *is* that guy?"

"Someone who could fry this town if he wanted," McNeal said, voice rough. "A level-ten who likes to play on the dark side."

Niol was definitely cold enough to kill, but he *wasn't* an incubus. And there'd been no knife wounds on his body.

So, as much as he wanted to put the demon away, he wasn't looking like the killer.

Which meant the bastard was still out there, somewhere. "We've been looking at this all wrong." They'd thought the woman was the primary, but Susan Dobbs had just been a pawn.

The real serial was still out there.

"I'm keeping Cara in protective custody until we catch the bastard." Probably should have asked permission from the captain first, but screw that, his woman was in danger, and he *would* be keeping her safe.

Colin cleared his throat. "Ah, how does she feel about that?"

"Doesn't matter." His stare was on the captain. "I think she's in danger." Those instincts of his were screaming at him. Cara would have said his *sensitivity* was charging up—hell, whatever it was, he *knew* that the lady was in danger.

And he was going to keep her safe.

The captain gave him an almost imperceptible nod. "Do we need to take her to a safe house?"

He walked over to the captain's door. Peeked through the blinds. Cara was still sitting in his chair. Mark was stationed at her side. "Yeah, I think so." He'd like to keep her at his place, but he knew someone could have already staked out his home.

No, better to take her someplace secret.

Even if she raged at him, and he was certain she would.

He reached for the knob. "I'd better go break the news to the lady—"

"Hey, Brooks!"

He glanced back at Colin's call, opening the door just a few inches. The rumble of voices from the bull pen drifted in to him. "What?"

"Before I came in here, I called the phone company, pulled a few strings." One brow lifted. "The last call Susan Dobbs made wasn't to your place."

Now *that* got his attention. "What? No, she called—"

"I know—I *know*—but the call to your place wasn't the last one she made." Colin stood, stepped toward him. "I got the number and guess who answered on the second ring?"

"Who?" Not Niol, it couldn't be—

"The newswoman. Holly Storm."

What?

"I sent a squad car after her. Ms. Storm should be here any minute for a little interrogation."

"Good." He was curious as all hell to learn just why Susan had contacted the reporter. Had she been offering Storm a tell-all interview? A scoop on the killer that the cops were try-ing so hard to keep under wraps?

Damn. Just how much did the reporter know? And how deep was she involved in this mess?

"She could—"

The silence hit him then. The absolute and complete silence from the bull pen.

The rumble of voices had quieted now. He saw Colin stiffen, and Todd turned back toward the door, peering through the crack he'd made.

Then he heard words that chilled his soul. "Put the gun down and we can talk."

What the fuck? He pulled the door open another two inches. Caught sight of a kid with long, greasy hair. As Todd watched, the kid turned in wide circles, a gun clutched in his trembling hands.

No, not a kid. The guy looked like he was in his early twen-ties. Too old to be pulling something stupid like this.

"What is it?" The captain's voice. McNeal had sidled across the room. He peered over Todd's shoulder and hissed out a breath. "I'm going to fucking nail some bastard to the wall for this!"

Because someone had left an unsecured weapon out in the open and now they were all in serious shit.

Then the punk with the gun made the mistake of lunging forward and grabbing Cara.

Todd's hand went to his holster as he ran out of the room.

Well, damn if her day didn't just suck.

She'd been watching the rumpled human male with half an eye, her mind on the murders, when the guy suddenly lunged for the desk on the far left.

He'd come up with a gun and every cop in the area had frozen.

Now he had a too-tight grip on her arm. The scent of fear and unwashed skin flooded her nostrils.

The barrel of the gun came dangerously close to her face.

No, not a damn good day.

"Stay back or I'll fucking *kill* her!"

The arm he'd looped around her neck tightened.

From the corner of her eye, she saw Todd. He was advancing on the man, *on them*, eyes narrowed, face hard with rage. He had his gun out.

Cara realized if she didn't do something, fast, her day was about to go from bad to sheer hell.

Because she sure wasn't just going to stand there, be strangled, threatened, and then watch her cop get hurt.

Not when she could so easily stop the jerk who held her.

Todd might not like the methods she was about to use, but there wasn't much of an option.

Besides, perhaps it was time for him to see that she truly wasn't the helpless damsel that he thought she was.

"I goin' out of here, and I'm takin' this bitch with me!" The guy snarled, spittle flying from his mouth.

Her hands lifted, yanked on the arm and freed her throat. "No," she told him softly, "you're not." Breathing deeply, she dropped her control and let her pheromones fill the air.

The guy was so close to her that he got a direct hit. He spun her around to face him, eyes wide, mouth open.

She smiled at him. Pitched her voice low and poured on the compulsion as she said, "Kiss me."

The gun hit the floor with a clatter as he locked his lips on hers.

The air pulsed with his sexual energy. It was an energy much darker than Todd's. And weaker. So much weaker.

But energy was energy—and the little bastard had threatened her.

So she'd take a bit of his power for herself.

Asshole.

Her hand rose. Touched his chest, and, with her kiss and touch, she pulled the man's lust and power right out of him.

The sweet rush heated her blood. Oh, but it had been so long since she'd just let herself go. Just let herself take and take and take.

His body trembled against hers. A strangled moan bubbled in his throat and the heart that thumped beneath her hand began to slow.

Then to skip beats.

She pulled her mouth from his. Watched his bleary green eyes drift closed.

And then man fell backward, landing on the floor with a thud.

Cara inhaled deeply and caught the power still floating in the air. A faint shine lit her skin.

Sweet, sweet power.

Her head turned. She saw the stares then. The slack expressions on many of the male officers' faces. Her gaze darted past them, caught sight of—

Smith. The ME stood near the elevator, hands fisted, mouth open, and eyes wide with horror.

Just great.

And a few feet away from Smith stood—

Another woman. A redhead. She waited between two cops, just a little past Smith. She stared right back at Cara. Not with the horror that Smith had, but with a kind of stark curiosity on her face.

As she focused on the woman's face, the flare of her hunger and rage began to fade, and reality slowly raised its head.

Hell.

But there was no going back now.

"What the fuck were you doing?" The roar came from Todd as he grabbed the gun, then secured the weapon. He caught her arms, pulling her close to him. "Cara?"

She blinked. Forced herself to meet his dark stare. Anger. No, fury. Jealousy.

Fear?

She could see it all. Swirling in those eyes.

She could feel the emotions beating at her.

"This is who I am." Gyth was on the floor next to the still man, checking for a pulse. "I told you, I can take care of myself." And punish those who threatened her.

Or those she cared for in this world.

"He's alive," Gyth said, jaw tight.

"Of course, he is!" She snapped. Did they think she had no control? "I wasn't trying to kill him." *Jeez.* If she had wanted the idiot dead, the guy would have been at hell's gate. "I was just trying to stop him from hurting anyone."

"Pull it back." Todd's whisper was laced with steel.

"I don't—"

"The scent . . ." He swallowed. "Pull it back before I have to start beating sense into this pack."

"I—it's not that easy. It'll take some time—"

"Then I'm getting you the hell out of here, baby." He grabbed her wrist, yanked her through the crowd, and took her down a long, winding corridor.

Glancing back over her shoulder, the last person she saw was Gyth. He watched her with the sharp eyes of a shifter.

One predator, measuring another.

He pushed Cara into the old interrogation room, the one that hadn't been used for anything but storage during the last six months. The door slammed closed behind them, then he pounced.

His hands locked around her upper arms as he held her against the mirrored glass on the left wall. "What the hell were you doing?" God, but the woman was beautiful. Skin seeming to fucking glow. Eyes sparkling. Mouth wet and red—

From another man's mouth.

He growled, and, not giving her time to answer, he crushed his mouth to hers. Took her lips. Drove his tongue deep inside in an act of possession.

No one else. No one.

She moaned, the sound making his fully erect cock twitch with hunger.

His hands tightened on her arms, fingers digging into her flesh.

The woman was making him crazy.

His mouth lifted as he dragged in a desperate gulp of air. God, but her scent was everywhere. Driving him wild.

Pushing him to the absolute edge of his control. Not that he'd ever had much to begin with, not with her.

"Why?" A stark demand ripped from him. She hadn't been forced to confront the perp. To use her powers. Damn it, why—

"I'm not weak. Not human." She licked her lips, her tongue snaking out in a quick move. "I am . . . what you saw. You have to un-understand that." Her voice was shook just a bit. Husky.

God but he wanted her naked.

The pheromones? Her magic?

Or just the woman?

"I know what you are." No question in his mind.

"I've walked this earth a long time." Her eyes faded to black. "Seen things, done things, that most wouldn't accept."

This was important, he realized. This moment. "I'm not most people."

Her lips began to curl, but then the smile that would have been vanished almost instantly. "You kissed me. Knowing what I can do, after you saw—you kissed me."

He kissed her again. Hard. Thrust his tongue past those perfect white teeth and savored the warmth of her mouth.

Not enough.

His hands dropped to her hips. She was wearing a dress. A slinky, sexy-as-hell black dress that fit her body like a second skin and skirted the top of her knees.

His mouth moved to her neck. He licked. Sucked. Bit. Whispered, "Hell, yeah, I still kissed you. *You're mine.*" Time for them to both realize that fact.

"But you don't know the real me, not—"

Her words had him pulling back, glaring down at her. "I know everything that matters. I know the demon. I know the woman. *I fucking want them both.*"

He grabbed the fabric of her dress, hiked it up to her waist. "And you want me."

A nod.

"Don't do it again, Cara. Don't take another when I'm near—"

Her black eyes widened. "I would *never* take another while I'm with you. *Never.* Back there, that was a succubus fighting. That is our way. We fight, we kill, with just a kiss."

Scary shit.

"I wanted you to see me," she whispered the words as his hands caressed the warm flesh of her hips. "Not the woman you think I am, but what I'm like inside. What I can do." She sucked in a sharp breath. "What I've done."

"You are *exactly* who I think you are." He was still furious as hell, but the rage was channeling fast into a white-hot need, a need that had been stirred in the bull pen, but ignited to a flash point once he'd gotten her alone and tasted her again.

"I'm not weak. Not some simple prey." She whispered the words again.

He stared into her eyes. Ancient eyes. Mysterious. "No," he agreed, "you sure as hell aren't."

"I can be dangerous—I don't want to hurt you—"

Was the woman trying to warn him off? Because it was far too late for that. "You won't." He eased down in front of her, bending to his knees.

"Todd? What—"

"God, but I need you, Cara, *I need you.*"

She touched his cheek, her fingers moving in a featherlight caress. "It really doesn't matter to you, does it?"

He turned his hand. Pressed a hot kiss against her palm. "Demon, woman, both are *mine.*" He stared up at her. "Just don't ever even think about making *me* prey."

"I never would." Her lips curved again and her stare softened as she gazed down at him.

"Good." They would have a hell of a lot more to hash out later. But that would all come, later.

Now, he wanted her. They were alone, and his cock felt like it was going to burst.

He hiked up her skirt a little more, found the small silk of her panties. He pressed a kiss to the crotch of the underwear, putting his lips close to her covered sex and enjoying the soft feel of woman and silk against his mouth.

But he knew he wanted more.

They wouldn't have long. Someone would look for them eventually. Track him down. Demand explanations.

Fuck that.

He caught the edge of her panties with his teeth. Tugged until the seam broke. Heard the delicious sound of her laughter.

Damn, but the woman had made him into a walking hardon.

She spread her legs for him, needing no urging. He touched her sex. Found her creamy and ready. Just the way he wanted her. Edging closer, he curled his fingers around the firm cheeks of her ass. Her hips rocked forward, and his mouth claimed the hot core of her body.

His tongue slid over her clit and a shudder rocked her. *So good.*

Yet it could be even better.

One hand slid down the curve of her ass, and his fingers curled between her legs. Found her tight opening. Todd pushed his index finger inside her.

Licked.

Another finger. Thrust harder.

A lick.

Then a slow suck on her tight point of need.

Her sex clenched around him.

Oh, hell, *yes.*

"Todd!"

A demand. Her fingers were buried in his hair. She pulled the strands once. Hard.

Growling, he lifted his head, tasting her, wanting more, and—

The lust on her face drove the breath from his lungs. The raw need.

The same need he felt.

He was up in a instant, hands flying to the buckle of his belt. Their fingers met, fought, and somehow they managed to get the top of his pants undone and his cock out.

He couldn't wait to be balls-deep in her.

Todd grabbed Cara, spun her around, and lifted her onto the old table in the middle of the room. The table groaned beneath her, the faded wood protesting, but right then, Todd didn't give a shit.

If they'd ended up on the ground, he wouldn't have cared. As long as he'd was inside her . . .

Her legs were open, the pink folds of her sex glistening and tempting him. He caught his cock in one hand. Lodged it against that creamy slit.

"Now, love," she whispered.

He thrust as deep as he could go.

Their eyes met.

He withdrew.

Thrust.

Again. Again. *Again.*

He covered her mouth to muffle her moans.

To muffle his own.

His thrusts shoved the table across the floor. Cara held on to him, her fingers digging into his arms, her nails scoring his flesh.

He felt her come, that same, wild, mad fury of passion that was hers, his. That joining that he didn't understand, but longed for with every breath.

Then he was coming, his semen pumping deep into her as he stiffened and fought to hold on to his sanity.

Her hand moved, drifted to his heart.

The pleasure seemed to double. Burning through him, to her, back to him.

The room swirled around him in a flash of colors. His body quivered, his breath panted out.

When the orgasm ended, he lifted his lips, pressed a kiss to her cheek. Tasted tears.

Cara stared up at him, and her skin was so beautiful it almost hurt to look at her with that magic light spilling from her—*from the inside, out.*

Energy pumped through his veins. The power she'd given to him.

Given, not taken.

The salt of her tears seemed to burn his mouth. "Cara?" He'd known only pleasure, and he'd thought she had, too.

Her lips parted. Then the hand still over his heart pushed against him. *Pushed him away.*

No. He didn't want to retreat from her. Not yet.

But she was pushing him, and time had run out. The passion had barely been sated, but he'd have her again.

Soon.

He eased away from her, hating the loss of the tight clasp of her body, but he'd already taken enough risks. Losing his control at the station—there were too many eyes in this place.

Both human, and as jerk-ass Niol had so recently pointed out, *Other.*

"Th-there's something I have to tell you." She stood, and the dress fell right back over her flesh.

Damn it.

He righted his clothes with a jerk. "I'm not apologizing for that."

Her eyes narrowed for a second, then widened with understanding. "Good."

He blinked.

She stepped away from him. "I-I should have told you this sooner."

The sound of footsteps echoed in the hall.

Time was definitely almost up.

He caught sight of her panties on the floor. Scooped them up. Enjoyed the feel of the cool silk against his fingers. "We need to think of a cover story. All those cops saw what you did and—"

She waved a hand dismissively. "Most won't remember."

"What?"

"The human men won't. The demons, well, they won't care."

"And the women?"

Frustration flashed across her face. "Tell them I hit the guy when we kissed."

The footsteps were louder now. Closer.

"Tell them whatever you want! It doesn't matter!" Her hands fisted. "But you have to know, there's something I should have told you before."

Now the woman wanted to make some kind of confession? And he'd always heard men were the ones with the piss-poor timing. "Look, we need to—"

"I-I did something once. Crossed the line—that weak line between right and wrong."

"What?"

Her eyes shifted back to blue as she stared at him. "I—ah, damn, this is hard." Her shoulders straightened. "But you deserve to know."

Oh, Jesus, what was the woman about to reveal? And why were his guts twisting into knots?

Because what she's about to say is going to be bad, real bad.

It didn't take psychic powers to figure that one out.

"Cara . . ."

A door slammed. Sounded like it was just a few feet away. Someone had to be in the small hallway now, heading straight for them. "This can wait, when we're someplace secure—"

"No! You have to hear this." She grabbed his arm. "Todd, I-I've used my powers before, *deliberately* to hurt—"

"*Cara* . . ."

"To try to kill."

The door to the interrogation room flew open. Todd turned to see Gyth standing in the doorway, and one look at those glittering eyes was all it took for Todd to know that his partner had just heard his lover's confession.

Shit.

Chapter 14

"Not another word, baby, not without a lawyer." Todd's face was rock hard. His voice grim.

"No, you need to hear this." Screw his partner. Todd deserved to know about her. All about her. When he'd touched her earlier, kissed her, it had been so much more than just sex.

Perhaps it had been from the beginning.

No more secrets, no more lies.

She was telling him everything. Her eyes slit as she frowned up at the shifter. "When I'm done, if you want to lock me up, that's fine." She'd be out in less than ten minutes once she got a guard under her spell, but he could sure try tossing her butt in jail, if that made the big, bad cop feel better.

Gyth gave a slow nod.

She caught Todd's hands. Because she needed to touch him again. Because holding him made talking about the past easier. "I-I had a sister once. A twin."

A dark look passed between the cops.

"We were close. Always close. But so different." The memory of Nina made her lips curve. "She was dark where I was light. Wild when I was careful. And she *knew* me. The hidden parts of me that even I didn't fully understand."

Not identical, but they'd been a perfect match. Nina with her long, straight dark hair and her golden skin. The smile that had always lit her face and the eyes that had shined, with and without glamour.

"It's hard to kill my kind." Her fingers tightened around his. "Damn hard because I'm a demon, and even harder because I'm a succubus." Not the run-of-the-mill demon blood. So few knew that dark secret.

But *he'd* known.

"Nina started seeing a human. She fell for him." A pause. "I thought he cared for her."

Todd swore, obviously knowing where her story was headed. Hell, of course. Not to a sweet, happily-ever-after ending.

Demons didn't usually get those.

The shifter remained silent, watching her carefully.

"I felt it when she died," she whispered. "It was like pain stabbed straight through my soul, and in my mind, I heard her scream." She could still hear it. Because in that last moment, her sister had cried out for her, helplessly, and Cara hadn't been able to do a damn thing to save her.

She swallowed back the grief that wanted to choke her. Years had passed, but the wound was still fresh to her. "Her human killed her. The one she trusted, loved."

Todd flinched.

And it was the shifter who asked, "How?"

It wasn't a question she would normally answer, but these were far from normal circumstances. One of her kind was out there, killing, and the cops, well, they needed to know how to take the demon down.

"We heal fast," she said, nodding her head toward Gyth. "Much like you do, I imagine."

He said nothing.

"Gunshots, knife wounds—they'll hurt us, but those weapons alone won't kill a succubus or an incubus." There was really only one moment when her kind became vulnerable. Her lips twisted as her gaze darted back to Todd. "I told you before, succubi believe that true power rests in the heart, not the mind." Her power certainly did.

He gave a grim nod of his head.

She lifted her hand, touched his chest and felt the strong beat of his heart beneath her palm. "In that one moment when we take from others," *or give to them,* but she wasn't going to mention her ability to give power, not in front of that dangerous shifter, "we are at our most vulnerable."

"Cara . . ."

"When I touch your heart," her voice dropped, "That is the time, the only time, when I'm vulnerable." When the power began to stir. That first moment, as the air thickened and magic fired her blood. Her hand never moved from his chest and her eyes held his. "In that instant, a human's weapons—guns, knives—they *can* kill my kind. A bullet in the heart. A knife. *In that one moment,* you can destroy a succubus or an incubus, forever."

As her voice trailed away, silence filled the room. Thick, heavy. Far too tense.

Her hand dropped from his chest and Cara stepped back.

"If Susan was working with someone . . ."

Cara stilled.

Todd's gaze met Gyth's. "A man—an incubus . . . if they were fighting and she was using her knife on him—" Todd broke off, shaking his head. "Shit. She had to be hitting close to his upper chest. You saw the spray—"

Gyth whistled softly. "You're right. *Damn it.* She attacked him, got too close, and he couldn't risk draining her. He had to kill her fast, to save his own life."

"Uh, th-that seems likely," Cara agreed quietly, her mind whirling. They thought an incubus had been working with the murdered woman?

She'd been the lure.

Her lips parted. *Of course!* A temptation to pull in the men. It made sense. They hadn't been bound for kinky fun, they'd been tied so they wouldn't fight when the incubus appeared.

No wonder she hadn't felt the draw of another succubus in the city—there wasn't another one around!

The killer was an incubus . . .

Oh, hell.

Cara took a deep breath. The men were still talking about the woman—Susan—and her death. "If she was working with an incubus, she might have known how to kill him, or maybe—maybe she just got lucky."

Either way, she'd wound up dead and her killer had gotten away.

Todd and Gyth glanced toward her in surprise. Okay, so "lucky" hadn't been the best word choice. She licked her lips then said, "Look, just remember what I've said, okay?. My kind—we aren't vulnerable often, so if you have the chance to strike at the killer, well, you'd better take it."

There. She'd done it. Given a human and a shifter the most prized secret of her kind. A secret they'd need in order to survive.

Todd's fingers reached out and snagged her hand. Held tight. "What happened to the man who killed your sister, Cara?"

Ah, now this was the part she'd dreaded from the beginning. Todd had just started to look at her as a woman, and now he'd see the killer lurking inside of her pretty shell.

But perhaps it was time. She'd carried this secret for too long. Seven years.

"I went to him in his dreams."

Todd's expression didn't alter. Those brown eyes of his were steady on her.

"I made him weak. Made him want." It had been so easy. And she'd been so furious. He'd never met her, didn't know that she and Nina had a bond beyond death.

Her sister had wanted vengeance.

Cara had given it to her.

"Did you know . . ." It was hard to say the words when he was so close, touching her. "That some can become addicted to the touch of a succubus?" Like a drug addict, needing a fix. If the magic was strong enough, the human was helpless.

She'd made Lance helpless. He'd come to her, eyes desperate, hands sweating. He'd tracked her to her home, screaming at her. Wanting her.

And she'd been ready for him. "I lured him to me." So easy. "When he found me, I touched him." She'd nearly drained the bastard dry. His skin had paled. His body had trembled. Tears rained from his eyes.

The rush of power from his body had been so strong. And so dark. Tainted. Twisted.

Lance had been evil. A monster beneath the flesh of a man.

He'd realized what was happening to him—*too late*.

His heart had lurched beneath her hand. So close to death. To the hell he deserved.

She'd held him there, suspended between the world of the living and the wisps of the eternal, and asked, "Why?"

He'd known what she meant. Knowledge had been in his eyes. He'd smiled at her. "B-be . . . cause the f-fucking . . . b-bitch wouldn't . . . give . . . m-me . . . p-power . . ." Then, he'd managed to gather his strength—she still wasn't sure how the asshole had done that—and he'd jerked a knife out of his back pocket. One of those stupid, small, Swiss Army knives that men always carried, and he'd plunged the blade right into her chest.

He'd missed her heart, but the attack had thrown her off guard and the bastard had gotten away.

For a time.

"Did you kill him?" It was Gyth who asked the question.

"Don't—" Todd snapped, shaking his head. "You don't have to say—"

She tugged her hand from his. "He got away from me." True. She'd regretted that, hated her failure for years.

"So the bastard's still out there?" Todd asked, mouth hard. "Tell me his damn name and I'll—"

"He's dead now." And that should really have made things easier for her. "The next day, his body was found in his apartment. Lance killed himself." That was the story that had been in the papers, anyway.

More silence. The thick, uncomfortable kind that made her want to squirm.

"Is that the whole story?" Gyth asked. She slanted him a look, saw the suspicion in his eyes.

No, it wasn't the whole story, but she'd told all of her part. She'd confessed to the Monster Doctor about her attack on Lance before.

And if Lance hadn't pulled that knife—

Well, she wouldn't have regretted his death. Did that make her evil? She really didn't know.

I'm a killer. Yeah, that's what she'd told the Monster Doctor. Because even though she hadn't been the one to take the last breath from Lance's miserable body and soul, she'd still been responsible for his death.

"Check the Miami papers. They ran the stories on him for a few days." She'd been living in Miami back then. The *Other* always liked the big cities. So easy to blend in with the throngs of people. "The article said that Lance Danvers slit his wrists and bled to death." Too messy for her taste.

But not for the demon who'd killed Lance.

Suicide. *Not damn likely.* Not for a man like him.

"Why did you tell me this?" Todd asked.

"Because I wanted you to know there's a point for humans *and* paranormals. We can all be pushed too far, and we can all become monsters." Because she'd truly been a monster that long-ago night. One without pity. Remorse. She would have killed him, and she would have loved every minute of his death.

Her chin lifted as she faced them. She'd just admitted to two cops that she'd attempted murder. "What are you going to do now?" Cara asked, voice soft.

Todd brought his mouth down on hers, hungrily taking her lips. Her hands wrapped around his arms, held on with all her strength.

Behind him, Gyth coughed.

Todd's dark head rose. "I'm going to thank God that bastard didn't kill you."

She pressed her lips together. Caught his taste. "And what about what I did?"

Todd turned slowly to face Gyth. "She didn't do anything." A challenge. Cara could feel the tension pumping through his body. "Isn't that right, Gyth?"

The shifter's gaze met hers. Held. Finally, he said, "No crime that I see." A pause. "And I would have done the same."

His head inclined toward her slightly.

One predator to another.

The breath she'd been holding expelled in a sharp rush.

"You should have told me sooner," Todd muttered, bending so that his words whispered into her ear.

Yes, she should have, but the guy had already been dealing with the fact that she was a demon. She hadn't wanted him to completely freak on her.

But Todd wasn't showing any signs of freaking. Or running. Or, well, hell, the guy was actually holding pretty tightly to her.

A stab of hope shot through her heart. Maybe, just maybe, Todd would be different.

More footsteps sounded in the hallway. Hard. Determined steps. The shifter tilted his head to the right, said, "McNeal," about five seconds before the police captain shoved open the door and stalked inside.

He pointed his finger at Cara. "You."

Her brows lifted. She'd seen the captain a few times, but never actually spoken with the guy.

"You just put on one hell of a show in my precinct, demon."

Not human. Not completely, anyway. The understanding dawned instantly. As she'd told Todd, the human males would have all forgotten.

Hmm. So just *what* was the tough captain? She took a step away from Todd, more than ready to defend herself. "What I did," she said, voice fierce, "was save lives and fix the screwup one of your officers caused!"

A grunt. Then his hands flew up. "Don't come any closer!" She saw his nostrils twitch. "I'm taken."

"Since when?" The words were a bare thread of sound as they slipped past Gyth's lips.

"So is she," Todd said.

Gunmetal eyes widened. "Ah, you poor bastard." McNeal sighed. "Don't you know demons can't be trusted?"

Now the guy was pissing her off. The air began to thicken around her.

"*She* can be." Her lover's voice sounded absolutely confident.

The captain's eyes weighed him. Her. "You willing to risk your life on that assumption?"

"Yes." No hesitation.

"Then bring your demon into my office. It's time to clear the air and catch this damn killer before I have another stiff on my hands."

McNeal's office was too quiet. The old phrase *as silent as a tomb* whispered through Cara's mind as she waited in the cramped quarters.

Cara stood near the captain's obviously fake plant, arms crossed over her chest. Todd was beside her. Gyth leaned against the edge of McNeal's desk. And McNeal, well, he was sitting behind his desk, glowering at the ME.

After what had to be at least five minutes, Smith finally cleared her throat and shifted a bit in the rather uncomfortable-looking leather chair she occupied. "Are you, um, sure I can talk about the case in front of her?"

Her. The ME hadn't made eye contact with Cara the entire time they'd been trapped in the silence of the office.

"This is off the record, Smith."

The ME opened her mouth to protest.

"*Off the record.*" McNeal ran a hand over his face. Exhaled hard enough to shake the room, then said, "We need her help, okay? She's got to know the facts of the case because she's the only damn one who can really tell us what the killer is like."

Because I'm just like the killer.

Smith's back was ramrod straight. Her shoulders far too stiff.

McNeal stabbed his finger toward Gyth. "All right—let's start with the knife. Forensics said—"

"No prints were on the knife," Gyth finished. "But the hair we found belonged to Susan Dobbs."

Todd glanced at her. "You sure you didn't know the woman?"

He'd shown her Susan's picture, and yeah, the woman looked freakily like her, but—"I don't know her."

"Yeah, but you didn't know Walters, either," Gyth pointed out, "and that guy had been going to Paradise for the last month to watch you."

She saw Todd stiffen. "I think we need to take a step back here." He motioned toward the captain. "Susan Dobbs was human. How'd she hook up with a demon?"

"Demons are everywhere," McNeal said. "Shouldn't have been too hard—"

"It would have been a hell of a lot easier for her if she'd been inside Demon Central."

Gyth began to nod, obviously understanding where Todd was going.

"Niol's place is a meeting point for the *Other*, and Cara told me once that some humans like to play in Paradise."

McNeal's head cocked to the right. "And you think Susan was the playing kind?"

The woman had been the killing kind, so, yeah, Cara thought she was definitely the type of human who would have enjoyed playing with the *Other*.

"Niol will know." Todd gave a quick nod. "No one gets in that place without his knowledge."

"And you think the guy will be in the mood to cooperate with the cops?" Gyth asked, looking damn doubtful.

"He'll cooperate," Cara said, voice clear. He would do it, for her.

"Who is this . . . Nee-ole?" Smith asked slowly, pronouncing the demon's name with care.

McNeal's fingers splayed over the desk. "You really don't want to know about him."

"Yes, I do." The ME's voice hardened. "I'm in this game now, and I want to know *everything*."

"Niol is the most powerful demon I know," Cara said, and Smith's head jerked toward her. Her eyes were wide, stark.

"And he's a serious ass," Gyth added.

Smith didn't glance back at him. Her gaze stayed on Cara. "Is he evil?"

Hard question. "I've never known him to hurt an innocent." The not-so-innocent, well, that was a different story.

"Niol knows every damn thing that happens in this town," McNeal rumbled. "With the humans and with the supernaturals."

"He can tell us if there are any incubi hunting on the streets." Gyth's features were tense with predatory anticipation. "He was the one who originally tipped me off about the Night Butcher."

Cara bit her lip. She knew of a few incubi in the area. One of the guys—well, she'd known him for years, and the thought of him killing—of any of them killing—*no*, she just couldn't see it.

But she couldn't lie to Todd about the men. Not with so much at stake. "You really think the killer is an incubus, don't you?"

Todd turned to face her. His eyes were cop sharp. "I do. A succubus wouldn't have needed a lure—not with the scent you can put out—and sure as hell not if all succubi are as sexy as you."

No two succubi looked alike—not even twins. Her kind came in all shapes and sizes, but they were all created with one purpose—to seduce.

A succubus would never need another woman to act as bait to capture the attention of human men.

If there was a chance that the killer was an incubus—and from where she was sitting, it looked like there was one big-ass chance Todd was right about that—then she had to tell him what she knew. Protecting the private lives of demons would have to come second to saving the humans and finding out who was setting her up.

She held Todd's stare and quietly told him, "I can give you the names of three incubi right now." The men might all be proved innocent—they were good men, two in high positions in the city—but she had to tell Todd their names.

Yet even after she told them, Cara knew that the cops would follow up with Niol and find out if any other incubi were hunting sexual prey.

Niol always knew exactly who was hunting in the city. That was the reason she'd gone to him after leaving Todd's bed. She'd asked him if there was another succubus on the streets.

He'd told her, simply, "No."

She believed him. Because while he might make a habit of lying to others, he'd never lied to her.

Cara realized that all eyes were on her now. She licked her lips. "I only know three, but there could be more."

Gyth stood up, fast.

Todd swore. "You could have mentioned their names sooner."

"I just learned that you were looking for an incubus and not a succubus less than half an hour ago!" Jeez, *she* had been the suspect, and she hadn't thought that a man was involved.

Until now.

"Trey Barker." She said his name clearly.

Smith's mouth dropped. "The newsman from Channel Twelve?"

"No wonder my mom likes to watch him so much," McNeal mumbled.

"Jody Rain."

Todd's eyes widened. "The assistant district attorney?"

A nod. There was a reason why the guy was so well liked by the women on his juries.

"And you've met the third demon."

Todd shook his head.

"Cameron Komak, the bartender at Paradise Found."

"I knew that asshole was too pretty."

Too pretty. A fairly normal description for an incubus.

"Gyth, start checking these bastards," McNeal ordered. "Track 'em down, get 'em in here, and find out everything you can about their lives for the last two months."

Todd stepped forward. "Captain, I told you I wasn't going to be shut out—"

"Brooks, get your ass over to Paradise Found and make Niol tell you everything he knows about the sex demons in this town."

A wide grin split Todd's mouth. "My pleasure, sir."

But she knew Todd would be in for one hell of a fight, because no one *made* Niol do anything he didn't want to do. "I'll go with you," she offered, because she knew the demon didn't exactly have a soft spot for her lover.

But he did for her.

"Good idea." McNeal looked so satisfied that she realized that had been his plan from the beginning.

"Captain . . ." Todd's face flushed with anger. "She's supposed to be in protective custody. I can handle Niol on my own—"

"But she can handle him one hell of a lot better." One finger jabbed at Todd. "You saw her, Brooks, the woman doesn't need protecting, but any fool who gets in her path just might."

Hmm . . . maybe the captain wasn't so bad.

His fist pounded against the desk. "Now, let's get this shit wrapped up before any more dead bodies pile up in our Crypt."

Smith was the last to exit his office. She waited for the cops and the succubus to leave, then she hesitated at the door.

McNeal sat in his chair, and she could feel the heat of his stare on her back. Her fingers tightened around the door knob—and she closed the door.

"Smith?" A thread of worry was in that rough voice.

She turned slowly and rested her back against the blinds on the door, not caring that they bent and snapped behind her. "You should have told me . . ."

He rose from his chair.

"From the beginning. Right after the first kiss." The kiss they'd shared here, in his office.

God, they'd had sex on his desk.

The memories were all around her in this room.

She hated coming to meetings in his office.

And once she left, well, she couldn't wait to get back inside the room again.

She still wanted him.

Damn it, a part of her still loved the asshole. A part she'd tried so hard to kill.

"I didn't want you to leave me." Stark.

"Why not?" He'd just left her in the end.

A muscle flexed along the hard line of his jaw. Her fingers balled into fists. She'd touched that jaw so many times. Felt the rasp of stubble on her palm.

On her entire body.

"Because . . . you mattered too much to me."

She held his glittering stare and saw raw honesty reflected in his eyes. "But *you* walked away."

Now he walked toward her. "You don't know how hard it is to keep secrets from the rest of the world. To live every day, hiding who you really are, and praying that no one else finds out your secrets—because if someone does find out, the *wrong* someone, well, then your life will go straight to hell."

She understood that. If the truth got out, God, she couldn't even imagine what life would be like in the world if all the humans realized what was *really* happening around them.

Yeah, she understood, but understanding didn't mean she forgave. "You didn't have to walk. You could have *told me the truth.*"

"And have you look at me the way you do at Gyth? Or Cara? Or, hell, I guess the way you're staring at *me* now?"

That stopped her cold. Gyth was a shifter, she knew that, but the man had saved her ass. He wasn't evil.

And as for the succubus, well, Smith didn't know that woman, but she didn't *seem* like she was a monster. She just seemed . . . normal.

Like any woman. Like . . . *Jesus, she seems just like me.*

Smith had even found herself admiring the woman's shoes.

"I'm not evil, Nathalia." He was close to her now. So close she could smell the crisp scent of his aftershave.

She'd given him that aftershave.

Her knees began to tremble.

"The bastard who took you—yeah, he was fucked up. As dark inside as they come, but you know, *you know*, we've dealt with human killers who were just as twisted."

She nodded. She'd worked on too many cases to deny the truth of his words. They hadn't all been *Other*. She knew that.

"We're not all bad, baby, understand that—"

"I do." Her nails dug into her palms. She understood, but *it was just so hard*. She woke up most nights, a scream choking her. She'd nearly died in that damn place and when she'd met the killer's stare, she'd known what hell looked like.

She saw Dan's throat work as he swallowed. His hand lifted then, as if he were going to touch her, but then he hesitated.

Pain danced over his face.

And she hurt.

He stepped back. Dropped his hand. "If there isn't anything else, Dr. Smith, I need to get back to work and—"

"There's something else." Her voice shook. Just like her knees.

He lifted a brow.

"I wouldn't have walked away from you." Her chin came up. "I mean, shit, Dan, I didn't care about the fact that you're white—did you really think I'd give a damn that you could go all Dr. Doolittle on me?"

His mouth dropped open.

Satisfied with that response and not really trusting herself to say more, Smith managed to turn around and open the door. Then she walked out, head held high, and didn't look back.

Her mama had taught her long ago how a lady made an exit.

Her mama just hadn't warned her that she had real wolves to worry about in the world, wolves who often wore the flesh of men.

The guards weren't at the door of Paradise Found, and the sight of the empty entranceway had Todd tensing.

Cara stilled beside him. "Todd? What's wrong?"

Everything. Cara shouldn't have even *been* with him then. She should have been in a safe house, protected by several guards—and he should have been casing the place alone. "When we go inside, stay behind me, okay? Just—"

Her bow lips turned down. "*Why . . .*" she drew the word out with obvious impatience, "do you have such trouble with the concept of me being a demon?" She pointed to her chest. "Look, nearly immortal me." She tapped him, a bit harder than he thought was really necessary, right in the middle of his chest. "And weak, human you."

He reached for his holster. He might be mortal, but he was armed. Todd wasn't forgetting for a moment that a potentially murderous incubus might be inside.

And then there was Niol . . .

His fingers curled around the gun. "Me—human, but ready to shoot. And don't forget," he offered her a brief smile, "I'm the one with the badge." Okay, yeah, he knew the woman was strong.

But she was *his* and he wanted to protect her.

Todd pressed a hard kiss to her lips.

Then playtime was over and he stalked toward the door. Cara followed on his heels, her seductive scent wrapping around him.

He pushed on the door. *Open.* No way was this Niol's usual operation.

The cop in him hesitated, but then Todd realized his internal alarm—that system that had never failed him before—it wasn't making a single noise.

What a fucking bad time for his instincts to fail him.

Shoving open the door, he went in with his gun up and his pulse steady.

Chapter 15

"The gun's not really necessary, you know," Niol murmured, not bothering to rise from his table. He sat in the middle of the club, a pair of dark glasses covering his black eyes, and offered them a cold smile. "Back so soon, are we?"

Ignoring him, for the moment, Todd swept his gaze across the bar.

"Where's Cameron?" Cara asked.

The smile tightened a bit. "Not here."

It didn't look like *anyone* else was there. "Where the hell is he?" Gyth had probably already sent a squad to the incubus' house and taken him into custody, but Todd asked the question anyway.

"I don't know." A shrug. "Don't really care."

"*Niol.*" A warning edge had entered Cara's voice. Then the woman stepped around him. Damn it, he'd told her to stay behind him for protection.

She strode toward Niol.

He grabbed her hand. "Don't get too close to him." She might be all warm and friendly with the demon, but it would be one cold-ass day in hell before he felt the same. His gaze snapped to Niol. "I'm here on business, Niol, and I'm gonna be nice and ask you again. Where's Cameron?"

"Why?" Niol's head tilted to the left. Mild curiosity flavored his voice.

"Because we've got an incubus loose in this city who's killed at least three men."

Niol raised his hand. Removed his sunglasses and cast his dark stare toward Todd. "An incubus, is it? I thought you boys in blue were looking for a succubus."

"Things have changed." That was all the info he'd give Niol. "Where is he?"

The black stare slipped toward Cara. "You think Cameron's a killer?"

He read the hesitation on her face. Before she could reply, Todd said, "Every option has to be explored."

"Um." A rumble. "Of course, it does." A shrug of the demon's shoulders. "Don't really know where Cameron is. His shift doesn't start until eight tonight."

"He was here earlier."

Another careless shrug. "He—and the two other bartenders who work for me."

"*Niol.*"

"Cameron came in for his check, okay, Detective? He told me he wasn't feeling too good, then left."

Todd shoved his gun back into the holster. "You don't seem particularly concerned about the fact that your bartender might have killed those men."

Niol's lips quirked at that. "Cameron's not really the killing kind. He doesn't have that instinct."

"You sure about that? Maybe when you look at him, you've just been seeing what good old Cameron wants you to see." He slanted his stare at Cara. "Maybe that's what both of you have been seeing."

Niol's eyes narrowed just a bit. "Cameron lives at 55 Corington Place. Go get him and drag him down to your station, if that's what you want."

No emotion on the guy's face or in his voice. And Cara was quiet now. What was with them? Todd took an aggressive step toward Niol. Maybe he should reveal a little more information and see just what kind of response he could shake out of the demon. "The incubus doing these killings—he's been setting up Cara."

The dark eyes didn't blink.

"Did you hear me? Cara was right—she's being set up—and this bastard is doing it to her! So you know—and what? You don't give a damn? I thought you cared about her! Are you just going to sit there while—"

"*Todd.*" Cara moved forward in a flash, putting herself between him and the demon. A good thing, because he really wanted to rip that guy's head off.

That had to be a surefire way to kill him.

"I do care for Cara." Niol stood slowly, his body a ripple of threat. "I'd never let anyone hurt her." His gaze raked down Todd's body. "Demon or *human.*"

Oh, was that supposed to be some kind of scary warning? Too bad, Todd wasn't exactly feeling intimidated. "Who are the other incubi in the city?"

Now Niol looked amused. "Didn't Cara already tell you?"

"*I'm asking you.*"

A shrug. "The ADA. The reporter. You obviously know about Cam."

"Any others?" He bit out, impatient. "Come on, Niol, you're the one who knows this city. Tell me who I'm up against so that I can damn well make certain Cara is safe."

The black eyes widened in just the briefest show of surprise. True emotion—*finally.* "You care for her."

Well, shit, of course, he did. He wasn't a fucking idiot, but he also wasn't about to have some kind of soul-baring fest with Niol. "I'm doing my job. Stopping killers and protecting the innocent."

"How great for you." The emotion was gone and—again, it didn't seem like Niol particularly cared.

Cara's mouth tightened. "Who else is hunting in the city?"

His gaze raked her. "I must say I'm a bit disappointed in you, Cara. Taking up with a human like him—he's so beneath you."

Yeah, Todd knew that, had known for a while now that he

wasn't good enough for her, but hearing the demon say those words enraged him. Cara was a damn goddess—and he was a detective who'd struggled too long with hell on the streets.

"You don't deserve her," Niol snapped. "You're not strong enough, you—"

Todd was on him. He'd dodged around Cara in a flash and then locked his hands on the demon. He slammed the asshole into the bar. Balled the front of the demon's T-shirt in one fist and raised the other, more than ready to punch the asshole right in the face. "I'd give my fucking last breath to protect her." Yeah, okay, so he wasn't a level-ten killing machine, but he wasn't going to back down from anyone.

And he sure as hell would never let anyone *or anything* hurt his woman.

Not when he'd just found her.

"What would you do for her, cop?" Niol's voice was pitched low, and not a hint of fear or worry so much as flickered in that icy pool of darkness that was his gaze. "Would you lie? Break your precious laws?" His voice deepened. "Would you kill? Die?"

"*Anything* for her." The words were ripped from him, almost helplessly, as Todd found himself unable to look away from that darkness. *Trapped.*

Good. Right answer, human. The words were in his mind, but Todd knew Niol hadn't spoken. Not out loud, anyway.

Shit.

"Don't hurt him!" Cara's fierce demand.

But was the demand given to Todd—or to Niol?

The demon smiled. "You should let go of me now, cop."

He didn't want to. He wanted to punch the bastard right in his smiling lips, but—

Todd found himself stepping back, dropping his hands.

"You're a strong psychic," Niol murmured, "but not strong enough to fight me."

The glasses behind Niol began to shake, just a bit.

"Stop it!" An order from Cara. "I'm not in the mood for your shit right now, Niol."

Neither was he.

"Just tell us the names of the others—"

"The sex demons?"

"*Incubi.*" Todd snarled.

"Um . . ." His lips twisted. "I suppose there could be a few male strays who've snuck into town. I'll have to check my sources—"

"You mean you don't *know*?"

"I'll know by nightfall." Absolutely confident. "Come back to me then, Detective, and I'll tell you the exact location of every incubus in the city."

Not much of a choice. "I'll be here." He glared at him. "And you better have the information." He finally asked the question that had been nagging at the back of his mind. "And where the hell is everyone?"

A shuttered expression. Then, "Hunting your sex demons, of course."

"What?" No way, that would be—

"Really, Detective, I *did* know you were coming." A shrug. "My men will be back, by nightfall as I told you, and we'll find your murderous demon."

Yeah, well, Todd was pretty sure he was staring at a murderous demon.

Why did Cara have a soft spot for the guy? Couldn't she see that he was ice cold all the way to the soul?

Todd straightened his jacket. Felt the reassuring press of his holster against the small of his back. "Let's go," he said to Cara.

Her gaze was on the demon.

A prick of jealousy stirred inside Todd. Those two—they shared a bond, a magic, that he'd never know. Did Niol understand Cara better that he did? Better than he *could*?

"You're making the same mistake she did." Niol spoke to Cara, voice ragged, as if the words had been torn from him.

A slight tremble rolled the floor.

Cara just stared at him. "Am I?"

"Humans can't be trusted, Cara. You saw what happened to Nina."

Oh, no, the bastard had better not be saying he was like the murdering prick who'd attacked her sister. "*Watch it, demon.*" No way would he ever hurt Cara.

"I don't need your warnings," Cara said at the same moment. "And I am *not* my sister."

"No, love." A touch of sadness there. The wisp of a memory in the blackness of his eyes. "You're not." Then he blinked, and Todd wondered if the emotion had ever been there. "But like her, you want something that demons, well, we don't always get to have."

Cara's gaze flickered to him—and Todd saw the yearning in her stare.

For him? Didn't the lady know she already had him? Every damn piece of him, good and bad?

"Don't trust the humans, not with your life." Niol sauntered forward, reached for his glasses. "I'll watch your back, just as I've always done."

Yeah, and he'd be watching her back, too. Front, back, every inch of her. "No one's going to hurt her," Todd said clearly, just in case the old demon wasn't understanding so well.

"No, they aren't." A certainty from Niol. "You protected me, I'll do the same for you." The words were directed to Cara.

Her head moved in a brief nod.

Niol pushed by him. "You know your way out, Detective."

"Yeah, I do." And his way right back in.

Because he'd be back at nightfall—and the demon had better be ready.

The Channel Twelve newscaster's face flushed dark red. "What the hell am I doing in here?" He demanded.

Colin leaned back in his chair and crossed his arms over his chest. "I've got a few questions for you," he said.

If possible, Trey Barker's cheeks became even redder. "I'm

the fucking anchor for Channel Twelve! We've got the largest market in the city—I *am* the damn market! You don't call me in here like I'm some punk off the street, you got that, Detective? You don't send your boys into my office to pick me up, you don't—"

Colin raised a brow as he listened to the guy rant. Yeah, this one looked like an incubus. Too good-looking—well, he *would* have been good-looking if it weren't for that crazy skin thing he had going on. Wide blue eyes. Dimples.

Perfect face, but his scent was off. Too strong. Overpowering.

Incubus.

"I'm a fucking star in this town!" Trey shouted, and his gaze darted around the interrogation room. "I'll have you walking the streets again, giving old ladies parking tickets, I'll—"

Colin exhaled. "I know exactly who you are, Trey. Or rather, *what* you are."

That shut up the newsman. Colin saw the guy's Adam's apple bob as he gulped. Then Trey muttered, "I-I don't know what you're talking about."

"Sure you do." Why was the guy even gonna waste his time with denials? "You're an incubus."

Trey flinched, then managed a faint, scratchy laugh. "Don't be ridiculous, I'm not—"

"You were using your scent on the female officer who brought you in to interrogation." And that annoyed him. "I gave orders only men were to escort you to the precinct, but I should have made sure the women stayed away once you got here."

"I wasn't doing a damn—"

"Bullshit." Colin said calmly. "You were pumping out that sick scent and trying to trick her into telling you about this case." He nodded toward the files spread before them.

"I wasn't read my rights! I wasn't asked if I wanted an attorney present—"

There was one sitting in the next interrogation room. But Colin would get to him, next. "Did you really want the cops telling everyone at the station that you were a demon and you were being brought in because you might be connected to a series of sex murders?"

The guy seemed to shrivel. His shoulders slumped. His chin fell to his chest.

Yeah, that was the way it always was. The ones who blustered the loudest fell the fastest. "So . . ." Colin drawled out the word slowly, aware that his captain and Emily were watching. "You admit you're an incubus." McNeal had called Emily in as soon as the incubi were found. The captain wanted her take on them. McNeal had stationed her in the observation room so that she'd be able to see their reactions to Colin's questions.

And Colin was damn interested in his doc's analysis of the guys. His Emily had a talent for getting good and deep beneath the skin of the *Other*.

"Do you admit it?" he asked again, still keeping his voice easy and calm.

A quick nod from Trey. A frantic glance up at the interrogation mirror.

He knows they're watching him. Just like Cara had known. Demons always made his job so much harder.

"How—how did you find out?" Trey asked.

"Doesn't matter."

"Are you . . . going to tell everyone?" Horror, in his voice, on his face.

"Depends."

Another bob of the guy's Adam's apple. "On what?"

Colin leaned forward. Opened the file and shoved the pictures at the demon. "On whether or not you're a killer."

"Not him," Emily said as Trey Barker vomited into the garbage can.

"You sure? Maybe he's just faking his reaction. He knows we're here, he could be—"

"No! No! I didn't do this!" Trey's frantic voice broke across the captain's words.

Colin began to rattle off the dates of the killings.

"No! Listen, damn it, listen to me!" He shoved the pictures away, looked like he might vomit again. "I didn't do this! Shit!"

"Then give me an alibi. Make me believe you." Colin started talking about the first victim, the date he'd been found and—

"I was in Boston!" Relief lit Trey's eyes. "I was interviewing for a job up there—call them! At Station Seven. I flew up and I—"

McNeal leaned forward and adjusted the volume control for the interrogation room. His gaze met Emily's.

"Not him," she repeated again, and he gave a slow nod.

"Then let's try demon number two."

"I'm not the Bondage Killer," Jody Rain said the minute Colin walked into the second interrogation room.

Colin blinked. Way to cut to the chase.

Jody shrugged. "I'm not an idiot, Gyth. You know what I am and I—" His lips curved. "I know you're not human, and that's about damn all I know."

Colin lowered himself into the chair across from the incubus. Jody Rain was tall, muscled, with skin tinted gold by the sun. No lines marred his face, so his age was close to impossible to guess.

"I wouldn't say that's all you know," Colin murmured, aware that he had to tread very carefully with the ADA. Jody was smart, tough, and not generally one for bullshit. "You know about the Bondage Killer, after all."

One dark brow rose. "I have my sources."

Colin wasn't really one for bullshit, either. "Or else you've been draining men dry in the city." A deliberate pause. "If you're the one killing the bastards, then, the way I figure it, you'd know exactly what was happening."

A bark of laughter. "I'm no killer." The smile still curved his lips as Jody said, "I know about the case because my boss knows—and my boss has a big mouth."

Yeah, that was true enough. Everyone knew the DA needed to learn how to slap a gag order on himself.

"Look, let's just cut the shit, Detective. I know when the men were killed, and I can provide airtight alibis for all occasions." That brow was still up as he murmured, "You ready for 'em?"

"Damn it." McNeal's only response as Jody Rain began to rattle off dates and locations—and, far, far too many names to back him up.

Emily watched the ADA quietly. She could a feel a hum of energy pulsing off him.

This one was dangerous. Much, much more dangerous than the last demon.

She had to point out, "Demons lie well, you know. And they can get humans to lie for them, too. A simple suggestion, the magic of an incubi's hypnosis—people would back up his alibi even if they didn't know who he was."

"Working these cases can be a bitch," McNeal grumbled, rubbing a tired hand over his face. "And, yeah, Doc, I know, if they're strong enough, demons can make the whole world lie for 'em."

Colin continued to grill the ADA about the alibis, asking question after question, and Jody never even came close to breaking a sweat as he replied.

"Shit." McNeal ground his back teeth together. "Where's the last asshole?"

Cameron Komak sprawled back in his chair. His face was hard with anger, belying his easy pose, and the eyes that locked on Colin's were narrowed.

"Where's your partner?" Cameron demanded.

"Doesn't matter." Colin stalked across the room. "You'll be dealing with me today."

Cameron leaned forward, eyes assessing, and after a moment, a wide grin broke across his face. "Good. I'm tired of those fucking humans."

Colin never changed expression. "Wanna run that by me again?"

The demon rolled his eyes. "Come on, I know you aren't like them. I've known from the first night when you came in with the sexy little Monster Doctor." He glanced knowingly toward the mirror. "She's watching me, isn't she? I can *feel* her."

The beast Colin carried roared to life. He clenched his hands—the better to leash the urge to punch the demon.

A laugh, high and grating, burst from Cameron's lips. "Ah, man, come on, I mean—you know what I am, right? If you didn't, well, *you* wouldn't be in here with me. One of *them*"—disgust laced the word—"would be."

Okay. So the guy wanted to play it with gloves off. Fine with Colin. "You don't like . . . *them* . . . too much do you?" His voice was without any inflection. Not good cop, not bad.

Not yet.

"They're weak." Cameron's lips twisted with distaste. "And they don't even know it. They go around, acting like they rule this damn world—and they don't even have a clue what's really happening."

"Or who is really running the show," Colin finished softly.

"Right! Yeah, that's right. They don't know." He nodded quickly, dark hair glinting under the light. "They think they're the smartest, the strongest things ever put on the earth." A hard exhalation of air. "They're dead wrong."

"Hmm." Colin pulled out the photos of Michael House, Travis Walters, and Simon Battle. "And sometimes they're just dead."

Cameron shot back in his chair. "What the hell?" His eyes almost doubled in size as he stared, almost helplessly, at the dead men.

"You hate them, don't you?" Soft voice, no pressure. Colin just watched the demon, and waited.

"I don't even *know* these guys!" Cameron shoved the photos away. "Is this why I'm here? You think I had something to do with those stiffs?"

"Humans," Colin drawled out the word, deliberately not

answering Cameron's questions. "You hate all of them, don't you?"

The demon blinked. "Don't hate 'em," he said slowly. "Just don't really care about 'em at all—"

"So you don't care that these men are dead?"

"I don't *know* them!" His fist slammed onto the table.

Ah, so Cameron had a temper.

And an obvious dislike of humans.

But did he hate them enough to kill?

Colin shifted gears, fast, needing to keep his suspect off balance. "What about Cara Maloan? Just how do you feel about her?"

His lips parted. "Cara? What—"

"How do you feel about her?" Colin pressed.

"I've known her for years. She's like—like a sister to me." Real worry appeared on Cameron's face. "Is she okay? Has something happened to Cara? Hell, I knew she shouldn't be dating that cop friend of yours! I knew it would be trouble—"

"Why?" Still soft.

Cameron swallowed. "Because humans and demons don't mix. Humans can't know anything but fear when they're with us. They aren't strong enough for more."

Colin thought of his Emily, and one word immediately sprang to mind. *Bullshit.*

"He'll hurt her." A fierce shake of his head. "I've seen it happen before. He'll take everything she has to give, then he'll destroy her."

As Cara's sister had been destroyed?

"Humans are *weak*," Cameron repeated. "They can't be trusted."

"So they just need to be killed?"

"No!" Cameron shot to his feet. "Damn it, stop putting words in my mouth! I never said—"

"Why did you think you were brought down here today?" Another rapid-fire question shift.

A blink from the demon. "I-I . . . don't know. Thought that Brooks bastard was trying to start trouble for me—"

"Why?"

"Cause he's always in Paradise, and the guy knows he's not wanted there. Not by Niol, not by me—"

"But he is wanted by Cara."

Cameron's mouth snapped closed. The handsome face turned almost ugly for a moment. "He's what she wants . . . *now*."

"Ah, so you don't think that . . . wanting will last?"

"Not for Cara." Absolutely certain. Then his gaze sharpened. "Wait, you never said—is Cara okay? *Is she?* Or has that asshole cop done something to—"

"She's fine."

His shoulders relaxed.

Colin's gaze raked over the demon's body. "I need you to lift up your shirt for me, Cameron." It was the same request he'd made to the last two demons. Right after they'd finished their explanations and alibis.

He wasn't going to wait for the alibi spin with this guy—he was ready to cut to the chase with old Cameron. No sense listening to false stories from this guy when a simple test would tell the truth about him.

Susan Dobbs had fought like a wildcat. Her knife had found its mark over and over on her killer. And, yeah, demons healed fast, but an incubus wasn't a level-ten, and it would take time—a hell of a lot longer than twenty-four hours–for the wounds to heal.

If Cameron *had* killed Susan, the marks would still be on his flesh.

Flesh that was currently hidden by a dark shirt, a shirt buttoned all the way to the demon's neck, and with long, thick sleeves that covered his arms and fastened at his wrists.

Cameron smirked. "Sorry, man, I don't swing that way."

Colin stared back at him until the little bastard lost his grin. Then he said, "Two ways to do this, demon. You can willingly take off your shirt—or I can take it off for you."

The demon's eyes darted to the mirror. "You can't do that! That's not legal!"

Yeah, the ADA had said pretty much the same thing, *but* . . . Colin let a smile shape his lips, one that showed the tips of his lengthening canines. "I don't really care about legal now. I just wanna stop the killing." Human laws weren't going to apply to this . . . situation.

Cameron's gaze darted to Colin's teeth. "Ah, shit, *shifter.*"

His smile widened.

"Thought you might be a charmer, hadn't pegged you for one of those animals." His hands went to the bottom of the shirt, and he jerked the material up, fast.

Revealing a completely unmarred stomach and chest.

Just like the flesh of the other two demons.

Well, damn.

"Satisfied?" Cameron snapped, and Colin saw the faint tremble in his hands.

"No." The wounds could have been to the killer's arms. Defensive wounds that were deep, and bled like a stuck pig. "Show me your arms."

A curse. Muttering. Todd yanked the shirt down, fumbled with the buttons at his wrists and finally managed to push up the sleeves.

Not even a scratch, on either arm.

"Now are you *satisfied*?"

Colin shook his head. Of the three demons, he sure as hell would have pegged this guy as the killer.

But it looked like there was another incubus out there in the city. Hiding in the dark, and killing at will.

And playing one deadly cat-and-mouse game with his partner's lover.

"I'll be satisfied," Colin said clearly, "when you give me your alibis for the murders." Then he sat down and pulled out his notebook and a pen.

"What? Shifter, damn it, I don't even know when those humans *died*!" He tugged his sleeves into place.

"You will." Colin tapped his pen against the table. "Now let's start with the first victim, Simon Battle."

*   *   *

McNeal looked like he was about to start screaming. His face had flushed beet red, and Emily could actually hear the sound of his teeth grinding together.

"Back to square one," he gritted. "Damn, but I hope Brooks and his demon have better luck with Niol."

Then he turned on his heel and stalked from the room.

Emily turned her gaze back to her lover, her brows pulling down into a frown.

Maybe it was just the demon's distaste for humans that had her stomach clenching. There had been such anger in him when he raged at Colin, and she'd been around Cameron before—actually, she'd known him for years—but she'd never felt that fury from him.

He'd always been seductive. A flirt. She'd known he was an incubus, of course, it would have been impossible for her *not* to know, but the rage in him—

It was new.

And that scared her.

Jesus, but when had he started to hate with such a consuming fury?

That much hatred, if it wasn't faced and *fought*, soon, it could destroy a man . . . or a demon.

Chapter 16

Time to face the devil.

When night fell, as the shadows stretched over the city and seemed to swallow the light in their hungry grasp, Todd returned to Paradise and to face his own personal demon.

The guards were at the door this time. He tensed when he saw them, more than ready to deal with their shit.

He'd been briefed by the captain. Their top three suspects appeared to be in the clear. That meant, as McNeal had told him, "We're back to jackshit with this case."

He needed a break, and Niol was going to give it to him.

"Don't mess with me tonight," he warned, voice cold. Cara wasn't with him. He'd dropped her off at her place, despite his lady's vehement and *loud* protests. But he didn't want her involved in the danger, superhuman powers or not.

The woman was *his,* and the way Todd saw it, as a cop, and as a man, he was supposed to do his damnedest to protect her.

Tall and Scary opened the door for him. "Not stopping you this time," he told Todd. "Boss wants to see you."

Todd grunted and shouldered past him. It was still early enough that the place wasn't packed. A few folks had wandered in, and Todd thought he caught the glimpse of fang as one guy turned away from him, but the club appeared mostly empty.

His gaze darted toward the bar.

"He's not here tonight." Niol's voice, coming from right behind him.

Christ. Todd spun around. Met those dark eyes. "Where is he?"

"I was going to ask you the same question, Detective." Niol cocked his head. "Did your partner decide to arrest my bartender?"

"No." No sense lying—and where was Cameron, anyway? "He's clear." The guy had provided Colin with alibis for the murders. The bastard said he'd been tending bar, and at least four people had already confirmed his story. Sure, the witnesses were humans, so they could have been hypnotized by the demon, but Colin had also told him that the bartender didn't have so much as a scratch on his body—and there was no way the guy could have covered the knife wounds.

It looked like the asshole bartender was off the hook.

"He's clear? Hmm. Interesting." But no interest showed in Niol's shuttered expression. "Cameron didn't check in for his shift. Should have been here at least half an hour ago."

The hair on Todd's nape rose. "The captain told me he left the precinct just before six." *So where was he?* His heart rate kicked up, but Todd drew in a deep breath in an attempt to keep his control.

Cara was okay. While she'd still refused the safe house, she'd finally agreed to accept guards. *Grudgingly* agreed and just to "satisfy you," as she'd said. A patrol car was stationed right in front of her house.

Nothing was going to happen to her.

Besides, Cameron had been cleared. He was an annoyance. Not a killer.

But something was pushing his body into alert mode.

Was it Niol? Or someone, *something* else? "What did you find out?" He demanded, wanting to get his information and get the hell out of there. His skin was prickling, and he wanted to see Cara again.

God, but the woman was always in his mind. Awake. Asleep. Her smell was on his skin. Her taste in his mouth.

He swallowed.

Niol shook his head. "You're addicted, you know."

Not the answer he needed. "What?"

"It can happen. The lure of a succubus is strong. She won't just take your heart. She'll take your soul, and you'll want her so much, you'll stop caring about the pain when she takes and takes."

But Cara didn't just take from him. She gave—passion, trust, strength, power. "You don't know what the hell you're talking about." And it wasn't the demon's business, anyway. "Forget about Cara. She's not yours to worry about."

Niol's face hardened, his lips firming. "Cara is the only thing resembling a family that I have left in this world. Believe me, human, she most definitely is *mine* to worry about."

Okay, now he was about to have to get real physical, real fast with the jerk. And to think, he'd promised himself he'd try to be the good cop tonight.

"I don't know why she chose you," Niol said, and his brow furrowed. "She could have anyone."

Yeah, like he didn't know that fact. But his goddess had chosen him, and he'd thank his lucky stars every day for the rest of his life.

A life he wanted to spend with her.

The realization was as shocking as it was sudden.

"I've got word of a few strays in the area." Niol shrugged. "Nothing too dangerous from the accounts, but—"

Strays? Niol had used that word earlier and—Jesus, what were the demons, some kind of unwanted cats?

"My men will be bringing them soon." Said with supreme confidence. "Then you can play your cop games with them, or you can just stand back, and I'll get all the information you need."

"*I'll* question them."

"If that's what you want." One shoulder lifted. "We'll play it your way."

Todd's gaze returned to the empty bar. Cameron's disappearance bothered him. So he had alibis and he didn't have wounds, that should have put him in the clear but—

But Todd didn't like the guy and he'd always felt that cold shiver of awareness when he was near the demon.

"How long have you known Cameron?" Todd asked as he paced toward the bar.

"Almost as long as I've known Cara."

And that told him jackshit. "How long?"

"Why?"

Still no answer. Niol just couldn't ever make things easy.

"Cara trusts him." But she also trusted the demon beside him—not exactly a ringing endorsement. "I want to know why."

Niol pulled up a bar stool. "Cameron's still pretty young—particularly so for a sex demon." His eyes swept the bar, lingered a moment on a couple swaying on the dance floor, then he glanced back at Todd. "Cameron's mother left his father for a human, and, well, his father—Dominic—he wasn't exactly the nurturing type."

Well, well. McNeal had told him that during the interrogation, Cameron had been all too vocal about his disgust for humans.

Now he knew why.

"His mother raised him some, when Cameron wasn't on the streets, but she had a new family to look out for."

A family that didn't include an angry young incubus.

"Cara found him one night. Brought him to me. We taught him the things he *should* have learned years before."

He could see Cara doing that. Helping the other man. "Was this before or after her sister died?"

"Before. Cameron helped Cara after . . ." Niol clenched his right hand into a fist. "I wasn't much good to her then. Cameron made sure she was all right."

So he should be grateful to the demon, but he wasn't.

Because his alarms were still shrieking in his ears.

"Damn it, when are your men gonna be here?" He wanted to get back to Cara. *Needed* to get back to her.

"Soon." Niol's black gaze flickered over him. "Relax, human. We'll have your killer before the night's over."

* * *

Cara cut through the water, her eyes wide open, her arms moving in fast glides as her feet kicked in quick arches.

She broke the surface, drawing in a deep breath and gazing straight up at the starry night. She'd needed this, needed to wash away the horrors of the day and—

"I thought you liked to swim in the mornings."

The voice had her spinning around, one hand lifting to her chest. Awareness came too late as the man stepped from the shadows.

Cameron stared down at her, the dim lighting from the patio lights flickering over his face. "You like the dawn, don't you? You don't usually swim at night."

Her heart thumped against her chest. Hard. She ignored his question, saying, "Cameron? How did you get back here?" The patrol officers were right in front of her house, and no way would they have just let him stroll around and—

A brief bark of laughter. "Come on, Cara!" He shook his head, a smile flirting around the edges of his mouth. "I'm a demon. It's not that hard for our kind to scale a fence." His gaze flickered to the nine-foot privacy fence that walled in her property. "Even one like yours."

Cara swam toward the ladder.

"The police picked me up today," Cameron growled, smile vanishing as he watched her with eyes that didn't blink. "Hauled me down to the station and that animal *shifter* questioned me."

Her fingers closed over the ladder. The metal felt cool to the touch. She climbed up quickly and reached for her robe, not bothering with a towel as the chill in the night air swept over her skin.

"You don't seem surprised."

She belted the robe in a quick move. "I'm not."

Anger swept over his face. "You're the one who told them about me, aren't you?"

She nodded. "Cameron, I had to! I had to tell Todd about any incubus I knew in the area. Someone's out there killing humans, leaving them with the death brand on their chests."

"And you think I'm that someone?" He shook his head. "Cara—I thought you knew me. Inside and out."

Hurt was in his voice. "Cameron . . ." She stepped toward him.

He immediately moved back. "*Do you think I'm that someone?*"

His voice blasted her. *Well, damn, shouldn't the cops hear that?* Her chin shot up. "It doesn't matter what I think, don't you see that? I knew of three incubi in the city—I had to tell Todd about them all! And if I hadn't, someone else would have. The killings have to stop! I couldn't just let—"

"I never told about you." Almost whisper soft.

"Wh-what?" Her arms wrapped around her stomach as the wind seemed to chill even more. She'd been so warm in the water. But the night had taken a turn on her.

"Not a soul." He raised a hand. Pointed his index finger at her. "I knew what you did to him, but I never told."

Maybe it wasn't the wind that was cold. Maybe the icy tendrils were coming from within her. "Told what, Cameron?"

"That you killed him." Said so quietly, so sadly.

Cara tried taking another step toward him.

Cameron stiffened.

"I didn't kill anyone," she told him, and ignored the pang in her heart. She hadn't, but it had been a damn near thing. "If you're talking about Lance, he killed himself."

She didn't see him move—the guy was on her in less than a second. His hands wrapped around her arms, fingers digging deep. "*Don't lie to me!*" A snarl of rage. "You killed him. You seduced him, slipped into his mind, and then *you killed him!*"

"No, I didn't—"

"He went to you that night. When his body was found, your scent was all over him." He shook her once, hard. "I know what you did!" A vein bulged near his temple. His eyes blazed black.

Not so handsome right then.

"Let go of me." Said calmly, but she wasn't feeling calm.

And if he didn't get his hands off her—right *fucking* immediately—she was going to forget their friendship and show him just how dirty a succubus could fight.

His mouth snapped closed and he blinked. "Cara?"

"*Let. Go.*"

His hands dropped immediately. "I-I'm s-sorry—"

"How do you know?"

But Cameron just shook his dark head. The black began to fade from his eyes.

"How do you know," she repeated again, swallowing and clenching her hands into fists, "that my scent was on him?"

"I went looking for him, after Nina died." Grudging. His eyes were now as blank as glass. "I knew what you'd want to do to him—"

"And how would you know that?" She demanded.

"*Because I know you!* You've been in my head, I've been in yours. I. Know. You." A ragged exhalation of air. "And if she'd been my sister, I would have wanted to do the same thing."

To make the killer pay. To scream. To beg.

To die.

"I was the one who found Lance's body." He backed away from her, began to pace along the edge of the pool. "I got there and caught the stench of death through the door."

"If you were there, then you saw that it was suicide and—"

"People who kill themselves don't have terror frozen on their faces, Cara! They don't die with their eyes wide open and their mouths twisted into a scream!"

Her nails bit into her palms. She felt the wet trickle of blood easing over her flesh. "You're saying—"

"Cut the crap! We both know Lance didn't kill himself, and damn it, I never told what I knew! I never said a word to anyone about you killing him, and you turned and ratted me out to your lover the first chance you got."

"I didn't." Said as softly as his words earlier had been. The wind caught her voice, carried it to him.

Cameron frowned. "You—you said you told him, that—"

"I did tell Todd." And she would make that choice again. "But I swear to you on my sister's grave that *I did not kill Lance.*" Truth time. The air she sucked in tasted bitter. "I was going to, but he got away from me. I *wanted* him dead, so badly—but I did *not* kill him." If he hadn't pulled that knife, she would have.

And she wouldn't have regretted the action for a moment.

He stopped, stared at her. "No, no, you killed him because of what he did to—"

"I didn't." She held his stare, eyes direct.

His hand trembled as he rubbed his eyes. "But if you didn't, who did?"

Niol watched the crowd as the humans and demons and God knew what else began to flow faster into Paradise Found.

There was a tension about him—a tightness around his mouth, a narrowing at his eyes—that worried Todd.

"Shouldn't your men have been here by now?" Over an hour had passed since he'd arrived at the club.

Niol lifted a brow. "Strays probably didn't want to come willingly."

Yeah, he imagined they didn't. "That won't really matter to your men, will it?" Of course, they weren't really men.

"It might slow 'em down a bit. Nothing too severe." Niol's shoulders stiffened then, and his head turned quickly toward the entrance. "*Shit.*"

A redhead stood just inside the door, her purse clutched tightly in her hand, and a *very* determined expression on her pretty face.

Wait a minute, that woman was—

The reporter. Holly Storm.

"Told 'em *not* to let her kind in."

"Her kind?" Was the lady *Other,* too?

"Reporters." Niol spat the word. "As if they ever know what the hell they're reporting."

Holly's gaze swept across the room. Locked on the bar. On them. Then she started marching forward.

The tension rolling off Niol seemed to double.

No way. The demon *couldn't* be scared of Holly Storm.

She stopped in front of them. Kept her eyes on Niol. "I want to talk to you."

He smiled at her then, more a baring of his teeth. "Looks like that's what you're doing."

Her cheeks flushed a bit, and her eyes darted to Todd. "Detective, what are you doing here?"

He tapped his fingers on the bar. "My favorite singer performs here."

"Bull." Her small nostrils flared. "You're just like he is, aren't you? Well, fair warning, I'm going live with this story. It's time the world finds out the truth about—"

Niol laughed. Hard.

Holly Storm glared even harder.

"I've got proof, you know. I've been following this Bondage case every minute. I *know* the killer isn't human. He's some kind of demon—like *you*—and he's sucking the life right out of his victims. He used that woman, Susan Dobbs, that he met *here* to trap them and—"

Todd jumped to his feet. "What the hell did you just say?"

Holly's mouth hung wide open. She clamped it closed and tossed him a hard stare.

"*What* did you just say?" He demanded, patience gone— well, it had never really been there.

"You already know this—"

He sure as hell hadn't known that Susan and the incubus had met at Paradise. Todd growled.

Holly started talking again, fast. "I got sources—*Other* sources—that place Susan here as a regular about four or five months back. She was coming in here plenty, until he"—she glowered at Niol—"gave a standing order that she wasn't allowed on the premises."

What would it feel like to break a demon's neck? Todd wondered as he eyed Niol and clenched his teeth. "You didn't mention that Susan was a visitor here." And the detective who'd been assigned the task of tracking Susan's connections to the case—Flint, a guy who'd been transferred up from Narcotics less than a year ago—was going straight to the top of his shit list.

"You didn't ask," Niol drawled.

"Flint sure as hell did!"

Niol just stared at him then, with those fathomless eyes. Todd remembered, too late, something Niol had told him days before.

A third of the officers on your force are demons. I know what's happening in this town every moment. Don't think I don't.

Hell.

The reporter watched them with green eyes that saw too much. Todd tried to rein in his temper—he sure would have liked to have rip into Niol, but now wasn't the time.

"Seems you've got some pretty interesting sources, Ms. Storm." He'd bet his next paycheck that Susan Dobbs had been one of those sources. "Do you realize that you've been getting information from a killer?"

She didn't blink. "Easy to lay blame on the dead, isn't it?"

"Yeah, real easy—when the dead was a murderer." He paused. "Are your other sources just as reliable as she was?"

Her eyes held his. "Well, at least they're better than the police department's."

Hit. He inclined his head. "Rest assured, we are doing everything possible to make certain that the Bondage Killer is stopped."

"Well, when I go live with my story at ten tonight, and tell everyone in Atlanta the truth about what's happening, *then* I think you'll start *truly* doing everything that's possible."

The woman couldn't be serious. "Lady, you don't even know what you're talking about." He didn't need crap from a reporter right then. The puzzle pieces were all dancing through his mind.

Susan had been in Paradise Found before Cara started singing, but she *could* have still been around when his succubus was performing, if she'd slipped past the guards . . .

Paradise Found.

Had she met the killer here? Seemed a damned good possibility.

A perfect place for humans who liked to play with the dark side.

From the reports he'd read on Susan, the woman had possessed one major dark side of her own.

"I know—I know about the demons," Holly said. "I know they're around us, cops, doctors, lawyers—"

"And you have proof, do you? Hard evidence?" He pinned her with his stare while Niol just well, looked bored. *Nothing new there.* "You think the station director is gonna just let you blast out your tale? Get real, lady. *News Flash Five* would be laughed out of the city." And so would she. People weren't ready to hear the truth yet.

He sure hadn't been. "And you mentioned just the demons— what about the others?"

Her face seemed to pale a bit. "O-others?"

"Yeah, you know, the vampires, the witches, the shape-shifters . . ."

Her eyes widened a bit with each name that he rattled off. He did not have time for this. "Lady, you don't even have a fucking clue about everything that's lurking out there—and do you really think all the supernaturals are gonna be happy that you're planning to blow the lid off their nice, secret world?"

He saw her throat work as she swallowed. Then her gaze shot to Niol's. He smiled at her, a smile that displayed a whole lot of teeth. "I don't care what you do. If exposing the *Other* is your plan, then do it."

Aw, crap. Niol *would* encourage her.

"Every demon in the city will go after her," Todd snapped. Maybe the woman's sources were setting her up for just such an event.

Niol's lips quirked. "I wouldn't."

And that just left what, a couple of thousand who would? Could he not just deal with one crisis at a time? "Go home," he told the reporter, injecting as much steel as possible into his voice. "This isn't a place for you—go back to your safe world and forget about this story."

"And what about the killer?" She demanded, voice rising.

"I'll handle him." And he'd handle Niol, too. "Don't report this story," he told her. "Just go home for the night, and we'll talk tomorrow—hell, I'll answer any questions that you have, *tomorrow*." In the bright, safe light of day.

She hesitated.

"I'm asking for just a little time, Ms. Storm. Just a little more time." And if she didn't agree, well, he'd have to toss her ass in jail—because no way was she airing her story tonight. He'd hate to lock the lady up, but he couldn't risk her blowing his town to hell, and now that he knew she'd been poking around in his case, well, the woman could very well have stirred up a whole mess of danger for herself.

Her lips pressed together. Her gaze flew between him and the ever-watchful Niol. "You promise to answer all of my questions, on the record?"

Ah, now she was pushing too much. "I'll give you an interview." That was as much of a promise as she was going to get from him. And once he got her in the station, he'd work on convincing her to see things *his* way.

Holly exhaled. "All right. You have until tomorrow afternoon, three p.m. If I don't hear from you, I'll go live at five."

And the woman would do it. He'd have to contact the captain ASAP and let him know they had another fire blazing.

She turned around, began to stride away from them.

"Oh, Holly . . ."

Niol's voice was soft, silken.

The woman stumbled to a halt. She glanced back over her shoulder, lips parted.

"Don't come to my Paradise again, unless you're willing to play with the devil."

Todd heard the sharp sound of her indrawn breath. Then she hurried toward the door, almost ran in her haste, and Niol watched her every move like some kind of hungry spider. *Creepy as hell.*

"Leave her alone," Todd warned. "Hell, I thought you didn't even want her 'kind' in here!"

Niol shrugged. "She's human, sexy, and hungry for a walk in the dark." A soft laugh. "Just the way I like my women."

Christ. Todd's stare shot across the room. Landed on the door marked PRIVATE. He pointed toward the door. "I wanna know every damn thing you've been holding back, and I want to know now." Before any more unexpected visitors showed up in Paradise.

Chapter 17

The closed door muted the growing hum of conversation and music from the club. Todd didn't bother to sit down. His hands rested easily at his sides and he pinned Niol with his gaze. "Talk, and, this time, save the bullshit."

Niol lowered his body into the chair behind the desk. "Just what do you want to know, Detective?"

"Why didn't you mention that Susan Dobbs had been in your place before?"

The demon's lips pursed. "Because I didn't want you to think I was involved with the killings. And I'm not, by the way."

Yeah, 'cause the guy just reeked of innocence. "So you've been hindering my case so you wouldn't look guilty?"

Niol frowned at him. "I've been *helping* you."

By withholding information. Right. "Cut the crap, okay? I really don't have time for this shit."

"Then what is it that you want to know?"

"Why'd you kick her out? Why let Susan come in, then suddenly bar the door to her?"

"Susan wasn't a woman who took well to rejection." Level stare. "And she was also very much not my type."

A woman who liked to kill—and she wasn't a perfect match for the demon? "So the lady hit on you, you rejected her, and then told her to keep her ass out of your place?"

One brow lifted. "Pretty much."

Todd felt an ache behind his right eye. "Let me go over this one more time, asshole."

The demon's brow lowered. His lips thinned.

"I've got four dead bodies now, all pointing to a demon's hand." Okay, so Monroe's pointed more to Susan's dead hand, but . . . "I'm staring at a fucking demon who knows what's going on, and I'm getting sick and tired of hearing his jackshit stories."

"Humans die every day," Niol said. "Not really my problem."

"*This* is your problem. The killer brought Cara into his game, and his damn accomplice was in your bar, right in your face and—"

The door to Niol's office flew open.

Todd jerked his head toward the entrance, automatically reaching for his gun.

"What the hell—Cara?" She stood in the doorway, her chest rising and falling quickly, her long hair wet. "What's wrong? What's happened?"

Her eyes were on Niol. *Only* Niol, and she asked starkly, "What did you do?"

The demon stared back at her.

Todd realized that his lady was trembling. He was by her side in an instant, catching her arms and pulling her against him. Damn but her skin was cold. "Cara?"

She looked up at him, and her eyes were pitch black. Her lips tried to curve into a smile, but the sight was so weak that he felt a hard clench in his gut. "Baby, what's going on?"

She blinked once, twice. "I-I need to talk to Niol. Please, Todd, let me talk to him for just a moment. Alone."

The clenching in his gut turned in to a hard kick. "Where are the patrols I put on you?" Because, yeah, the lady was strong, but she wasn't invincible.

And he didn't want to take any chances with her life.

"They're in the club. They brought me here." Her skin was

smooth. No makeup. No jewelry. She wore jeans, a pair of high, strappy sandals, and a light blue shirt. She looked so casual, so very perfect.

And a bit afraid.

No, a *lot* afraid.

What did you do? Her question rang in his ears. He wanted to stay there with her. His mouth opened as he began to demand that she tell him exactly what in the hell was happening.

"Todd, please, this isn't about the Bondage Killer, okay? Just—just trust me a moment and let me talk to Niol."

Trust. So simple to ask for, so hard to give.

He leaned forward. Kissed her chilled lips. He wanted to keep kissing her, until the heat and warmth flowed back into her.

Something had spooked her, and he wanted to find out exactly what had put the fear into his lover's eyes.

He raised his head. Gazed into her turbulent gaze. "I'll be on the other side of the door."

A soft sigh slipped past her lips. "Thank you."

He brought her hands to his lips. Kissed the palms. *Too cold.* His lady wasn't cold. She was fire. Passion.

Not ice.

"You're gonna tell me what's going on. You're gonna tell me everything." He didn't want any secrets between them, not ever again.

A slow nod.

"Cara . . ." A hard edge cut through Niol's voice. "Some things the human doesn't need to know."

"And there are some things that he does." Her voice was fierce. "Wait for me, Todd. I-I'll be right out."

Another kiss. One from her this time as she stood on her tiptoes and pressed her mouth against his. Her breasts brushed against his chest, the soft weight of her body an intimate caress.

Desire reared its head—*as it always did when she was near.*

The urge to pull her against him, tighter, harder, flared through him. But now wasn't the time.

Soon.

She pulled away, and though he wanted to hold her fast, he stepped back. Cast one last look at Niol, then stalked out the door.

Cara's past wasn't going to stop him from wanting her.

And it wasn't going to stop him from trusting her.

Now, if she would just start trusting *him* a little more.

The door closed with a quiet squeak. Cara's heart pounded so hard her body seemed to shake and the fierce drumming echoed in her ears.

"What's got the fear in you, love?"

Love. He used that endearment with everyone, but with her sister, well, she'd thought he actually meant it then.

"I have to ask you a question, Niol, and I really, *really* need you to give me a straight answer."

"You and your cop—always asking questions—"

"Niol, damn it, I'm serious! I need the truth!"

He stilled. "Have I ever given *you* anything else?"

She didn't respond to that. Instead, she got to the question that was ripping her apart. "Did you kill Lance?"

No change of expression. He was far too good at deceit for that. "Why are you asking me this now, Cara? Haven't you known the answer to this question for years?"

Had she? "I thought it was you," she admitted as her hands balled into fists. "I didn't say a word all this time because *I thought it was you.*"

There was a crack in his expression. The barest hint of worry that appeared in his eyes. He rose from his chair. Crossed slowly to her side. "Cara? Love, why are you so scared?"

Niol—he'd always been able to read her so well.

Because she was scared right then, fucking terrified.

* * *

Todd fought the urge to shove his ear against the wooden door and listen for all he was worth. His partner's shifter senses sure would have come in handy right then and—

From the corner of his eyes, he caught sight of a familiar figure.

Todd spun around. His gaze raked the crowd *There*. Striding away from the bar. Black hair. Cocky-as-hell walk as he sauntered toward the back exit.

Cameron.

Oh, no, the guy wasn't getting away from him that easily.

Now that he knew about the guy's history, he had a few more questions for the incubus.

Jaw locked, Todd headed after him.

"I've got to know," Cara said, shaking her head. "Tell me, *did you kill Lance?*"

Niol's hand lifted and pressed against her cheek. "Who've you been talking to, love?"

"Cameron." The name seemed torn from her. "He found the body. Said he caught my scent on him and—"

"*Cameron?*"

She ignored his surprise, her words coming faster and faster as she told him, "It doesn't make sense to me. I mean, why would Cameron have gone to Lance's place? He barely knew the guy." But Cameron had always been protective of her.

Too protective at times.

He'd said that he knew what she had planned—but, damn it, *why go to Lance's apartment?* If he knew that she was seeking vengeance, then why hadn't he just confronted her instead of going after Lance himself? Cara swallowed back the pain and demanded, "Did you kill my sister's lover, or did Cameron?"

"*When did you see Cameron?*" Fierce, growling.

"*Damn it, answer my question!*" A demand as fierce as his.

Niol flinched. "I went to his place, is that what you want? I knew what had happened between the two of you—"

He always knew. *Everything.*

"I went to stop him before the little bastard could hurt anyone else that I—" His jaw clenched, then he growled, "The fool stood in front of me—looked me in the eyes—and told me that he was going to hunt you down and kill you. Just as he'd killed Nina." A pause. "He had to die."

Her shoulders fell. That was as close to a confession as Niol was ever going to give, and she knew that he spoke the truth.

After her confrontation with Lance, she'd known that the man would come after her. As soon as he'd gotten his control back, yeah, she'd figured he would come gunning for her. There'd been so much fury in his eyes.

As much fury as she'd had.

In her heart, when she'd heard the news of his death, she'd always suspected Niol. She knew that he cared for Nina—knew that the bond he felt hadn't disappeared when the two had parted ways.

And Niol was a man long used to the power of vengeance.

She'd suspected, but she'd never spoken of the crime to him.

Now, she knew everything. Well, almost. Niol had killed to make certain she was safe, and Cameron . . . "I-I thought—" She cleared her throat. "When Cameron said that he'd been there and caught my scent, I didn't understand. Didn't know what to think." The certainty she'd felt before about Lance's death had become a confused blur. "I never knew that Cameron was at Lance's place that night, and if he'd been there—well, I thought maybe *he'd* been the one to kill Lance."

Slowly, she uncurled her fists. "I guess—I guess Cam was there—trying to protect me, too, huh? But he just arrived too late—"

"I think he arrived too late, all right." Niol's eyes blazed with a dark fire.

Cara felt the power swell in the air around them. Her breath caught. "Niol?"

"Did he think it was you, Cara? Did Cameron think *you* killed Lance?"

She could only nod.

"Fuck."

The chill she'd felt back at her home iced her veins again. "Niol—what is it?" What was she missing? What—

He pushed her to the side, yanked open the door. "Brooks! Brooks!"

But her cop didn't answer.

And that numbing cold spread within her.

The alley was empty. *Impossible.* Todd tracked his gaze to the left, then the right.

The incubus had to be there. Cameron had exited barely ten seconds before him—and no way was he buying that the guy was powerful enough to just vanish.

A whisper of sound. Fabric. Clothes? From up ahead, near the Dumpster.

Instinct had him reaching for his gun even as he called out, "Cameron Komak, is that you?"

Silence.

The gun was heavy in his hands, a weight he'd grown used to years before. The weapon was up, pointed into the darkness. Just in case the guy hiding wasn't the incubus he was after, he said, "Listen up! I'm an officer with the Atlanta PD. I want you to come out now, where I can see you." Shit, but it was dark. He caught the fast scuttle of bugs as he advanced. "I said, *come out.*" Where were the two officers who'd been trailing Cara? He sure could have used some back up right then.

Every nerve in his body revved up, and with his instincts screaming danger, Todd was definitely on full alert.

So when Cameron stepped from the shadows, a smile on his face and his hands up, the gun never wavered.

"What do you want now, cop? Your partner's already cleared me."

Not really. Gyth had told him that he was suspicious as hell of the three incubi he'd interviewed, but since the guys didn't have any wounds to match the injuries Susan had given her attacker . . .

"Can't a guy just take a piss anymore without the cops getting called in?" Cameron drawled and began to lower his hands.

"*Don't move.*"

The smile widened. "I saw your lady earlier. Cara sure looks good when she's barely dressed, doesn't she?"

A flash of fire heated his veins. *Cara had been frightened.* He'd seen the fear in her eyes.

Had she been afraid of Cameron?

"What did you do to her?" he demanded.

"Not a thing." He rocked back on his heels. Shadows fell over his body, concealing too much. "Where is Cara? Shouldn't she be with you, right by her lover's side?"

Todd's hold on the gun tightened.

Cameron laughed. "Ah, I see. She didn't run to you, did she? After our talk, she went to . . . him. I always wondered about them, you know. Was Niol really in love with Nina? Or was it Cara all the time?"

The bastard was trying to push his buttons. "I want you to step out of the shadows and come fully into the light." The guy's hands were clearly visible, and he wasn't holding a weapon, but Todd knew a threat when he saw one.

"How does it feel to know that when the chips are down, Cara turns to him instead of you?"

The bastard's shitty mind games weren't going to work with him. "*Step into the light.*"

"If that's what you want . . ."

Cameron stepped forward.

The back door of Paradise Found shot open and slammed against the side of the building.

"*Todd!*"

His head jerked at Cara's cry.

"Get away from him!" Niol's order blasted through the night.

Cameron turned to run.

What the hell? Todd's gaze snapped back to him as he sprang forward. "Freeze! Damn it, don't you—"

A woman stepped into the mouth of the alley. For a moment, the streetlight fell over the fire of her hair.

Todd's lips parted to shout a warning.

Cameron barreled into her and knocked her onto the ground. Their bodies tangled, twisted.

Todd rushed toward them, Cara and Niol on his heels and—

The incubus rose with a sneer on his lips and his arms tight around Holly Storm. One hand locked around her neck, the other rose around her waist, so that his fingers pressed right against the middle of her chest. "Don't take another step," he snarled.

In that moment, Todd knew that things had just taken a serious shit turn. He froze, but didn't lower his weapon so much as an inch. "Cameron, I don't know what's gotten you so upset, but you just need to *calm down.* I only want to talk to you. Let go of the woman and let's go back inside." He pitched his voice low, tried to sound soothing. A hard task with alarms shrieking in his head.

The incubus shook his head. Holly twisted against him, struggling, cursing, but he easily held her prisoner.

Too easily, and with that damn demon strength of his, Todd knew that Cameron could snap her neck long before he'd be able to reach the reporter.

Hell. Hadn't he told the woman to *go home?* Why couldn't anyone take a simple order anymore?

The soft tap of a footstep had his eyes widening. He saw Cameron's gaze fly to the left.

To Cara.

Oh, no damn way was he about to risk her. "Go inside, Cara. Go inside, *now.*"

"*Stay, Cara!*" Cameron's scream of fury. "After all, this is all about *you.*"

Aw, fuck.

Todd looked into Cameron's black eyes and saw madness. Fury. Hate.

Love.

All directed at Cara.

Shit. He'd seen that same look before—in the eyes of men who'd murdered their girlfriends. Men who'd slaughtered their wives. Their whole damn families.

He was staring at a killer.

A killer too fixated on Cara.

The signs had pointed to the obsession from the beginning. He just hadn't figured out the case fast enough.

No, the incubus wasn't clear in the Bondage Killings—he was guilty as hell.

Todd took a step toward Cara.

"Stay away from her!" A shriek of fury.

Todd froze. *This bastard's past control.* He knew he had to distract him—no way did he want Komak focusing on Cara right then. "How'd you do it?" he asked, still keeping his voice easy while rage and fear pumped through his blood in a boiling mix. "How'd you fool Gyth? You should have been covered with knife wounds and—"

Cameron laughed. *Laughed.* Then bent to press his nose into Holly's hair.

Her struggles stilled, *as if the woman finally understood just how much danger she was in.* About time.

"It's them." He inhaled slowly, as if savoring her scent. "I never knew how much power humans had."

"Cameron, no . . ." Cara. Horrified. Disbelieving.

"When you take everything from them, the fucking rush is unbelievable." He turned his head, smiled. *Madness.* "I'm stronger now. So much more damn powerful." Another laugh, one that floated on the wind and twisted the air. "And I can heal ten times faster than before."

So fast there hadn't been a trace of the wounds on him. *But Niol had said the guy was sick that morning.* He hadn't fully recovered by then, but—

But he had by the time Gyth found him and hauled his ass into the station.

Shit.

"Cara isn't the one you want." Niol's voice and damn if the demon didn't just saunter forward from the darkness. No weapon, well, hell, Todd guessed that wasn't totally true. If he really was a level-ten, then Todd figured the guy's powers were all the weapon he needed. Niol stopped just to Todd's right, standing nearly shoulder to shoulder with him.

Just what I need, the devil for backup.

The incubus blinked. Shook his head. "Thought it was . . . her." His voice was slower now, a bit confused. "For years . . . thought she'd done it."

"Done what, Cameron?" Maybe if he lunged forward fast enough, he'd be able to break the demon's hold and free Holly. Unlikely, considering how strong the guy was, but if he caught him off guard—

"I thought . . . she killed . . . my brother."

Snap. The last puzzle piece fell into place. Much too late.

Niol had told him, but he hadn't fully understood . . . *"Cameron's mother left his father for a human."*

". . . she had a new family to look out for . . ."

The words played through his head, too loud.

Todd would bet that *new family* included a brand spanking new human brother named—

"Lance." Cara breathed the name. "You—you're the one who told him how to kill Nina!" The agony in her voice pierced Todd like a knife.

The incubus was going down.

But first, he had to keep Cara safe.

And save the hostage.

Hell. Talk about not having an easy job.

Cameron's hold tightened around Holly's neck. "The bitch deserved it! She was always shaking her ass in front of me, acting like she was too good for my touch, but she laid down fast enough for Lance—and then she tried to get him addicted—"

"She loved him!" A scream of fury. Todd flinched, unable to control his emotional response to the pain coming from Cara.

"I told him what she was. Told him just how to stick the bitch so she'd go down and not lift that demon head again—"

"You sonofabitch." Niol's voice was ice cold, where Cara's words had been fired with the heat of her rage. Niol stood, hands clenched, attention fully focused on Cameron. "You sold out your own."

"Lance was *mine*—*my brother,* human, but *mine!*" The blasting rage matched Cara's.

Todd could feel the change in the wind. The slight increase in temperature, the additional pressure of the air on his skin. Power was gathering. But whether it was Cara's, Cameron's, or, *Christ Forbid,* Niol's level-ten hell, he wasn't sure.

And he really, *really* didn't want to find out.

"I was gonna make you pay, Cara!" The fury was leashed now, but Cameron's eyes were still pitch black. The demon was out and ready to kill. "I waited—all these years, *fucking* waited until I was strong and you were weak. I found the perfect way to get back at you." He licked his lips. "I was gonna turn your world upside down and leave you with nothing!"

"You bastard—you did that already! You and your brother destroyed my world when you took my sister away from me. She was all that I had! My flesh, my—"

"He was all that I had! The only one who understood me, the only one who—"

Todd risked a small step forward.

"Don't fucking move!" Cameron's hand jerked around Holly's neck and her eyes bulged as she fought for breath.

"Let her go, Cameron!" Todd fired a glance toward Niol and found the demon standing with his legs braced apart, hands loosely at his sides.

Holly's nails scraped over Cameron's arms. Her legs kicked out, her hips twisted—

"Stop fighting me! I don't need this shit and—" He broke off, lips curving. "Humans are so damn easy," he said, but his voice wasn't the enraged killer any longer, it was the soft lover now.

"No . . ." Cara. "His scent . . ."

Oh, hell. The guy was about to make Holly a *willing* hostage. One that might do just about anything for her captor.

No, he wasn't about to do it—*he'd done it*. As Todd watched, helpless, her struggles stopped. She blinked and stood docilely in Cameron's grasp.

"So damn easy," he repeated.

"Yeah, they are," Niol agreed, voice taunting. "That's why your bastard brother was so quick to die."

"*You* were the one I should have hunted," Cameron yelled. "*You*. I should have known Cara wouldn't have the guts to kill him!"

"Oh, I've got the guts to kill." A promise was in Cara's voice. "Now let the woman go and stand on your own to face us!"

"You really think you can take me down?" A sneer twisted his mouth. "A low-level succubus and a human?"

"Hell, yeah, we can." No doubt in Todd's mind. His gun was still trained on his target. Ready for a head shot.

"*I'm* about to kill you in the next ten seconds," Niol said, voice like a breeze. "So what they can do, it doesn't really matter."

For the first time, Todd saw a flicker of fear in the incubus' eyes. "You move on me, I'll kill the human."

"You're not killing her!" Todd yelled.

But Niol just said, "Either way, you're dying tonight."

Shit. If Niol started using his powers, he was going to have a dead reporter headlining the stories on the news for the next two weeks, and the *Other* world really would be out in the open for all to see.

He turned his head toward Cara. He needed her help, and they'd have to move fast, before Niol attacked.

A distraction.

Her eyes met his. Black as the other demon's, but shining with trust. Her head moved in the slightest of inclinations.

She stared at the reporter, then dropped her voice low as she said, "Fight him. You don't want his touch. You don't like his smell. He's evil, and you want to fight. *Fight.*"

Magic flowed in Cara's voice. Power. Would her suggestion work on Holly? Hell, Todd didn't know—and from the way Komak was responding, it didn't really matter. The bastard was breaking, crumbling apart. Rage flashed in his eyes as—

"Shut up, you bitch! Just shut the hell up—"

"Now!" Todd growled. Komak's focus was divided, just like he'd wanted.

The perfect time to strike.

"Burn, you bastard!" Cara screamed at Cameron, just as she conjured one of her sweet balls of fire and threw it at the incubus.

As the fire spun toward him, Cameron cursed and lifted one of his hands as he struggled to send his own power at the swirling light.

And Holly Storm sprang to life then. She snarled, screamed, and twisted like a hellcat.

Her body fell to the ground when she broke his hold.

Todd was ready. As the flame disappeared into a wisp of smoke, he aimed and fired.

The blast rocked the alley, making nearby car alarms scream in the night.

The bullet thudded into Cameron's head and the demon stumbled back. But he didn't go down. "Fucking human, you'll have to do better than—"

Todd fired again. And again. Now aiming dead center for the guy's chest. Would he still live? Didn't know—Cara had said there was only one way to kill an incubus, and this wasn't it—but he was just trying to do his level damn best to take the bastard down.

The clip emptied and the soft *snick* of the pull on the empty chamber froze Todd's fingers. He stared at the demon—the still-standing demon—heart pounding, blood churning in his body and—

Cameron fell to the ground, landing on his back as a pool

of blood began to spread under his body. Todd reached for the extra magazine he made a habit of carrying. Reloaded the weapon. Cara started forward. He snagged her wrist. "Wait, baby." Her body trembled and he didn't know if it was fear or anger or some twisted mix of the two that caused her reaction, but he wanted to get Komak first—just in case the bastard had any more surprises waiting for them.

The reporter pushed herself up. She stared at the incubus with wide eyes.

"He's not dead," Cara said. "Down, but not dead."

Good enough for the time being. "You okay?" He asked her. She was pale, and still so beautiful that she stole his breath.

Even in hell.

"I-I didn't know it was him. I swear, Todd, I—"

"I know." Soft. If he didn't have a homicidal demon about ten feet away, he would have taken her into his arms and just held her until that fear and pain vanished from her face.

But holding her—that would have to wait for later.

"Niol's the one who figured it out, he knew that Cameron had a brother, just didn't know his name until I told him how—"

The incubus' body moved, just a bit. Twitched.

Damn it, the bastard better not be getting ready to rise like one of those B-movie horror freaks.

And why the hell hadn't the backup boys arrived? Two cops were somewhere in Paradise Found—hadn't they heard the gunshots?

"It's going to take more than you've got to kill him." Niol slipped forward, moving like some kind of cat as his feet made no sound on the cement. "An incubus—"

So much for the bullets, but then, he'd known that. "Can only die in the middle of one of those weird-ass power drains, yeah, I know."

Niol paused. "Cara just tells you everything, doesn't she?"

No, not yet.

After all, she hadn't told Todd how she felt about him yet.

Another twitch of the demon's body. Todd stalked forward, stopping only when he stood directly over the body.

Cara marched at his side.

Niol took up a position near the demon's head.

Holly stood, rather unsteadily, just a few steps away.

And as they watched, Cameron's eyes opened. Blood trickled from his mouth as he smiled—then lunged upward.

Todd fired six more shots. Two into his forehead and four into his heart.

The demon went down once more.

Holly choked out a cry of disbelief.

Todd spared her the briefest glance. "Yeah, and this is what you thought the city was ready to see." He shook his head in disgust. "Still think that, Ms. Storm?"

"N-no, I—"

"Detective Brooks!"

Glancing over his shoulder, he saw the two uniforms storm out of Paradise's back door.

Finally.

"How long will he stay down?" He demanded, knowing that Cara or Niol would be able to tell him. If there was enough time, they could secure the scene, call McNeal and get some kind of transport and security setup ready.

Niol whistled. "Well, considering he's got a hole the size of my fist in his chest and his head's not looking so pretty anymore, I'd say you've probably got a few days before our boy here so much as twitches again."

Good. A savage smile of satisfaction curled Todd's lips. "That's what I wanted to hear." He lowered his weapon. "Back up my story," he ordered softly, realizing there would be a ton of explanations needed.

Niol shrugged.

Holly bit her lip, then nodded.

Cara didn't take her eyes off the body, but he knew she would agree. He could count on her.

He put his gun in his holster. "Stay there!" He shouted to the uniforms. There was no second weapon on the scene, so they'd wonder why the hell he'd blasted an unarmed suspect with bullets—and they'd also probably want to know how the guy was still breathing.

'Cause he was. Todd had seen the light rise and fall of the demon's chest.

"I'm gonna keep 'em back. Cara, hell, baby, I hate to ask . . ."

The faintest of smiles curled her lips. Her eyes were haunted, but a hint of humor slipped over her face. "You wouldn't be asking me to distract police officers, now would you, lover?"

God, but she was gorgeous.

"Just this once . . ."

Her head inclined. After one final glance, she turned away from the demon. Just turned her back on the man who'd tried to set her up for murder and who'd arranged the death of her sister.

Todd couldn't help it. The detective knew he should stand back, keep it professional with so many eyes watching them, but—

He pulled her into his arms. Kissed her and tasted the sweetness of her fire on his tongue.

Her hands curled over his arms. Chilled, but so right.

He lifted his head. Forced himself to take a deep breath—but he just smelled her.

"Go." A whisper that slipped from the lips he'd reddened. "Do your job. We'll talk—later." There was the faintest glint of moisture in her eyes and he knew she was fighting for her own control.

Hell, the woman had just faced her sister's killer with stunning fury. Yeah, he *knew* she'd be able to keep her control now.

Giving a grim nod, he let her go. Then they began walking toward the officers and his nose twitched as he caught the deepening scent of her pheromones. Oh, damn, but this had better—

A sudden blast of flames erupted behind them, and the fury of the fire ripped through the alley with the force of an explosion, sending Todd and Cara flying through the air.

Chapter 18

Cara hit the ground hard. She felt blood pour from her knees, felt the trickle of the liquid on her palms. As fast as she could, she shoved to her feet, and her first thought was of—"Todd!"

Then she saw him, rising a few feet away from her, face cut, hands dripping blood just like her own were.

Relief had her shaking.

Her gaze flew toward the back of the alley, but she knew what she'd see. She *should* have known all along, really.

"*Christ!*" Todd's voice was stunned and she knew that he'd just caught a glimpse of Cameron's charred body.

He took off running, heading straight for the still-flickering flames.

Cara didn't move, but her gaze tracked over to the left. Niol rose, his arms around the pale reporter. Cara's eyes met his.

She hadn't told Todd, because it would have been impossible for him to manage the feat, but there *was* a second way to kill a succubus or an incubus. A way only the most powerful demons could master.

Complete incineration, an incineration that started from within the body. If the fire began in the heart, then blasted outward, the demon could be destroyed.

But there were so few who could manage that much power. *So few.*

Niol held her stare.

He'd loved her sister, in his way. And he'd wanted vengeance just as she had.

A vengeance he'd achieved.

A vengeance he'd given to her.

Cara's head moved in the briefest of nods. Her heart ached as she thought of Nina. Of the life that had been cut far too short by the darkness in demons and men.

Justice had finally been given to her twin. Perhaps now, the nightmares would stop.

And Nina could rest.

"Holy shit!" A stunned male voice.

Ah, the other officers. She'd nearly forgotten about them.

Todd jerked off his shirt, and he battled against the flames. Didn't really matter—she knew the fire would die away in moments.

But the two uniformed officers, they *did* matter. She closed her eyes, let her power stir inside her, and Cara pushed her scent hard into the air. Her eyes opened—one last look. Then, for the second time, she turned away from Cameron. The man she'd once called friend. The man who'd tried to destroy her.

This wouldn't be the last time she would think of him, she knew that. Turning away—it didn't mean she could shut him out or stop the memories. Her heart ached, her soul raged.

But it was over.

He was gone.

Nina was at peace.

Cara took careful steps toward the cops. The heel of her left shoe was broken, and her clothes were torn. She probably didn't particularly look *sexy*, but how she looked, well, that really wasn't the issue. The closer she got to the men, the more dazed their expressions became.

"Gentlemen," she pitched her voice low, injecting a strong dose of hypnotic power, "remember this. When you arrived at the crime scene, the body was already burning and Detective Todd Brooks was fighting as hard as he possibly could to stop the flames." Truth mixed with deception always worked the best.

Good-bye, Cameron. Hope you enjoy the hell that's waiting . . . wonder if it's as hot as Niol's flames . . .

Sometimes, fate had a way of giving people exactly what they deserved.

"*Shit.*" The next evening, McNeal sat at his desk, glaring down at the neatly typed report before him. "That woman from *News Flash Five* saw everything?"

Todd cleared his throat. "Uh, yes, sir." Since she'd been less than five feet away and had wound up with singed hair, it would have been hard for Holly Storm to avoid the whole self-combusting incubus scene.

McNeal's eyes rose, then pinned Todd in his chair. "And she's gonna keep quiet?"

He hoped. "I think so." The woman had been shell-shocked, but before the ambulance attendants loaded her up, she'd grabbed his hand and told him, voice hoarse from the fire and Cameron's powerful grip, "You're right. No one's ready for this."

"And the two uniforms?" McNeal demanded. "Billy Mane and Tyler Johnson? They're both backing up the story about the fire?"

With a little help from Cara. "Yes."

McNeal grunted.

"Todd secured the scene," Colin said. "He did the damn best he could under the circumstances and—"

"Hell, stop defending him, Gyth." McNeal closed the report with a snap. "I *know* he secured the scene the only way he could."

Hmm. Nice of Colin to back him up. Maybe he'd finally forgiven him for the whole your-lover-might-be-a-killer thing.

The bastard *should* have forgiven him—Todd wasn't holding a grudge against Colin for suspecting Cara. Mostly because he'd thought she was guilty in the beginning, too.

They were both idiots.

But it looked like they'd officially gotten past the twisted shit in their lives and gone back to being a team again.

"I just want to know," McNeal growled, "if Brooks here thinks that bastard Niol was involved in the torching." His lips pursed. " 'Cause that part wasn't in this neat little report."

"Sir." He kept his voice calm. "This *is* the report that you want presented to the DA and the mayor, correct?"

Another grunt.

"The report tells, clearly, that when I entered the alley, I discovered Cameron Komak, burning. I tried to put out the flames. Several other witnesses"—that would be Niol, Cara, and Holly Storm—"soon entered the alley. The police were notified. Unfortunately, the heat from the flames was so intense that Cameron died on scene."

"And when I went to Cameron Komak's house after I was informed of the incident," Gyth picked up the story with barely a pause, "I found undeniable evidence to link him to the killings of Simon Battle, Travis Walters, Michael House, and Susan Dobbs." Now, that part was actually true. The guy had made a whole fucking wall in his place dedicated to the crimes. He'd had clothing belonging to the victims, photos—a fucking sick shrine.

Gyth shook his head. "The man apparently had an obsession with Cara Maloan, and in his twisted mind, he was punishing Cara by attacking the men who showed interest in her."

"And framing her for their deaths, right." A hard exhalation of air from McNeal "Nice little package you've got for me." He leaned back in his chair. "Nice pretty bow you put on the case."

Todd's shoulders stiffened. "Komak was the one who tied things up with that damn wall." He'd gone to the apartment after Gyth had notified him and seen it for himself—*fucking insane.*

"This report will be fine for the mayor and the DA and any of those other vulture reporters who want info on the case." McNeal picked up a pen, began to tap it casually against the desktop. "But you left out a few details . . . like, oh, say, *just how the hell did Cameron Komak catch on fire?*"

He pissed off a demon. Todd didn't speak those words, because he didn't have proof. He had a suspicion that went straight to his soul, but there was no way anyone would ever be able to prove Niol's involvement. "We don't know how the fire started. Smith's looking at the body. She'll be in soon to brief you on what she's got."

"And what about his alibis? They checked out and—"

"The alibis were given by humans," Colin reminded him.

"And Komak planted the memories in their heads," Todd said. "They never actually saw him those nights—he just used his demon power," which was pretty damn scary, "to make them *think* they had."

"*Hell.*" Disgust coated McNeal's voice. "These cases just get harder and harder."

Todd shrugged. " 'Cause the criminals are a different breed." One that he'd be ready to face now, head-on.

He rose slowly, pushing up from his chair. He was bruised and sore as hell from the fall he'd taken in the alley, and he couldn't wait to go home and curl up in bed with his succubus.

"Where the hell are you goin'?" McNeal demanded.

"Don't you know, Captain?" Colin asked, and a smile lifted his lips. "The man's got a date waiting."

"Hmm." McNeal's dark brows bunched. "With the succubus?" No censure. Just curiosity.

Todd gave a stiff nod.

"Be careful with that one, Brooks. A woman like her, if she gets away from you, you'll spend the rest of your life kicking your own ass."

Then Todd was the one to smile. "Don't worry, Captain, I don't have any intention of letting her go."

"Um." He tracked his gaze over to Colin. "You gonna finish filling me in?"

A nod.

McNeal jerked his thumb toward the door. "Then get the

hell out of here, Detective. I think you've more than earned some rest . . . or a night off with your lady."

Todd didn't have to be told twice.

He found her sitting at the edge of her pool, staring down into the glowing water. She wore a loose, flowing top and a pair of dark shorts. In the faint light, her pale legs gleamed.

He'd kept his distance from her all day, knowing that the media glare would be on the case, and needing to wait until he'd presented his report to the captain before he got close to her again.

But, at least for him, the case was over now. The killer had been caught.

Killed.

Not by his hand, and not in a way that he understood. Because he could have sworn when he battled those flames—they had been coming from *inside* Cameron's body.

Impossible.

Or, at least that's what he would have thought, once.

Cara didn't glance up at his approach, but he saw her shoulders stiffen, and he knew that she was aware of him.

He walked toward her slowly, stopping only when he was close enough to reach out and touch her—and he did, lifting his hand to smooth over the long silk of her hair.

"Are you . . ." her voice, husky, sexy, made him ache, "going after him?"

Todd blinked. Not the question he'd been anticipating.

Cara turned her head, glancing over her shoulder so that their eyes met. "You know it was Niol, don't you?"

"Yes." He'd known the minute he saw the flames that Niol was responsible. When Cameron had threatened to kill the reporter, Niol had been too calm, too certain when he'd said, "*Either way, you're dying tonight.*"

And Cameron had died.

But Cara needed to understand something. He stared into her eyes, and told her the truth. "If I could have killed Komak, I would have." Because the bastard had gone after her. Killed her sister, and, in his gut, he knew Cameron wouldn't have stopped until Cara had suffered the same fate.

And anyone who threatened his woman's life—well, Todd intended to take them down, by any means necessary.

Yeah, he was a cop. But he was also a man.

"I can't prove that Niol was behind Cameron's death." And no matter how long Smith looked at the body, he doubted she'd find any evidence to link the demon to the crime.

Her feet lifted from the water's edge. After a moment, she rose slowly and turned to stand before him. "You're going to let him go?"

A grim nod. "For now." If the bastard fucked up in the future, he'd go after him. But, for now, with this case—well, there really wasn't a choice.

"And what about us?" Her eyes matched the darkness of the night. "Now that the case is over, are you just going to let us go, too?"

What? He grabbed her arms, holding her tight and helplessly noting the softness of her skin. "Is that what you want? To get rid of me now?" God, he hoped not, because if she left him now—

He'd never be the same.

"Am I what *you* want?" She asked, voice just as hard and desperate as his had been. "Am I really what you want, Detective Todd Brooks? A demon to take home to the family? A woman who will always be different, one who will always—"

"Be mine." Not a question, a statement of fact. In his heart, she was his. Would be his. Always. "And I don't really give a shit about what the rest of my family thinks. Not that I've got much of one left, anyway." A few cousins, spread across the United States. "Hell, baby, *your* family is the one I'm more concerned about." How would they feel about having a human in their fold?

"All day," he continued, "I've thought about you. Wanted you. Wanted to touch you and taste you and—" He broke off, because he had to feel her mouth under his. The kiss was too fierce, bruising in its intensity, but she met him, her lips feeding on his with a wild hunger—a hunger he knew well.

The thought of losing her—it ate away at him. His hands worked on her clothes, all but yanking the fabric away. Todd needed to feel the softness of her flesh against his, needed it more than breath right then.

He had to show her how good it was between them. How good it would *always* be.

But her hands rose and pushed against his chest. His head lifted.

"Todd . . . it's more than sex to you, isn't it?"

The question pierced his heart. "Do you even need to ask, baby?" This time, when he kissed her, his lips were soft. "You're *in* me, Cara. So deep inside me. Hell, I didn't think anyone would ever know me like you do." And he hadn't believed he'd ever need anyone the way he needed her. "I told you once that I would follow you into hell." His hands lifted and he framed her face. "I meant that. I'd do anything for you."

"You're not—not just saying—" She stopped, shook her head. Her face was wistful, her eyes watchful.

He tightened his hold on her. "Don't you understand, baby? You're mine—the woman I've always wanted, and never thought I'd find." Todd had to swallow before he said, "I know I should be better. More, for you, but I'm just a man, a man who touched the best thing he could have ever imagined one night." Time to drop his pride. "I love you, Cara. Love every part of you, and if you'll let me, I'll spend the rest of my life showing you just how damn good a human and a demon can be together."

Her lips curved upward slowly, and the darkness in her gaze seemed to lighten. "You love me?"

"More than anything in this world or any other." Stark truth. And, damn, but he was praying she felt even a fraction of the same way about him. She *had* to feel something, and if she gave him enough time, he'd show her how great they could be together.

"I know things started the wrong way between us." Extreme understatement. "I wish I'd met you without the case. Just seen you singing one night." He would have felt the same way about her, but the suspicions and accusations wouldn't have been between them.

Her right hand lifted, and she traced the lines of his face. "Do you know that before I met you, I was ready to give up sex?"

He slowly shook his head, shocked. Could a succubus even do that?

She laughed softly. "Then I met you, and everything changed for me. *Everything.*"

He hoped she meant—

"I love you, Todd Brooks, and I will keep loving you for all the very, very long years of my life."

She loved him. Fucking miracle. He crushed her against him, drove his tongue deep into her mouth, and tasted the paradise he'd been craving.

It should have been a soft, tender mating. Their feelings were spoken now, real, but the emotions were too raw, as was their hunger.

Their hands fought, ripped at the clothing. Fabric gave way quickly beneath the assault.

Then his mouth was on her breast. Licking, sucking, kissing, loving the sweet flesh. His hands shoved down her shorts. Tore away her panties to find the creamy flesh that waited for him.

Her fingers unsnapped his jeans, pulled down the zipper, and his arousal sprang out, hard, ready, so eager for her that moisture coated the broad head of his cock.

There was no waiting. He stumbled over to the chaise longue. Nearly fell onto the cushions and dragged her down over him.

Her thighs were parted, so when she fell onto him, she straddled him and her hot, wet sex slid over his cock.

Another kiss. Lips, tongue. Tasting. Taking.

His hands touched her—frantic touches, caresses all over her flesh.

Her fingers wrapped around the length of his erection. Squeezed, stroked, and had his eyes rolling back into his head.

His lips tore from hers. "Can't . . . wait."

Her smile would have tempted a saint—and it sure as hell tempted a cop. "Good."

Then *she* was positioning his length, lifting her hips, and pushing the head of his arousal into the tight opening of her sex.

He thrust up, jerking his hips off the chaise at the exact moment her hips drove down onto him. Their moans filled the air as his cock lodged deep within her.

When her sex clenched around him like a hot fist, there was no stopping him. Todd's hands dropped to the cement for balance and his hips began to piston up against her. Harder. Faster. The night sky glinted above—a million shining stars winked over Cara and he thrust, sinking into the hottest paradise he'd ever know and starring at stars—and his succubus.

Her eyes were shining. A glow inside the darkness. Her hand was on his chest, right over his heart.

The heart that had always been hers. He just hadn't known—

Her sex contracted, a ripple of movement that had Todd gritting his teeth and choking out her name.

Release was moments away, but damn it—he never wanted the passion to end.

Never wanted to leave her.

Her thighs clamped over his legs. The site of her bare breasts tormented him, and his head jerked up. Todd caught one nipple in his mouth, then slammed deep into her again.

The warmth of her palm seared his skin. Power filled the air. Danced over his body.

The climax hit him, and the world exploded into a shower of those stars he'd seen. Millions of stars. Pleasure flooded him as he pumped into her, driving as fully into her honeyed clasp as he could go, and filling her with the hot essence of his release.

Her magic roared through him and she called his name. Her hips bucked, her sex clenched, and the quiver that shook her body shivered through him.

He licked her breast as the aftershocks of pleasure hummed through his system.

His hands rose from the cement and wrapped around her.

Todd's head lifted and he stared up at her face.

His Cara.

The spark of her energy danced in the air, the spark that even now was heating his flesh and sending energy pumping inside him.

When he kissed her again, he tasted the magic and he tasted the power of the woman he'd gladly fight the devil to possess.

And, well, perhaps he already had.

The bull pen was all but deserted when Smith knocked lightly on Danny McNeal's office. It was well after 11 P.M., but she knew he was still working. Though the blinds were drawn in his office, faint light glowed from beneath his door.

"Come in." His voice was gruff, hard, as it usually was.

Her shoulders straightened and her left hand rose automatically to smooth over her hair.

Then she walked inside, keeping her head high and her strides long and easy.

She saw his eyes widen, just the tiniest fraction, when he caught sight of her.

"Dr. Smith."

Ah, so she was back to *doctor*, hmm? Smith placed her report onto his desk. "My notes on Cameron Komak's body."

He dropped his pen. "That was fast."

Well, there hadn't exactly been a lot left to work with.

"What's the determination?"

Now this was the tricky part—but she had a feeling she'd probably be dealing with a lot of tricky cases from now on.

The thought wasn't as unsettling as it had once been. In fact, now, well, the cases almost seemed . . . challenging.

The visits she'd been secretly having with Emily were starting to pay off.

All of the *Other* weren't evil. She was understanding that. Accepting that.

Smith met his stare directly. "Off the record, my belief is that Mr. Komak self-combusted."

He didn't blink. "Self-combusted."

"Um. The fire appears to have originated internally—as opposed to an external stimulus like gasoline or—"

McNeal held up a hand. "Go back to the internal part."

Simple enough. "I think the fire started inside Mr. Komak's body. Specifically, in the region near his heart."

"Shit."

Yes, she'd expected that response. He pointed toward her notes. "That's not in the report, is it?"

"My notes list a fire of undetermined origin." And that was true. She didn't know how the fire had started—just *where* it had flared to life.

"Thanks, Doctor. That should be all I need, for now."

A dismissal. Her eyes narrowed. "Does that mean the case is closed?"

"My detectives discovered indisputable proof to link Komak to the killings." His lips twisted. "Shortly after Komak died from that fire of *undetermined origin*, Gyth searched the guy's apartment and found one of those hell walls that the serials like to keep. So, yeah, the case of the Bondage Killer is closed."

"But there will be more, won't there? More cases like . . . this."

His chair squeaked as he rose. His shoulders were so wide, so strong, and his face—she'd always thought he had the face of a warrior. "There have *always* been cases like this. The only difference is that now we aren't transferring them away from you anymore, they're coming *to* you." He stalked around the desk. "That gonna be a problem for you?"

The *Other*, they still frightened her. Or, some of them did. Whoever had managed to burn Cameron Komak from the inside out, that guy scared her, but Smith realized she had to start trusting the supernaturals that she knew well. Like Colin.

And it was definitely past time for her to trust the one she'd let into her heart so long ago. "They won't be a problem." Deliberately, she looked him over, running her gaze from his gleaming head down to his too-big feet. "But you will be."

Her eyes returned to his face just in time to catch his wince. "We've been over this. I'm not gonna bother you, personally, anymore, Dr. Smith—"

"Ah, see, now *that's* my problem." She closed the distance between them. Wrapped her hands over his shoulders. "I want you to keep on bothering me." She kissed him. Mouth open, tongue ready.

His arms locked around her, jerking her tight against his chest—his heart.

Just where she liked to be held.

The kiss was hungry, wild, and held a desperate need—his need, *hers.*

Oh, God, but she'd missed him.

Her hands pushed between them, began to fumble with the buttons on his shirt.

McNeal dragged his mouth from hers. "Nathalia . . . Hell, babe, don't tease, don't let me think you want me again when—"

"I've always wanted you." Her nails stilled against the white front of his shirt. "Even when you were such a damn idiot." Because a little thing like her man talking to animals, well, that wasn't going to push her away.

Time to claim her lover again.

She glanced over at his desk and didn't even try to stop the smile that rose on her lips. "Feel like taking a walk down memory lane?"

His hungry growl was more than answer enough for her.

Cara watched Todd while he slept. Stared at the shadows beneath his eyes and the faint stubble on his jaw.

The sun rose slowly, and still she watched him. There was more that she needed to tell Todd, and she knew that when his eyes opened and he stared at her in the morning light, it would be time to share another secret with him.

She'd never told another human what she would tell him, but Todd deserved to know.

So when his eyelids finally opened and he gazed at her with sleepy brown eyes, she felt a moment of fear.

Then he lifted his hand and smoothed his fingers over her cheek.

He won't leave. The knowledge was certain in her heart.

"Todd." His name whispered from her lips. "I need— there's something I have to tell you."

He smiled and rolled onto his side. They'd made love again during the night. Sweet love, slow.

"I—you haven't noticed it yet, but you will, soon." She licked her lips. "Being with me, if we stay together, long term, um, you're gonna start seeing some side effects."

The sleep disappeared from his gaze as his body began to stiffen. "Side effects?"

"Uh, yeah." This wasn't the easiest conversation to have with a lover. She'd known that, and put it off as long as possible.

"Just what kind of side effects are we talking here?"

Okay, he didn't sound overly worried. Good. "You've never asked me how old I am, Todd."

"You're twenty-eight. I saw the age on the license we found and—"

"I'm not twenty-eight."

He blinked. "You look twenty-eight."

Yeah, and she'd keep on looking that way—for a long time to come. "The power that succubi get from sexual energy— well, you see, part of that power—it renews us."

A line appeared between his brows. "I don't think I'm following you, baby."

"Okay, follow this." A quick breath. "Sex for a succubus, it's like dipping into a fountain of youth." And that was one of the reasons her kind were so hard to kill. Frozen forever at a perfect age of health and vitality—yeah, it was hard to take 'em down.

His eyes widened and a soundless whistle passed from his lips. "Holy shit." Another whistle, a quiet one this time. "You're saying—you're some kind of immortal?"

Something like that. "When I'm with you and we share the power, you get dipped into that fountain with me." A pause. Okay, she was starting to sweat. "If you keep staying with me, and I don't take, and we both exchange the power—your body will start renewing like mine." He'd never be as strong as she was, because he hadn't been born an incubus, but when she poured the magic and power into his body, he would renew the same way.

They wouldn't live forever. She wasn't a true immortal. There were few of those guys left. But she and Todd, well, they'd sure live more than their share of days together.

"Those side effects I mentioned—well, you won't have as many gray hairs and wrinkles and—"

"You're fucking kidding me!" He'd shot upright and astonishment was clear on his face.

Cara shook her head. "No, I'm not."

She gave him a minute to take that in. Cara rose beside him, tugging the sheet up to cover her breasts.

His lips pursed. "Hmmm. Are women gonna start following me around now because my scent is supersexy?"

They'd better not, or she'd kick their asses. "No. The longer life span and physical appearance—those the only changes you'll have." The only ones she'd ever known a human mated with one of her kind to have. The renewing power was secret and sacred, and custom dictated that it was to be shared only with the mate of a succubus or an incubus.

Todd *was* her mate, forever.

"So now you know another of my secrets," she told him, and raised her chin. "And the choice to stay or go," *because it wouldn't be easy, having a longer life when so many that surrounded him—so many that he cared for—weren't able to walk the earth with him for those days.* "That choice is yours."

"Go?" He repeated, then he caught her arms, rolled fast, and pinned her beneath him on the bed. "Trust me, baby, there's no going for me." His kiss was warm and hungry. "I'm right where I want to be, with the woman I want, for the rest of my damn life."

Her heart slammed against her chest at his words. "Are you sure? Think about it, Todd. I can't just take from you— it's not an option." Long-term mating with a succubus without the exchange of power would result in death for a human. "You'll be different. From your family, your friends." He needed to understand the road he would take with her.

"We can end things now," she told him. "Before you change, before anything else happens—"

"Too late." Said simply. "I've already changed."

What? No, he hadn't—

"When I met you, I changed." He shook his head. "I don't ever want to go back to being the guy I was before. I want to spend the rest of my days—however many I get—with you."

Oh, but that sounded good to her. She tried to smile, because it was either smile or start crying like a baby. "Then I guess you're okay with my latest secret, huh?"

His lips hitched into a half-smile, a smile that showed off the dimple she loved so much. "Baby, I'm fine with all your secrets—and I *know* you've got more."

Her breath caught. "Do you?"

"One day, I'll discover them all." He pressed a kiss to her lips. "Every." Another kiss. "Last." A swipe of his tongue. "One."

"You . . . ah . . . know my secrets."

"Not all of them." Whispered against her mouth. "But one day, one day I just might . . ."

Then he lowered his head and pressed his lips against the sensitive skin of her neck, and the passion Cara felt for Todd rose once again in her body.

As she arched against him, Cara realized Todd was right. She did have a few more secrets. Nothing *too* dangerous.

And maybe—maybe he *would* discover them all.

But first, well, first she'd make certain she discovered his.

She could hardly wait for the games to begin.

Good thing they had plenty of time ahead of them.

Long days, longer nights, great sex, and a few secrets.

Things might get a bit wild for her and her detective, but that would be just fine for Cara.

In fact, that was the way life for a succubus *should* be.

Wild, sexy . . . and so damn satisfying.

Try MAXIMUM EXPOSURE,
Alison Kent's latest,
in stores now from Brava . . .

"Tell me what you're hoping to find, and I'll tell you everything that I know."

Finn McLain lowered his digital Rebel with telephoto lens and glanced at the woman who'd joined him at the bistro's very small table for two—the table where he'd been working his coffee more than his camera since setting up shop at nine.

She was hot, Miami hot, Latina hot, hot like chilies beneath the Florida sun. Exotic. That was the word. No. Sizzle. She sizzled. Was sizzling. Water droplets on an iron skillet. Empanadas scorching his tongue.

He set the camera on the scrollwork tabletop, stretched out his legs, and wishing for a glass of water, laced his hands low on his belly. Outwardly, he was cool, a pro. He knew his business.

It was his insides that were scrambling to figure out how badly he'd fucked up. If she'd pegged him as more than a tourist, how great was the chance that he'd also been made by his mark?

His dark lenses hiding anything she might see in his eyes, he finally came back with, "Guess you won't buy it if I say I'm just taking in the sights?"

She shook her head, her hair a colored mix of brown sugar and honey. "You want to sell me on anything, sweetheart, you'll have to do a better job than that."

"What gave me away?" he asked, still not admitting to any particulars.

She settled into the chair, which looked like it was fashioned from licorice strings, crossing her legs and revealing a whole lot of thigh where her skirt fell open at the side. And not just thigh, he quickly came to realize, just as quickly tugging his gaze from all that bare skin back to hers.

"This is the second time this week I've seen you and your phallic equipment in front of my store," she said.

"You don't say."

She inclined her head, indicating the designer boutique across the way. "Either you're a competitor looking to see what's selling, or you're keeping tabs on someone who frequents the area." The area being a ritzy and exclusive shopping spot near Miami Beach. "Which is it?"

He reached up, pushed his sunglasses a half inch down his nose, glanced over, and winked. "I just like taking pretty pictures."

She narrowed her eyes, her long dark lashes as thick as the bristles on an artist's brush. "More like you don't surveil and tell."

He shrugged lazily. He wasn't one to commit. "You mentioned telling me everything you know. Whenever you're ready . . . I'm all ears."

She looked across the street, where cars no longer drove, where trees now grew in beds lush with shrubs and tropical flowers, her mouth twisted up as if she wasn't sure she wanted to say anything at all.

He studied her while her attention was elsewhere, certain she knew exactly what he was doing, while not the least bit bothered by the invasion of her privacy.

It was ten a.m. It was early October. Meaning it wasn't hot enough or far enough into the day for her to look as disheveled as she did.

She'd said the store across the street, Splash & Flambé, was hers, and that led him to believe that she had an intentional reason for looking like she'd just tumbled out of bed, her caramel hair swirling this way and that where it fell free from the clip holding it.

She leaned forward, then propped an elbow on the table's edge and rested her chin in her hand as she met his gaze, daring his to keep from drifting into her cleavage.

But he was a guy, and it was there in the deep V of her neckline, where the lapels of her jacket gaped over her blouse, and he wasn't going to pretend otherwise.

He managed not to swallow his tongue and didn't even bite it when she used the tip of one slender finger to stroke his big lens.

"What would it cost to hire you?" she asked, and he started to tell her she could have him for the price of a post-coital cigarette.

But he didn't smoke, and because he still wasn't sure if she knew he was a PI and wasn't spying for a competitor, he asked, "Hire me for what?"

She inclined her head, her long gold earrings dangling against her neck. "You do this professionally?"

He nodded, still avoiding commitment.

"I need to have some portraits done."

"Www.yellowpages.com."

"Cute," she said, with a smirk. "I don't want a random photographer. I want you."

She thought he was a photographer . . . or was this some sneaky female test to trap him into admitting otherwise? "You don't know me. You haven't seen my work. You're picking me up on the street. How is that not random?"

"I've seen you. You've seen me."

Oh yeah. Understatement.

"I'd say that qualifies as the start of a beautiful friendship."

He sat straighter, cupped his hands around the metal seat, and lifted the chair, turning it so he could better face her. The legs scraped against the concrete of the sidewalk as he sat, scraped again as he scooted closer, conducting a sneaky-man test of his own.

"Is that what we're doing here? Becoming friends? You,

me, and my camera?" Something was going on here. He needed to know what the mystery was.

She uncrossed her legs, then crossed them the other direction, her foot swinging in the space between his calves, her skirt leaving nothing to the imagination where the side slit opened. Her thigh was bare long past the spot where it became her hip, and her skin was bronzed and sleek.

"I have a friend," she began, back to toying with his lens, her nails long and painted with a coat of clear shine. "He owns an art gallery. He's been after me for a while to hire a photographer before he hires one for me."

Like he'd thought. *A mystery.* "Why haven't you let him? Save yourself the cost and the hassle."

"True," she said, her head still inclined, her fingers now fondling the charms on her earring. "It's just the nature of the pictures he wants. The nature of his gallery. I don't do what I do for just anyone, and so only the right photographer will work."

His antennae twitched. He wasn't sure this was anything he wanted to know. But he had to ask. "What do you do?"

She cut her eyes to his. "I let people look."

Uh, whoa. Just whoa. Finn found his head nodding, like he couldn't keep it still with that picture bouncing around inside.

She let people look.

The next question should probably have been, "At what?" But the way she'd said it, he didn't need to ask.

He knew.

If you liked this book, you'll love Karen Kelley's
MY FAVORITE PHANTOM,
coming next month from Brava . . .

Hell, he knew the real reason he didn't want her in the house, he had a weakness for women. Always had. His siblings had teased him unmercifully, calling him Don Juan—more so now that he was teaching that other class.

Kaci hadn't looked like she would be that hard to resist, though. Not when she wore baggy clothes and that cap. He snorted. It hadn't been that long since he'd gone on a date. Okay, he was safe. No worries.

"I just wanted to let you know I'll be coming in and out of the house as I bring my equipment in," a voice spoke behind him, softer than before but still with a slight edge.

"Good. The sooner you can rid me of my problem the better." He set his soda can on the table and stood, turning around to face her.

His mouth dropped open. No, no, no! What happened to the baggy clothes and the baseball cap pulled down low and she hadn't looked like this and . . . Damn it!

He waved his arm in front of him. "You changed." Where were her other clothes? The ones that made her safe. Hell, the ones that made *him* safe.

She wore short-shorts that showed off long, wrap-around-his-waist-and-pull-him-in-closer legs, and a little blue tank top that stretched across her full breasts. And no more baseball cap. Now her long beautiful blond hair tumbled over her shoulders.

She glanced down, then shrugged. "I'm cold natured in the mornings. By afternoon, I get hot. I'll start getting my equipment." She turned and left the patio.

His glanced dropped to her sweet little ass. His mouth started to water.

By afternoon she got hot? Is that what she'd said? That was the understatement of the year. He wasn't sure what was going to be worse, the ghost or keeping his hands off the sexy exterminator.

Damn, he hadn't bargained for this. It seemed the hole he was getting precariously closer to falling inside just kept getting deeper and deeper.

Damn, she'd had a really nice twist in her walk, though.

No, he would not seduce Kaci. She was off limits—at least until she got rid of the ghost. But his mouth was already starting to water.

When his cell phone rang, he pulled it out of his pocket and flipped it open. He glanced at the number. His older brother. Great. He frowned. Things just got better and better.

"Hello."

"Hey, Peyton. How's it going? Has your ghost exterminator arrived?"

Peyton heard the unmistakable laughter in his brother's voice. Why had he even told Joe about his ghost? "Yeah, she's here."

"She?" The humor immediately vanished.

"Yeah."

"Get rid of her. You know how you are with women. It'll be the same as the last town."

He shook his head. "The last town, as you like to refer to it, was nothing more than a young woman who was infatuated with her professor. Nothing happened. I only left because I wanted to teach this other class as well as my history class and the dean offered me that opportunity. Have a little faith. Besides, I do have a ghost, and she can get rid of it."

"She stalked you." His sigh came over the phone lines. "A

woman to you is like someone on a diet crashing into a candy store. You know you can't change. At least tell me she's ugly."

Okay, he could do that. "She's ugly." He wasn't lying or anything. Just telling Joe what he'd asked to be told. "I can't get rid of her until the ghost is gone."

"Please, just be careful."

"I'm always careful." Joe was acting as though he had a disease or something. Hell, maybe he did, but he really enjoyed a woman's company.

"If you need anything, I'm only a phone call away."

"Yeah, thanks, bro." He closed the phone, then slipped it into his pocket as he walked toward the front door.

Man, he should've told Joe not to tell his other brother or his sister. If they got wind there was a woman living with him, even if it was business, he'd never hear the last of it.

Could he help it if he loved women? It wouldn't matter if Kaci had been old or young. There was just something about women that he loved. All women.

The baggy sweats and cap had made her safer, though. Sort of.

But he would stay on guard around her. Just as soon as he helped her carry in the rest of her things. A slow grin curved his lips. She was damned sexy.

For just a moment, he closed his eyes and lost himself in the fantasy of her body pressed against his. Her naked body. His hands caressing her.

He quickly shook off the image.

Damn it, he was not going to sleep with her.

He wasn't.